IT'S NEVER TOO LATE

Sue Woolley

Published by PPR Publishing,
19 Kingswell Road, Northampton NN2 6QB

www.pprpublishing.co.uk

A CIP catalogue record for this book
is available from the British Library.

ISBN: 978 1 0685176 2 4

June: *Divine Secrets of the Ya-Ya Sisterhood* by Rebecca Wells

Meg

"I've no idea," John said as he rummaged through the little cupboard next to the fridge-freezer they kept their over-the-counter meds in, "why I'm waking up feeling so knackered. It's not even as though there's an alarm to wake me nowadays."

"I'm sorry you didn't sleep well," Meg said, fighting to keep her tone neutral, rather than accusing. "What are you looking for?"

"The Recovery sachets. Where the hell have you hidden them?"

"You used the last one yesterday morning. Don't you remember?"

Why ask? She knew very well he wouldn't remember. He rarely did, now. How much booze was he getting through anyway? She suspected he was drinking alone in his study during the day, as well as in the evenings when they were together, although she had never caught him at it. Yet he seemed to have no clue about the harm he was doing to himself, to them.

John slammed the cupboard door, then winced at the bang it made. "Could you nip down the chemist and fetch me some?"

No 'please'. No 'would you mind'. Just the placid assumption she would jump to do whatever he wanted.

Not this time. "It's Sunday," she said with some

1

asperity. "There won't be anywhere open until 10.30."

He sank down into the chair opposite her. "Get me a coffee, would you, Meggie?"

Her heart softened as she took in the paleness of his face, the lines which pain had drawn there.

"Okay," she said, "and you'd better have some ibuprofen too. What d'you want for breakfast?"

"Nothing to eat. Just coffee. Thanks, love."

Nothing to eat. He never seemed hungry these days. Time was, he would eat whatever she put in front of him – he'd always enjoyed her cooking. Was there more wrong with him than she thought?

She put the kettle on, reached for his usual mug, with its 'World's Best Grandad' logo in curly purple lettering. It had been a present from Katie and Becky last Christmas and he'd used it every day since.

"Here you are, love," she said. "What are you doing today?"

"Golf with Nick and Martin, probably. I'll see how I feel later."

"Well, supper will be at six. Make sure you're back in good time."

He stood up with the mug in his hand and kissed the back of her head in passing. "Thanks, Meggie."

They always had a roast dinner on Sundays. But she needn't start it until after lunch. What was she going to do with herself until then?

Ginny

Ginny was putting away the last item from her fortnightly visit to the farmers market, some gorgeous sprouting broccoli, when the phone rang.

"Coming, coming," she lilted, as though the caller could hear. She walked out to the hall and picked up the handset.

"Hello, Ginny speaking."

"It's Meg. How are you?"

"Fine, thanks. How about you?"

"I'm sorry to bother you on a Sunday."

"No worries," Ginny said. "I'm just back from the farmers market at Wychbold. I'll be spending the afternoon batch cooking, to make the most of it."

"That sounds lovely," Meg said. "But isn't it awfully expensive?"

"I guess it costs a bit more than supermarket produce, but it tastes so much better." And at least I know where it comes from. And it isn't all packaged in plastic.

"Have you heard from Rose?" Meg said.

Ah, so that's why she's ringing. "No, not since the funeral," Ginny said. "How about you?"

She sauntered through to the living room, enjoying the caress of the parquet floor on her bare soles. Ever since California, she had loved going shoeless, starting as early in the year as she could, and continuing as late. Failing bare feet, she wore either rope sandals or boots made from pineapple leather. Her inner hippy was alive and well, even after all these years.

"Nothing. But I was wondering whether we should get in touch with her about our June book group meeting. It's been five weeks since the funeral and our next get-together is on the 26th."

"Yes, it wasn't the same without her last month," Ginny said, sitting down in her favourite rocking chair. "But like I said, I haven't heard from her, apart from that one e-mail saying she wasn't coming to our May meeting."

"I'm sure it's not good for her to be cooped up at home, alone. Will you give her a ring?"

If it mattered that much to Meg, why hadn't she rung Rose herself? She was a funny little soul, so lacking in self-confidence.

"Hmm, I'm not sure whether a phone call would be the best idea. I don't want to intrude on her grief. I'll send her an e-mail. Then I'll let you know what she says. Will that do?"

"Thank you, that's a weight off my mind. I don't know how you manage all that computer stuff – it's beyond me."

"I'm sure you could get on with it if you tried. Have you thought of enrolling on a silver surfers course?"

"Silver surfers?" Meg echoed, her voice full of puzzlement. "What on earth are they?"

Ginny had to laugh. "It's what people call older folk who use the internet. They run courses at the library sometimes."

"I suppose I could," Meg said. "But I've always left that sort of thing to John. He loves his computer. But I'm terrified of it… what if I pressed the wrong button and broke it?"

"Oh, they're a lot tougher than that," Ginny said. "You like your Kindle, don't you?"

"Oh, yes! But John has to order the books for me, off Amazon."

"Well, if you can use a Kindle, you can certainly manage e-mails. How many computers do you have in the house?"

"John's got a big computer in his study," Meg said, "and a laptop in the lounge. "Why?"

"Maybe you could use the laptop sometimes."

"I guess I could ask him, but I don't think he'd be awfully keen."

Ginny suppressed a sigh. She'd never met Meg's husband and wasn't sure she ever wanted to. He sounded like a classic MCP. "Remind me what our next book is, and I'll send Rose an e-mail."

"It's *Divine Secrets of the Ya-Ya Sisterhood* by Rebecca Wells, the one that Jessica recommended. I'm really enjoying it."

"I've downloaded it, but not started it yet. I'll e-mail Rose later."

"Thank you, Ginny. I'll leave you in peace. 'Bye now."

"See you on the 26th."

She, Meg and Rose were an unlikely trio. They had shared a table at the first session of a reading group at Worcester Library the previous spring and had hit it off, partly on account of being the only three pensioners in the room.

When the group had folded at the beginning of the

school summer holidays, they had decided to carry on meeting once a month, to share books, and something of their lives. Over the past few months, in spite of the disparities in their lifestyles, they had grown close to each other. When Rose hadn't made it in May, it had felt like the beginning of the end. She would miss the monthly meetings, if the group fizzled out. At the very least, they got her out of the house and into congenial company.

Yet she could not suppress a pang of unease. She had long ago learned the dangers of allowing herself to get too close to anyone… forget it, Ginny. Maybe it was time to get over that particular fear, however well-founded it was. She powered up her laptop and opened Outlook.

> Hello Rose,
> Meg and I missed you last month – it wasn't the same with only the two of us. I wonder whether you feel up to coming along for our get-together this month? Usual time, usual place.
> The book we're reading is *Divine Secrets of the Ya-Ya Sisterhood* by Rebecca Wells – Meg's choice. I've checked on Amazon, and it is available.
> Hope to see you there,
> Love,
> Ginny x

Hopefully, she would get a response. Meg was right – it wasn't good for Rose to stay home alone, with only her grief for company. As she knew from old experience.

Rose

Rose had believed that nothing would be worse than that dreadful period between Graham's death and the funeral, nearly three weeks later. After the first devastation, she had felt totally numb, locked behind a plate-glass wall, unable to connect with anyone.

It was only when his coffin was being lowered into the earth that the first cracks had appeared. Then the grief had hit her like a sledgehammer and since then, she had been barely functioning. If only she had still been working. Then at least, she would have had that to distract her. As it was, the long empty days stretched out ahead of her. She could not conceive how she was going to carry on with her life without him. What she had now was not a life, merely an existence.

Why had he left her? The downright unfairness of it made her so angry. If he'd been overweight, hadn't taken care of himself, at least she would have had some warning. But no. Bam! Heart attack out of the blue. And now she was alone.

She had slept in. Again. Having nothing to get up for. She had a shower, then puttered downstairs in her dressing gown to eat breakfast at the kitchen table. A big bowl of gluten-free cereal, coffee, four slices of gluten-free toast slathered with butter and strawberry jam. Yawn.

Sometimes she felt as though the house was stifling her. Everything around her reminded her of Graham. Without him, it felt echoingly empty. She'd considered selling up, moving somewhere new, simply to escape the memories.

But everyone she'd mentioned it to had told her to give it a year before making any big decisions. A year! She could hardly see further ahead than next week.

Yet at other times, it was her only refuge – the only place where she could show her true feelings, be herself. Even if Bonnie was the only living being to know it. On those days, all she had the strength to do was huddle on the sofa, wrapped in a soft velour throw, Bonnie purring on her knee, offering her unique brand of feline comfort.

She was eating for England, desperate to fill the emptiness which ached inside her. In her rare objective moments, she knew it wasn't doing any good, that it wouldn't work. But numbing the pain seemed to be the only option left to her. She was bingeing alternately on stem ginger cookies and vanilla ice-cream – the proper stuff, with real vanilla in it – and on classic detective novels – Arthur Conan Doyle, Ngaio Marsh, Margery Allingham, even Agatha Christie. But not Dorothy L. Sayers, much though she loved the Wimsey novels – she identified with Harriet too much to risk that. The intricacies of the plots diverted her mind for a while, even made her forget her sorrow, at least temporarily.

What to do today? She knew she had to try to keep busy and tire herself out, so she would sleep tonight. She powered up her iPad to check her e-mails. One from Matthew – he checked in every day, to make sure she was okay. Which was sweet of him, she supposed. No, it was. But he had no idea how she was really feeling. She had to maintain the façade of being 'over the worst' – she didn't want to worry him. She really appreciated her elder son, now that Graham... Again, the pit of black emptiness opened beneath her.

Stop thinking about it. Back to the e-mails. One from Ginny…

Dear Ginny. Always so tactful. Maybe she should make the effort. It had been more than a month, after all – and three weeks since the funeral. It was about time she got back into circulation, picked up the threads of her life. Graham would have expected it of her.

Divine Secrets of the Ya-Ya Sisterhood – such an intriguing title. She'd get it on her Kindle and make a start later. It would be good to see Meg and Ginny again, but she was afraid of Meg's sympathy. She couldn't bear it right now. Maybe if she asked Ginny to warn Meg not to introduce the subject…

> Dear Ginny,
> Good to hear from you. Thank you for not
> giving up on me. I'll get it on my Kindle
> and start reading it later.
> But… I don't want to talk about
> Graham.
> Could you let Meg know, please?
> See you on the 26th
> Love, Rose x

Then she answered Matthew's e-mail and closed the iPad down. She was looking forward to seeing him on Saturday, when he came round to help her with her weekly shop. Such a blessing that he lived nearby. With her gammy knee, she couldn't manage it on her own.

Time to get dressed, then order that book. Half an hour later, she was on the sofa, her legs supported by the recliner flap, a steaming mug of tea by her side, *Divine Secrets of the Ya-Ya Sisterhood* open on her Kindle. At first she found it a little confusing – it seemed to be about a daughter who had done an interview revealing family secrets and had fallen out with her mother in consequence. But as she read on, she began to realise that it was a story of four women in their sixties, who had been friends since childhood. Now she understood why Meg had chosen it.

The evening of the 25th, exactly one month since Graham's funeral, Rose set her alarm for the first time in weeks – it wouldn't do to be late. Up at eight the next morning, she chose what to wear – navy and white skirt, the one with pleats in, a white blouse, her favourite navy cardigan with the tiny flowers embroidered in shades of blue round the neckline. And of course, her pearls. She applied her usual lipstick carefully. That would have to do; she was only going to see Ginny and Meg, after all.

She drove into Worcester, blessing the automatic gearbox which meant she could still drive in spite of her knee, and parked in the St Martin's Gate car park off the City Walls Road. She walked slowly through Reindeer Court to the Shambles, then turned left. Capuchin's was a few doors down, on Friar Street.

They had found it through a friend of Meg's. It was a small, off-beat, café-cum-bookshop, an idea which worked surprisingly well. The bell tinkled as she walked in through the red painted front door. The walls were lined with bookshelves stained a light grey, full of the 'gently used' books that Capuchins specialised in, and there was another floor upstairs which was entirely given over to books. The counter with its cake stands and plates of home-made biscuits – such a treat – was at the back. The centre of the room was filled with six tables, four low and two at normal height, each surrounded by armchairs or chairs, covered in soft, deep brown leather. There were some beautiful banners on the walls, in the shop's colour scheme – deep blue, red and silver, which had quotations about coffee and reading on them. Rose's favourite was by Francis Bacon: 'Some books should be tasted, some devoured, but only a few should be chewed and digested thoroughly.' There were also some gorgeous black and white photos of Worcester and the surrounding countryside, which the shop's owner, Karen, sold as a side-line. The delectable scents of roasted coffee, old leather and second-hand books filled her nostrils, wafted through the air by the old-fashioned ceiling fans.

She was the first to arrive, as usual.

"Hello, Rose!" Karen said with a smile. "Good to see you back! What will it be today?"

So nice to be remembered. "A large latté and a slice of your gluten-free carrot cake, please," Rose said. She had missed Capuchins' wonderful cakes. "How are you? I hope business has been good?"

"Fine, thanks. We've had quite a busy month. I'll bring your coffee over when it's ready. Are Ginny and Meg coming too?"

"Yes, they should be arriving soon."

Managing a smile, Rose turned and walked over to

their usual table, in the back corner. They always sat here, because the table and chairs were higher than most of the others, and neither Meg nor Rose herself could get up easily from the low ones. One of the many prices of ageing.

By the time Karen had brought her coffee and cake over, Meg had arrived. She was looking tired and drawn, her back a little more hunched than usual and her flyaway grey hair looking limp and uncared for. Something was wrong.

"Rose! It's so good to see you! Ginny and I really missed you last month."

"Hello, Meg. Sorry about that, I didn't feel up to much..."

"That's okay, we quite understood. I'd better get my coffee. Ginny should be here any time." And Meg bustled up to the counter.

Ginny arrived on the dot of eleven, exactly on time, as always. How beautiful she was! So tall, so slim, so elegant. She moved so gracefully. You'd never think she was in her seventies.

"Hello, Rose. I'm glad you could make it. Is Meg here yet?"

"Yes, she's up at the counter."

"I'll go and order my tea."

Five minutes later, they were all seated around the table with their drinks. Rose sipping her latté, Meg with an Americano and Ginny with her usual herbal tea. Rose and Meg both had cakes in front of them, but Ginny never ate at these meetings. No wonder she was so slim.

"How have you both been?" Rose said.

"Oh, so-so," Meg replied. "But I'm beginning to

worry about John."

What now? Rose did not have a high opinion of Meg's husband, a real alpha male, who kept her friend firmly under his thumb.

Unaccountably, Meg was blushing. She looked... ashamed?

"What's wrong, Meg?" Rose said, leaning forward in her chair.

"It's... I'm – I'm getting really worried about his drinking," Meg blurted out, flushing even redder, not able to meet her gaze.

Rose and Ginny exchanged a glance. This did not sound good.

"He's not violent towards you, is he?" Ginny said.

Meg's head came up. She looked shocked. "Oh, no!" she said. "Nothing like that. He's always been a big social drinker, usually when he's out with his mates. But now, I'm pretty sure he's keeping a bottle of scotch in his study, where I won't find it. But I can smell it on his breath sometimes. He's struggling to get up in the mornings and he's off his food. Which isn't like John at all."

Meg bit her lip. Rose could sense that tears were near. What to say?

"Could you persuade him to visit your GP?" Ginny said.

"He hates doctors," Meg said, "and I'm sure he doesn't think that anything's wrong with him. But *I* know there is. I'm at my wits' end."

"Have you tried talking with him about it?" Rose said.

"No," Meg said. "To be honest, I haven't dared. He's

been in such a foul mood lately."

"Then have you spoken to Jessica?" Rose said.

Jessica was Meg's daughter, who lived on the other side of Worcester. To Rose's relief, Meg's face brightened up.

"That's a really good idea," she said. "I'll do it. He listens to her far more than he does to me. Thank you."

"You're welcome." Time to move the conversation on. "And how's life treating you, Ginny?"

"Oh, not so bad, thanks." Ginny sighed. "I'm still missing my teaching, although I do an hour's yoga every morning. It's not the same as doing it with a class. I'm at a bit of a loose end, to be honest."

"Oh, me too," Rose said. "I haven't known what to do with myself, these past few weeks. I get up, eat meals, try to keep myself busy, read, stroke the cat, and that's about it. My life seems so empty now."

The black hole loomed. Stop it. She squared her shoulders. "But enough of that. What did you all think of *Divine Secrets*?"

"I loved it," Meg said. "When Jessica recommended it, I got it on my Kindle straight away. At first, I found it hard to get into, but by the time I was half-way through, I couldn't wait to find out whether Vivi and Sidda would be reconciled, and how the other Ya-Yas would support Vivi."

"Yes, I found it difficult at first too," Rose said, "but I fell in love with all the Ya-Yas. Such a wonderful story of friendship between women. It made me realise how much I appreciate you two." She paused. "I don't have many real friends. Graham – Graham and the children were all I wanted, all I needed, for so many years."

She blinked hard to keep treacherous tears back, but they began to meander down her cheeks, in spite of her best efforts to dam them. She scrabbled in her handbag for a handkerchief.

"Oh, Rose," Ginny said softly. "Cry if you need to, my dear. We're here for you."

"Of course we are," Meg chimed in. "You can ring me any time." She reached across and touched her hand briefly.

After that, the tears fell harder. *Cry if you need to.* She hadn't expected that from pragmatic Ginny. How did she know? At length, after much lip biting, she managed to get herself back under control. She felt obscurely better – she had felt so held by her friends, in spite of the fact that neither of them were touching her. So very kind.

She wiped the tears away once again, then gave them both a tremulous smile. "Thank you, Ginny. Thank you, Meg. You don't know how much that means to me. Sorry, I didn't mean to cry. What must you think of me?"

She blew her nose, dabbed her eyes, but did not put her hanky back in her bag.

"That you're grieving, and life is hard at the moment," Ginny said. "But you will get through it. It just takes time."

"Thank you," Rose said again. *It sounds as though she really knows. I wonder why?* "So, what did you think of the Ya-Yas, Ginny?"

To her relief, Ginny accepted the change of subject. "Well, having been brought up Catholic, a lot of it resonated with me. Which is why I'm not religious now. Spiritual, but not religious. And I loved the deep friendship between the four of them... it must be such a blessing to have friends you have known all your life, that you can rely on for anything."

Rose sighed. Meg sighed. Ginny sighed.

"After today," Rose said, "I think *we* could be those friends, each for the others. Although we haven't known each other long, I feel that I can tell you two things that I can't share with the boys. They're too close to Graham."

"I agree," Meg said. "Jessica's lovely, but she's John's daughter. And I hardly ever see Andrew. He and Richard seem to be so happy in London, but I wish he'd come up a bit more often."

"At least the two of you do *have* family," Ginny said. "I've been alone for more than twenty years, ever since Laura died."

"Laura?" said Meg. "I don't think you've ever mentioned her before. Who was she? Your sister?"

Ginny took a deep breath. "Laura was my partner, the love of my life. We had nine precious years together, before AIDS took her from me."

So that's why she knows what grief feels like.

"I'm so sorry," Rose said. "When did she pass?"

"In 1993. So many of our friends died in the eighties and early nineties, before they found out how to treat it. It's made it hard for me to trust, to reach out to new friends... I'm always scared they will leave me, too."

"I can understand a little how that might feel," Meg said. "When Andrew first came out as gay, I was terrified he was going to catch AIDS. But Richard was his first partner, and Andrew was *his,* so they were okay. I'm so sorry."

"Thank you both for not judging me," Ginny said. "I'd never have thought that people our age would be so understanding. There is still so much prejudice against the gay community, even now."

"We're your friends," Rose said. "Friends don't judge."

Ginny's blue eyes brimmed with tears. She groped for Meg's and Rose's hands. "Thank you," she said softly. "I won't forget it."

They were silent for a while, three older women holding hands in a coffee shop. Then Ginny squeezed their hands and let go.

"Well," she said. "I've got a treat in store for us next month. My book choice is *Big Magic* by Elizabeth Gilbert. You know, the woman who wrote *Eat, Pray, Love*."

"Oh, I loved that film!" Rose said. "I've got it at home on DVD. Julia Roberts was amazing in it."

"Me too," Meg said. "*Big Magic*. What's it about?"

"I'm not going to tell you that," Ginny said. "I don't want to spoil it for you. But I'd recommend getting it in paperback, rather than on your Kindles. It's a book you'll want to flip backwards and forwards in, while you're reading."

"Okay, I'll stop off at Waterstones on the way back to the car," Rose said.

"I'll come with you," Meg said, "and buy my copy too."

Meg

Meg and Rose walked up Friar Street to The Shambles in the warm sunshine. Ginny had gone in the opposite direction, heading for home on her bicycle.

"Gosh," said Meg, "we definitely let some cats out of bags today, didn't we?"

"Yes, your worries about John, my loneliness without Graham, and Ginny's revelation. But I'm glad – I feel closer to both of you, having shared some of what I'm going through."

She's being so brave. "I know you didn't want to talk about Graham," Meg said, "but Rose, please know that I'm always there at the end of the phone, if the loneliness gets too much."

"Thank you," Rose said. "I appreciate that. Here we are, Waterstones. Let's hope they've got two copies in stock."

But they were out of luck – there was only one copy on the shelves.

"You have it," Rose said. "I can always order mine off Amazon."

"Thanks. I really must learn to use the computer. Ginny was going on to me about it when I rang her a couple of weeks ago. She said something about a silver surfers class."

"That's a good idea!" Rose said. "They sometimes run them at the St. John's Library. They teach you the basics – how to use the internet, how to set up an e-mail account, and how to use Word and so on."

"Word?" Meg said. "What's that?"

"It's the word processing package on Microsoft

Office. It's what you use for writing documents – letters, poems, even books."

"You've convinced me," Meg said. "I'll give it a go. I'm going to ask John to let me use his laptop."

"Good for you! It's never too late to learn something new. And John will be on hand to help if you get stuck."

"I guess so," said Meg. "He's been on at me for ages to learn to use the computer, but when he tries to explain anything to me, he goes so fast, I can't understand what to do."

"Yes, I had that problem too, with Graham. They've been using computers for so long they find it hard to think themselves back to the time when they were beginners. You could always ring me, if you have a problem. I promise not to patronise you!"

Meg laughed. "It's a deal. I'll give the Library a ring when I get home."

Ginny

Ginny sat in her rocking chair, her Siamese cat, Sofi, on her knee, front paws kneading Ginny's thighs. She stroked her gently, and a deep purr began to rumble in Sofi's chest.

"I never thought I'd tell them about Laura," she told the cat. "And I couldn't believe how well they took it. I think Rose was a bit shocked, but she hid it well. And of course, Meg having a gay son helped her to understand."

Sofi purred on, oblivious. Ginny continued to rock gently, her thoughts going back to those nine wonderful years. If she could ever tell Rose and Meg *that* story, she'd know she had found some true friends.

But did she dare? Could she take that risk? Let it go for now – there was plenty of time. She hoped they'd enjoy *Big Magic* as much as she had.

Rose

Rose let herself into the house, feeling better in herself than she had since Graham's passing. It had done her so much good to spend some time with Ginny and Meg. To get out of the house. She'd even managed to talk about Graham, a little.

She was sitting at the kitchen table eating her lunch when the phone rang. Mentally cursing whoever was disturbing her meal, she levered herself to her feet and picked up the receiver, so glad for the kitchen extension – it would have taken too long to get through to the hall.

"Rose Anderson speaking."

"Mum, it's Matthew. How did book group go?"

"Fine, thank you. I'm fond of Ginny and Meg. We had a good chat. I'm glad they're in my life."

"I'll be round a bit later than usual on Saturday," Matthew said. "Sarah's away for the weekend, so I've got to drop Rosie off at ballet before picking you up."

Rosie, her darling grand-daughter. It had made her so happy when Matthew and Sarah had named their youngest child after her. Now six, she was a golden-haired bundle of sunshine.

"I thought her ballet class was on a Wednesday?"

"Yes, but they're doing a recital next month, and Miss Rogers wants them to do an extra rehearsal on Saturday. It takes two hours, and Sarah has arranged for one of the other parents to pick her up afterwards, so I can still take you shopping."

"Bless you, Matthew. I do appreciate it. Where's Sarah?"

"Oh, she's off at a hen party with an old school friend, who's finally getting married."

"What time will you be arriving? I'll make sure I'm ready for you."

"The rehearsal starts at ten, so I should be with you by about twenty past, traffic permitting."

"Thank you, love. I'll see you then."

She put down the phone and finished her lunch. Dear Matthew, he had been such a solid rock for her since Graham... It was a godsend that he and Sarah lived so near. She must find out when the recital was and ask him to get her a ticket.

She was so glad she'd made the effort to meet Meg and Ginny. For the first time since Graham's death, she had felt almost normal, almost her old self. Even though she had broken down in front of them. Most unlike her. But they had seemed to understand. She'd better order that book. Ginny had been so mysterious, it had piqued Rose's curiosity. Clever Ginny.

Meg

"John," Meg said one evening, while they were in the kitchen eating supper, "I'd like to learn how to use your laptop. Could you show me how?"

He frowned at her. "What's brought this on? You've always refused to have anything to do with it before."

"Oh well," she ducked her head and blushed. "I was talking to Ginny and Rose the other day, and they both think I should learn how to do e-mails and use Word."

"But do *you* want to?"

"Yes, I really think I do," she replied. "It would be good not to have to rely on you if I need to look something up. And Jessica was on at me last week about getting a Facebook account, so that she can keep in touch with me that way."

"All right," John said. "But you'll have to be careful with it – if you can't work out how to do something, call me. Don't try to sort it out yourself. The first thing to do is set you up as a user, then sort out a new e-mail account."

Meg pressed her lips together. She didn't want to start an argument, not now he'd agreed. But why was he always so negative?

As soon as they'd finished eating, he fetched his laptop from the sitting room and powered it up. "Username: Meg Jeffries. What password do you want to choose? It should be something you find easy to remember, because you'll need it every time you log on."

Meg thought. Then inspiration came. "I'll use the children's initials," she said. "I won't forget *those*."

"Fair enough," he said. "But you ought to have some numbers and symbols as well, to make it less easy to hack."

Meg thought again, then told John what to use.

"Okay, that's done. Now, I think it would be best for you to have a Gmail account," he said. "That way, you can access it from anywhere."

Within minutes, Meg had her own e-mail account, and had sent her first message, to Jessica:

> Dear Jessica,
> Your Dad's helped me to set up an e-mail account, and this is my first message.
> When you come round at the weekend, can you help me to set up a Facebook account, please?
> Love,
> Mum xx

"There, you see," John said, "that wasn't too difficult, was it?"

"I guess not," Meg said, "but how will I know when she's replied?"

"You'll need to check it regularly, like opening the post, every time the postman comes. That's all e-mail is – an electronic postal service."

"I hadn't thought of it that way, but I suppose you're right."

"Let's see how you get on with it. If you take to it, the family could buy you a laptop of your own for your birthday."

Meg could hear the unspoken words behind that well enough. 'So you won't break mine'. But all she said was, "Oh John! That would be wonderful!"

The next morning, after her housework was done, Meg

settled down in her corner of the sofa to read *Big Magic*. And was instantly enchanted. Liz Gilbert seemed to be speaking to her, Meg Jeffries, challenging her to live more creatively. But what could she do? The only ways in which she was creative were cooking, crochet and occasional knitting. She loved inventing new recipes and trying them out. Sometimes the results tasted wonderful, sometimes the exact opposite, like Mrs Cropley's in *The Vicar of Dibley*. Well, perhaps not quite that bad. She was looking forward to the return of *The Great British Bake Off* in a couple of months – her all-time favourite programme. And she always had a crochet project on the go. It was her favourite way to spend an evening, sitting in the lounge with John, watching the television, her crochet on her knee.

She'd need to think about this… but for now, just carry on reading. It seemed to be mainly about writing. Meg had loved English at school and had enjoyed writing essays and book reviews. Since then, she had only written poetry and that not often, or at least, not recently. There always seemed to be so much other stuff to do.

But now the yearning filled her to write something… maybe even a whole book. She read on. Then, on page 108, there it was. Her call to new creativity. Liz Gilbert was telling her that as she had lived for a long time, she had experienced life, and there were things that she needed to share with the world, with the people she loved.

She sat there, reading that same paragraph over and over. That was it. That was *it!* She would write a memoir of her life, for the grandchildren. She could aim to finish it by their Golden Wedding anniversary, in September next year.

This was so exciting. She knew she could do it. There was so much to write about… growing up in the fifties and sixties, marrying John, her job as a nursery school teacher, the arrival of the children, all the griefs and joys of bringing them up. She hugged herself. This was going to be fun!

July: *Big Magic: Creative Living Beyond Fear* by Elizabeth Gilbert

Ginny

Ginny was at a loose end, an all too frequent sensation these days. She felt antsy, restless. The house was immaculate, she'd done all the batch cooking with the fresh veg from the farmers market and frankly, she was bored. What to do?

She ought to re-read *Big Magic*. She had adored it when it came out in 2015 but hadn't read it since. Now where was it? A moment's thought located it in the bookcase in her study and she hooked it off the shelf and walked back downstairs. Curling up on the sofa, she began to read.

Like Liz Gilbert's friend, Susan, she couldn't remember when she had last felt light, joyous and creative. Not since Laura had died, anyway. What could she do? She'd never enjoyed English that much at school, except for the poetry, and was hopeless at art. She threw the book down in disgust. She'd chosen it because she'd thought it would be a good stimulus for all three of them and now, here *she* was without an idea in her head. This was no good. She'd cycle into the centre of Worcester and have a wander round, in the hope of spotting something that would enthuse her.

Half an hour later, she had locked her bike to a hoop in the Commandery Gardens and set off in search of inspiration. She wandered through Crowngate and Reindeer Court, looking in shop windows, trying to find something that appealed. No joy. Finally she walked into W H Smith and browsed in the hobbies section of the magazines. She didn't have the patience for cross-stitch or knitting or crochet – too much like hard work, and the paper crafts looked too finicky. She had nearly given up hope when she spotted a copy of *Outdoor Photography*.

Hmm. That was a possibility. She began to leaf through it. There were some stunning photographs in there. She had a little compact camera at home. Maybe she could start to take it with her on cycle rides and photograph what she saw. She took it up to the counter and paid, then left the shop with a new sense of purpose, the spring back in her step.

Rose

Rose was pleased to have something positive to share when Matthew picked her up.

"I had a wonderful time with Ginny and Meg last week," she said, as she put on her seat belt. "It was so good to see them again. I'd missed the May meeting – just didn't feel up to it. But I think it's time now."

"Time for what?"

"Time to start living again. I'll never stop missing your Dad, but I can't stay locked away in the house forever. So I'd like you to get me a ticket for Rosie's ballet recital, please."

His face lit up. "That's so good to hear. I'm sure Rosie will be thrilled to have Granny there. I'll ask Sarah to buy you a ticket."

An hour later, the shop was done, and they were driving back to the house.

"I do appreciate your help," Rose said. "This blessed

knee of mine isn't getting any better and it's a struggle to carry heavy stuff these days."

"You're welcome, Mum. I'm happy to help. You're on the waiting list, aren't you?"

"Yes, but goodness knows when the operation will be – the NHS is so under-funded these days. Do you want a coffee before you go?"

"Sorry, I can't. I have to go and pick Rosie up from Amanda's. I expect she'll be hungry and it's nearly lunchtime."

"Oh, of course," Rose said. "But bring the children round to see me soon, will you? I haven't seen any of them for weeks."

"Better still, why don't you come round to ours on Sunday afternoon? I can't offer you Sunday lunch, because James has a football match in the morning, and we'll be eating in the evening."

Sometimes, Matthew reminded her so much of Graham, it was hard to be around him. He had the same shaped body, the same beautiful brown eyes. Would she ever get over this?

"That would be lovely, dear," she said. "Thank you."

After unpacking the shopping and eating her solitary lunch – she still couldn't get used to catering for one rather than two – Rose sat down to begin reading *Big Magic*. So, Ginny was on the crusade path. But yes, why not? From what Liz Gilbert was saying, creativity could bring some joy back into her life, a quality that was sorely lacking at the moment. She had never thought of herself as particularly creative, having spent most of her time instilling creativity into others, as head of the English department at St Jude's. What to choose?

An idea came into her head. She dismissed it. It refused to go away. She gave it a second chance. She'd love to learn to play the piano again. Making music was creative, wasn't it? But she hadn't played since she was twelve. She glanced over to where Graham's upright piano stood against one wall of the living room, its wood gleaming gently in the sunlight. Surely she was too old to learn.

"Well," she said aloud, "you'll never know if you don't try!"

But how to find a piano teacher? None of the grandchildren played… Perhaps one of Meg's did. It wouldn't hurt to ask. She picked up the phone.

"Meg, Rose here. Do either of your grandchildren learn the piano by any chance?"

"Yes, Katie does. Why?"

Rose took a deep breath. "Well," she said, "I've been reading *Big Magic,* and the one thing I really want to do is to learn the piano again. So I need to find a teacher."

"Oh, good for you! I'll e-mail Jessica and ask her."

"What's this?" Rose teased. "You, on e-mail? I thought you didn't like computers?"

Meg laughed. "Me neither! But I've decided to join the 21st century. John's set me up on his laptop, and I've not only got an e-mail account, I'm also on Facebook, so that I can keep up with what the grandchildren are doing, through Jessica's posts."

"That's great news. Well done you!"

"Thanks. I'm really looking forward to our next

meeting. I can't wait to tell Ginny that I've taken her advice."

"Why don't you send her an e-mail? Hang on, I'll look up her address…." She powered up her iPad and found Ginny's last e-mail. "Here it is," and she read it off to Meg.

"Thanks, Rose. What's yours?"

"rose underscore anderson1943@hotmail.co.uk. All lower case, no spaces."

"What's an underscore?"

"If you look on your laptop's keyboard, it's the key to the right of the zero at the top – not the short hyphen, the long one, so you'll need to use the Caps Lock."

"Hang on."

There was a pause – Rose guessed Meg was opening John's laptop. Then, "Okay, I've got it."

"Let me know when you've heard back from Jessica, won't you?"

"Of course, I'll ask her now. See you on the 29th."

Ginny

Ginny was startled to receive an e-mail from Meg, of all people.

Dear Ginny,

Meg here! Yes, I've taken your advice and got an e-mail account. John's set me up on his laptop. I can't understand why I was so frightened of it – it's much easier than I expected.

And I've set up a Facebook account too, so that I can keep in touch with Jessica and Andrew.

Big Magic is amazing… I can't wait to tell you what I've decided to do.

See you on the 29th

Love, Meg x

Oh, good for her! She replied straight away:

Hello Meg,

Well done! I'm so glad for you. You'll find it easier and easier as you go on.

Yes, *Big Magic* is special. I've thought of something too.

Looking forward to seeing you then,

Love, Ginny x

She walked upstairs to find her camera, an ancient Zenith LOMO she'd bought more than thirty years ago. She found it, then hesitated. Of course, it took film. She wasn't sure it was even possible to buy films for cameras these days – everything seemed to be digital. Maybe she'd need to buy herself a new camera. This could be more expensive than she'd anticipated.

Back downstairs, she turned to the adverts section at the back of *Outdoor Photography* and was dismayed by the price of cameras. And the camera specs were so much gobbledegook to her. She googled 'camera shops in Worcester' and found one in Pump Street. She'd go there next time she was in town, after meeting Rose and Meg.

When she arrived at Capuchins, Meg and Rose were already there, both looking very pleased with themselves. She ordered her tea and walked over to the table. It was hot outside and she mentally blessed the ceiling fans, which at least kept the air circulating.

"You two look like cats who've stolen the cream!" she said. "What's up?"

"Oh, Ginny!" Meg said. "Thank you so much for introducing us to *Big Magic*. I've come up with a brilliant idea for doing something creative, and so has Rose. How about you?"

"Yes, me too. That's excellent news. So… spill the beans."

Rose smiled at her, the first true smile Ginny had seen on her face since Graham had died. Her grey eyes had recovered some of their sparkle and some of the dark shadows underneath them had disappeared. She was always well turned-out, but today her inside seemed to match her outside.

"I'm not sure my idea really counts as creative," she said. "I've decided I'd like to learn to play the piano again. I've not played since I was about twelve, but we do have a piano at home." She grimaced and corrected herself. "I mean, *I* have a piano at home. It was Graham's."

"That's wonderful! Of course making music is

creative. Are you going to try to work it out for yourself, or get a teacher?"

"Oh, get a teacher, I couldn't imagine learning again without one. Luckily, Meg's grand-daughter, Katie, learns, and Meg asked Jessica for her teacher's phone number." She took a deep breath. "And, my first lesson's next week! I have to say, I was horrified by the cost," she added with a laugh, "but I really want to do this. I've promised myself I'll give it a go for six months, then if I don't make any progress, I'll try something else."

Meg hugged her. "Of course you'll make progress, so long as you practice regularly. Jessica has to nag Katie sometimes, but she does love it. She's going to be doing her Grade I exam this November."

"Exams?" Rose sounded startled. "I hadn't thought that far ahead. We'll have to see how I get on."

"How about you, Meg?" Ginny said. "What creative idea have you come up with?"

"It was a paragraph in the book, about half-way through, which really spoke to me." She was positively bubbling with enthusiasm. "Something about if you've lived this long, you've got a lot of experience of life, and you have a duty to share what you know with the world. Hang on, I'll find it."

She fished her copy of *Big Magic* out of her shopping bag, found the place and read it out to them both.

"So," she continued, "I've decided to write a memoir of my life, for the grandchildren. I'm hoping to finish the first draft by our Golden Wedding by August next year – our anniversary is on September the 11th. I've already started jotting down ideas of what I want to include… I'm so excited about it!"

"Wow!" Ginny said, forcing herself to respond with enthusiasm. She couldn't help contrasting her own life with Meg's: she had no-one to write her own memoir for. "That's fantastic. Are you going to write it longhand, and then type it up or write it straight into the computer?"

"Oh, longhand," Meg said. "I can't imagine writing freely on a computer yet. But John said that the whole family's going to club together to buy me a laptop of my own for my birthday on the 5th of August. It's a big birthday – I'll be seventy. So I'll be able to type it up on that."

Meg was so lucky, having a loving family of her own. Be pleased for her.

"That's marvellous. I hope we'll get to read it too."

"Yes," Rose chimed in, "we can be your first readers."

"Now," Meg said, "how about you, Ginny? What have you thought of?"

"I've decided to take up photography, specialising in outdoor stuff – landscapes, flowers, birds and wild animals, that kind of thing. But the only camera I possess is an old Zenith LOMO, and it only takes film, and everything seems to be digital these days. I suppose I could use my phone for the time being, but I'd really like to have a proper digital camera of my own." She sighed. "But they're so expensive, and I haven't got a clue what to look for. I bought a photography magazine, but they use so much jargon when they're describing the cameras, I feel lost. I'm going to go to the camera shop in Pump Street after we're done here, to see if I can get some advice. But I don't have a huge amount of money to spend."

"You don't need to do that," Rose said, to Ginny's surprise. "Graham was a bit of a photography buff, and I could lend you one of his cameras. I've used his Canon a time or two myself, and it's quite user-friendly. And the lens zooms from landscapes to close ups. Why don't you come home with me afterwards, and you can have a look at it?"

"Wow, thank you," Ginny said. "But I've got my bike with me..."

"Not to worry," Rose said, "Where do you live? I'll put the postcode into my satnav and meet you there. Then we can drive to my house."

"I do have a car," Ginny said. "I'll cycle home, then drive over to yours. Where do you live?"

"In a village north-east of Worcester – Crowle." And she gave Ginny her postcode.

"Goodness," said Meg, "we seem to be taking off in all directions. Me writing, Rose and her music, Ginny taking photographs. I can't wait to see how we all get on."

"I'd like to think of something else to do besides learning the piano," Rose said. "I know that playing music is creative in one sense, but I'd like to have a tangible end product."

"What do you fancy doing?" Meg said. "Do you knit, or crochet?"

"I used to knit sweaters and suchlike for the children when they were small, but I find knitting so boring – it takes so long to grow to a respectable size. Or at least it does, the way I knit! And the weather's far too hot at the moment."

"I decided on nature photography by having a wander round the magazine section of W H Smith," Ginny said. "Why don't you give it a try?"

"That's a good idea. I'll do that tomorrow."

They ordered another round of drinks and cakes, feeling that there was something to celebrate.

When Karen brought them over, she said, "You're all looking very happy today... what's happening?"

"We've been reading a book by Liz Gilbert called *Big Magic*," Meg said, "and we've all decided to do something new and creative."

"Oh, I loved that book," Karen said. "What are you all going to do, or is it a secret?"

"I'm going to write a memoir of my life," Meg said. "I can't wait to get started."

"I haven't quite decided yet," Rose said, "but probably something with wool or thread."

Why didn't Rose want Karen to know she wanted to play the piano? Surely she wasn't afraid of being mocked? Oh well...

"I'm going to start taking a camera with me, wherever I go," Ginny said, "and take photos of landscapes and things in nature."

"Do you all want me to keep an eye out for books on your subjects?" Karen said.

"That would be so kind," Meg said. "Thank you,"

Once Karen was back at the counter, Ginny said, "Okay, Rose, what's our book for August?"

"I've decided on *The Book Thief* by Markus Zusak. It's officially a book for teenagers, but I absolutely love it."

Rose

When Ginny drew up on the drive, Rose was waiting for her, the kettle already boiled. Her first non-family visitor since the funeral.

"Come away in!" she said. "Would you like a drink? I can offer you tea, coffee, or camomile tea."

"Camomile tea, please," Ginny said. No surprises there.

Once they were sitting in the living room, Ginny said, "Why didn't you want Karen to know that you're planning to learn the piano?"

"I don't really want anyone to know," Rose said, "in case I don't get on with it. I haven't played for more than sixty years, apart from the occasional carol at Christmas. That's why I'm planning to do something else as well."

"I'm sure it will come back to you," Ginny said, "I bet it's like learning to ride a bike – you never forget how."

"Hmm, I'm not so sure about that. But at least I know what the notes on the keyboard are, and where middle C is! And I can vaguely remember how to read music – at least the notes within the staves. I've got my first lesson next Thursday."

"You can do it, I'm sure of it."

"Thank you. Now, I'll go and fetch Graham's camera."

A few minutes later she returned with a camera bag, which was more of a small backpack, over one shoulder.

"Here it is," she said, "I'm sure it's all in working order... Graham was pretty good at looking after his possessions." A pang of sadness.

"Thank you," Ginny said, giving her a hug. "I really appreciate it. Can you show me how it works, please?"

"Blimey, this is going to be a case of the blind leading the lame. I haven't used it for ages. Like I said, Graham was the photographer in the family. I used to borrow it sometimes to take photos of the grandchildren, but that's all. Let's see… I *think* the manual's in here somewhere." She rummaged in the camera bag. "Yes, here it is."

Ginny leafed through it. "Ah, here's a labelled diagram. That's useful."

"It's a DSLR," Rose said, "so if you look through the viewfinder, what you see is what you'll be taking a picture of. Much better than those cameras where you have to look through the back."

"What does DSLR mean?" Ginny said. "I saw that acronym so many times in the photography magazine, but all the writers assumed their readers would know."

"The D stands for Digital and I think the L stands for lens, but I only know that much because Graham explained it to me once."

She passed the camera to Ginny, who took it gingerly. "Gosh, it's quite heavy," she said. "I wasn't expecting that."

"Well, it's a proper camera, not a little point and click thing."

"May I take it out into the garden and have a play?"

"Of course you can. This way," Rose said, leading the way to the French windows. "If you hold it with your right hand – you *are* right-handed? – you can alter the zoom on the lens with your left."

She showed Ginny how to do it, then walked back inside. Ten minutes later, her friend came back in, her eyes glowing.

"It's wonderful!," she said. "I can't believe how much you can zoom in and out. I'm going to have fun with this. Thank you so much!"

"Do you want to take the camera bag, too? That way, it will be safe."

"Yes, please, that would be great. I'm so grateful."

"That's what friends are for."

Half an hour later, Rose rang Ginny. "I forgot to ask you, do you know Meg's home address?"

"No, why?"

"Because she told us it's her 70th birthday on the 5th and I'd like to send her a card."

"Good thought," Ginny replied. "I'll do the same. I don't have her address, but I'm sure they'll be listed in the phone book. You can get it online now."

"Failing that," Rose said, "I'll e-mail Jessica and ask her for it."

"Jessica?"

"Meg's daughter. She was the one who sent me the piano teacher details."

"Shall we send her some flowers too?" Ginny said. "After all, it is a big birthday."

"That's an excellent idea. I'll order some and we can split the cost."

Meg

Meg had treated herself to a special book from Paperchase to do her writing in, an A4 spiral-bound hardback journal. Sitting at the kitchen table with it open in front of her, she felt somehow reluctant to sully its pristine pages. Maybe she should use an ordinary writing pad instead. No, that was ridiculous! She had a feeling that using this book would make her writing time more special.

When she had been inspired with the idea of writing a memoir, she had thought it would just be a matter of sitting down in front of the blank page and letting the words pour out of her. But here she was, biro poised above the page, not having a clue where to start. She wrote a sentence, crossed it out, wrote another, then crossed that out too.

This was stupid. Maybe she'd better do some planning first, so as to have some idea of what she wanted to write about. She fetched the note pad she used for her shopping lists, and started a new page. Let me think... She sucked the end of her pen, and slowly the ideas came.

- Birth (something about parents, and mother dying. Auntie Enid)
- Siblings – Geoffrey, Jack, Philip, Nan
- Early years – any memories? Where we lived
- Primary school & Sunday school
- Secondary school – Grammar – love of English – friends

- The sixties – what it was like to be a teenager then
- Meeting John – marriage & house moves
- Nursery school teaching
- Children – Andrew, Jessica
- Children growing up in seventies and eighties
- Changes in society
- Getting older
- Retirement & grandchildren

She looked at it with satisfaction. That was better! Now she knew where she needed to go. She tore the list off the pad, folded it up, and put it inside the front cover of her journal. That was enough for today. She'd start properly tomorrow.

That evening, she started to sort through their extensive stash of old photos, which had been sitting in the bottom of her wardrobe for years. Each picture brought back another memory. She fetched her journal and began to write them down. After an hour or so, her hand began to cramp. She wasn't used to writing for any sustained period. She remembered how her hand used to ache at the end of an exam, back in her schooldays. Better take care, she didn't want to end up with wrist strain or something.

John looked up from his magazine. "What are you doing, Meggie?" he said, taking a swig from his glass of bitter. "You've been quiet as a mouse all evening."

"I'm sorting through all our old photos," she said, "so that I can remember the important things. I'm going to write a memoir for the grandchildren."

"What brought this on?"

"It was a fabulous book called *Big Magic*," Meg said, "which Rose and Ginny and I were reading for book group this month. It's all about living a creative life, and I've decided I want to write. You know I used to write poetry, years ago. Well, there was a bit in the book which spoke about sharing the wisdom of your life, your experiences, with the world. And I thought – hey! I could write a memoir of my life – not for publication, just for the family."

"Blimey, that could be a major undertaking," John said, negative as usual. "Are you doing it longhand?"

"At first," Meg said. "I don't think I could compose anything on the computer. But I'll type it up on there."

"Then we definitely need to get you a laptop of your own," John said. "I'll get in touch with Jessica and Andrew tomorrow, and see whether they'd be willing to put towards it."

"I haven't got very far yet, no more than chapter headings," Meg said. "I've bought myself a special writing journal, and I sat in front of it for ages, paralysed. It wasn't till I thought of doing some planning first that I could write anything."

"You can do this." He kissed the top of her head. "I'm looking forward to reading it."

That was a surprise. "Thank you, John. But you may have quite a long wait."

Rose

Rose showed up for her first piano lesson after nearly cancelling several times. She had never met this woman – Lesley Flynn, her name was – but Meg's daughter, Jessica, had spoken highly of her and she'd seemed pleasant enough on the phone. She rang the doorbell and a short, plump woman with auburn hair and brown eyes answered it.

"You must be Rose Anderson," she said, "I'm Lesley. Come on in."

Rose followed her nervously into the room to the left of the hall. Which was dominated by an enormous, black, grand piano. She stopped in her tracks. She had been expecting an upright, like her own piano at home, not this monster.

Lesley saw her look of apprehension. "Don't worry, it won't eat you!" Her eyes twinkled. "Come and sit down and tell me what your experience of playing is. I think you said on the phone that you'd played as a child. Have you kept it up at all?"

"No, not really. I learned with the woman next door until I was about twelve, but never took any exams. And that was a very long time ago."

"That's fine," Lesley said. "At least you know your way around the keyboard. Do you have any particular goal in mind?"

"I hadn't really thought about it," Rose said. "I just want to be able to play again – perhaps some classical pieces."

"Okay, let's start with something simple." Lesley said, fetching a music book from her white-painted bookshelves.

Rose looked at them in wonder – they covered the whole of one wall, from floor to ceiling, and were filled with dozens of box files containing what she presumed were music books. "I usually start adult learners with this."

It was called *Masterwork Classics: Levels 1 – 2.* Rose opened it and began to leaf through it. The first few pieces were quite short – only a few bars long.

She sat down at the piano and looked at Lesley. "What do I do now?"

"Find middle C," she said, "then place your right hand on the keys so that your thumb is on middle C and your little finger on G."

Rose did that. "Now put your left hand an octave below, with your little finger on the C."

The lesson went on. By the end of the half hour, Rose was playing a very short piece, very slowly, hands separate.

"Well," she said, smiling at Lesley, "that wasn't too bad."

"You did really well," Lesley said, "considering it's so long since you've played. I'll order you your own copy of the book, but it will take a couple of weeks to arrive. You can borrow this one in the meantime. You can practice that piece, hands separately at first. Then if you feel brave, you can try to put them together. You can also have a go at a couple of scales, if you like. I'll get you a scales book too."

"I always enjoyed doing scales when I was younger," Rose confessed, "because I didn't need to read the music."

Lesley laughed. "It *will* come back to you. By the end of the year, you'll be surprised how far you've come."

"I'll believe you," Rose said. "Thank you, Lesley, I

really enjoyed that. How much do I owe you?"

"£17.50. If you're planning to come regularly, I usually ask my students to set up a monthly standing order. It saves having a lot of cash in the house."

"I'll let you know next time," Rose said. "I'll see how the practising goes, first."

"Fair enough," Lesley said. "See you next week."

Rose walked back out to the car with a light heart. That had been fun. Maybe she could do this, after all.

Ginny

Ginny took Graham's camera out with her the following weekend. She decided to go for a walk on the Malvern Hills. It was a warm and sunny Saturday and the car park at British Camp was crowded. She shouldered the camera bag, with a water bottle in one of the pockets and a granola bar and apple for lunch in another, and set off, up the first rise to the Herefordshire Beacon. The view from the summit was fabulous – the rolling countryside with its neat patchwork of fields on the Worcestershire side, and the wilder, less inhabited landscape of Herefordshire on the other, with Wales in the far blue distance.

There seemed to be something to photograph everywhere she looked. It was like she had been given a new pair of eyes. She had always walked in nature – it was one of her favourite ways of exercising but, more often than not, she'd be concentrating on her number of steps and pace, rather than on the beauty around her. She breathed in deeply, and closed her eyes, feeling the warmth of the summer sunshine against her skin. It almost felt like a rebirth, as though she had just emerged into the world, full of awe and wonder.

She was still getting used to Graham's camera. There was much more to it than simply pointing and clicking. But she was gradually feeling her way and couldn't wait to upload the day's photos onto her laptop. Rose had explained the little gadget in the front pocket of the camera case – you loaded the memory card into it, then plugged it in to one of the USB ports to upload the photos. She'd tried it once and had been amazed when it had worked. So different from taking a film to Boots and picking the prints up a week or so later.

She was feeling pleasantly tired by the time she got back home. She took a portion of the homemade leek and potato soup she'd made a couple of months earlier out of the freezer and microwaved it warm. That and a couple of wholemeal rolls provided a filling evening meal.

Then she uploaded her photos. All in all, she was quite pleased – there were some lovely panoramic shots of the landscapes from the Hills, and the close-up shots of some wildflowers – buttercups, foxgloves, and others she'd have to look up to identify – had worked better than she had hoped. Satisfied, she shut her laptop down and snuggled down on the sofa to read *The Book Thief*.

After a while, she was filled with a sense of haunting familiarity. She was certain she'd never read it before, but something in the style of Zusak's writing rang a bell with her. She was enjoying it, but its close resemblance to... something was getting on her nerves. *Who* did the writing style remind her of? It was so familiar... then she had it. Hermann Hesse.

That was it. She remembered reading *The Glass Bead Game* as a student and falling completely in love with it. Of course, she hadn't been reading the original German, but the translation had been superb.

And this *Book Thief* was so like it. The slight detachment in the narration. As though Death was entirely objective about the lives he observed. Dispassionate – that was the word she was looking for. At the same time, Zusak was a wonderful story weaver. She read on and on, dying to find out what happened to Liesel, to Rudi, to Liesel's foster-parents Hans and Rosa, and to Max, the hidden Jew with the hair like feathers. She might have sat there all night, enthralled, has not Sofi jumped onto her knee, reminding her that it was high time for her evening snack.

"Okay, Sofi, I'm coming," she yawned. "Goodness, it's late! Good job I don't need to get up tomorrow."

The next morning, she was stiffer than usual, feeling the effects of her Malverns walk. She eased into her yoga routine, making sure she did enough stretches to allow her abused leg muscles some chance to recover. Sunday. What to do today? Until recently, Sunday had been her paperwork day, when she tallied up all the classes she had taken the previous week and brought her accounts up to date. She still hadn't relaxed into the new rhythm of retirement. It had only been four months, after all. She had finished at the end of the Spring term, which had handily coincided with the end of her financial year. It was a joy not to have to do accounts anymore, but there seemed to be rather too much free time in her new life. She had always been a doer, choosing walking holidays or exploring a new city, rather than sitting by a pool, sunning herself and reading.

"Get a grip, Ginny," she said aloud. "You're seventy-five next month. It's about time you took life a bit more easily."

At least she didn't have to worry about money. When her parents had died, thirty years before, Ginny, as an only child, had inherited the entire estate. She had sold the house, not wanting to live among old memories, and invested the proceeds (minus the tax man's far too generous cut) in her yoga business, and paid off the mortgage on her little house in Barbourne. The rest had gone into a savings account and, managed sensibly to supplement her pension, it should be enough to last the rest of her life. So long as she was prudent and didn't splurge too much, or too often.

It had been so kind of Rose to lend her Graham's camera. It made such a difference to the types of photos she was able to take. She vowed to make good use of it, suppressing the small, nagging voice in the back of her head that kept asking, 'But what are the photos *for*? What are you going to do with them? There's no point in taking photos just for the fun of it.'

"Shut up!" she said aloud, startling the cat. "I'm doing it for my own pleasure. Because being able to make a record of the beauties my eyes see is enough. It doesn't have to be *for* anything!"

She sighed. This was her all over. She had always been so driven, always needing to have a project on the go, to be in control. But she knew from experience that life had a habit of throwing obstacles in your path. Let it go. The three most difficult words in the English language.

Eleven o'clock. She'd have a mug of tea, then go out and mow the lawn and do some weeding. The garden was looking more than slightly scraggy at the moment. She hadn't been out there for a fortnight, and it showed.

August: *The Book Thief* by Markus Zusak

Meg

Meg's seventieth birthday was on the 5th of August. The weekend before, the whole family – she and John, Andrew and Richard – were invited to Jessica and Mark's to celebrate it.

"I'm so excited," she said as they drove over the bridge to St. John's, the sunlight dancing on the River Severn below them. "I haven't seen Andrew for ages. Not since Easter. And phone calls just aren't the same. I've missed him so much."

"Even after all this time?" John said. "He's 48, for heaven's sake. And he's got his own life to lead, in London. You can't expect him to come trotting home to mother every couple of weeks."

Meg sighed. John simply didn't understand how much the Andrew-shaped hole in her heart still ached, even after all these years. "Oh, I know, but I'll never stop missing him. It's not the same with Jessica – she lives so close that I can see her and the grandchildren regularly. But Andrew's so far away."

"Well, you'll see him and Richard today."

"I can't wait!"

Everyone was waiting for them when they arrived. "Come on in," Jessica said, throwing the front door open wide, a big smile on her face. "Happy birthday for tomorrow, Mum!"

Meg hugged her daughter. "Thank you, darling. It's

50

gorgeous to have everyone together."

Andrew rose from his chair as they entered the sitting room and gave her a huge hug. "Happy birthday, Mum!"

Meg's heart contracted. *He's looking thin. I hope he's eating properly.* "Andrew! It's so lovely to see you!"

"Happy birthday, Meg," Richard said.

Meg smiled up at her son's tall partner. "And it's lovely to see you too, Richard. I haven't seen you two since Easter."

"You'll have to come and stay with us in Crouch End one weekend," Andrew said.

"That would be marvellous. It's a date." *John could look after himself for once.*

Jessica had prepared a sumptuous birthday lunch for them all – a buffet of delicious finger food, including all Meg's favourites, and a huge chocolate cake, with two candles shaped like a seven and a zero. The whole family joined in singing *Happy Birthday* to her – even little Becky added her small, true voice to the chorus.

"Now," Mark said, once they were back in the sitting room, "close your eyes, Meg, and we'll bring your present down."

Meg obediently shut her eyes but couldn't resist sneaking a quick look as the seconds ticked by.

"Nana, stop peeking!" Katie said.

"Sorry, Katie," Meg said with a smile, and put her hands over her eyes.

"Okay," Jessica said, "you can open them now. Here you are – happy birthday from all of us."

A large, heavy, rectangular parcel was deposited in her

lap. She took the paper off carefully. Inside, as John had promised, was a laptop of her very own.

Tears came to her eyes. "That's fabulous – thank you all very, very much!"

"I was so surprised," Andrew said, "when Dad rang to ask us to put towards a laptop for your birthday. It's your Big Seven Oh, so we all wanted to buy you something special, but I thought you hated computers."

"Well," she said, "I've made two new friends, and they've persuaded me that I've been silly. We meet once a month to share books and our lives, and one of the books was *Big Magic* by Liz Gilbert, which is all about being creative. Ginny challenged Rose and me to do something new."

"Why do you need a laptop for that?" Richard said.

Should she tell them? Would they think it was silly? Go for it. She took a deep breath. "I've decided to write a memoir of my life, mainly for the family, especially Katie and Becky. Because the world's changed so much since I was born, and I'd like them to understand how different things were when I was growing up, and about Andrew and Jessica when they were children."

"Wow, Meg, you're a dark horse!" Mark said, his dark eyes lighting up. "I'd no idea. I can't wait to read it."

"It's only at a very early stage yet," Meg said. "I've been going through all our family photo albums and making notes about what I remember. Then I'm going to put them all in chronological order and start writing. I've made a rough list of chapter headings and started on the first chapter."

"Are you writing it by hand first?" Andrew said, "or are you going to write it straight onto the laptop?"

"Oh, I'm going to write it longhand first. I don't think I could write creatively on a laptop. So at first, it will be a glorified, much more efficient typewriter. And it will be great not to have to keep borrowing John's. whenever I want to look something up."

"I'll set it all up for you when we get home," John said.

"Thank you all, so much," Meg said, her heart full. "This will be a birthday to remember."

Rose

Rose was ready to scream with frustration. She had managed to play the piece Lesley had given her, first the right hand, then the left, with few problems, albeit slowly. But as soon as she tried to put both hands together... disaster! It was like trying to rub her head and pat her stomach at the same time, or whatever the damn fool saying was. Her fingers simply would not do what her brain was telling them to. It was driving her mad.

But she'd been here before. When she sat and thought about it, she remembered how aggravated she used to get, when she had learned the piano all those years ago. She remembered old Miss McCrae saying in her soft Highland voice, "Practice makes perfect, Rose. It's the only way you're going to improve."

But at the moment, as soon as she sat down at the piano, her fingers became two unrelated bunches of bananas, over which she had little or no control. She'd have to ask Lesley, when she went for her next lesson. *If* she went back.

The way she was feeling now, she wasn't sure whether she'd bother.

That afternoon, she went round to visit Matthew and Sarah, and to see the grandchildren. Ben was twelve and would soon be taller than she was. Every time she saw him, he seemed to have grown some more. His voice was beginning to break, and it was disconcerting to hear a deep rumble replacing the boyish treble she had loved. He had finished his first year in secondary school and left his childhood behind.

James, just nine, would be in Year 5 at the local primary school in September, and thought about little else apart from football and swimming. He was so like Matthew had been at that age. Such a strong little boy, but always ready with a hug and a kiss for his Granny. And Rosie, the youngest, was simply a darling. Rose knew she shouldn't have favourites and she adored all her grandchildren, but with two boys of her own, this was the first time she'd experienced a little girl close up and she'd fallen in love with her straight away.

As soon as she walked into the house, the two younger children rushed to meet her, demanding hugs, which were given with a will. Rosie grabbed one hand, James the other, and they towed her into the living room. "Granny's here!"

"Hang on, you two," Sarah said. "Don't be so rough. Let your Granny go at her own pace."

Rose smiled. "Thank you, Sarah. Let me sit down, you two, and you can tell me all your news."

James said, "I won Most Improved Player of the Year

at football. D'you want to see my cup?"

"James! That's wonderful. Yes, please, you go and get it." He rushed out of the room and she heard him galloping up the stairs at his usual headlong speed.

"How about you, Rosie?" Rose said. "What's my favourite grand-daughter been up to?" She wouldn't be able to say *that* much longer; her other daughter-in-law, Debbie, was expecting a girl shortly after Christmas. Better make the most of it.

"Silly Granny," Rosie said, echoing her thoughts, "I'm your only grand-daughter!" She beamed. "We're doing a real live ballet recital, next weekend. Are you going to come and watch me dance?"

"Yes, I've asked Mummy to buy me a ticket."

"I'm doing two dances," she said proudly.

"That's wonderful, darling. I'm looking forward to it very much."

After a while, once their news had been shared, and the cup admired, the little ones went back to their own ploys. Time to ask Sarah how Ben was. She had only seen him at a distance when she arrived. Then he'd disappeared into his room.

"Ah, he's changed so much," Sarah said, sounding so sad. "I was warned it would happen, once he was at senior school. And they were quite right. He's not my little boy anymore."

"I know, love," Rose said. "They grow up so quickly at that age. I can remember the same thing happening with Matthew and Daniel. The only thing you can do is let them go. You've provided good roots, now it's his time to learn to fly."

"But he's only twelve…" Sarah wailed, "and the world's a lot rougher these days. I want to protect him for a while longer."

"I'm sure it will all work out fine," Rose said, pretending an optimism she didn't feel. She knew exactly how Sarah felt – she had been the same, all those years ago.

Ben came down just before she was due to leave. "Hello, Granny," he said.

"Hello, Ben. How are things going for you?"

"Oh, not bad, thanks."

"That's good." Rose knew better than to ask anything more. His father had been just the same at that age – almost monosyllabic, living in his own private world, in which neither parents nor grandparents had a part. She sighed.

"Well, it's nice to see you, anyway."

He gave her a peck on the cheek. "Thanks, Granny."

Meg

The memoir was going swimmingly. Or at least, planning it was. Meg even found herself neglecting the housework, so she could concentrate on it. So many memories came flooding back as she looked through the photos and the diaries she had kept as a teenager, one seeming to trigger another. She'd decided to scribble a few words down on five by three record cards to summarise each event, with approximate dates, then file them chronologically. She'd even treated herself to a red plastic card index box with a set of dividers for the purpose. Which meant she'd be able to reorganise them in a logical order later.

So far, she'd gone through her early years, and was about to embark on the most exciting decade of her life, the sixties. Being a teenager then had been so magical. She'd been an avid Beatles fan, like most of her peers, and had actually seen them in concert once. She snorted... she had *seen* them, but hadn't heard very much for the screaming. In fact, she'd screamed a bit herself.

It had been a magical few years, when people her age had claimed the right to be young and carefree, not under parental thumbs. Not that it had worked particularly well in her case. Her father and Auntie Enid had been horrified by the 'dirty, unwashed yobs' they saw on their television screen and had been reluctant to let Meg go out with friends, unless they knew exactly where she was, who she was with, and when she would be getting back. Pumpkin time had been ten o'clock during the week, ten-thirty on Fridays and Saturdays.

She'd managed to have fun, nonetheless. Life had been simpler in those days – she remembered having brilliant times just sitting on the floor of a girlfriend's bedroom, listening to records on her Dansette, talking about boys and fashion and other girls. Her best friend had been Linda, tall and slim, her hair cut in a madly smart bob. Meg had been so envious – Linda's mother had allowed her to wear make-up.

Her own father and aunt had been so Victorian about it. "I'm not having my daughter looking like a cheap slut," her father had fumed. So she'd had to keep her make-up at Linda's and put it on round there, being sure to take it all off again before she went home.

She'd managed to get three good A levels, in spite of

all the distractions, and had decided to train as a nursery school teacher, spending three years achieving her B.Ed. She'd always wanted to work with children, especially little ones. They were so rewarding at that age.

Maybe she'd better start to write some of this up, before it got too unwieldy to manage. Then type it up on her gorgeous new laptop. And she still had to read *The Book Thief*, before she saw Ginny and Rose again. First things first. She opened her writing journal and turned to page one.

> "I was born in a little village in the West Riding of Yorkshire, on August 5th, 1948, exactly one month after the establishment of the National Health Service…"

Ginny

Ginny finished *The Book Thief* for the second time a couple of nights before they were all due to meet. And had re-read *The Glass Bead Game* in between. Both had held her enthralled, all else forgotten. It must be so wonderful to be able to write like that. Ah well, we all have different talents. Carrying Graham's camera with her was becoming a habit, and her eye for a good shot was getting sharper. She was even considering setting up a blog to share some of the best ones.

Rose was sitting alone when she got there, sipping her usual latte.

"Hello, Rose, where's Meg? She's usually here before I am."

"I don't know," Rose said, "I spoke to her a couple of

days ago, and she was looking forward to coming. I hope nothing's happened to John."

Ginny frowned. "Hmm, me too. I know she's been worried about him. Let's wait a bit longer."

Meg rushed in at a quarter past eleven. "I'm so sorry I'm late," she said, "John kept me talking and I missed the bus."

"Don't worry," Rose said, "we were going to wait for you."

"Catch your breath and place your order," Ginny added. "We've got plenty of time."

Soon they were gathered round their usual table.

"Well, my dears," Ginny said as she looked at them both, "How is the creative spirit showing itself?"

"I've spent so much time looking through old photos and diaries," Meg said, "and trying to plan what I want to write, that I've hardly done any actual writing. But at least I've got a clearer idea of what I want to include now, and some clue as to what order it all happened in. And the family bought me a laptop, for my birthday three weeks ago. So lovely of them. It's so exciting to have my very own computer, that I don't have to share with John. I'm still getting used to it, it's got a different version of Windows than his, but I just love it! And thank you both so much for your cards, and for the lovely flowers."

"Good grief!" Ginny said. "You've still got your old diaries? I put mine on a bonfire years ago."

Then bit her lip as Meg looked hurt. "Yes, I've kept them in an old attaché case in the loft," she said. "Reading back through them has made me blush, sometimes, but at least they're first-hand reports of what I was doing and thinking at the time."

"How wonderful!" Rose said. "Mine got mislaid in one of our moves. I'd love to be able to read over them again."

"Anyway," said Meg, a little stiffly, "to answer your question, Ginny, it's going okay. What about you?"

Oh dear. I didn't mean to upset her. "Sorry, Meg. I'm glad you've got them for the record."

Meg nodded but did not say anything.

Ginny shot her an uneasy glance, then continued, "I've been learning how to use Graham's camera. It's a lot more complex than my old one, but I'm beginning to feel my way now, and I've been quite pleased with some of the photos I've taken. I'm thinking of setting up a blog to share some of the better ones with the wider world."

"I'm glad you're getting the use of it," Rose said. "It was sitting upstairs gathering dust at home."

"It's marvellous," Ginny said. "I'm so grateful for the loan."

Rose smiled at her. "You'll have to let us know when you've got the blog up and running," she said, "so that we can follow it. Have you thought of a name for it?"

"What's a blog?" Meg said.

"It's short for 'web-log'," Rose said. "Lots of people publish them, on all sorts of subjects. They write short articles, often with illustrations, about whatever they're interested in."

"Oh, I see," Meg said. Her face brightened. "I bet there are loads of writing ones. I'll have to have a look."

"Good idea," Ginny said. "And," she told Rose, "I've racked my brains and can't think of anything that isn't banal and obvious. So at the moment it's 'Blank Spot at the Top of the Page'."

"Oh dear," Rose said. "Let's all think about it, and let you know our suggestions next time."

"You could e-mail me if you have an inspiration," Ginny said, "I really don't want to wait another month."

"Okay, I'll do that," Rose said, and Meg nodded.

"How about you, Rose? How's the piano playing going?"

Rose groaned. "It's so damned hard," she said. "I'm beginning to remember how to read the music – at least in the right hand, but the left hand has me stumped every time. I keep having to say, 'Grizzly Bears Drink Fizzy Ale' in my head."

"Grizzly bears *what?*" Ginny said.

Rose laughed. "It's a mnemonic to remember the notes on the lines in the left hand – G, B, D, F, A. The other one is 'All Cows Eat Grass' for the spaces between. Lesley's given me a couple of very simple short pieces to practice, and I can just about manage them hands separate, but as soon as I try to put them together, it all goes pear-shaped. She says that's quite normal, and that I just need to slow down and place each note carefully. Easy for her to say, really *not* easy for me to do. It's difficult not to beat myself up about it, but I *think* I'm making progress. I don't remember it being so challenging when I was young."

"But are you enjoying it?" Meg said.

"Good question!" She took a sip of her latté. "I've

only had two lessons so far and, like I say, it's more frustrating than enjoyable at the moment. But I can dimly begin to see that in a few months' time, when I'm a bit more competent, it will start to be more fun. Once I can actually *play* something."

"They say that the piano is the most difficult instrument to play," Ginny said. "Give it some time before you write yourself off."

"I guess so," Rose said. "Anyway, I went down to Smiths, like you suggested last month, and I've decided to give cross-stitch a try. I've never been very artistic, but I've bought a magazine, and it seems as though it's a matter of following the chart – a bit like paint-by-numbers with a needle."

"Have you decided what design you want to stitch?" Meg said.

"I've visited Hobbycraft in Wychbold and picked up a couple of kits for cards. But I'd really like to try something a bit more ambitious – a sampler, or a big picture. I'm going to see how I take to it, and then choose something."

"I've got a friend who started off doing small cards," Ginny said, suddenly remembering Jo. "She's ended up stitching endless samplers for friends and family – for christenings, big birthdays, weddings and anniversaries. They make lovely mementos."

"That's a great idea," Rose said, her face lighting up. "Matthew and Sarah will be celebrating their Silver Wedding next May. I could stitch something for that. I can't believe they've been married that long! I don't feel old enough to have children celebrating twenty-five years of marriage!"

"There you go then," Meg said. "Problem sorted." She grinned at Rose.

"Thank you both," Rose said. Then she said, "What did you both think of *The Book Thief?*"

"I couldn't put it down," Ginny said, "I loved it. In fact, I've read it twice. But the first time through, it was driving me mad. Zusak's style reminded me of someone else, and I couldn't work out who. Then I finally got it – Hermann Hesse!"

"Goodness," Rose said, "I'd never have made that connection. But I see what you mean."

"I thought the idea of having Death as the narrator worked really well," Meg said, "but I found all the time-jumping a bit confusing at first. The way he tells you what's going to happen through Death's knowing everything, and then you watch it unfold. It took me a while to work out what was going on. But I did enjoy it – such a sad story."

"Yes, it really is. But full of hope at the same time," Ginny said. "It's definitely been added to my re-reading list."

"That's good to hear," Rose said. "What's our book for next month, Meg?"

"I've decided on *Eleanor Oliphant is Completely Fine* by Gail Honeyman. I've been seeing it all over the place, and the title's weirdly fascinating."

"Okay," Ginny said, "we'll give it a try."

Meg

Ginny had been in an odd mood. And she needn't have been so mean about her keeping her diaries. Rose had been kinder.

Meg shrugged. Let it go. Life's too short to hold grudges.

"Hello," she called, taking off her jacket, and hanging it up in the hall. "I'm home."

Silence.

"John? Where are you?" She walked into the kitchen to find a note on the table.

> Meggie:
>
> I got a phone-call from the GP, and they wanted to see me straight away, so I've gone down to the surgery.
>
> Back soon. Don't worry!
>
> John x

'Don't worry!' Yeah, that was going to happen. Her mind went into panic mode. She didn't even know he'd been anywhere near the doctor's. He hated doctors. Why hadn't he told her? And 'straight away' sounded serious. Her mouth was dry, her vision narrowed. Oh God! Should she walk down there herself?

She groped for a chair and sat down. Nothing like this had happened before. What should she do?

She was about to put her jacket back on and head down to the surgery, when she heard the front door open. She flew out into the hall. John. Thank God!

"What's wrong? Are you okay? I was so worried!"

He hugged her. "Woah, Meggie, slow down! But, we need to talk."

He led her through to the kitchen, sat her down at the

table.

"What's wrong? You're frightening me."

"Let's get a cup of tea first."

This consideration, which would usually have surprised her, now scared her. He was obviously setting the scene for some bad news. Trembling all over, she sat at the table, watching while he made them some tea. He plonked a mug down in front of her, the hot liquid spilling over the top, then sat down facing her.

He took a sip from his own mug, using both hands to hold it steady, while the tension shrieked inside her. What was going on?

"I told you I've been down to the doctor's," he began. "What I *didn't* tell you, was that this was a follow-up visit."

No, he hadn't told her. It hurt that he would hide something this important.

"A follow-up visit? Why didn't you tell me? Didn't you think I'd want to know? I'm your wife, for God's sake."

"I didn't want to worry you," he said. "But now, you've got to know."

She wanted to scream – getting information out of him was like pulling teeth – slow and agonising.

"John, would you please just tell me what's wrong," she said, proud that she able to keep her voice down. So far.

"A few weeks ago," he said, "I had a blackout, and it wasn't the first."

A blackout. Oh, God! Meg cradled the mug in her hands as though her life depended on the heat radiating from it. What was coming?

"And you know I've been feeling rough lately – tired,

off my food and so on. And there have been other symptoms too – my feet and ankles have been swollen, My stomach's been upset and my hair's been falling out. So I thought I'd better get it checked out," John said. "They did some tests a couple of weeks ago, and today I got the results."

"And?" She could scarcely breathe.

He met her eyes. "And," he said, "I've been diagnosed with ARLD."

"What the heck is that?"

"It stands for Alcohol Related Liver Disease," he said quietly.

Meg shook her head. She couldn't take it in. She knew he'd been drinking too much and too often, but this… This she hadn't expected. She set her mug back down, as she was now shaking so much the tea was slopping over the rim. He was watching her, waiting for her response.

She cleared her throat, forcing the words past the fear which was clogging it. "What – what does it mean?"

He took her hands in his. "It means my liver's been damaged by my drinking," he said in the same quiet voice.

"What can we do?" she said. "Is there a cure for it?"

"There's no cure," he said.

No cure. That couldn't be true – it just couldn't. Tears sprang from her eyes – he couldn't die, not now. The thought was unendurable.

"Don't look like that, Meggie," he said, leaning across the table and wiping the tears away with his thumb. "Although they can't reverse the damage I've already done to my liver, I *can* stop it getting any worse by quitting drinking. Now."

She was on an emotional roller coaster – terrified one minute, bathed in relief the next. It was almost too much for her to process. But she seized on the one positive: he could stop it getting worse. It wasn't too late.

"Will – will you be able to do that?"

He frowned. "It's going to be hard," he said. "I can't remember the last day I didn't have a drink or three. I'm going to need help."

"Anything I can do, you know I'll do it."

"I know, and that helps more than you know. But I think I'll need to go to AA or something like that. I'm not sure I can do it on my own."

AA? Oh, of course, Alcoholics Anonymous. He was an alcoholic. Oh God. She stood up, walked round the table and put her arms around him. "You can do this, I know you can."

"I hope so. God! I need a drink."

Which gave her an inkling of how tough the next weeks and months were going to be.

"Don't you dare. I can't do without you, John Jeffries."

Rose

Such an odd title for a book. *Eleanor Oliphant is Completely Fine*. She'd seen it in the book aisle in Tesco's a couple of times but hadn't been tempted to buy it. She logged on to Amazon and bought it for her Kindle.

But first, some piano practice. She was now playing two pieces from the *Masterworks* book, *Carefree* by Türk and

Melody by Kabalevsky. And four scales, C, G, D and A, two octaves each. Start with the scales. A was new this week and had three sharps. She looked at the scales book first, to check the fingering, then tried to memorise it. She always found it difficult to do scales with the music in front of her; it was easier to learn them by heart. Then she could look at her fingers. As ever, her right hand was far more obedient to her will than her left. Lesley had told her this was normal. She smiled in relief when both hands managed it without a mistake. She'd have another few goes hands separate, then try to put them together before her next lesson. Now for the pieces.

She'd just finished her practice when the phone rang.

"Rose? It's Meg. Such an awful thing…"

"What on earth's wrong?"

"I got home from Capuchins this morning to find a note on the table. The doctor wanted to see John straight away. I didn't even know he's been to the surgery."

"What's wrong with him?"

"It's – he's – he's got Alcohol Related Liver Disease," Meg said, all in a rush.

Oh, no. So Meg had been right to be worried.

"Oh, I'm so sorry. That's hard. What can they do about it?"

Meg gulped, and when she spoke, her voice was very wobbly. "They – can't reverse the damage he's already done, but he can stop it getting worse, if he quits drinking straight away."

"That's good news, isn't it?"

Meg sighed. "I suppose so. *If* he manages to stop

drinking. He's upstairs now, looking for local AA groups."

"I'll be holding you both in my thoughts," Rose said. "And you know where I am if you need me."

"Bless you. It's so hard to take in…" Meg's voice changed, "Got to go, he's coming downstairs."

Ginny

Her 75th birthday was coming up fast… on the 18th of next month. Perhaps she should invite Rose and Meg round for a meal. She didn't go in much for entertaining. In fact, she couldn't remember the last time she'd had guests. Normally she and Sofi had the house to themselves.

Inviting them into her home seemed a vulnerable thing to do – it would move their friendship into a new, deeper level, past the simple pleasure of the monthly meeting at Capuchins. Could she take the risk? It had been years – no, decades – since she'd allowed anyone past the barricades she'd spent so long constructing.

But they had been so good to her, so good *for* her. It would be an appropriate way to show her appreciation of them, her new friends. Do it, Ginny. She flipped her wall calendar over to the following month. The 18th was a Wednesday, so she could visit the farmers market the Saturday before, to stock up on goodies.

What to cook? She took a pile of vegetarian cookbooks through to the sitting room and began to browse. Problem was, she didn't know their tastes, apart from cake. She'd better drop them both an e-mail… so good that Meg was online now.

Hello Rose and Meg,

I'm going to be 75 on 18th September, and
I'd like to invite you both round for a meal.
It will be vegetarian, because as you know,
I don't eat meat. Do you have any
particular likes or dislikes?

I hope you can come,

Love,
Ginny x

Done. There was no going back now.

The responses soon came back. Both could come –
excellent. But she had forgotten Rose was coeliac. Which
would add a whole layer of complication to the recipe choice.
She googled 'coeliac diet' and learned that anything
containing barley, rye, oats or wheat was out. But potatoes
and rice were okay, so that was a start.

After browsing through her recipe books for about
half an hour, she came up with her menu: slices of honeydew
melon to start, a vegetarian risotto for the main course, and
Bosh's aquafaba chocolate mousse garnished with fresh
raspberries for dessert. Yum! And the handy thing was, she
could prepare the watermelon and mousse in advance, so
would only have to worry about the main course in the
moment.

She put the books away with bookmarks in the
relevant pages, then settled down to read *Eleanor Oliphant is*

Completely Fine. And nearly gave up in disgust after the first few pages,. Such a weird character. Such a boring life. But there were some odd sentences, which hinted that there was more to Eleanor than met the eye. Her stockpile of medication, her vodka drinking. She read on. Why did Eleanor find social interaction so hard? At least she could empathise with her loneliness, her denial that she *was* lonely. It had been her own default state for so many years.

Meg

"Hello, love," Meg said, "come on in."

"Hi, Mum," Jessica said, "I came as soon as I could."

They walked through to the kitchen and Meg re-boiled the kettle and got the biscuit tin down from its high shelf.

"Tea or coffee today?"

"Tea, I think. I've been drinking too much coffee lately, and it's giving me headaches."

"Tea it is then. Help yourself to biscuits. Hang on, I'll get the plates out."

"It's okay, Mum, I know where they are," Jessica said, opening the cupboard.

Five minutes later, they were in the sitting room, sipping their tea, the plate of biscuits between them.

Jessica took one. "What's up? Why did you want me to come round when Dad was out?"

Meg took a deep breath. "It's about your Dad," she said. "He's been to the doctor and had some bad news."

Jessica turned pale. "Oh, God! Not – not cancer?"

Meg took her hand. "No, love, nothing as bad as that. But still serious."

"Mum, for God's sake, tell me! What is it?"

"It's – he's been diagnosed with liver damage."

Jessica met her eyes, anxiety radiating out of her. "He's not going to die, is he?"

"Not yet," Meg said. "But if he doesn't start taking it seriously, he may not have many years left."

Tears sparkled in her daughter's eyes. Damn, she shouldn't have told her. But Jessica would never have forgiven her for leaving her in the dark.

"What's the treatment?"

"He's got to stop drinking straight away," Meg said. "It's the only thing that will help. That's where he is now – at an AA meeting."

Jessica drew back. "You mean, he's an alcoholic?"

Meg winced. "Not exactly," she said. God forgive her the lie – she couldn't bear the expression on Jessica's face – a mixture of fear and contempt. "But he can't do it on his own, so he's giving AA a try."

"What can we do to help?"

"I've stopped drinking myself – not that I drank much, or very often, but I wanted to be in solidarity with your Dad. We've cleared all the booze out of the house to remove temptation."

"So he *is* taking it seriously?"

"Yes, love, and so am I. If he manages to quit and keep it up, he should be fine."

I hope.

Jessica took a tissue from her bag and blew her nose.

"Well, please keep me in the loop," she said, "I *am* your daughter. I need to know these things."

Meg hugged her. "I will," she said, "I promise. Now, how are my beautiful grand-children?"

Rose

Rose was finding *Eleanor Oliphant* quite creepy. On the surface, the main character seemed socially inept, almost autistic. Such odd opinions and habits. Such stilted vocabulary. She went to work, came home, didn't seem to know how to interact with anyone. And that horrible mother… how could any mother speak to her child like that? She read on, trying to ignore the huge silence all around her. The house seemed so empty without Graham.

Slowly, the truth began to be revealed. Rose paused to make herself a meal – cheese on toast, something quick – then ate it absently, her mind on Eleanor. How could one person undergo so much? Now she could understand why the young woman was so odd, and drank so much. Which made her think about Meg – she was being so brave. Hopefully John would be able to stop drinking.

The *Bad Days* section made her cry. So raw, so very, very sad. But Raymond… so kind. She reached the end with a sigh of relief, got up and stretched. She was stiff, from sitting in one position for so long. It didn't take long for that to happen, these days.

What a book! She'd have to re-read it, slowly, to take it all in properly. This book group was certainly broadening her literary horizons. Which was good. At least it took her mind off being so alone. Eleanor's aloneness was much worse.

September: *Eleanor Oliphant is Completely Fine* by Gail Honeyman

Rose

Rosie's ballet recital, held in the hall of one of the local primary schools, had been wonderful, if unintentionally hilarious. The older girls had danced beautifully, but Rose had struggled to keep her face straight as she watched the younger ones going through their paces. Some, her own Rosie among them, hadn't been bad at all... you could see that in a few years they would be quite good. But a couple of the youngest had been a hoot... following on as best they could, getting their feet mixed up, such serious expressions on their young faces. Bless them!

A pang of sadness – how Graham would have enjoyed this. Then she caught herself in the lie – no, he wouldn't – he'd have made some excuse not to attend. But she would have enjoyed telling him about it. It was so hard to have no-one to share these special moments with. Let it go, Rose.

Rosie rushed up to them afterwards, "Did you enjoy it, Granny? Was I good?"

Rose hugged her. "Yes, darling, you were wonderful. My clever girl!"

"Thank you, Granny." Rosie flushed with pleasure. "Mummy, Daddy, did you like it?"

"You did really well, my precious," Sarah said. "Now off you go, time to get changed."

Rosie beamed and rushed off to the changing rooms.

"Thank you so much for inviting me," Rose said. "I wouldn't have missed that for the world."

Once Rosie had re-appeared, resplendent in flowery lilac leggings and matching tee-shirt, they walked out to the car park together.

Back home, she rang Meg.

"I've just been to Rosie's ballet recital. It was such fun, watching them all dance. Some of the older ones were very good."

"How did Rosie do?" Meg said.

"Ah, she was so sweet. And did very well. Some of the younger ones were quite funny to watch, but we all clapped like mad."

"Bless them," Meg said, "they need all the encouragement they can get at that age."

"You're so right." Rose changed the subject. "How are you? and how's John?"

"I don't know," Meg said, her voice changing, becoming low and hopeless. "The first few days were awful – he was quite poorly. I nearly rang for an ambulance. But somehow, he got through it. We've thrown out all the booze and he's attending an AA meeting every day, but he won't talk to me about how he's feeling."

"I'm sorry to hear that – it must be so hard for you. You know you can ring me, any time?"

"Thank you – that helps. Jessica took the news badly, so I can't talk to her about it."

What else to say? – she knew so little about alcoholism. Thank God. Time to talk about something else.

"How are you getting on with *Eleanor Oliphant?*"

"I haven't read it yet – I've been so worried about John. So I've been distracting myself by writing. It's been a good way to forget, throwing myself back into the distant past, rather than having to face what's happening right now."

Rose couldn't have agreed less – she was throwing herself into the present, in a vain effort to forget the past. But she understood what Meg meant. Any distraction helped.

"I'd love to see what you've written so far. Is it ready for sharing yet?"

"I think I'd rather leave it for now, sorry. I'm in the very early stages yet, just scribbling down whatever comes into my head. When I've typed up the first couple of chapters, I'll share it then."

"Fair enough."

"How about you? How's the piano going? And the cross-stitch?"

"The cross-stitch is going better than the piano," Rose said. "I've stitched two cards so far, and I'm planning to do another for Ginny for her birthday."

"Oh, she'll be thrilled! What a lovely idea."

"It's hard to go wrong with it. Like I said before, as long as you can follow a chart, and remember to start your crosses from bottom left to top right every time, and keep an even tension, it's simple enough."

"How about the piano?" Meg said again.

"It's not getting any easier," Rose said. "Perhaps I'm expecting too much too soon. But I can't help feeling a bit discouraged. Lesley will play a couple of bars to show me how to do something, and I feel like I'll never be any good.

Her fingers just do it, effortlessly."

"You'll get there. Just give yourself a chance."

"That's what Lesley says. I suppose you're right. But I'm not sure I'm going to carry on with it. It reminds me too much of Graham."

"Graham? Why?"

"It was his piano and I used to love listening to him play. He was really good."

"So we're both having a fairly rubbish time at the moment."

"Yes." Rose took a deep breath. "But life goes on, regardless. What are you giving Ginny for her birthday?"

"I've knitted some fingerless mittens for her, using fine four-ply wool, to use when she's out taking photos. What are you getting her?"

"I'm sure she'll appreciate them. I've got her something photography-related too – a new memory card for the camera."

"I hope John will have an AA meeting to attend that evening. I don't like leaving him on his own in the house."

"Perhaps you could arrange for Jessica to visit him."

"Hmm, not sure about that. Like I said, she took it hard. But it's a thought – thanks, Rose."

"I'll collect you at ten past six. 'Bye now."

Ginny

Seventy five today. Oh my. Three quarters of a century. And it felt like she'd spent most of those years alone. Snap out of it, Ginny! She was lucky to still be here.

She did her yoga and meditation practice, had a shower, then ate breakfast. Rose and Meg would be arriving at 6.30 this evening and she had loads to do before then. She set to, wanting the house to look its best for her visitors. Knowing that they probably wouldn't care. But she did. Everything had to be perfect.

By the time she was done, her back was aching, and she was glad to sit down. She re-read the risotto recipe and reckoned it would take about an hour and a half from start to finish. So she'd need to be ready to roll by half-past four, to give herself time to change afterwards. The mousse wouldn't take long – maybe she'd better do that first, so it would have time to chill in the fridge. And the melon couldn't be simpler: slice, dice and serve.

As the clock's hands crept round to 6.30, the butterflies in her stomach were fluttering madly. It had been so long since she had entertained anyone.

She changed swiftly into one of her favourite floaty, Indian cotton dresses in warm earth colours, and selected her rings – all silver, all beautiful. She liked to wear one on each finger and both thumbs. An amber bracelet and earrings provided the finishing touch. She put her long silver hair up in a loose bun, then nodded to her reflection. That would do.

Then sat down with a mug of camomile tea, for soothing.

She knew Rose was picking Meg up on the way, as Meg didn't drive, and the evening bus services were infrequent. The doorbell rang at 6.30 on the dot.

"Hello, you two! Thank you for coming. Come on in."

Meg thrust a bouquet of flowers into her hands, "These are from both of us. Happy birthday!"

Such beautiful autumn colours – orange and deep yellow alstroemeria, white carnations, Chinese lanterns, and some dark red roses. They took her breath away.

"Thank you both, so much. They're gorgeous." She gave them each a hug. "Come on in. I'll just put these in water."

She led them through to the sitting room, then said, "Make yourselves comfortable. What would you like to drink? I've got sherry, red wine, white wine..."

"Do you have any soft drinks?" said Rose. "I don't drink and drive."

"Of course. I can offer you elderflower cordial or red Schloer." Good job she'd thought to buy something alcohol-free.

"The Schloer will be fine, thank you."

"I'll have the same, please," Meg said, glancing at Rose.

What was going on? Ginny brought them their drinks, then arranged the flowers in a vase. They really were gorgeous. Such a kind thought. She took them through to the sitting room and placed them on the coffee table.

"Dinner will be at seven," she said, "I've got a few last-minute things to do in the kitchen, then I'll be with you."

"That's fine," Rose said. "It smells delicious."

"I hope so. It's a new recipe I'm trying out."

Twenty minutes later, they were seated round her kitchen table. She brought the melon from the fridge.

"Melon!" Meg said. "My favourite starter."

"Enjoy," Ginny said.

"You may be wondering," Meg said, as they began to eat, "why I'm not drinking, even though Rose is driving."

"I was. Why aren't you?"

"We've – we've had some bad news," Meg said, her lips quivering. "John's drinking has damaged his liver and he's been told to quit, so I've done the same in solidarity."

"Oh, God. I'm so sorry. That must be awful for you. What's the treatment?"

Meg's eyes sparkled with unshed tears. "There isn't any," she said. "His only hope of avoiding any further damage is to stop drinking altogether, forever."

"I hope he manages it." What else was there to say?

"I'm sorry," Meg said. "I didn't mean to put a damper on your birthday. Let's talk about something else."

"How are things with you, Rose?" Ginny said.

"I've made a lifestyle change too," Rose said. "I'm trying to eat more healthily. When Graham first passed, I was eating for England. Comfort eating – anything sweet and filling and fattening. I put on more than a stone before I realised what I was doing." She grimaced. "But it's proving difficult to lose it again."

A sharp pang of recognition. "I remember it well," Ginny said, "I did exactly the same thing after Laura died." She paused. Did she want to tell them the rest? What would they think of her? What would they say?

She took a deep breath. "Problem was, when I realised I was putting on weight, I took control of my eating rather too well." She paused again. "I'll just dish the main course, then I'll tell you the story." Maybe it was time to trust a little.

She saw Meg and Rose glance at each other. Would they judge her? Hopefully not.

"Here we are," she said, "Ratatouille risotto."

"Mm. It smells scrumptious," Rose said. She took a forkful. "And it tastes wonderful! Thank you."

"Yes, it's delicious," Meg agreed. "So, what's the story?"

Ginny was silent. This felt vulnerable. But they were her friends. The first close friends she'd had in... oh, years.

"You don't have to tell us if you don't want to," Rose said, touching her hand.

"Thank you, Rose. But I think I know you both well enough now... I met Laura when I was in my early forties. I'd known for years that men didn't interest me and was more or less reconciled to spending my life alone. I'd been practising yoga since my return from the States in the late sixties, and built up a small business, teaching yoga to women. Then Laura joined one of my classes. I noticed her straightaway – she was so beautiful, all fire and darkness. A few weeks later, I'd dismissed the class and was packing away my yoga mat and cassette player, when I realised that someone was hovering behind me, waiting to speak to me.

"It was Laura, and she asked me out for a drink. We had a wonderful evening together, and ended up at her flat, in bed. I think it was then that I found out for the first time what love really meant. I adored her. Within a year, she had moved in with me, and we spent a blissful few years together, growing closer and closer..."

This was difficult – she hadn't shared this much of

herself for years. She looked up and saw that Rose and Meg were listening attentively, plainly waiting for her to go on. She took another deep breath. "Laura was so good for me. You may have noticed that I'm a fairly serious person, left to myself, but Laura brought laughter and fun into my life." She paused. "Then it all started to go wrong. She kept having stomach problems and lost a load of weight. All her beautiful energy disappeared, and she took more and more time off work. She caught every cold doing the rounds, and had trouble fighting them off.

"I was worried sick about her and marched her along to the surgery. Our GP listened to Laura's symptoms, and took some blood from her. A couple of weeks later, when I arrived home at the end of work, Laura was waiting for me. I'll never forget it... She told me she'd had a phone call from the doctor's secretary, and that the doctor wanted to see her 'as soon as possible'. I'll never forget how she clung to me, whispering, 'Oh, Ginny, I'm so scared!'

"The doctor broke it to us as gently as she could. She said, 'I'm so sorry – I'm afraid it is bad news. You have the AIDS virus.'

Ginny's eyes were full of tears, remembering. "We were stunned; we couldn't believe it. We'd been together for several years after all, and I knew Laura had never looked at anyone else. I remember the doctor asking, 'Did you have any partners before Ginny? The HIV virus can remain dormant for several years, before evolving into AIDS.'

"And she had. A bisexual man who had died years before. The diagnosis shattered us both – she'd been carrying the HIV virus for ages without any symptoms at all. After that, it was just a matter of time. I had to watch my darling girl turn into a shadow of her former self, wracked by coughs, struggling for breath, her body almost skeletal, her muscles ropey, dark tumours blooming on her beautiful face. I nursed her through it all and was devastated when she died.

"Of course I thought I'd be infected too, but it turned out I was one of those rare people who was immune. But my life was over. I couldn't understand why I had survived. My reason for living was gone. I felt like I didn't deserve to live, not without Laura."

Ginny paused again, then continued. "I'd never been that interested in food, being someone who ate to live, rather than living to eat, to coin a cliché. But after Laura's death, I ate everything that wasn't actually nailed down, trying to fill the huge hole in my life with food. It didn't work, of course – I gained two stone, and added disgust to the despair I was already feeling. And I still felt empty. One morning, I looked in the mirror and was filled with self-loathing. I didn't understand how I could have done this to myself.

"So I took back control," she went on, addressing the salt and pepper. "I managed to lose the weight I'd gained fairly quickly. I counted every calorie religiously and beat myself up each time I slipped. Over time, it became easier and easier to make my portions smaller, and before I knew where I was, I was subsisting on a very low calorie diet, and the weight simply fell off me. It felt wonderful to be in control of something… I'd felt so helpless since Laura had died, and so guilty for not having seen soon enough that she was really ill. I didn't want to live without her and needed to punish myself for still being here… To cut a long story short,

I ended up with anorexia. It wasn't diagnosed until I fainted one day at a yoga class and one of the class members was a nurse and recognised the signs. She marched me along to my GP the next day."

Ginny stopped, scanning her friends' faces, expecting... what? Revulsion? Disgust? To her relief, she saw nothing but kindness and sympathy in their expressions. Tears were sparkling in Rose's eyes.

"Oh, Ginny," Rose said, taking her hand. "I'm so sorry. What happened next?"

"Well, I was taken straight to hospital, to stabilise me, and then, because I had private health insurance, I was transferred to another hospital which specialised in eating disorders and other addictive behaviours. It was a long haul, but through a combination of a controlled eating programme and a lot of therapy, I gradually began to understand that I had been punishing myself for still being alive, and that Laura's death hadn't been my fault. I found that I did want to live after all, and eventually graduated to day-care at the local hospital. I'm still really careful about what I eat and how much I eat, but I can live with that. And here I am," she finished, "seventy-five today."

There was silence round the table for a few moments.

"Thank you for sharing this – it was so brave of you," Rose said, leaning across and touching her hand. "I know how hard it is to come through such grief. I'm still in the middle of it, to be honest. But hearing your story has helped me to realise that I need to take hold of myself and start to move on."

"Oh, God! I'm so sorry. I didn't think..."

"No need for apologies. Like I said, it's helped, hearing your story."

"We're here for you, Ginny," Meg said, "and Ginny and I are here for you too, Rose."

"Bless you both," Ginny said. "I'm so lucky to have found you." Time to change the subject. "Now, let's finish our meal, and I'll bring out the puds."

Meg's eyes lit up at the sight of the chocolate mousse. "Oh, heaven!" she said, "Chocolate! Such a treat. Thank you."

When they'd finished eating, they cleared the table, and Rose and Meg insisted on washing up. Then they all went back through to the sitting room.

"Now," Meg said, "it's present time."

Rose delved in her bag and brought out a small, flat parcel and a large card. "Here you are," she said, "Happy birthday!"

Ginny opened the parcel first. "A new memory card for the camera – excellent! Thank you."

Then she opened the card. It was a cross-stitched rose, in varying shades of peach, with the words 'Happy Birthday Ginny' done in back-stitch. "Rose! That's beautiful. Thank you so much." She hugged her friend.

"My turn now," Meg said. "I hope you like them." She handed over a small, squishy parcel. What on earth?

"I'm sure I shall," Ginny said, opening it carefully. Inside she found a pair of soft, woollen fingerless gloves in variegated autumn colours, with a mitten flap to cover the fingers.

"They're gorgeous, Meg," she said, "Where did you

get them from?"

Meg blushed. "I knitted them myself," she said. "I thought they'd be useful when you're out taking photos in the cold weather, because you can slip the mitten flap off to use the camera without removing your gloves."

"That's so thoughtful – I'll use them all the time."

Then she opened her card. Meg had written 'To my dear friend, Ginny. Happy 75th Birthday, Love Meg xx'. She hugged her.

She smiled at both of them. "Thank you both, so much," she said. "It's been a while since I've really celebrated a birthday. You two have made it so special for me."

"You're more than welcome," Rose said. "You're special to us too."

Rose

Back in the car on the way home, Rose said, "Ginny's story moved me so much. And it's made me realise the danger I'm in, at the moment."

"Danger?" Meg said.

Deep breath. "Yes, of trying to fill the emptiness inside me with food. But it doesn't work. I'll never stop missing Graham, but overeating isn't going to make the pain go away. It's just adding physical discomfort to all the rest of it."

"I'm so sorry," Meg said, "I can't imagine what you're going through at the moment. But you seemed be dealing with it so well."

"Ah, that's the public face I put on. I've found that

after the first few weeks, most people seem to expect you to have 'got over it' and are 'ready to move on'." She lifted two fingers off the steering wheel to sketch the speech marks, "and I don't want to add to Matthew's and Daniel's grief by talking about it with them, so I've bottled it all up and eaten my feelings. I'm only just realising that's what I've been doing."

"You know that you can always ring me?"

Bless her. She genuinely wants to help, in spite of her own problems. "Thank you. I may well take you up on that. I'm going to clear out my cupboards tomorrow. Healthy eating starts now."

Rose stopped the car outside Meg's house. "Here you are, safe and sound. See you on the 25th."

Meg leaned across and kissed her cheek. "'Bye now. Remember what I said – I really meant it."

"Thank you, Meg. The same goes for you."

Back home, Rose made herself a mug of tea and sat down in the living room, Bonnie on her knee. It had been such a special evening. She was so glad that Ginny had trusted them enough to be able to share her story. It had been a real wake-up call. It was five whole months since Graham had passed, perhaps it was time to try to move on. Or at least, to stop comfort eating. Even her loosest clothes were getting uncomfortably tight and the extra weight was doing her dicky knee no good at all.

"Well, Bonnie," she told the cat, "it's time to take hold of myself. Like I told Meg, I'll never stop missing your dad, but eating for England isn't going to bring him back. I'll go through those cupboards tomorrow."

Bonnie purred on, happy to be on Rose's lap. It must be wonderful to be a cat – no emotional upheavals, no grief.

Rose took Bonnie in her arms and gently set her down on the floor. "Time for bed, my precious. Come along."

Meg

Meg was the first to arrive at Capuchins, for a change. She ordered her Americano and a chocolate brownie from Karen, then sat down to wait for the others.

Rose walked in just before eleven. "Hello, Meg, you're here early!"

"Yes, John was coming into town for a haircut, so he dropped me off. How are you?"

"Good, thanks. I'll just place my order."

"Well," Rose said as she sat down, "I've done it."

"Done what?"

"I've cleared out all my cupboards. Anything still in date has gone to the food bank, and I've lobbed the rest."

"Oh, good for you. How are you feeling, now that you're eating more healthily?"

"It's only been a few days, so I'm not seeing much benefit yet. But I'm feeling less lurgy in the evenings. I expect I'll start to lose some weight soon."

"I'm sure you're doing the right thing."

Ginny arrived. "Hello, you two! See you in a minute." And she walked up to the counter.

"Ginny," Rose said as her friend sat down, "I've thought of a good name for your blog. 'Ginny's Nature

Journal'."

"Hmm," Ginny said, "I've done some googling about blog titles and there's one with a similar title... I couldn't believe it. I had no idea there were so many people with photography blogs!"

"Oh! Well, never mind." Rose said. "It was just a thought."

She sounded deflated. Ginny could have been a bit more tactful.

"I'm finding that I'm getting an almost spiritual pleasure from taking photographs," Ginny continued, "so I'd like to use some sort of poetic or spiritual quotation for it, I think."

"Why don't you google nature quotes?" Rose said.

"That's a brilliant idea," Ginny said. "Why didn't I think of it?" She paused. "Would the two of you mind if I did it now?"

"Of course not," Meg said.

Ginny fished her mobile phone out of her back pack. A couple of minutes later, she whooped with delight, startling both of them.

"That's it!" she said. "Listen to this: 'Nature is so powerful, so strong. Capturing its essence is not easy – your work becomes a dance with light and the weather. It takes you to a place within yourself.' It's by Annie Leibovitz. I'll call the blog *A Dance with Light and the Weather*. Thank you, Rose. That was an excellent idea."

"A dance with light and the weather... I like it!" Rose said. "You'd better google that too, to check that nobody else is using it. And check out Annie Leibovitz too. If she's still alive, you may have to ask her permission to use the quote."

"Good thinking," Ginny said, "I'll do that when I get home."

"How's the memoir going, Meg?" Rose said.

"I'm really enjoying it. I'm finding that every time I remember one incident, it triggers another memory, of a place or person. The problem is choosing what to include and what to leave out."

"What a lovely problem to have," Ginny said. "How are you dealing with it?"

"That sounds sensible," said Rose, when Meg had explained her method to them. "I hope we'll get to hear some of it soon."

Meg shook her head. "I've started writing the first chapter, which is mainly background about the era I was born in, and about my parents, but I'm not sure I'm ready for that just yet. I'd like to work on it a bit longer."

"Fair enough. Now for my news. I've found a gorgeous website dedicated to cross-stitch, which has thousands of charts and kits covering every subject you could think of. I've chosen a silver wedding sampler for Matthew and Sarah and ordered the kit. Matthew's crazy about Charles Rennie Mackintosh and it's based around those roses. I can't wait for it to arrive."

"Oh, that's marvellous," Meg said. "You'll have to bring the kit in to show us, once it's come."

"Yes, I'd love to see it too," Ginny chimed in. "I'm so pleased that we've all found something creative to do, that makes our lives happier."

"Yes, Liz Gilbert has a lot to answer for," Meg said,

"I'm so glad we read *Big Magic*. Good call, Ginny."

"What did you think of *Eleanor Oliphant*?" Ginny said.

"I absolutely loved it," Rose said, "once I got past the first few pages. At first, I couldn't understand what all the fuss was about. She seemed to be the most boring, maladroit person ever. But then, as I read on, her story broke my heart."

"Yes, I felt that too," Meg said. "I think it was very brave of Gail Honeyman to open her book with those early chapters. I kept thinking 'there must be more to it than this'. And of course, there was."

"It's one of the most unusual books I've ever read," Ginny said. "Like both of you, I nearly gave up in disgust after reading the first few pages, then the odd sentence kept cropping up, like her vodka buying habits and her stash of medication, which made me realise that there was more going on than met the eye. But I didn't see the end coming at all."

"Oh, me neither," said Rose. "I found it so moving that she gradually learned to trust people and to allow herself to reach out for help. The *Bad Days* section made me cry."

"It just goes to show," Meg said, "you can't judge people by the faces they show to the world."

"That is so true," Rose said. "Look at the three of us. If anyone glanced across now, they'd see three old ladies, meeting for a quiet coffee. But underneath, we're three powerful women, with the creative spark burning brightly inside us." She grinned.

Meg smiled back. "Three powerful women. I like that, Rose."

Ginny nodded. "Long may it continue," she said.

"I'm so grateful for that blog title. I can't wait to get started on it."

"Let us know when it's up and running," Rose said.

"Yes, I will," Ginny said. "I've decided on *Wild* by Cheryl Strayed for next month's book. It reminds me of my year in California."

"I think I've heard of it," said Rose, "wasn't there a film version with Reese Witherspoon?"

"Yes, but it wasn't nearly as good as the book."

Rose

So, Ginny had spent a year in California. There was still so much they didn't know about each other. Maybe she'd tell them more next month.

The post had already been delivered when Rose reached home. Including a Jiffy bag parcel with the label of the cross-stitch company on the back, propped up against the front door. She took it through to the kitchen, where the letter opener lived in a jar on the side, and slit it open. Inside was the kit, in a neat, resealable plastic bag, with a full-colour photograph of the finished design at the front. A frisson of excitement. She opened it up and began examining the contents.

A large chart. All the threads were pre-sorted and arranged on card thread holders. That would save some time. Such delicate colours. And the fabric, cream 16 count Aida. It looked gorgeous. She'd start it this afternoon. Good job she'd bought a larger hoop from Hobbycraft. Her small one, the one she'd used for the cards, would be no good for a big project like this.

She read the accompanying instructions over lunch, then sat down in her favourite armchair, folded the material in four to find the centre, then put it in the hoop and counted down from the centre to the top of the heart. She'd decided to leave the lettering in the middle until the end. Once she'd done a few stitches, she re-positioned the hoop, so that the portion she was stitching was in easy reach. This was going to be fun.

How she would have loved to use her new-found skill to stitch something for Graham. Now she never would. She put the hoop down, suddenly blinded by tears.

Meg

"I love the time I spend with Rose and Ginny," Meg told John when she got home. "Being with them makes me feel young again."

"How d'you mean?" John said.

"Well, we talk about all kinds of things, apart from the books we're reading. And those have been an eye-opener too. I'm reading books I'd never have picked up for myself, and have really enjoyed them. The most important one was *Big Magic*, which was why I've started on my memoir."

"How's it going?" John said. "Every time I look up lately, you're either going through old photo albums or scribbling something down on a record card."

Meg's face lit up. "It's been such fun! Looking through all our old photos has brought back so many memories and every time I've remembered something, I've jotted it down. The next stage is going to be sorting the cards into chronological order and starting to write. I've started the first chapter."

"What are you calling it?"

"*In which I was born,*" Meg said. "I'm setting the scene by sharing a bit about Mother and Father, and what was happening in the world in 1948. I've had to do quite a bit of research. I'm so glad I've got over my computer phobia – otherwise, I'd have had to spend days and days down at the library. Now it's all at my fingertips." She laughed.

"Good for you, Meggie!" John said. "But I meant, what are you calling the memoir?"

"Oh! I hadn't even thought of that. I suppose it has to have a title…"

"I guess you could just call it *The Life and Times of Meg Jeffries.*"

"That sounds so boring," Meg said. "I'd like to think of something a bit more original than that. Thanks for bringing it up. Now, what would you like for lunch?"

After the meal, John went off to his AA meeting, so Meg logged on to Amazon, and searched for autobiographies. To her dismay, there were thousands of them. She wasn't going to copy anyone else's title, but she needed some inspiration. Lots of them had subtitles, which referred to the person's role in life or had a 'how I did x' or 'how I survived y' sort of wording. This was going to be harder than she'd thought. She hadn't done anything out of the ordinary; she'd grown up, got married, worked as a nursery school teacher and had children. But she'd been happy, by and large. What on earth could she call it? Then inspiration struck – perhaps she should look up quotes with the words 'ordinary life' in them. She closed down Amazon and went back to Google, checked some quotations websites. There seemed to be an answer to everything on the internet. Why had she been frightened of it for so long?

Meg shrugged and carried on scrolling. John had bought her a mouse with a little wheel on the top, which made it easy. Bingo! A gorgeous quote by William Martin, advising parents to introduce their children to 'the wonder and the marvel of an ordinary life.' She scribbled it down, then searched again to find his blog site so she could send him a message, asking for permission to use the quote as the title of her memoir.

She hugged herself. It would be perfect. She just hoped he'd say yes.

When John returned, she told him, "I've thought of a title for my book: *The Wonder and Marvel of an Ordinary Life.*"

"Where on earth did you get that from?"

The scorn in his voice made her doubt herself straight away. "Don't you like it? I thought it was perfect. I found it by googling 'ordinary life'. Because that's what I've had. I haven't done anything extraordinary – climbed any mountains, jumped out of aeroplanes. Nothing. But I've been happy."

He hugged her. "Sorry, Meggie – I was a bit surprised, that's all. Where's all the wonder and marvel going to come in?"

"I may have had an ordinary life," Meg said with dignity, "but there has been plenty to wonder at, plenty to marvel over."

"Such as?" he said. He really didn't understand.

"The children, for a start. Not only Jessica and Andrew, but all the children I taught down the years. Each one unique, each one with their own special gifts, their own personalities. And the places we've been on holiday. The beauties of nature. The history we've lived through. Lots of things."

"Good for you," he said. "I'm off upstairs. See you later."

October: *Wild* by Cheryl Strayed

Meg

Meg was fuming. John could be so infuriating sometimes. Why did he have to pour cold water on her idea? There was only one solution for times like this: make some bread.

She slammed the dough down onto the well-floured worktop, before pummelling and kneading it into submission with her strong fingers. Slam, pummel, knead. Slam, pummel, knead.

It was the best stress buster she knew. By the time the dough was ready to be put into the proving drawer, her mind was calm.

Or calmer… why did she put up with him? And why did he get under her skin so much?

She set the timer for twenty minutes, then made herself a cup of tea, fetched the biscuit tin out of the cupboard and sat down at the kitchen table, pillowing her chin on her hands.

Why wouldn't he take her seriously? They had been married for 49 years, and he still drove her mad as often as he kept her sane. When he was in a good mood, Meg couldn't think of anyone she'd rather be with – he could charm the birds off the trees. But it felt like a long while since he'd made the effort to charm her.

Meg sighed, took a long swallow of her tea and helped herself to another custard cream. She tried to make allowances for him, knowing how much the shock of the ARLD diagnosis had affected him, and how difficult he was finding it to not drink. But there was no excuse for this morning's bad behaviour. Somehow, he had to learn that her life, her ideas, were as important as his.

As soon as the bread was in the oven, she rang Rose.

"Rose. It's Meg. I'm so furious with John."

"What's he done?" Her voice changed. "He's not drinking again, is he?"

"No, nothing like that," Meg said. "I was wondering what title to give my memoir and looked on Amazon to find some inspiration. But all the autobiographies seemed to be about people who'd done something remarkable. And I haven't. So I decided to google 'ordinary life' and found a brilliant quote by William Martin 'The wonder and the marvel of an ordinary life'. And John made fun of it."

"Oh, Meg," Rose said, "I'm so sorry. I think that's a brilliant title. Because just bringing up children has so much wonder and marvel in it, it should be enough for a lifetime."

"That's exactly what I was thinking," Meg said, "but he just didn't get it."

"Oh dear. Men often don't, I've found. Graham could never understand, when I came home from school, full of joy about a breakthrough by a particular pupil. In the end, I stopped sharing them."

"That's it!" Meg said, "I had that too, with my little ones at nursery school. Thank you for understanding. I was beginning to think it was a stupid title."

"Not at all. It's perfect. You go for it."

"Thank you, I will. I've found William Martin's website and sent him a message asking his permission to use it."

"I hope he says yes. Let me know when you hear back from him, won't you?"

"Of course I will."

Thank goodness for Rose. Meg had forgotten she'd been a teacher too. Now, back to the memoir. She'd better sit down and think of some wonders and marvels, to justify the title. She reached for her faithful notepad, sat back down at the kitchen table, and began to write.

Wonders and marvels:

- The children being born and events in their lives
- Being a teenager in the 1960s
- Seeing Paris for the first time
- Nursery school – some of the children there
- Scenery in Austria and Wales – mountains and lakes and waterfalls
- Books I've read
- Music I've loved
- Events in history – first man on the Moon, medical breakthroughs, technological changes

Plenty to be going on with there. That would show John.

Ginny

Ginny was determined to carry on going for walks or cycle

rides with Graham's camera, trying to capture the beauty all around her, even though the days were getting shorter and the weather more inclement. It was fascinating to watch the world change as summer turned into autumn. Autumn and spring were her favourite seasons. Spring because that was when everything was coming out of hibernation and growing and blossoming with a myriad shades of green, from the vivid lime green of young oak leaves in sunlight, through the countless greens of the grasses and flower stems with their infinite variations, to the darker greens of evergreens like holly. And the gorgeous pinks and whites and yellows and blues of the flowers and blossom. Autumn because of the glorious colours of the trees – their leaves all the shades of yellow, gold, copper, bronze, red, burgundy and brown as they prepared to fall, and the reds, oranges, blues and purples of the fruit. Her file of uploaded nature photos was filling up fast. In fact, she'd decided to create several sub-folders – one for flowers, one for trees, one for landscapes and so on.

She loved walking by the River Severn, past the Cathedral in all its gothic majesty, watching the endlessly changing water, the ever-present swans – so white and elegant – the feel of the warm sunshine caressing her skin, and the clean scent of the air. She was so lucky to have all this beauty on her doorstep.

But she was also frustrated. She'd looked everywhere she could think of and couldn't discover a way to contact Annie Leibovitz. She had found out a lot about her, but no website, no contact details. There was a Facebook page, with a message link, but Annie did not seem to want to use it to send a reply. Ginny was tempted to use the title anyway…

she really wanted to get started on the blog. But she didn't want to get into trouble... maybe she'd better think of something else. She thought and thought, and eventually came up with *A Dance with Words and Nature*. It didn't have the same ring as the Leibovitz quote, but it would have to do. She'd ask Rose and Meg – perhaps they'd be able to come up with something better.

Meg

Meg was finding *Wild* hard going. For more than one reason. First, Cheryl Strayed's life was so wildly (ha, ha!) different from her own, she was struggling to empathise with her. Apart from losing her mother. Her own mother had died when she was eight, and she had been brought up by her Auntie Enid. At least Cheryl had experienced a loving mother for all her growing up years. Auntie Enid had done her best, but it had fallen to Meg to mother her siblings, to provide the love her maiden aunt had been unable to give.

Second, she couldn't understand why anyone would choose to endure such physical discomfort. Meg didn't mind an occasional stroll in the countryside, but to walk all day with a heavy pack, which rubbed her back and shoulders and hips raw, wearing boots which gave her blisters and destroyed her feet. Well, she just couldn't do it. Wouldn't.

But if she was honest, the primary reason was sheer, green-eyed envy. *Wild* was a superb memoir, vividly written. It made her doubt her own ability to write anything even vaguely approaching acceptable. Her life had been so boring... why on earth would anyone want to read about it?

She read over what she had written so far, tore the pages in two, and flung them in the bin. It was no good. Why had she ever thought she could write?

She rang Rose. "It's no good," she wailed, "I need to find something else creative to do."

"Why on earth?" Rose said, "I thought it was going well? That you were enjoying writing it, bringing your memories to life?"

"It's *Wild*," Meg said. "I'm about half-way through, and it's brilliant. I could never write like that in a hundred years, and anyway, I've never done anything interesting like that."

"Oh, Meg," Rose said, her voice warm and reassuring in Meg's ears, "don't compare yourself with Cheryl Strayed. Remember what Liz Gilbert wrote in *Big Magic*? The bit when she said we all have our own unique experiences to bring to the work? Well, you're you, you're not Cheryl Strayed. You're writing your book for your grandchildren, to share your life with them. Only you can do that. And it's worth doing."

"Do you really think so?"

"I *know* so!" Rose said. "Please don't give up on yourself. So long as you write from an authentic place, from your own unique point of view, you can't go wrong."

"But I've ripped up what I've written so far."

"Oh, Meg!" Now Rose sounded exasperated. "Why did you do that? Have you still got the pieces?"

"They're in the bin in the kitchen."

"Then get them out, tape them back together, and type them up. Or start again, fresh. But please, keep going. Stop doubting yourself. I can't wait to read it."

"Really?" Meg said, desperate for reassurance.

"Really," Rose said, with a different inflection. "I can't wait to read about your life, how you grew up, the people who have influenced you, your joys, your sorrows. All of it."

Tears filled Meg's eyes. "Thank you. You've made me feel much better. I'll get those pages out of the bin and start now."

"That's more like it," her friend said. "You do that. It's going to be fine – I know it."

Rose

Poor Meg! Rose knew exactly how discouraging comparison could be. Every time Lesley showed her something on the piano, Rose would watch her fluent fingers dancing across the keys and feel so bad about her own playing. Maybe she'd better take her own advice and stop comparing her performance with her piano teacher's. After all, if she played as well as Lesley, she wouldn't need lessons.

Thinking of which, she'd better do some practice. She'd been learning for a couple of months now and was gradually gaining some confidence. She was starting to play slightly longer pieces – 16 or 20 bars – and to put them together more easily. But her left hand was still her Achilles' heel. It wasn't too bad when she could concentrate on it, but when she had to play hands together, it was so difficult. She wished so much that Graham was still around to encourage her. He had been quite a good pianist. He'd never learned with a teacher but had a natural ear and had taught himself to read music. Her own stilted attempts at playing seemed very feeble in comparison.

There she was again, doing precisely what she had told Meg not to do. Comparing herself with others. She sighed. At least the cross-stitch was going better. She'd made a good start on the sampler for Matthew and Sarah and was thrilled with what she'd stitched so far. And she'd found a gorgeous book in Capuchin's, *Traditional Samplers* by Brenda Keyes, which had some wonderful projects in it, using other stitches as well as cross-stitch. She was very tempted to try one of them, perhaps the *Band Sampler*, once she'd finished the anniversary one. Although perhaps she'd better find a birth sampler instead – Daniel's wife Debbie was due to give birth after Christmas.

It would certainly stretch her and fill those long winter evenings. Which she wasn't looking forward to, not even slightly. Last year, the quiet, dark evenings had been spent watching television with Graham, or reading together in companionable silence, side by side on the sofa. Now she only had Bonnie for company. She missed Graham so much. So very much... They'd had more than fifty years together and she had thought there would be many more. Well, perhaps not *many* more, but at least some. He'd always been healthy, had taken good care of himself, exercising regularly and eating (mostly) healthily.

Until that April afternoon, when her life had fallen apart. They had just returned from a walk and were sitting in the living room, when his face had turned grey, his lips blue.

"My chest," he had gasped. "Can't breathe. So heavy."

She'd phoned 999 immediately, but by the time the ambulance crew arrived, it had been too late. The paramedics had fought to resuscitate him, but in vain.

"I'm so sorry, Mrs Anderson," the paramedic had said gently. "There's nothing more we can do for him."

"No! That can't be true," she had protested, shaking her head in instinctive denial. "There must be something…"

"I'm so sorry."

She hadn't cried. Not then. Not when they'd taken Graham's body away in the ambulance. Not until Matthew had arrived, an hour later. When she had felt her son's strong arms around her, she had finally been able to weep. And then had been unable to stop. She had cried herself to a standstill. Just thinking about that day had brought the hot tears to her eyes.

So she had found reading *Wild* a challenge. The author's grief over losing her mother had brought it all back. The anger, the feeling of emptiness, the lack of purpose in her life. She had to keep reminding herself that she had survived, she was here, that life went on. That she had Matthew and Daniel and their families. Ginny and Meg too. But it wasn't the same. Graham had been her best friend as well as her husband, and she missed him desperately. She scrubbed at her eyes, trying to stop the tears from falling, but it was no good.

"Graham!" she wailed to the empty house, "why did you have to leave me?" She collapsed into a chair and cried until her head ached and her eyes were red and sore. Would there ever be a day when she didn't miss him? A day when she would feel whole again?

Meg

Meg had followed Rose's advice and typed up what she had written so far – just the first chapter, and then printed it out. It had been kind of John to link her laptop to his printer in the study. Seeing her words as a typescript rather than a handwritten scrawl made them seem more real – more legitimate, somehow. She read the chapter through, and immediately came across some words and sentences she wanted to improve – both typing errors and parts she could have expressed better. She fetched a red biro from the pot by the phone and began to jot the changes down in the margins. Then she re-opened it on her laptop and made the alterations, before printing it out again and stapling the pages together.

Perhaps she would be brave enough to read it to Ginny and Rose next week. She'd take it along in her bag and see how she felt.

At least they'd be an attentive audience. Unlike John. She'd tried to share something with him a couple of nights ago – just a few sentences, to ask his opinion about them.

"Not now," he'd growled. "I've got an AA meeting to go to."

He wasn't sharing anything with her. She had no idea how the not drinking was going, except he wasn't drinking in front of her. But she suspected he was still having the occasional drink, from the smell of toothpaste on his breath. Why else would he be cleaning his teeth in the middle of the day, if not to disguise the smell of booze?

He'd always had a short temper, but now it had evolved into a hair-trigger one. Anything she said seemed to be wrong. She'd offered to listen whenever he wanted to talk, but he seemed not to want to talk – at least, not to her. Which hurt. She felt so helpless, so desperate to help him, but was being rebuffed at every turn.

Ginny

Ginny arrived at Capuchins early on purpose, so she could browse the bookshelves before Meg and Rose arrived. She was feeling discontented – her new blog wasn't going well. In fact, it wasn't going at all. She had drafted several blog posts, but hadn't yet had the courage to publish one. She was in two minds about continuing with it. Compared to other nature photography blogs she'd seen, hers was rubbish.

Perfectionism. Her besetting sin. She found it impossible to stay out of judgement, to have compassion for herself. It was easier with other people. She stalked over to the arts and crafts section and began to look along the shelves. Karen must have been a librarian in a previous life; all the sections were neatly arranged in alphabetical order by author. She'd got all the way to 'S' before she came across *The Secret Lives of Colour* by Kassia St. Clair. Intrigued by the title – how could colours have secret lives? – she took it off the shelf and began to skim through it. Even glancing down the contents list, she could see that this was a whole new way of looking at the world around her. She walked up to the counter.

"I'd like to buy this, please."

Karen's eyes lit up. "That book," she said. "I absolutely loved it – it's made me see colour in a completely different way."

"What do you mean?"

"I don't want to spoil it for you," Karen said, "but it's like having a new pair of eyes."

"It sounds fascinating." She gave Karen a ten pound note. "Here you are."

"Thank you, Ginny. I hope you get as much out of it as I have."

"Well, I'll certainly give it a go. May I have a camomile tea too, please?"

"Of course. Here's your change. I'll bring your tea over in a moment."

She had just sat down when Rose arrived.

"Hello, Ginny," she said. "You're early."

"Yes, I wanted to have a browse along the shelves before you arrived."

"Have you found anything good?"

Ginny showed her *The Secret Lives of Colour*. "Karen said it's going to change the way I look at the world."

"Sounds like a good title for all of us," Rose said, "It could help with my cross-stitch and Meg's crochet."

"I'm going to take it home and read it, and if it's as good as Karen says, I'll might make it my next book choice, in January."

"Good idea," Rose said, "I'm going to order my coffee and cake."

Then Meg arrived.

"Am I late?" she said, seeing Ginny sitting there.

Ginny smiled at her. "Not at all. I came early for once to look at the books."

A few minutes later, they were ready to start.

"What did you both think of *Wild*?" Ginny said.

Rose frowned. "I found it quite challenging," she said, "I think I was too close to losing Graham to read a book about loss. Cheryl's grief over losing her mother really hit home."

Ginny's cheeks grew hot as the guilt flooded through her. How could she have been so insensitive? "Oh, I'm so sorry. I should have thought. I chose it because of the setting."

"That's okay, I'm not blaming you. I've got to come to terms with it sometime and, in a way, reading about someone else's grief helped. But her way of dealing with it is definitely not mine."

"What do you mean?" Meg said.

"Well," and Rose paused, "I think the world is divided into two types of people. Those who find strength and centredness in being alone, and those who need support from friends and family, who need other people to help them deal with strong emotions. Cheryl Strayed is obviously one of those who find themselves in solitude. I need the support of others, like Matthew and Daniel and their families, and you two."

"Hmm," Ginny said, "I hadn't thought of it like that. You're right. Perhaps that's why *Wild* appealed to me so much. When Laura died, I shut myself off from other people. I couldn't bear their sympathy, however well-meaning. Not that being alone did me much good... you both know what I did with my solitude. I wonder whether going on a long-distance hike would have helped me to heal without punishing myself."

"I struggled with it too," Meg said. "I lost my own mother when I was eight and was brought up by my Auntie Enid. She did all she could for us, but she didn't have any experience with children. She kept us warm and fed, and drilled good morals and manners into us, but she wasn't much good at hugging. I had to be mother to the younger ones, in that respect. So *Wild* struck chords with me too."

Ginny bit her lip, suddenly on the edge of tears. It sounded as though *Wild* had been a dreadful choice, for both Rose and Meg.

"I'm so sorry," she blurted out. "I'd no idea that *Wild* would be so hard for both of you. I just wanted to share how wonderful California is."

Rose took her hand. "Like I said," she said softly, "there's no blame here. I loved reading about her experience of lugging Monster all those miles. It was great to read about such a strong woman. So tell us about your time in California."

"You really want to know?"

They nodded.

"Okay. I took a gap year after university and travelled out there in September 1966. I had no idea how much it was going to change my life. I wandered around from place to place for a couple of months, working in bars to keep myself, then gravitated to San Francisco and became a full-time hippy." She laughed. "I attended the first Human Be-in at Golden Gate Park in the January of 1967, and took Timothy Leary's invocation to 'Turn on, tune in and drop out' to heart. Then spent a blissful few months immersed in the counter-culture of Haight-Ashbury, smoking dope and taking LSD, part of a community of free spirits who shared everything. I had some amazing trips and was one of the lucky ones, surviving with my mind intact. I learned about Krishna Consciousness at the Mantra Rock Dance and started a lifelong love affair with the music of Janis Joplin. In the April, I marched against the Vietnam War with thousands of others. We marched for civil rights too, inspired by the words of Martin Luther King." She paused and sighed. "We were so idealistic, so willing to believe that if we protested hard enough and long enough, things would change.

"But then a dear friend, Michelle, died after a heroin overdose. Which brought me to my senses with a bang. I booked the next flight home, in the August of '67. My parents scarcely recognised me at the airport; my hair was bleached with blonde streaks from long days in the California sun and my skin was walnut brown. It took me a while to get my head together and decide what I wanted to do with my life. I'd learned yoga in the States and resolved to set up my own business as a yoga teacher. My father provided the initial finances to rent a small studio, and there were many young women in Moseley who wanted to learn from me. Some years later, I met Laura and my life changed forever."

"Wow!" Rose said, "that sounds awesome. I was teaching in a school by then… far less exciting. I watched a documentary about Haight-Ashbury recently, and it looked amazing."

"It was life changing," Ginny said. "I took on values that year that I've never lost. I was so young, so full of certainty that everything was going to go right. But now everything's going wrong again, and I don't know what to do."

"Why do you say that?" Meg said. "What's going wrong? Can we help?"

"Ah, that's sweet of you. It's the blog. I can't find a way to get hold of Annie Leibovitz, so I can't use *Dance with Light and the Weather* as my title. I thought of *Dance with Words and Nature* first, but it didn't sound right. So I googled nature quotes, and found some gorgeous words by Ralph Waldo Emerson: 'Nature always wears the colours of the spirit.' So I've decided to call it *Colours of the Spirit.*"

"Colours of the spirit – I like it," Rose said, and Meg nodded in agreement.

"Yes," Ginny huffed, "that's all very well – at least I've got a title for it. But I've been looking at other people's nature photography blogs, and they're brilliant. It's made me lose confidence about posting my own photos... compared to them, mine are very ordinary."

To her astonishment, Rose and Meg were both smiling. "What's so funny?" she snapped.

"Sorry, Ginny," Rose said, putting her hand on top of hers. "It's just that both Meg and I have been struggling with the demon of comparison too. When Meg read *Wild,* it discouraged her from writing her memoir, because she felt she could never write as well as Cheryl Strayed, and I keep looking at Lesley's fingers when she shows me how to do something on the piano and getting depressed about my lack of ability."

"Yes," Meg said, "we're both realising that as soon as we compare what we're doing with other people, we get fed up and down on ourselves."

"Oh, I see," Ginny said. Of course Rose and Meg wouldn't exclude her – why had she thought they would? "Okay, let's ban the word 'comparison' from our lives. We are us, and they are them. We can only do the best we can."

She just wished she believed that.

"That's a good idea," Meg said. "We'll do our best and to hell with the rest of them. Talking of which," and she delved into her bag, "I've brought my first chapter along to share with you."

"Oh, that's great," Rose said. "We're all ears."

"Do you want me to read it aloud?" Meg said. "I thought you'd read it to yourselves."

Ginny glanced around the café. "There's no-one else in earshot. I'd like to hear it in your own voice, please."

Obediently, Meg began to read, "I was born in a little village in the West Riding of Yorkshire, on August 5th, 1948, exactly one month after the establishment of the National Health Service…" Ginny and Rose listened in silence.

"Well, what do you think? Is it any good?"

"It really took me back," Rose said. "All those little details about life in the early 1950s. Of course, I'm a bit older than you – I was born in 1943 – so I can remember the privations of rationing very clearly. The whole make do and mend ethos. It's good stuff, Meg. You write very vividly."

"Thank you, Rose. I was only six when rationing ended, but I can remember the thrill of being able to buy sweets at the corner shop again."

"I remember all the bombed buildings," Ginny said. "I grew up in south Birmingham, and we used to play among the ruins. I can remember the excitement when somebody found the fin of a bomb. We were very lucky… it could have gone off, but being kids, that never occurred to us. It took until the end of the sixties for Birmingham to be rebuilt."

"But did you like what I wrote?" Meg said.

"Yes, I did," Ginny said. "Keep on with it. I'm sure the grandchildren will love it."

"They're growing up in a very different world," Meg said. "It was Katie's ninth birthday last weekend, and Matthew and Sarah bought her a tablet. Can you imagine having a hand-held computer of your own at the age of nine?"

"The closest I got to that was a slide rule," Rose said with a grin. "Yes, it's a whole new world. But I'm not sure the kids of today are any happier than we were. Those were simpler times. I spent my childhood in the Highlands, playing outside or reading. I didn't go to a cinema until I was in my teens; we lived too far away from the nearest town. So we had to make our own entertainment."

"We're beginning to sound like Monty Python's four Yorkshiremen!" Ginny said, "But I *do* think life was simpler back then, and not necessarily the less happy for it."

"You're right, Rose said, and Meg nodded in agreement.

"I've got something to show you, too," Rose said, changing the subject. "I've brought my sampler along."

She took it out of her bag and unfolded it for them to see. "I haven't done that much yet," she said, "but I'm really pleased with how it's turning out. This…" and she showed them the cover photo, "… is what it will look like when it's finished."

"Oh, that's gorgeous," Meg said, "such delicate colours."

"I love the font of the writing," Ginny said, "it's so Charles Rennie Mackintosh. How clever!"

Both Meg and Rose were producing fantastic work. And here she was, afraid to publish even one blog post. Get a grip. She'd tweak one of the ones she'd already drafted and publish it when she got home.

"What's our book for next month, Rose?" Meg said.

"I've decided on *Testament of Youth* by Vera Brittain, because it's November next month, and Remembrance Sunday. I read it when I was in my teens and have never forgotten it."

"I think I saw the TV series, back in the seventies," Meg said.

"Yes, I remember that," Ginny said, "with a very young Cheryl Campbell playing Vera. But I've never read the book – it's quite a doorstop, isn't it?"

Rose grimaced. "Yes, but it's worth it. And if you get it on your Kindle, it shouldn't make a difference."

Rose

Rose hoped Ginny and Meg would like *Testament of Youth*. It was one of her favourite books of all time, and she'd re-read it more than once. It had forced her to think about deep issues, such as militarism, pacifism and feminism, and had a huge influence on her.

She could understand so very much better, these days, why Vera had been so devastated by Roland's death, on that long-ago Christmas Eve. Now the central axis of her own life had been ripped away, and she was floating around, rudderless and disconnected. Even now, six months after Graham's death, she could not accept the fact that she was never going to see him again. Would never hear his voice, his booming laugh. Would never feel his arms around her, his lips on hers. Would never feel... whole.

Or was that being melodramatic? Her generation had been taught that feeling deep emotions, particularly negative ones, was for sissies; "wallowing" was the dismissive word. Having been born at the tail end of the Second World War, which her parents had experienced as adults − her father serving in the Army, her mother working on the land − she had grown up in a world where bad things happened, and you just dealt with them and carried on. Very much as Vera had, in the Great War and its aftermath. Her own father had spent the last eighteen months of the war in a POW camp in Poland, and had returned as thin as a rake, with a persistent cough. But he had never spoken of his experiences, at least, not to little Rose.

The phone rang, jolting her back into the present.

"Mum? It's Daniel. Debbie's gone into labour."

"What? But she's only thirty weeks!" Rose's stomach started to churn.

"Thirty-one." Daniel sounded terrified. "The ambulance has just picked her up. And Jake and Davy are on half-term. Could you drive over and look after them? I need to get to the hospital."

"Of course, Danny," Meg said. "I'll be with you in an hour. Is there a neighbour you can leave them with, till I arrive?"

"Yes, I'll ask Sharon next door. Be quick, Mum, please."

Meg

Meg was back to enjoying writing her memoir, buoyed up by the kind words of her friends. It was her great escape from worrying about John. She'd covered her childhood years and was planning to tackle her teens next. Which meant that wonderful decade, the sixties. She'd been eleven when the sixties began and had met John in 1968. Such a lot to cover. Even if she hadn't been to California, like Ginny. Where to begin?

Better start with secondary school. She sat down at the kitchen table, a mug of tea at her elbow, and made a list of all the things she could remember about it – her favourite subjects, her most-hated subjects, teachers ditto, her best friends and worst enemies, how important pop music had been. Then she skimmed through her teenage diaries, retrieved from a case in the attic weeks ago, occasionally blushing at her own naïveté. And remembering incidents she would rather have forgotten ever happened. She wouldn't be writing about *those*. Oh well, she'd come through it.

Now, how to weave it into one narrative? This could be tricky. She decided to pick one favourite pop song for each year of the sixties and relate it to her experiences. She went hunting for their battered old copy of *The Guinness Book of British Hit Singles* but it wasn't where she expected to find it. Disappointed, she returned to the kitchen.

Then John walked in to make himself a coffee.

"Do you know where our copy of *The Guinness Book of British Hit Singles* is?"

"We threw it out years ago, when we had that big clear out. Why?"

"I wanted to find some favourite music from the sixties for my memoir."

"Why don't you just look it up online?"

"Will it be on there?" she said doubtfully.

"My darling Meggie," he said, in the patronising tone she hated, "you can find *anything* on the internet these days. Let's have a look."

He sat down, dragged her laptop across the table without so much as a 'by your leave'. "D'you want me to look it up for you?"

Pick your battles, Meg. Biting her tongue to suppress her annoyance, she said, "Yes, please."

He brought up Google and put in 'British singles 1960s'. Right near the top of the results was a Wikipedia listing covering all the number one singles throughout the decade.

"Ah, that's just what I wanted… thank you."

Taking the laptop back, she began to scroll through the list. So many wonderful songs… so many memories. She picked a few and started to write. No doubt the grandchildren would be surprised that dear old Nana had once loved pop music so much.

Perhaps she'd better talk about the sixties with Ginny and Rose, to see what their memories were.

Ginny

Ginny decided to write her first blog post about flowers. How had it taken this long to pluck up the courage? Damned perfectionism! Blog, Ginny. Just do it.

She'd taken quite a few close-ups since she'd had Graham's camera and decided to select the best and look up their meanings in the language of flowers, then say where she'd found them and when. Good job she'd saved the photos on her laptop by date. She had an ancient copy of *The Concise British Flora in Colour*, inherited from her mother, which was brilliant for identifying flowers she didn't recognise.

Now for their meanings. A quick search brought up a couple of brilliant websites which listed the flowers and their meanings in alphabetical order. But, damn it, the listed meanings didn't always match what they meant to her. She'd taken a lovely photo of a vivid red poppy in a wheat field, but the website listed its meaning as "pleasure", whereas it was inextricably linked in her mind with remembrance of the dead. And the sunflower was supposed to symbolise "pride, false riches." But seeing the bright yellow flowers with their central whorl of dark brown seeds always made her feel happy. This was no good. What should she do? Write about their meaning for her, or the "official" meaning? She'd ask Rose.

The phone rang and rang. No answer. At this rate, she'd never get a blog post published. Disgruntled, Ginny closed her laptop down and plunged straight into the first chapter of *Testament of Youth*. Thank goodness she'd got it on her Kindle.

November: *Testament of Youth* by Vera Brittain

Rose

Rose threw a few necessaries into an over-night bag, shoved her arms into her coat, grabbed her bag, and was out of the door in ten minutes. Hurry, hurry, hurry. She drove on auto-pilot, her mind in a whirl, a cold weight on her chest. Up the M5, onto the M6, then the M54. Oh God, this was so unfair. She knew how much Debbie had been longing for a little girl of her own. She adored her boys but had been so happy when she knew they were having a girl.

Thirty-one weeks. Rose had no idea what complications might arise from such a premature birth. Please, God, let Debbie be okay. Let the baby be okay. Please, God. May she be spared the grief I had, when Joshua...

It had been so long since she had thought of that dark chapter in her life. She had fallen pregnant again, when Matthew was two, had carried the baby almost to term. Had gone into labour so full of joy...

In those days, no father was allowed to be present during the birth. So she had coped with the pain alone, fortified by the happy prospect of another son or daughter. But her perfect child, her precious son, had been born dead. Even now, she could remember the scream of pain that had ripped its way past her clenched teeth, the hollow emptiness that had invaded her mind and heart.

And later, the tiny white coffin, the graveyard of her hopes.

Not again, please God, not again. She couldn't bear it.

She wasn't sure she'd be able to cope with any more grief. Not now. Not so close to losing Graham... Please God, let the baby be okay, let Debbie be okay. Please God.

Never had the drive to Shrewsbury seemed to take so long. She cursed each slight delay, desperate to get there. But when she checked her watch, after drawing up on Daniel's drive, it hadn't taken any longer than usual – just over an hour. It had seemed like an eternity. She hobbled down the drive as quickly as she could, ignoring the protest from her knee, to knock on the door of Daniel's neighbour. She had met her once before, at Daniel and Debbie's housewarming party.

"Hello, Sharon. I'm Rose, Rose Anderson, Daniel's mother. I've come to pick up the boys."

"Come on in," Sharon said. "They're playing outside with my three."

"Do they realise what's happening?" Rose said.

"They know that Debbie's had to go into hospital because of the baby, because of the ambulance arriving. But I don't think they understand the implications. After all, they're only eleven and eight. I've tried to keep them busy."

"Thank you so much," Rose said, "I came as soon as I could."

"Would you like a cup of tea?" Sharon said, showing her into the kitchen. "Have you come far?"

Rose collapsed into a chair. "From Crowle, just north-east of Worcester. And yes, please, I'd love one."

"I'll put the kettle on. Try not to worry. They've had to go to the Princess Royal at Telford because the maternity unit in Shrewsbury is closed. But she'll get good care there."

"Oh, God! I'm so frightened. Debbie's forty-one…"

"You mustn't think like that. She didn't have any problems with the boys, did she?"

Rose tried to get a hold of herself. "That's true, but she was much younger then."

"Hospitals can do amazing things, these days."

By the time Jake and Davy came inside, Rose was calm, at least outwardly.

"Hello, Granny," Jake said, "what are you doing here?"

"I've come to look after you two until Daddy gets back from the hospital. You know he's gone in with Mummy, because of the baby?"

"Is the baby being born now?" Davy said. "I thought she wasn't coming till after Christmas."

"I'm not sure, Davy," Rose said, evading the question, "so let's wait until Daddy gets home. Now, say your goodbyes and we'll go back to your house."

"'Bye, Sharon," Davy said, giving her a hug.

"'Bye, Sharon," Jake echoed.

Daniel had left the spare key with Jake, so they let themselves in.

"Now, you two," Rose said, "how would you like pizza for tea?"

Food would be an excellent distraction. Hang the diet for once. And sure enough, the boys' faces lit up. "Can we go to Pizza Express, Granny?" Jake said.

"I think we'd better get one delivered. I'd like to be here in case your Dad comes back."

Forty-five minutes later, they were sitting round the

kitchen table, sharing a huge pepperoni pizza straight out of the cardboard box. So lucky they did a gluten-free version. Rose had no appetite, but forced herself to eat. She mustn't worry the boys.

"Thank you, Granny," Davy said, "Mummy makes us put it on our plates."

"Oh, well. I expect she'll forgive me this once."

After tea, she let the boys watch *Spiderman,* and pretended to read a magazine. The pizza was sitting uneasily in her stomach. Time crawled by, and no word from Daniel. The labour must be going ahead. She had no idea of the boys' bedtimes. Better ask them.

"What time do you have to be in bed?"

"Not yet, Granny," Davy said indignantly, "it's half-term."

"Okay, I suppose I can let you watch something else. But you'll have to promise you'll go straight up then. Bath and bed."

So they watched *Minions,* which she found oddly compelling. Then she sent Davy up for a bath. Once he was safely out of earshot, Jake turned to her, his young face serious.

"Granny, is Mummy okay?"

What to say? "I'm sure she is, Jake. The baby has decided to come early, so I don't expect your Dad will be home before you're asleep. We should have some news in the morning."

He nodded. "But will the baby be okay? Ben's Mum had her baby early last year, and they were in hospital for ages."

Rose took a deep breath. If he's old enough to ask the question, he's old enough to hear the answer. "I don't know, Jake. She should be. But because the baby's coming early, they'll need to take great care of her. So I don't expect she'll be coming straight home."

His lip started to quiver, and she could see tears standing in his eyes. "Granny, Mummy will be okay, won't she?"

Rose opened her arms, and he came in for a hug. "Of course she will," she said, praying that this was the truth. "Try not to worry, Jake. Like I said, we'll hear some news in the morning."

She let him cry out his worries on her shoulder. When he stiffened in her arms, she let him go.

"Okay, Granny, I'll be good. I won't say anything to Davy."

"That's my brave boy," Rose said. "Now off you go, it's bath time."

She followed him slowly up the stairs and found Davy towelling himself dry in the bathroom.

"Come on, Davy, into bed," she said. "Do you want me to read you a story before you go to sleep?"

"No, thank you," Davy said with great dignity. "I can read for myself now."

"Okay, but only for fifteen minutes. Then it's lights-out." She kissed the top of his head.

Half an hour later, both boys were in bed. Rose hoped Jake would be able to sleep. She was sure she wouldn't. She made herself a mug of tea and settled down to wait. Good job she'd brought her Kindle with her. She suddenly remembered she hadn't asked her neighbour to feed Bonnie in the morning. Better ring her while she remembered.

"Joyce? It's Rose from next door. Sorry to ring so late. I'm over in Shrewsbury looking after my grandsons because my daughter-in-law's gone into labour early. Would you be able to feed Bonnie tomorrow morning please?"

"Yes, of course. Let me know if you won't be back tomorrow, and I'll feed her tomorrow evening too."

"Bless you! I really appreciate it."

"I hope it all works out for the baby."

"I'm sure it will, but thank you."

But she was far from sure in her heart. Time passed, and no word from Daniel. When it got to nearly midnight, Rose went up to the spare room, undressed and went to bed. She felt exhausted but could not sleep. Her knee was aflame with pain, her mind full of dark imaginings. She tossed and turned and turned and tossed. Sleep would not come. In the end, she turned the bedside light on and read for a while. Then, eventually, fell asleep.

The next morning, she was shaken awake by Davy.

"Granny, Granny! Daddy's not home yet. Where is he?"

She sat up, rubbing her eyes. "What time is it?"

"Nearly seven o'clock…. Where's Daddy?"

"I'm sure he'll be home soon. Let me get up, precious, and I'll get you some breakfast."

The next couple of hours dragged by. Daniel's car drew up at just after nine o'clock, by which time Rose was running out of ways to distract the boys. They raced to the front door.

"Daddy! How's Mummy?" Davy said, as Jake said, "Dad, is the baby okay?"

"Hang on, you two, let me get in the door," Daniel said. He came in and saw Rose, hanging back.

"Hello, Mum, thank you for looking after these two."

He looks so tired. But not sad. Please God... "I'll get you a coffee," she said, as he walked into the living room, followed by his sons.

A little while later, the four of them were sitting together, the boys either side of Daniel on the sofa, and Rose in an armchair. He took a sip of his coffee and smiled at his mother.

"Thanks, Mum, I needed that. Now..." and he hugged the boys, "I've got some news for you. You have a new little sister. She was born at quarter-past six this morning and is very tiny. Mummy's very tired, but she's fine. The baby is being looked after by all the doctors and nurses, but they think she'll be able to come home in time for Christmas."

"When's Mummy coming home?" Davy said.

"When can we see the baby?" Jake said, "and is Mummy all right?"

Daniel smiled at them. "Mummy should be coming home in a few days, Davy. Like I said, she's very tired at the moment, but we can go and see her this afternoon. And might be able to see your little sister too... would you like that?"

"What's she called?" Jake said, then more urgently, "Is Mummy really okay?"

"Yes, Jake, Mummy really is okay. Don't worry! And

we've decided to call the baby Natalie Grace."

Rose caught his eye. "That's beautiful, Daniel. May I come and visit too?"

"Of course. Debbie can't wait to show off our new daughter. Off you go, you two. I want to talk to Granny."

Once the boys had left the room, Daniel's face fell. "Oh, Mum, she's so tiny – only three and a half pounds. And Debbie had a really hard labour this time – much worse than with the boys. They took Natalie straight to the Neo-natal Unit, so we haven't even been able to cuddle her yet." He rubbed his eyes. "I'm so tired, I can hardly think straight. And Debbie is so upset. That's why I'm only just home. She needed me there."

Rose's heart melted. "Oh, darling. I wish I could just give you a kiss and make it better. But Natalie is alive. You have to hang on to that. They can do amazing things with premature babies nowadays. I'm sure she'll get through this…. What did the doctor say?"

"So many things… that she will be taken great care of, that they have to monitor her closely for the next few weeks, until she can eat, breathe and stay warm by herself. She hasn't got all the immunity she needs from Debbie, and she can't breathe by herself yet, so they've got to protect her until she's fully grown. We'll be able to visit her every day, and Debbie should be able to feed her herself in three weeks or so. At the moment, she's a mass of tubes and monitors. They *say* there's every chance that she'll be completely okay, but they need to keep her in a warm, calm environment so that she can use all her strength for growing." His voice changed. "Mum, why did this happen to us?"

"You mustn't think like that," Rose said, taking his hand. "Try to concentrate on the fact that she's here and alive and in the best possible place for her continued health. You'll need to be the strong one in the weeks ahead. I expect Debbie is beating herself up badly over this. But it's nobody's fault, it just is as it is. Try to think what a joyful Christmas it will be, when you've finally got her at home."

Daniel squeezed her hand. "Thanks, Mum. I'll try."

"Now, eat a bowl of cereal, then go and have a nap for the rest of the morning. I can look after the boys, and you'll feel much better for a few hours' rest."

"Okay, you're the boss." He stood up and kissed her cheek. "Bless you for being here. I'm not sure how I would have managed without you."

"That's what mothers are for," Rose said. "Off you go."

Later that day, Rose, Daniel and the boys drove to the hospital. Then walked along a seemingly endless series of corridors to the post-natal ward. Debbie was in a cramped, curtained-off cubicle, her face pale, dark circles under her eyes, emphasised by the harsh fluorescent lighting. Rose found her daughter-in-law tired and emotional, but doing her best to hide it for the sake of her sons. So sad that her own mother was no longer around. Then they had gone down to the Neo-Natal Unit to visit baby Natalie. Such a little dot, so many wires and monitors. Please God she would come through this.

When they got back to Daniel's, she said, "Daniel, do you want me to come and stay for a few days? Or have you managed to get some paternity leave?"

"Oh, Mum, that's a lovely thought. But I've phoned my boss, and he's agreed that I can start my paternity leave today and stay at home for two weeks. So that's okay. But it would be great if you could come and look after the boys on a couple of odd days, while Debbie is still in hospital."

"Of course I will. I'm sure my neighbour won't mind looking after Bonnie, if I explain why. When do you think Debbie will be back home?"

"I'm hoping she'll be back by the end of the week, or the beginning of the next. Davy's accepted that Mummy's poorly and needs to rest, but Jake's been asking questions, which I don't know how to answer."

"I think he's old enough to hear the truth," Rose said. "He's at secondary school now, after all. And it would be better for him to know what's happening, than to imagine all kinds of horrors for himself. He was talking yesterday about a friend of his, Ben, whose Mum was in hospital for ages after having a premature baby."

"I guess you're right," Daniel said, "but my instinct is to protect him."

"I know, but I think I'm right this time."

"Okay. I'll find a time to talk to him alone."

"You're a good father. I'm sure it will all work out. I'll get off now and come back.... When?"

"Could you come back over tomorrow?" Daniel said.

"Of course," Rose said, her heart sinking. Her knee was not going to like this at all. It had been aching badly, following yesterday's journey. Oh, well. Needs must when the devil drives.

Rose let herself in, gave Bonnie a fuss, made herself a cup of tea, then collapsed into a chair in the living room, propping her leg up on the pouffe. All the fears she'd been hiding from Daniel were swirling around her mind. The main one being that Natalie would not survive. She'd looked so tiny, so fragile. Rose put her hands together and said a short, heartfelt prayer. "Dear God, please look after Natalie. Give her the strength to survive, to grow, to thrive. Be with Debbie and Daniel in the days and weeks to come. Thank you, Amen."

She decided to stitch a birth sampler for her and pray every stitch of it. She found a gorgeous kit on the same website she'd used to find Matthew and Sarah's sampler, which showed a baby bear in a pink romper suit, surrounded by hearts in varying shades of pink. It didn't look too complicated, so she ordered it, paying a little extra for next-day delivery. She was so tired.

The phone rang. She snatched up the receiver, terrified that it was Daniel with bad news.

"Rose? It's Ginny. Is this a good time to talk?"

Ginny. Thank God for that. Rose pulled herself together. Her friend sounded very fed up.

"What's up?"

"It's the blog. I was going to do the first post about flowers, saying where I'd seen each one, and then a bit about their meanings."

"Meanings?"

"Oh, you know," Ginny said, "the language of flowers."

"Ah, I see," Rose said. "That sounds like a great idea

– what's the problem?"

"I found a couple of websites that give meanings, and they don't match with my associations."

"I don't quite understand… what do you mean?"

"Well, one of them said the red poppy means pleasure," Ginny said, "but I always associate it with Remembrance Day."

"Oh, me too," Rose said. She thought for a moment. "You know what? It's your blog, and I'd go with what the flowers mean to you. But use the language of flowers if the meaning matches with your association."

"Thank you, I'll do that. You've no idea how wound up I've been getting about it. I tried to ring you yesterday, but you were out."

"Yes, I was over at Shrewsbury," Rose said. "Daniel's wife, Debbie, went into labour eleven weeks early, so I had to look after the boys."

"Eleven weeks? Oh God! Are they okay?"

"Well, yes, I suppose," Rose said, "for a broad interpretation of 'okay'. Debbie's exhausted; she had a hard time. And baby Natalie is alive, but so tiny. They've got her in the Neo-Natal Unit, with loads of tubes and wires and monitors."

Her lips started to quiver, her eyes to fill with tears, as all the fears she'd been suppressing in front of Daniel flooded her mind. "They say… they say she's got a good chance of surviving and growing up normal. But oh, Ginny! I'm so scared. What if she doesn't?"

"You mustn't think like that," Ginny said, her voice soft in Rose's ears. "Hospitals can do so much, these days. If *they* think she's got a good chance, then she must have. Try to hang on to that, my dear."

"Oh, I know," Rose said, "but it seems so unfair. I feel so much for Debbie and Daniel. And Jake, my older grandson, has been asking all sorts of questions. It's been hard to sound upbeat, when my own heart is so full of fear. I'm not sure I could deal with another death, so soon after Graham."

"D'you want me to come over?"

"Ah, that's sweet of you, but I think I'm going to have some lunch, then go to bed for a nap. I got precious little sleep last night, and I'm exhausted. And Daniel wants me back over there tomorrow."

"Fair enough. But don't nap for too long, otherwise you'll never sleep tonight."

"Thank you, that's good advice," Rose said, "I'll set my alarm for two hours."

"Okay, I'll let you go. But if you need to talk, you know where I am."

"Thank you, my friend, I appreciate that."

Ginny

Poor Rose. Such an awful thing to happen. Hope the baby will be okay. Ginny shook herself. Back to the blog.

She walked upstairs to her study to make a start on it, past the small mahogany bookcase on the landing, which she'd inherited from her parents. It held the books from her childhood she had kept for sentimental reasons. Her eye was caught by a row of thin, colourful spines – Cecily M Barker's

Flower Fairies books. She'd been enchanted by them when she was little, particularly by the illustrations. She hooked one of them – *A Flower Fairy Alphabet* – off the shelf, took it through to the study and sat down at her desk.

Such a simple idea… that each flower had a fairy to look after it, dressed in the same colours and style as the flower's petals and leaves. The accompanying words were a bit twee to Ginny's adult eyes, but she'd loved them when she was small… Wait a minute. Brilliant! She could choose a poem to accompany each of her photos, then add a bit about the flower's meaning.

She turned her PC on and googled 'Remembrance Day poems'. And found *In Flanders Fields* by John McCrae. That would do nicely. She clicked on her blog's icon, which opened a new window, and began to type. "The poppy, pictured here in a wheat field this summer, is always associated in my mind with Remembrance Sunday, when we commemorate all those who have died in the service of our country. One of the first poets to make this association was John McCrae, who wrote *In Flanders Fields* in May 1915, during the Second Battle of Ypres…."

She found out a bit more about how the poem came to be written, on a website about World War One, re-wrote it in her own words, then copied and pasted the poem itself.

She read the post through critically a couple of times, took a deep breath, and clicked Publish. Her first blog post was out in the world. She clicked on the View link and surveyed it with satisfaction. Then noticed the little icons at the bottom and realised that she could share it on Twitter and Facebook. Was she ready to do that? Yeah, why not? She sent the link to Rose and Meg for good measure.

Rose

Debbie came home the following Tuesday. Rose had decided to stay at Daniel's until then; the driving back and forth was too much for her knee. Fortunately, Joyce was willing to look after Bonnie for a few days, so she'd packed a case and driven back over on the Friday morning.

The news continued to be positive. Little Natalie was holding her own, although she still wasn't breathing by herself, and was fed by a tube. But they were assured that this was normal and that she was making good progress. She would need to remain in the Neo-Natal Unit until she could breathe without oxygen and without any interruptions, take all her feeds by mouth rather than through a tube, and maintain a stable body temperature. The staff explained that these milestones varied from baby to baby, but that if all went well, she ought to be allowed home by the end of the year, maybe even for Christmas.

Debbie too was recovering slowly. She'd had a stressful labour, tearing badly at the end. The guilt she felt about letting her baby down was proving obstinate. No matter how many times Daniel, Rose and the nursing staff explained that the early labour was nobody's fault, she continued to blame herself. When Daniel brought her home on the Tuesday morning, after the boys were at school, she looked around the living room and sighed.

"It's good to be home," she said to Rose, while Daniel was taking her case upstairs. "But it's so hard, leaving

Natalie at the hospital. I feel so torn… I want to be with her every minute of the day, willing her to grow and thrive. But I need to be here for the boys too."

"And the boys need you," Rose said. "Natalie's in the best place for her, at the moment. Try to concentrate on what a joyful Christmas it will be when she finally comes home."

Debbie's eyes filled with tears. "Why did my body let me down? If only I'd been able to hold on to her a few weeks longer."

Rose sat down next to her and took her hand. "I can hear how hard it is for you at the moment. But you must stop thinking like this. It's just one of those things. You need to look after yourself and the boys and Daniel and look forward rather than back. The doctors are happy with Natalie's progress so far, aren't they?"

"Yes, they are. I'll be going back in every day, to spend time with her. Thank goodness the boys are back at school. Oh, Rose! I know you're right, but it's so hard, trying to stay positive."

"I know." Rose paused. "I'm going to tell you something now, that Daniel has probably forgotten he ever knew. Between Matthew and him, I had another pregnancy, but he – he was a stillbirth, at thirty-seven weeks." Rose resisted the surge of grief filling her heart. She must be strong for Debbie.

"Like you," she continued, her lips quivering in spite of all she could do to remain composed, "I beat myself up badly, wondering what I had done wrong, why this had happened to me. Graham was sympathetic for a while, but eventually lost patience. He told me that Matthew needed me, that *he* needed me. And I realised I had to concentrate on my living family and let the baby go. But your Natalie is alive and is likely to remain so. For her sake, as much for Daniel's and the boys', you need to concentrate on the positive. Every day, she's growing stronger. Keep thinking about that. And try to keep a brave face, especially in front of Jake and Davy. Davy's too young to understand, but Jake's well aware of what's happened. Can you do that? For them?"

The younger woman wiped her eyes. "Th-thank you. That helps. I'll do my best."

"No-one can do more than that. If you need to talk about it, I'm always on the other end of the phone. Now," Rose said, standing up, "would you like a cup of tea?"

"I'd love one." Debbie caught her hand and squeezed it. "Thank you, Rose… for everything."

Ginny

Once Ginny had thought of the idea of using poetry to complement her photos, she was on a roll. She'd gone through her photo folders and found several which made her think of particular poems. By the middle of November, she'd published four blog posts and was relaxing into the process. She couldn't wait to share the news with Rose and Meg. Wonder how Rose's grand-daughter's getting on?

"Hi, Rose. Ginny here. I was wondering how the baby is?"

"Thank you for asking," Rose said. "She's doing well – three weeks old yesterday. The doctors are happy with the progress she's making and we're hoping she'll be able to come home for Christmas. I'm stitching a gorgeous birth sampler for her."

"Ah, that's excellent news. I'm so pleased for you."

"Thank you. How are things with you?"

"Really good, thank you," Ginny said. "The blog's going swimmingly... I've published four posts now and have ideas for a few more. And," she said with a warm glow of satisfaction, "I've been getting some likes for them on Facebook!"

"Well done! I really enjoyed the first one... I'd no idea that *In Flanders Fields* was written as early as 1915."

"Yes," Ginny said, "that surprised me too. I'd always thought of it as a sort of requiem at the end of the Great War."

"Well, thank you for ringing. I'd better get back to the stitching, if I want to finish it by the time Natalie comes home. See you a week on Wednesday."

Meg

"Hello, Meg," Rose said as Meg walked in to Capuchins. "I've got some news for you."

"Ooh! What?"

"I have a new grand-daughter, Natalie. She was born on 24th October, the day after our last meeting, eleven weeks early."

"Eleven weeks?" Meg said, her expression changing from joy to alarm. "Is she okay?"

"Well, she's still in the Neo-natal Unit, but she's beginning to breathe on her own, and we're hoping that she'll be home in time for Christmas."

"That's wonderful news! Does Ginny know?"

"Yes, she happened to ring me a couple of days later, so I told her then."

"I wish you'd let me know," Meg said, fighting down a wave of jealousy. Enough already, she's telling you now.

"I'm sorry," Rose said. "I've been backwards and forward to Shrewsbury the last few weeks."

Meg forced a smile. "It doesn't matter," she lied. "Are you stitching her a birth sampler?"

"How did you guess?" Rose smiled. "Yes, I've found a gorgeous one – a little teddy bear in a deep pink romper suit, surrounded by hearts. It's really cute and I should have finished it by the time she comes home."

"I'll go and order my coffee and cake," Meg said, and marched up to the counter, fighting back tears. This was ridiculous. Rose had the right to tell whoever she wanted, whenever she wanted to.

Just then, Ginny walked in. So tall, so elegant, so self-assured. Everything that she wasn't. And now, apparently, Rose's best friend.

"Hi, Meg," Ginny said, "how are you?"

"Good, thanks," Meg said. "Isn't it good news about Rose's grand-daughter?"

"Yes, she seems to be making excellent progress," Ginny said. "See you in a minute."

Meg walked back over to their table, her mind in a whirl. She hadn't felt like this since she was a teenager. How silly. Better pull herself together.

She and Rose waited for Ginny to sit down.

"How's the memoir coming along?" Rose said.

"Well, I'm a bit stuck at the moment," Meg said, glad for the change of subject. "The chapter I'm on is about the sixties, and I have so many memories, I'm finding it difficult to string them into one narrative that hangs together. I was going to ask you two what your memories were, to see if I could identify a few important events to hang the story on."

"Oh dear," Rose said. "I'm afraid my memories aren't very exciting. I was seventeen at the beginning of the sixties, living in the Highlands, and working hard for my A levels, so that I could go to university and train to be a teacher. I met Graham at university, and we got married in 1965. I spent most of the decade teaching in a grammar school, so the whole hippy revolution thing rather passed me by." She smiled at Ginny. "Of course I noticed that my male pupils were growing their hair and so on, and I did rather like the Beatles. And Simon and Garfunkel. But I remember the sixties more by personal landmarks – getting married, setting up home, learning to drive, acquiring our first television – things like that. I can remember the excitement when BBC2 was launched and I'll never forget watching Churchill's funeral or the moon landing."

Meg was scribbling furiously in her notebook. "Thanks, Rose, that's really helpful. How about you, Ginny?"

"Well," Ginny said, "you've already heard about my year in the States. Unlike Rose," and she smiled at her friend, while Meg fought down another pointless stab of envy, "I was deeply into the hippie revolution – it changed my life. If I hadn't gone to the States and spent those months in California, I'd never have been a yoga teacher, to start with. I was fifteen at the beginning of the sixties and loved the music so much. But it wasn't until I went to the States that I really got into it in a big way. And my time there opened my mind to all sorts of issues that had never been on my horizon – feminism, the environment, all that. By the end of the decade, I knew what I really cared about – finding myself through yoga and meditation and music, and about women's rights and green politics."

"Gosh," Meg said, "the two of you had such different experiences. I was younger than you, of course – only eleven at the beginning of the sixties. But I was a teenager for most of it, and the music was so important to me. Oh dear. Now I'm more confused than ever."

"Meg," Rose said gently, "it's your memoir, not ours. It's what you experienced that matters, not what Ginny or I did. What have you written about so far?"

Did she really want to tell them? Would they laugh? Deep breath. "Well, it's been mainly about my teenage life – school, boys, music, going out to dances and the cinema – that sort of thing. Nothing significant, really." She sighed.

"But it was significant for you," Ginny said, "and that's what matters. Think about the people you knew, the songs you loved, the films you saw, stuff like that. Don't think about what we did, unless it resonates for you."

Meg gave her a small smile. "You're right. Okay, I'll do that."

"Now," Rose said, "What did the two of you think of *Testament of Youth?*"

"I loved it," Ginny said. "It's brought the Great War alive for me, which no other book has. And I could resonate with Vera's feelings after first Roland, then Geoffrey and Victor and finally her beloved Edward, died. I cried buckets when I read about her losing Roland and Edward. I can't imagine what it must have been like to lose your fiancé, your two dearest friends, and your only brother, in the space of three years. No wonder she had mental problems at Oxford."

"Yes, I found the death scenes difficult... they reminded me too much of losing Graham," Rose said. "But like you, I could imagine myself there. She writes so vividly and in such detail about those days. How about you, Meg... what did you think of it?"

"I'm sorry, Rose, I didn't finish it," Meg said. "Maybe I'm stupid or something, but I got bogged down in all the detail, and the font was so small. I loved the TV series, but her world was so alien to my experience that I gave up after she left Oxford. I found all the politics as dull as ditch water." Meg Jeffries, dimwit.

"Don't worry, I understand," Rose said. "It's not for everyone. And you're not stupid, far from it. It would be a funny old world if we all liked the same things."

"What've you chosen for our December read, Meg?" Ginny asked. "We'll be meeting a week early next month... Christmas Day is on the fourth Wednesday."

"Ironically," and Meg gave them both a tepid smile, "something that has a lot of politics in it. But it's bang up to date – in fact, it's only just been published. It's *Becoming* by Michelle Obama."

"I've been waiting for it to come out; thanks, Meg," Rose said.

"Yes, me too," Ginny said. "I've read Barack

Obama's two memoirs and they were beautifully written. It'll be interesting to see how she writes."

"I've only read *Dreams from my Father*," Rose said. "I really must get round to *The Audacity of Hope*. It might cheer me up in these dreadful Trump days."

Meg's heart sank. She hadn't read either of them. What must they think of her? She was an unwanted third here. She stood up.

"Well, got to go now. I've got to cook John's lunch. 'Bye Rose, 'bye Ginny."

She walked out, her head held high, blinking to hold back her tears.

December: *Becoming* by Michelle Obama

Rose

Rose was worried about Meg. Something had definitely been on her mind at Capuchins. She hadn't been her normal sunny self at all. Better ring her, so that whatever it was didn't have time to fester.

"Hello Meg, Rose here. You seemed very down yesterday. Anything I can help with?"

Silence on the other end of the phone. Then, without warning, the unmistakable sound of a sob.

"Meg, my dear, what's wrong?"

"Oh, it's just me being s-silly," Meg said, "take no notice."

"Of course I'm taking notice. You're my friend."

"I can't tell you on the phone," Meg said. "Would you come round for a cup of tea? John's out playing golf."

"Of course. I'll be with you in half an hour."

When Meg opened the door, she wouldn't meet Rose's eyes. "Come on in," she said, "the kettle's boiled."

When they were sitting at the kitchen table, basking in the warmth of the range, Rose said, "Now, what's up?"

"It's hard to tell you. It sounds so childish." Meg's eyes filled with tears.

"Better out than in, whatever it is. Come on, Meg, please tell me."

"Well… it's you and Ginny," Meg said in a rush. "You seem to be so close, and you're both so much cleverer than me, and I feel… I feel like a dim and unwanted third."

Whatever Rose had been expecting, it wasn't this. Meg – jealous? Oh dear. What to say… She breathed a quick prayer before answering.

"That's simply not true. We're all vital parts of our group – me, you, Ginny, all three of us. It wouldn't be the same without any one of us. You're my friend, and I value that friendship highly."

"But you told Ginny about Natalie ages ago," Meg blurted.

Ah, that's what the problem is. "I'm sorry. I should have thought to ring you. But it was only because Ginny rang me, had been trying to get hold of me, that I explained where I'd been. I had no intention of leaving you out. I'm so sorry."

"And then, yesterday, you were both talking about the Barack Obama books you'd read, and I hadn't, and I felt so stupid."

This mustn't be allowed to go on. "Meg," Rose said, taking her hand, "what did we all agree about comparing?"

Meg's face crimsoned. "Oh!" she gasped, "I didn't think of it like that."

"You really ought to," Rose said gently, "All three of us are very different and we each have various facets of our personalities and lives in common with the other two. Ginny and I may share more in terms of reading tastes, and that we've both lost the people we love, but you and I are both mothers and grandmothers, neither of which Ginny shares with us. Each of us has qualities to bring to the table of our friendship, and no single one of us is more important or better than the other two. You must understand this. I'm very fond of both of you, for different reasons."

"Oh! I'm so sorry. I've been so silly. If you knew how I've been torturing myself…"

"You silly sausage!" Rose said. "Friendship isn't a limited quality. It's like love – there's always enough to go round."

"I know. Oh! I'm so ashamed of myself…"

Rose held up her hand. "Enough already. We're done with that. Now let me have another one of those delicious biscuits and I'll tell you the latest about Natalie."

Meg

"Imagine my surprise," Meg said as she stalked into the study, "when I found *this* in the back of your wardrobe."

She flourished a three-quarters' empty bottle of scotch under John's nose. He shrank back in his chair, his face pale, a picture of guilt. Good – so it should be.

"It's not what you think," he began.

"Don't give me that, John Jeffries!" Trembling all over with the force of her anger, she could hardly get the words out. "You *promised* me you'd stop."

John surged up from his seat and snatched the bottle out of her hand, the colour flooding back into his cheeks.

"What the hell were you doing in my wardrobe anyway?" he snarled.

"I was looking," Meg said, "for some more family photos. For the memoir. But instead, I found family betrayal."

He flinched and Meg was glad to see it. She'd really believed that his daily attendance at the AA group was working. It hurt so much to realise he'd fallen off the wagon so soon.

"Do you really care so little about me, about Jessica and Andrew, that a drink is more important than your survival?"

He set the bottle carefully down on his desk, then reached for her hand. She allowed him to take it, but part of her wanted to punish him some more.

"Well?" she snapped. "I'm waiting for an explanation."

"You don't understand how hard it is," he said in a low voice, his eyes trained on the carpet. "I think about it all the time, day and night. I'm not sleeping and the cravings were so strong I couldn't resist any longer."

She could see how much it was costing him to admit how addicted he was, and couldn't help softening towards him. She took his other hand and brought both of them towards her breast, cradling them in both of hers.

"Aren't the AA meetings helping?"

"Sure, sometimes," he said. "At least, when I'm there. Even if all the God language gets on my nerves. I do come out of each meeting feeling stronger in myself, determined to beat this. Then it wears off and the cravings start up again. I'm sorry, Meggie, so sorry."

"So what now?" she said.

He sighed, a deep sigh which seemed to come from his boots. "I don't know. I'll have to tell my sponsor, ask their advice. They're going to be so disappointed in me."

"Don't they say something about taking it one day at a time?"

"Where did you hear that?"

"I'm not stupid, John," Meg said. "I've googled AA and I know what happens at their meetings. I've read the booklets they hand out."

His look of surprise was comical – his eyebrows shot up and his jaw dropped. "Why would you do that?"

"Because, strange as it seems, I care about you. Don't you understand? I love you, and I want you in my life for as long as possible. But I know I can't force you to do anything about this. It has to come from you. You have to *want* to quit."

"I don't deserve you," he said. "I'm so sorry. I really will try."

"That's all I ask," she said and, gathering up the rags of her dignity, determined not to cry in front of him, she left the room.

As she closed the door behind her, she heard the metallic sound of a bottle cap being unscrewed. All hope left her.

She pulled on her coat, wound a warm scarf around her neck, snatched her handbag from the hall table, and walked out. She couldn't bear to be in the house with him a moment longer.

Rose

Rose parked in the St Martin's Gate car park and hurried to Capuchins as fast as her knee would allow. Meg had sounded distraught.

And sure enough, when she sat down opposite her

friend, the traces of past tears were plain to see. Thankfully, they were out of earshot of other customers and Karen was busy with the book stock.

"What's wrong?" she said.

"It's John," Meg said.

She might have guessed. "What's he done now? He's not drinking again, is he?"

"How did you know?"

"It wasn't difficult," Rose said. "I couldn't think of anything else that would drive you out of your own home at this time on a Thursday." She took Meg's hand. "Tell me what's happened."

Out it all came, how Meg had been searching for some more family photos for the memoir, and had come across a nearly empty scotch bottle in the back of John's wardrobe. And the dreadful row that had followed.

"So I walked out," Meg finished, "and as I left the room, I heard the sound of the bottle cap coming off. He's betrayed my trust."

Rose squeezed Meg's hand, not sure how to respond. It was obvious that John was an alcoholic and she knew her friend was right – it would be impossible for him to stop drinking unless he really, really wanted to. And it seemed that he didn't, ARLD diagnosis notwithstanding.

"I'm so sorry," she said. "That must be hard to bear."

"I just don't understand," Meg said in a small, hopeless voice. "Doesn't he care about the damage he's doing to himself? To the family? To me?"

Rose winced. "I've never met an alcoholic in real life," she said slowly. "But I've read about it and it's a really tough addiction to battle. I've heard that they have to find something that is important enough to them to trump their desire to drink."

"Aren't I enough?" Meg said. "Aren't the children enough? What's wrong with him, that we aren't a good enough reason?"

"You mustn't look at it like that," Rose said. "Of course he loves you and the rest of the family. But from what I've read, the cravings are intense and urgent. It takes a very strong person to resist them. Isn't the AA helping?"

"Evidently not. I don't think I've ever been more furious with him. We've had our ups and downs in the past – what couple hasn't? But this, this is different."

"I'm so sorry," Rose said again. "What are you going to do?"

"I don't know," Meg wailed. "Just now, I can't stand the thought of being anywhere near him. I can't trust myself not to shout at him some more, and I know that would be pointless. It would only make him even more stubborn. And there's nowhere else I can go – I can't involve Jessica. I owe him that much."

"You could come home with me, if you like."

Meg's face brightened. "Could I? Oh, that would be marvellous. But I don't have anything with me."

"I could lend you a nightie, and we could buy you some toiletries and clean undies on the way home."

"Then yes, please, I'd like to. I'll ring him when I get there, and tell him I need some time to think about what's happened."

"Good idea," Rose said. "We don't want him to

report you as missing."

"I'm not sure he'd even notice."

Rose hugged her. "Don't say that. You know it's not true."

Meg

It had taken Meg hours to fall asleep in the unfamiliarity of Rose's spare bedroom and she woke up with gritty eyes and a dry mouth. She stumbled along the landing to the bathroom to splash some cold water on her face. Better. She'd skip a shower for once, having enjoyed a deep, soaky bath the evening before, at her friend's insistence.

Rose was so kind, taking her in like this. She'd tried to ring John the night before, to let him know where she was, but he hadn't picked up. She'd left messages on both the answerphone and the voice-mail of his mobile. God only knew where he'd been. Out drinking, probably.

She was half way through dressing when her mobile rang, startling her. She jammed her glasses on her nose, then picked it up. Not a number she recognised. Who the devil was ringing her so early?

"Good morning, is that Mrs Meg Jeffries?" A cool, official voice. How had they got hold of her number?

"Who is this?"

"I have your husband on the line."

Meg sat down abruptly on the bed as her legs gave way beneath her.

There was a click, then she heard John's voice, "Meggie?"

151

"John! What's wrong? Where are you?"

"Oh, Meggie, I've screwed up so badly." He sounded so upset.

Alarm bells began ringing in Meg's head. "What's wrong?" she repeated. "Where are you?"

"Worcester Police Station."

Oh no. Not again. Get a grip, Meg. You need to be the calm one now.

"Tell me what's happened."

"It's – I – oh, Meg! I nearly hit someone. Last night."

Oh my God. He'd been drinking and driving. Again. Meg's nails bit into the palm of her free hand.

"In the car?"

"Yes."

"You said you *nearly* hit someone. Were they all right?"

"Yes, I think so."

Thank God for small mercies. "Are they keeping you in?"

"What? No, I don't think so. They said I could ring you, let you know where I am."

"I'll be with you as soon as I can," Meg said, and rang off.

Rose

As soon as Meg walked into the kitchen, Rose knew there was something badly wrong. She had heard her friend's mobile go off. Had it been John?

"Come and sit down," she said. "I'll make you a cup

of tea."

Meg pulled a chair out from the table and dropped into it. Rose busied herself with boiling the kettle, putting three teabags into the old-fashioned teapot she still preferred, then left it to brew.

"Would you like some breakfast?" she said.

Meg raised her eyes to meet her gaze and Rose's heart was pierced by the sadness she saw in them.

"Oh, Meg, don't look like that," she said, sitting down opposite her. "What's happened?"

"It's John," Meg said in a flat voice. "I just got a phone call. He's – he's in Worcester Police Station."

"Oh, no, I'm so sorry." Rose took her friend's hand, unsure how to respond to this news.

"He's been arrested," Meg continued in the same monotone. Rose could tell how hard she was fighting to keep her voice under control. "They let him ring me and he said... he told me... oh, Rose! He said he'd nearly hit somebody."

"He was in a fight?" Rose hadn't been expecting this.

"What?" Meg said, sounding shocked. "Oh, no, nothing like that. He was in the car."

Rose didn't know what to say. She stood up, poured the tea into two porcelain mugs, added milk, then brought them to the table. "Drink this," she said.

Meg took the proffered mug in her hand, raised it to her lips. But she was shaking so much that the hot liquid slopped over the rim.

"Sorry," she muttered. "Let me get a cloth to mop it up."

"Leave it," Rose said. "It doesn't matter. What

happens now?"

"I told him I'd be with him as soon as I could. I don't know what's happened to the car, but it sounds like they're letting him come home on bail."

There was no hint of shock in Meg's voice and Rose jumped to a curious conclusion. "This has happened before."

"Yes, eight years ago. He *promised* me he'd change his ways." Meg paused, then continued, "I should never have left him on his own."

"You mustn't think like that. It's not your fault."

"I need to ring for a taxi."

"Nonsense, I'll take you there, then drop you both home."

"You've done enough already," Meg said.

Rose couldn't tell what her friend wanted. She could understand why Meg would rather she kept out of this tangle. But a taxi from here to Worcester, then back home, would be expensive.

"It's up to you," she said, "but I'd be happy to help."

Meg's shoulders slumped. "Then yes, please."

"You should try to eat some breakfast first," Rose said. "I can offer cereal or toast, or both."

"I couldn't eat anything, not now."

Rose knew better than to push it. "Okay," she said. "You go and get ready while I have my cereal. It'll only take a few minutes."

Meg stood up, then met her eyes. "Thank you for everything."

Ginny

For the first time in… she couldn't remember how long, Ginny found herself daring to care about other people. She was worried about Rose and Meg. Rose, who would be spending her first Christmas without Graham, and Meg's problems with John.

She thought of them as she made her way round the pre-Christmas farmers market, its stalls bright with wreaths and cards, Christmas trees and Yule logs, as well as the usual produce. A group of carol singers, well wrapped up in coats and scarves, gloves and bright woollen hats with pom-poms, were filling her ears with the Christmas message of joy and peace. It was a bitterly cold morning and she became mesmerised by the music – it was as though she could see their notes in the puffs of air as they sang.

She was glad she had come, even though she didn't need to buy much – she'd be spending Christmas at the Buddhist Retreat Centre, as usual. She'd booked her place on the Winter Retreat months ago, having attended it for the past several years – it was a lovely way of re-centring herself for the year to come. An opportunity to spend time in awareness and loving-kindness meditations, and to remind herself of the importance of compassion and mindfulness in her life.

Above all, it meant that she wouldn't be spending Christmas alone. She sighed as her gloomy thoughts broke into the pre-Christmas mood in the market – she could do with some of that compassion and mindfulness in her life right now. All around her, people were getting ready for

Christmas. Even Meg and Rose would be spending the time with their families, however hard that would be, this year.

She was with Scrooge – she simply couldn't be bothered. Why would she? She had no family to share it with, after all.

God! Life was so unfair. When Laura had been alive, their Christmases had been so special. This was the time of year she missed her darling girl the most, when everyone else was playing happy families. It sometimes felt like she was the only person in the world without a loved one to buy presents for.

She shook herself – enough of the self-pity party. She'd enjoy the Winter Retreat, same as always. But it wouldn't hurt to buy Rose and Meg a small present each... Better let them know, perhaps.

Rose

Her first Christmas without Graham. She was going to spend Christmas Day with Matthew and his family, then drive over to Shrewsbury to have Boxing Day with Daniel and his. And maybe even little Natalie, if she was home by then.

But it wouldn't be the same. Not in any shape or form. For the past more than fifty years, Christmas had meant time with Graham – even when he was still working, he'd always taken the week between Christmas Day and New Year off. Both Daniel and Matthew had fallen into a pattern of spending Christmas Day with them one year and Boxing Day with their wives' families, reversing it the following year. It felt so odd having no food preparation to do. She couldn't bear the idea of spending either of these days at home without him, so she'd asked her sons if she could come to their homes instead. Fortunately, Danny was a good cook, so it wouldn't be putting too much pressure on Debbie.

She'd forced herself to go through the motions, buying and wrapping presents for everyone, and was stitching against the clock to get Natalie's birth sampler finished in time. The tiny girl was feeding from Debbie's breast now, or from a bottle with her mother's expressed milk, and was starting to put on a bit of weight, to lose that awful air of fragility. The doctors were speaking optimistically about discharging her by Christmas.

Wonder what Ginny does at Christmas? So far as Rose knew, Ginny didn't have any family of her own. *And poor Meg... better count her blessings.* She glanced at the clock – quarter to two. Time to drive over to Lesley's for her piano lesson.

"What are your favourite carols?" Lesley said.

"I'm not sure... *Unto us a boy is born* and *O little town of Bethlehem*, I think. And *The Zither Carol* – we used to sing that at school."

Lesley produced two books of carols with a flourish. "Would you like to be able to play them?" she said. "We've got four lessons to go before Christmas, so there should be time for you to get your fingers round them."

"That would be wonderful," Rose said, "but I won't have anyone to play them to... I'm at Matthew's on Christmas Day and Daniel's on Boxing Day."

By this time, Lesley knew all about the family. "Don't

any of the children play?" she said.

"No, Jake and Davy are real outdoor types, and Jamie's football mad. I rarely see Ben these days, and Rosie loves her ballet. I've no idea how little Natalie will turn out."

"How's she doing?"

Rose smiled. "Much better, thank you. They're hoping she'll be home in time for Christmas."

"Well, do you want to learn to play them anyway?" Lesley said.

Rose nodded.

"Okay," Lesley said. "Let's start with *Unto us a boy is born*. It's in the key of C, so you've got no sharps or flats to worry about. Try the left hand first."

By the end of the lesson, Rose could play both hands separately, if slowly. "Thank you, Lesley, that was fun!" she said. "It really helps, knowing the tune already."

"Keep practising it this week, and put it together if you feel like it," Lesley said. "We'll add O *little town of Bethlehem* next week."

Rose left Lesley's feeling Christmassy for the first time this year. When she got home, she checked her e-mails. Something from Ginny...

Hello Rose and Meg,

I was wondering about Christmas presents. I know we didn't exchange them last year, but we've all got a good deal closer this year, and I'd like to buy you both something to appreciate that. But I thought I'd better check, in case you

weren't planning to. Please let me know.
Ginny x

What a good idea. Better reply straight away…

Dear Ginny and Meg,
 That's a wonderful idea – thank you for thinking of it.
 Looking forward to seeing you both on the 18th.
Love,
Rose x

Ginny

Ginny had enjoyed *Becoming*. She'd had no idea that Michelle Obama had been such a force for good in her own right. Wonder whether she'll stand for President herself, one day?

 Politics. Another subject she didn't know Rose and Meg's views about. Ginny herself had always been left-wing and liberal in her views, ever since her time in the States, which had played such a formative role in her life. But she had no idea whether Rose and Meg shared them. This meeting was going to be interesting. And she was looking forward to giving them their presents.

 The rain was drumming against the window, pouring down the panes. She hated using the car for local trips, but on the other hand, she didn't want to catch pneumonia. She shrugged on her winter coat, picked up her backpack and headed out to the car.

When she reached Capuchins, she was grateful to walk into its cosy warmth. She hated to think how much it must cost Karen to heat it adequately at this time of year. Her friends were already there, sitting at their usual table, talking quietly. Rose looked up and smiled when she saw her.

"Ginny, I'm so glad you're here. I've been looking forward to our get-together for days."

Meg smiled too, but the smile did not reach her eyes. Something wrong there. Ginny bought her herbal tea, then walked over to join them. "Well, my friends, how have you been?"

"I've brought the finished baby sampler to show you both," Rose said, delving into her shopping bag. "I'm really thrilled with how it's turned out."

"It's gorgeous," Ginny said, "your stitches are so neat and even."

Rose blushed. "Thank you. I had to buy a custom-made frame though, which cost a fortune. I was horrified."

"It's worth it," Meg said. "It sets off the stitching beautifully."

"Thank you."

"Is something wrong, Meg?" Ginny asked. "You don't seem to be your normal, cheerful self." Then cursed her own lack of tact, as she saw Meg's lips begin to tremble, tears to fill her eyes. "God, I'm sorry... what's up?"

Meg met her gaze. "It's John," she said. "He – he was arrested for drinking and driving a week or so ago."

Ginny sat back in her chair, shocked. What a selfish swine John was. Why did Meg stay with him?

"I'm so sorry to hear that," she said. What else could

she say?

"Thank you," Meg said with simple dignity. "He's back home now, and we'll have to wait until the New Year to find out what happens next."

Rose squeezed Meg's hand. "We'll both be here for you, whatever happens."

The tears were now running down Meg's cheeks and she was scrabbling in her handbag, presumably for a tissue. Ginny passed her a packet. "Here."

"Thank you. I'm sorry, you two, I didn't mean to spoil our meeting."

"You haven't spoiled it at all," Rose said, soothing her. "That's what friends are for, to support each other in times of trouble."

Meg blew her nose, wiped her eyes. "That helps. Thank you, both of you. I expect it will all work out in the end."

Ginny took the unspoken cue and said, "So, what did you think of *Becoming*?"

"I absolutely loved it," Rose said. "The more I read, the more I liked her. She is such a strong person in her own right. It must be difficult to be married to someone so prominent, to have every aspect of your life open to public scrutiny. But she seems to have risen to the challenge so well."

"Me too," Ginny said. "I loved the way she fought for the issues she was passionate about, whether or not Barack agreed with her."

"I liked how protective she was of her girls," Meg said. "I got a bit lost with all the politics, because I don't understand how the American system works, but I really admire her. I'm glad I chose it. Jess recommended it. I'm also glad," and her voice got stronger, "that I got it on my Kindle. I find it difficult to read hardbacks these days – they're so heavy and my hands begin to ache. And the print is so small."

"Have you been to the optician recently?" Rose said.

"Not for years," Meg said. "I manage well enough with the glasses I've got."

"You really ought to go for an eye-test," Ginny said. "Your eyesight is so precious, you don't want to strain it."

"Oh, I suppose you're right. Okay, I'll book an appointment. I can always come into town on the bus."

"Good," Ginny said. Time to change the subject.

"I've chosen the book for our next meeting – *The Secret Lives of Colour* by Kassia St. Clair. Karen recommended it to me a while ago, and it's fantastic."

"I'm looking forward to it," Rose said. Then she said, "What are you all doing over Christmas? Lesley's got me playing Christmas carols on the piano – such fun. But," and she sighed, "it's going to be so strange spending Christmas without Graham."

"Where are you going to spend it?" Meg said. "If you're going to be at home alone, you'd be welcome to join us."

"Thank you, Meg, that's very sweet of you. But I'm going to spend Christmas Day at Matthew's, then drive over to Shrewsbury on Boxing Day to see Daniel and his family. We're hoping that little Natalie will be home by then."

"How is she?" Ginny said.

"Coming on by leaps and bounds, thank God. The

doctors are really pleased with her progress."

"Ah, that's good to hear. What about you, Meg? How will you be spending Christmas?"

"Usually, the whole family come to us on Christmas Day," Meg said, a quaver in her voice, "but this year, I don't know how that's going to pan out. Unless John gets his act together, it's going to be really difficult."

"How about you, Ginny?" Rose said hastily. "What do you do over Christmas?"

They didn't know how lucky they were, having families to spend Christmas with – even a loser like John. Ginny tried not to feel bitter, strove to keep her tone light, as she answered, "I'll be in the same part of the world as you. I always go to a Buddhist Retreat Centre in Shropshire over Christmas, rather than staying at home alone."

Rose's face softened. "I hope you have a lovely time there. Whereabouts in Shropshire is it?"

"Near Whitchurch. I've been going there for years, ever since... ever since Laura died."

Rose took her hand, squeezed it gently. Ginny felt that her friend understood. Such a blessing.

"Now," she said, "it's present time." She rootled through her backpack and brought out her two presents. After thinking long and hard, she had decided on books for both of them, to support their new hobbies. "Here you are, Meg," she said, passing one parcel over.

"Thank you," Meg said. "May I open it now, or would you rather I waited until Christmas Day?"

"Oh, you can open it now."

Meg carefully unwrapped it, then beamed. "That's

fabulous – thank you so much!"

"What is it?" Rose said.

"*Writing the Memoir* by Judith Barrington." Meg started to look down the contents page. "It's exactly what I need. Thank you, Ginny." She gave her a hug.

"You're welcome," Ginny said, well pleased with her gift's reception. "And here's yours, Rose."

Rose opened it. "*The New Cross Stitcher's Bible*," she read aloud, "Oh, that's super. It's going to be so useful."

"I looked at the contents list before I bought it," Ginny said, "and it explains how to do other stuff too, like blackwork and Hardanger, and how to design your own sampler. I thought you'd like it."

"Oh, I do! Thank you so much." Rose looked through it carefully, a broad smile on her face. Then closed it and reached into her own bag.

"Here's your present, Ginny," she said, "two minds with but a single thought." And she handed her a suspiciously book-shaped parcel.

Ginny grinned back at her. "Excellent." Unlike the other two, she tore the paper, eager to see what was inside. She read the title, *The New Art of Photographing Nature*. She opened it straight away and began to browse through it – the illustrations were stunning. "This looks gorgeous. Thank you."

"I hope it will be right for you," Rose said, a hint of worry in her voice. "I had a good look through it when it arrived, and it seems to be good on technique, but also inspirational."

"I'm really looking forward to reading it."

"And here's yours, Meg," Rose said, passing over her gift. Once again, Meg opened it carefully. It was a beautiful A4 hardback journal. "For finishing the memoir," Rose said.

"It's lovely – thank you very much. Oh dear, I hope you both like what I've bought you…"

"Of course we will," Rose said.

Meg gave Rose her present first, while Ginny looked on, curious to see what Meg had chosen. Rose opened it to reveal a bright orange music book, *The Young Pianist's Repertoire, Book One.*

"I know it says, 'young pianist' on the front," Meg said, an anxious expression on her face. "But I asked Jess to ask Lesley what would be suitable for you, and she said you should be ready for this now."

Rose hugged her. "Thank you. That's super. I'll take it with me to Lesley's after Christmas, to see what she recommends I should start on."

"And here's yours, Ginny," Meg said, passing it over – it felt like another book. She ripped off the paper, then beamed. "Another BOSH! cookery book – that's fantastic. I love the original one – it will be great to have another."

Meg's shoulders sagged in relief. "Oh, I'm so glad you like it."

"I really do," Ginny said. "Wow, we've really spoiled each other, haven't we? Bless you both."

Silence reigned for a while as they examined their presents more closely. The strain had left Meg's face and she was looking contentedly at her book. Good.

Then Rose stood up. "Time to go, I'm afraid," she said, "I've agreed to meet Sarah this afternoon, to get some advice on what to buy the children. Their interests change so quickly these days, I find it hard to keep up. And buying the wrong thing is worse than anything. I hope you both have a gorgeous Christmas." She gave them each a hug.

"I suppose I'd better be getting back too, if I'm to talk some sense into John," Meg said, an uncharacteristically determined note in her voice. "Have a lovely Christmas, both of you."

Ginny felt a bit flat but tried to hide it. "I hope you both have a good time with your families," she said, trying to ignore the surge of envy running through her. "See you next year."

Rose

As she had expected, Christmas was difficult for Rose. She had a private weep on Christmas Day morning, waking up alone. Would she ever get used to this solitude? But she had bucked herself up and driven round to Matthew and Sarah's late morning. To be met by Jamie and Rosie, both wild with excitement that Christmas had finally arrived.

"Granny, come and see what Mummy and Daddy gave me." Jamie said, towing her into the living room, which was chaotically untidy, with brightly-coloured wrapping paper strewn everywhere.

"Look!" he said, and she obediently admired the large, blue, plastic box sitting in the middle of the floor.

"What is it?"

"It's a K'Nex set – I can make all kinds of things with it."

"That's lovely." Rose guessed it was similar to Lego, and mentally wished Sarah the best of luck with keeping track of all the pieces.

"What about you, Rosie? What did Mummy and Daddy give you?"

Rosie beamed at her. "My very own art set, with crayons an' felt tips an' paints an' paper an' stickers. It's lovely."

"I hope you'll draw a picture for me, sometime."

Another big grin. "Of course I will. What do you want me to draw?"

"Anything you like, sweetheart."

Bless them both. She could remember Matthew and Daniel at the same ages, so thrilled by the simplest things. No sign of Ben – she guessed he was still asleep.

"Mum, here you are," Matthew said, giving her a hug. "Let Granny sit down, you two. Would you like a drink?"

"I'd welcome a cup of tea, thank you, love."

"Sarah's in the kitchen, getting the veg on. Thank God we do the turkey on Christmas Eve – the gas pressure's low, as usual."

"Does she need any help?"

"I don't think so. You just sit and relax. I'll be back with your tea in a minute."

By the time they had eaten lunch, Rose was feeling tired. Ben had eventually appeared just before they'd sat down, but had sloped back off to his room after they had all exchanged presents. She was glad she'd asked Sarah's advice about what to get him – the latest edition of *Grand Theft Auto*. He'd even given her an awkward hug.

The rest of them, she, Matthew, Sarah, Jamie and Rosie, had sat down together to watch *Inside Out,* one of the many Pixar films she hadn't seen. To her surprise, she thoroughly enjoyed it.

When she reached home, she felt both happy and sad – which made her smile as she thought of Joy and Sadness from the film. It had been lovely to spend the day with Matthew and the family but coming home to an empty house was hard – at least she had Bonnie for company. With the cat purring on her knee, she settled down to watch *It's A Wonderful Life*. But had to turn it off part way through, as it brought back too many memories of Christmases past, when Graham had been there to share them.

So she took herself off to her lonely bed with a mug of hot chocolate. It would be an early start in the morning – she couldn't wait to see baby Natalie, who had finally come home on the 22nd – such a wonderful Christmas present.

January: *The Secret Lives of Colour* by Kassia St. Clair

Meg

"What's wrong?" Meg said, as John stomped into the kitchen a few days before Christmas. She was icing the Christmas cake, but what she saw in his eyes made her put the palette knife down.

"Everything," John said.

"What do you mean, 'everything'?"

He ignored her, opening cupboard doors then slamming them shut again. "Where's the bloody coffee?"

Meg pulled out a chair and sat at the table. Why was he in such a foul mood? "In its usual place in that cupboard," she said, nodding her head towards it.

Then held her peace by dint of biting her lip until he'd made himself a mug of coffee, hot, black and strong. It wasn't until he was heading for the door that she broke the silence.

"John," she said with some asperity, "you can't just march in here with a face as black as a thundercloud, then disappear back upstairs without telling me what's wrong. Because something obviously is."

"It's nothing to do with you," he growled. But he came back and sat down opposite her.

She reached over and touched his hand. "Please tell me."

His shoulders slumped. "I've been doing some research on the internet, and trying to find out what my sentence will be."

"Sentence?" Meg said, her stomach clenching. "You can't mean you might have to go to prison?"

Oh, God. How was she going to tell Jessica? It had been bad enough when they'd had to ask for her help to bring the car back home, now that John wasn't driving. She hated to think how her daughter would react to this.

"It depends," John said, and Meg winced at hearing the bitterness in his voice, "on how lenient the magistrate is feeling on the day. Apparently it's not enough that I'll be disqualified from driving for at least a year – it could even be three. There will also be a hefty fine to pay and I could get sent down."

"Where have you found all this out?"

"By googling 'drink-driving offences', of course. It's a bloody good job I didn't hit that pedestrian, otherwise they'd be locking me away for sure."

"But you didn't," Meg said. "You didn't damage anything except the car and that waste bin. So I'm sure they won't send you to prison."

"That's all you know. Don't forget, I've been disqualified before."

"As though I could forget." She'd thought it had taught him a lesson – evidently not. "There's only one thing for it – we need to find you a good solicitor."

"Have you any idea how much solicitors charge?"

"I don't care," Meg said, some useful anger surging through her. "Don't you understand? I'd pay *anything* to avoid that. And we've got savings, haven't we?"

His face softened and he reached out for her hand. "What have I done to deserve you, Meggie?"

"I'm your wife. Nothing you do or say can change that. We'll get through this somehow. You simply can't go to prison – I couldn't bear it."

"Let's hope it doesn't come to that. Okay, you win. I'll go back online and try to find a solicitor."

Rose

It had been such a blessing to spend Boxing Day with Daniel and Debbie. The journey over to Shrewsbury had been a bit of a nightmare – the roads were chock-a-block with cars, all full of people heading out to visit their relatives – but she had got there in the end.

"Mum! It's so good to see you," Daniel said, giving her a hug before relieving her of the heavy bag of presents. "Come and sit down. I'll get you a cup of tea."

"Be careful with that," Rose said. "One of the presents is breakable."

Daniel grinned at her, his eyes twinkling. "Trust me. I'm a big boy now."

When she walked into the living room, Jake and Davy surged up from the sofa, rushed over and hugged her.

"Guess what, Granny?" Davy said, "Baby Natalie's home."

"Is she?" Rose said, feigning surprise. "That's wonderful, Davy."

"You knew," he said, disappointed. "Did Daddy tell you?"

"I'm sorry, he did. But I haven't seen her yet."

"She's asleep upstairs," Jake informed her. "She's still

really tiny."

Rose could see the shadow of anxiety in his eyes. That must stop. "Well, you'd expect that," she said. "She wasn't supposed to be born until around now, so it's not surprising that she's still only the size of a newborn baby."

To her relief, his shoulders relaxed. "I suppose so."

"I know so," Rose said. "So, what have you two had for Christmas?"

As she hoped, this question diverted them both nicely. By the time they had showed her all their loot, it was nearly time for lunch. They were all seated round the dining table and Daniel was just beginning to carve the turkey when a loud squall came through the baby monitor.

"Natalie," Debbie said, standing up quickly. "Her timing is impeccable. I'll be back soon. You all carry on."

Rose was itching to rush upstairs after her, but knew it would alarm Jake. "Would you like me to dish your vegetables, Davy?"

"Yes, please. But no sprouts – they taste horrible."

Rose grinned – he was so like his father. "Okay, no sprouts."

By the time they all had well-filled plates in front of them, Debbie's footsteps could be heard on the stairs.

"I've changed her," she said, "but I'll need to feed her before I eat myself."

"I've dished your lunch," Rose said, "and you can microwave it warm again when you're done."

"Thanks, Rose."

They had nearly cleared their plates by the time Debbie re-appeared. "She's fed well," she said, "and I've put her down in the Moses basket in the living room. She should sleep for a while now."

"When's she going to get interesting?" Davy said plaintively. "All she does is eat and sleep."

"Give her a chance," Daniel told his son. "She's only little. She'll be awake much longer in a few weeks."

Once they'd all finished eating, Rose helped Daniel to clear the table and load the dishwasher, before they moved back into the cosy warmth of the living room. It was present time. Debbie knelt in front of the Christmas tree, under which all the family's gifts were stacked.

"Here you are, Rose," she said, handing her mother-in-law a flat, rectangular parcel. "Merry Christmas!"

Rose opened it curiously, then gave a cry of delight. It was a photo of Natalie and the boys, Jake holding her carefully in his arms. "Oh, that's fantastic! Thank you so much. I'll put it in pride of place in the living room."

Her own presents – a white England rugby shirt for Jake, a Playmobil set for Davy, a tiny, soft, white teddy bear for Natalie, and books for Daniel and Debbie, were well received.

"I have a little extra present," she said, meeting Debbie's eyes. She handed over the parcel containing the completed birth sampler, which she'd stretched and laced herself, following a YouTube tutorial, before placing it behind a pale pink mount and white painted wooden frame.

Debbie opened it. "Oh, Rose," she said, a little catch in her voice. "That's so special. Look, Daniel."

"That's gorgeous, Mum," Daniel said. "I didn't know you could cross-stitch."

"It's my new hobby," Rose said. "I'm so glad you like it."

"Like it? I love it!" Debbie said. "Thank you so much."

A little later on, Natalie woke up and Rose was able to hold her in her arms, marvelling at her dark grey eyes, her perfect little fingers.

"She's so beautiful, Debbie," she said softly. "You must be so happy."

"I am – now," Debbie said. "I'm so glad she's at home with us."

Ginny

Ginny's time at the Buddhist Retreat Centre had gone a long way towards restoring her soul. As always, it had been wonderful, in the true sense of that word, to be there, spending her days in quiet meditation, combined with peaceful rituals, simple yet delicious vegetarian meals, renewing old friendships and making new ones. There was plenty of time to walk in the beautiful Shropshire countryside, and the weather was blessedly dry and sunny, if cold. She was so glad she'd brought her winter coat along, and the fingerless gloves Meg had made her.

This year, she'd also decided to bring her camera, and a notepad to record any reflections for blog posts. She rose early one morning and watched the sun rise, lost in the glory of the slowly lightening sky, starting black with pinpoints of starlight, fading into deep purple and navy. Then, as the sun began to come up, all the shades of red and orange and gold, even a hint of green. She hurried back inside, eager to capture the experience on paper – she'd already taken several photos.

She'd followed her usual practice of bringing an 'improving' book with her, so that she could begin the new year as her best self. This time it had been *The Gifts of Imperfection* by Brené Brown, and she had found it life-changing. Perhaps she'd offer it to Rose and Meg next April.

Her thoughts often returned to them – how were they getting on? She guessed that Rose at least would be finding this first Christmas without Graham difficult. She hoped that spending time with the two sons and their families would help to fill the yawning emptiness. And Meg – had John been able to stay sober?

She'd find out soon enough.

Meg

Meg had waited until after Christmas to have the conversation with Jessica – no point in both of them being miserable over the festive season.

But when her daughter decided to drop in for a cup of tea on her way to the supermarket, Meg seized the day. John was at his AA meeting, so they wouldn't be interrupted.

"I have some news for you," she said, once they were sitting comfortably at the kitchen table, a plate of freshly-baked stem ginger biscuits between them.

"News? What kind of news?"

"It's about your Dad."

"What? What is it now?"

"He did some research on the internet before

Christmas," Meg began, "and he's found out what might happen when he goes to court."

"I expect he'll have to pay a fairly hefty fine," Jessica said.

"Yes, but that may not be the worst of it."

Meg bit her lip. This was more difficult than she had expected. She watched the colour drain from her daughter's cheeks.

"Then what *is* the worst of it?" Jessica whispered. "Not... prison?"

Meg reached across the table, took her daughter's hand. "I'm afraid it might come to that," she said, "because it's not his first offence. He got away with being disqualified for a year and a fine last time, but they're almost bound to take it more seriously this time."

Jessica looked dazed. "But why?" she said. "He didn't hurt anyone, only the car."

"I know," Meg said, "and I hope it won't happen. But we – we have to be prepared for it."

"He needs to find himself a good solicitor," Jessica said, sitting up straight, switching from shock to action in a heartbeat.

Meg nodded. "We've already done that," she said. "He, that is, the solicitor, thinks that your Dad will probably not be sent down, so long as he pleads guilty."

"Does that make a difference?"

"Apparently so. He thinks that your Dad's ARLD diagnosis may help too, so long as he agrees to keep on attending AA every day and doesn't start to drink again."

"Is that where he is now? At the AA meeting?"

"Yes."

"How long will it be until we know when he goes to court?"

"We haven't got a date yet, but I'm hoping we'll know fairly soon."

Jessica stood up. "I must go," she said. "I've got the supermarket run to do before I pick the girls up from school."

Meg knew that wasn't the reason for her daughter's haste. That she needed time alone to process what she'd heard. It had always been her way when something bad happened.

"All right, love," she said, standing up and giving her a hug. "I'll see you soon."

She waited until she heard Jessica's car drive away, then sank back down onto her chair, feeling exhausted. Had she been right to share this with her? Yes. She knew that if John did go to prison and Jessica had had no warning, that would be infinitely worse. But God! It had been hard.

Rose

"Hello, Mum," Matthew said. "What's up?""

"I've finally had a letter from the hospital," Rose said. "They want me to go there next week to assess whether I'm ready for the knee replacement, and whether it would be suitable. And they've asked me to go for an x-ray beforehand."

"About time too. How long have you been waiting?"

"Nearly eighteen months. But now it's come, I'm

feeling a bit afraid. What if they don't find me suitable?"

"Don't worry, I'm sure they will. Will you need a lift? I could take a couple of hours off work if necessary."

Rose picked the letter up off the table and scanned it quickly. "No, I don't think so, love. It doesn't say I have to be brought there by someone else. But thank you, that was kind."

"Let me know how it goes, won't you?"

"Of course I will."

Next week came rather too fast for Rose. The letter from the hospital had included two forms to complete. The first asked for general information about her health and lifestyle. The other was headed, *Finding Your Oxford Knee Score,* and was a multiple choice set of questions, asking whether and how much pain she felt when she did various things, such as getting in or out of the car, getting up from the table, when walking, in bed, walking down a flight of stairs, and so on. One made her hoot with laughter: "Could you kneel down and get up again afterwards?" She hadn't been able to do that for years. From her answers, she suspected she might be in more trouble than she'd thought. Now she was at the hospital, waiting to be called in.

"Mrs Anderson?"

Rose struggled to her feet and followed the doctor into the consulting room.

"I'm Dr Robertson," the young woman said. "What would you like me to call you?"

"Rose, please."

"Have you filled in the forms you were sent, Rose?"

"Yes." Rose passed them over. A couple of minutes' silence followed as Dr Robertson read them through, while Rose's heart went twenty to the dozen.

"May I examine you please?"

"Of course."

The next few minutes were quite painful as Dr Robertson felt around her left knee, and asked her to stand up, sit down, walk, and show how far she could bend and straighten her knee.

"Well, Rose," the doctor said, meeting her eyes with a smile, "it seems as though you are a good candidate for a knee replacement. Your knee arthritis is severe – I'm glad we can do something about it. I'll send a letter to your GP with my report, and we'll put you on the waiting list for an operation."

"Thank you," Rose said faintly. She hadn't expected such a swift result.

"But in the meantime, I suggest you use a stick all the time, to take as much pressure as possible off that knee. And if you could lose some weight, that would also help. Otherwise, the replacement knee won't last so long."

Rose flushed. She should have thought of that for herself.

"When is the operation likely to be?" she said.

"Sometime in May, I expect," Dr Robertson said. "I'll be writing to your GP."

"Thank you."

Ginny

The morning of January's book group meeting was cold but sunny, so Ginny decided to risk going on her bike. When she arrived at Capuchins, invigorated by the exercise, Rose and Meg were already there. She ordered her usual camomile tea, then strolled over to where her friends were sitting. It seemed an age since they had last met, and of course it had been a week longer than usual, because of Christmas. Already warm from the exercise, she had to shed her coat, whereas the other two were still wearing theirs.

"How are you both?"

Meg grimaced. "I'm fine," she said, "but John isn't."

Oh dear. "What's up with him?"

"He's still struggling with the temptation to drink," Meg said. "It's making him really foul tempered."

"Even after the arrest?" Rose said.

"I know. You'd think that would have brought him to his senses. He is trying, but I'm not sure the AA meetings are doing any good. I'm at my wits' end."

Selfish sod. He didn't deserve her. But Ginny knew better than to say so, out loud.

"That must be so frustrating," Rose said. "But in the end, it's up to him. If he doesn't want help, you can't force him to accept it."

"Oh, I know," Meg said. "But it's so infuriating."

"How about you, Rose?" Ginny said.

"I have some news," Rose said, sitting up a little straighter. "You know I've been having trouble with my left knee? Well, it got abruptly worse over Christmas. It's quite swollen and gave way entirely a couple of times. I was lucky not to fall. But the timing is good – last week, after an eighteen month wait, I finally had a consultation at the General, and they're putting me in for a knee replacement."

"Wow! That's good news?" Ginny said, not sure whether it was or not.

"Yes, it is," Rose said. "But I'm feeling quite scared, just the same. It's a major operation, especially at my age."

"What's the next step?" Meg said.

"I've been told to lose some weight, so there's less pressure on my knee, which is why I'm not having cake today."

"I did wonder about that," Meg said. "That makes sense. I'm glad *you're* taking your health seriously."

"And," Rose continued, "I've got another appointment with the consultant during the second week of March, when I'll find out the date of the operation, I hope. I'll keep you both posted."

"If you need someone to take you to appointments, or with anything else," Ginny said, putting her hand on Rose's arm. "I'd be happy to help."

Rose smiled at her. "Thank you. I might well take you up on that. But enough about me – how have you been?"

"Oh, not so bad. The days at the retreat centre were good for me – they helped me to centre myself again. And I've signed up for a Photoshop course, to learn how to edit my photos." She paused. "But it still seems weird not having to plan my yoga classes. You'd think I'd be used to it by now, eight months in."

"I know how you feel," Rose said with a laugh. "I

remember my first year of retirement – I didn't know what to do with myself." She turned to Meg, "I expect you felt the same?"

"Not really," Meg said. "I was looking forward to retirement, to spending more time with John."

Ginny changed the subject. "Well, my dears, what did you think of *The Secret Lives of Colour*?"

"I found it enchanting," Rose said. "I've learned so much from reading it. I love the way the author combines history, art, the science behind how the colours were made, with fascinating snippets about people in her descriptions of each colour, and random facts too. Good choice, Ginny."

"I'm so glad you enjoyed it," Ginny said. "I absolutely loved it, so much that I wanted to share it with you both, then worried that it wouldn't appeal to either of you."

"I enjoyed it too," Meg chimed in. "I had no idea there were so many different names for shades of the main colours."

While they were talking, Rose had taken the book out and was leafing through it.

"Here's one," she said, "under minium." She read the passage aloud. "I had no idea that the origin of the word 'miniature' came from the colour used by scribes used to illuminate their manuscripts. And that's just one example."

"It's going to be useful for my memoir too," Meg said. "It'll help me to vary how I describe things."

"I'd thought of that as well," Ginny said, "for my blog posts. It's enabled me to describe the colours of flowers and fruits more accurately – and more poetically."

"I found some parts of it pretty gory," Rose said.

"How they tortured various creatures in their quest for particular colours."

"And how the ingredients of some colours were poisonous," Meg added.

"Talking about the use of colours," Ginny said, "how did Daniel and Debbie like the birth sampler, Rose?"

Rose's face lit up. "They were thrilled with it," she said, "and I got to give Natalie a long cuddle when I spent Boxing Day there. She's up to the normal weight for a newborn now, and is making good progress."

"That *is* good news," Meg said. "I'm so pleased for them."

"Me too," Ginny said. "You must be so relieved."

"Yes," Rose said simply. "It's a good end to a worrying few months."

"So what's our book for February?" Ginny said.

"I'm afraid I've not been terribly original," Rose said. "When I'm feeling stressed, like now, I tend to go back to my roots and re-read one of my old favourites. So I've chosen *Jane Eyre* by Charlotte Brontë."

"Oh, I loved that when I was a teenager," Meg said.

"It will certainly make a change from all the up to date books we've been reading in the last few months," Ginny said.

Meg

As she made her way back to the bus stop, Meg had to fight down the all too familiar sense of inferiority, which kept resurfacing whenever she was with Rose and Ginny at the same time. The two of them seemed to be so much cleverer than she was, interested in things she knew nothing about. If she was honest, she'd found *The Secret Lives of Colour* more hard work than enjoyable, but hadn't dared to admit as much. At least she knew something about *Jane Eyre*. And she hadn't dared tell them about the possibility of John's being sent down. Not until he'd seen his solicitor again. It wasn't her news to tell.

She remembered what Rose had told her about not comparing, but it was so hard not to when they were all together. And now Ginny was going to be looking after Rose when she'd had the operation – she just knew it. Which of course *she* couldn't offer to do, because she didn't drive and Rose lived in a village, and because of John.

At least the memoir was going well. The book Ginny had bought her for Christmas had been really useful, giving her all sorts of new ideas, and tips on how to approach her story. The book Ginny had bought her... when was she going to realise that Ginny was not her enemy? She flushed, ashamed of her uncharitable thoughts. Stop it, Meg. You're being pathetic. Cross with herself, she boarded the bus home.

Rose

Try as she might, Rose was finding it nigh on impossible to shift her excess weight. She'd made all the obvious changes to her eating habits – cutting out cakes and biscuits, not snacking between meals, and switching to no sugar almond milk (and then switching back a week later when she realised she was only saving a handful of calories). But in the couple of weeks since her consultation, she'd only managed to lose a pound. And she knew that could be down to water fluctuations.

Jake's twelfth birthday was at the end of January, a few weeks before her own, so she drove over to Shrewsbury the weekend before, her knee well strapped up in a support, to take part in the family celebration.

"I'm so glad you could make it," Debbie said, as she welcomed her in. "We're all in the living room."

Daniel and Debbie had treated Jake to the latest X-Box for his birthday, so Rose had settled on a voucher from Game Station as his present. That way, he could choose a new game for himself. She would rather have given him something tangible, but children seemed to grow up so quickly these days, and she didn't really know what he liked.

"Thank you," he said, giving her a hug.

It was a long tradition in the family – started by her and Graham when the boys had been small – that the person whose birthday it was could choose their favourite food for the birthday meal. Both Matthew and Daniel had carried it on in their own families. This year, Jake had opted for Debbie's special lasagne, which came out of the oven with the cheese and meat juices bubbling. Followed by a rich and delicious chocolate, rum and raisin cheesecake. Oh dear, all those calories.

Once the meal was over, Jake and Davy went back to their rooms, while the adults settled down for an enjoyable chat. Natalie was awake and gurgling.

"May I hold her?" Rose said.

"Of course," Debbie said. "But would you mind

washing your hands first? We're having to be extra careful that she doesn't catch any bugs. There's some hand sanitiser in the downstairs loo."

Rose obediently did so, then sat down again. Debbie put the baby girl into Rose's arms. In which she seemed to be a much more solid presence than on Boxing Day.

"I can't believe how much she's grown in the few weeks since I last saw you," Rose said.

Debbie beamed. "Yes, she's making excellent progress now, and has started to smile at us all. She's such a little poppet."

"I'm so glad," Rose said. "And you're looking so well too. How have you managed to lose all your baby weight so quickly?"

"Through intermittent fasting. Why do you ask?"

"Because I've been told to lose some weight before my knee operation and I'm really struggling."

"How much do they want you to lose?" Daniel said.

"As much as I can. Which is infuriatingly vague. I've been trying for the last couple of weeks, but I've only lost a pound."

She turned to Debbie. "What's intermittent fasting? I've never heard of it."

"It can mean two different things," Debbie said. "You can either limit the hours in the day when you eat, so that you only eat during a short period in the day and fast for the rest of it. Or you can be super strict a couple of days a week, and eat normally, but healthily, on the others."

"Which one did you go for?"

"The five-two option."

"Five to what?"

Debbie laughed. "Two as is T W O, not T O," she said. "The other way is far too restrictive when I have the rest of the family to feed."

Rose laughed too. "Oh, I see. How does it work?"

"You have to limit your intake to five hundred calories on the two fast days, then eat whatever you like on the other five."

"That sounds awfully strict," Rose said. "How have you managed?"

"I start the day with a bowl of cereal and a coffee – but I weigh the cereal and only use skimmed milk. Then I have a ready-made fruit salad for lunch, and a very light meal for tea. They recommend only having two meals a day, but I found that made me too grumpy, so I've fudged a way of doing it that works for me. And the weight has fallen off."

"So I can see. Do you have a book about it?"

"Yes, I'll fetch it for you."

"Thank you."

Rose looked at the cover, *The Fast Diet*. Such a clever title, with its dual interpretations of 'fast'. "D'you mind if I take a quick look, to see whether I think it might help?"

"Sure," Debbie said. "I'd lend it to you, but I'm still using it for the recipes. Now I've got down to a weight I'm happy with, I'm maintaining by having a fast day once a week. I feel so much better for it."

Rose read the introduction and began to feel enthusiastic. "I'll order it when I get home," she said. "Thank you."

Daniel smiled at her, picking up two envelopes from

the sideboard. "Here are your birthday present and card," he said. "You might like to open the present early, if you're going to be ordering a new book."

Inside, Rose found a generous Amazon gift voucher. "Thank you, both of you," she said. "I'll save the card until my birthday."

Ginny

Why had Rose chosen *Jane Eyre*? Ginny remembered reading it as a teenager, and feeling actively nauseated by the saccharine-sweet happy ending. Oh well, it wouldn't do her any harm to give it another try – Rose and Meg had been so good at reading the off the wall books she'd recommended. Although she suspected that Meg hadn't really enjoyed *The Secret Lives of Colour*.

She was looking forward to spring – there wasn't a huge variety of new plants growing for her to photograph during these short January days. Yet she still went out for either a cycle ride or a walk as often as the weather permitted. And found that when she really used her eyes, there was always something interesting to photograph – the striking silhouette of a tree's bare branches against a moody sky, the first buds and catkins appearing in the hedgerows, and some gloriously colourful sunrises and sunsets.

She couldn't wait to begin the Photoshop course. Talking of which… She picked up her phone and sent Meg an e-mail.

Hello Meg,

I think I mentioned that I've signed up for an online course in Photoshop, which helps you to edit your pictures. And it occurred to me that I could help you scan in some photos for that memoir of yours – how's it coming along?

Let me know if you're interested and we can arrange a get together.

Love,

Ginny x

Meg's reply came thirty minutes later:

Dear Ginny,

Thank you so much! That would be wonderful. I'm not quite at that stage yet, but it's so kind of you to suggest it.

Love,

Meg x

PS I haven't written much recently – too much stress about John. But you've given me a nudge to get back to it – thank you!

Meg

Meg had really wanted to include some photos in the memoir, but had no clue how to do it. And now Ginny was offering to help her. So kind. She hadn't written much – or anything, if she was truthful – since Christmas. Time to get back to it.

The next section would be about meeting John, and getting married.

She waited until the evening, when John was sitting in the lounge, biting his nails and trying to read the paper. But, as usual these days, he was restless, unable to relax. He'd try to read for a while, then throw the paper aside, stand up and prowl around the room, or twitch the curtain aside and gaze out of the window. Or he'd ask her questions without either listening to or really caring about her answers. Or make himself yet another cup of tea. Then he would sit back down and the cycle would repeat. She guessed he was finding it difficult to settle to anything without a drink in his hand. And she knew that distraction was important for him.

Should she ask him now? She knew he found evenings hardest of all. Perhaps it would take his mind off not drinking.

"Can you spare a minute?"

"What for?"

"I'm about to start writing about how we got together and I'd love to have your memories of that time."

John folded the paper and gave her his full attention. "I remember it well," he said, his eyes beginning to twinkle in the way she loved, and had almost forgotten. "We met in The Dolphin in Angel Place. I was there with some of my mates and you walked in with a couple of friends."

"Yes," Meg said, "Linda and Pamela. I'd forgotten they were there. I wonder what they're doing now."

"And I saw this tiny girl with a cloud of golden brown hair and deep brown eyes," John continued, "in one of the tightest pairs of flared jeans I'd ever seen."

Meg blushed. "I'd forgotten about those. They were my pride and joy – the first pair of Levis I'd ever owned."

"They certainly caught my eye." John grinned at her, and for a moment she could see the gorgeous boy he had been in his lined face.

"I fell for you immediately," she said. "So tall and handsome. I knew straight away that you were the one. And my father was thrilled that you were training to be an accountant – so respectable!"

"Yes, it didn't take us long, did it? Engaged after six months, married the following year. Very different to the kids these days, who live together for years before they even think about getting married – if they ever do."

"My father wouldn't have stood for it," Meg said. "He was so square he was practically cubed."

"He terrified me," John said. "So Victorian."

"Well, he gave his consent. And here we are nearly fifty years later, with Andrew and Jessica happy in their own lives, and grandchildren too."

"Will it be fifty years in September?" he said. How could he have forgotten? "We should do something special to celebrate."

"I'd like to throw a party for our family and close friends," Meg said, "with a cake and everything."

"If I'm still around," John said, with a return to his usual pessimism.

"Of course you will be," Meg said. "I'll see to that."

But would he be? Even if he managed to stay sober, he might be in prison. Which didn't bear thinking about. She remembered what her Auntie Enid always used to say, "Don't borrow trouble."

So she forced herself to smile at him, before standing up and kissing his forehead. "Thank you. That's given me some good memories to write about."

"Where are you going?"

"To fetch my journal, so I can write it all down while it's still fresh in my mind."

"Fair enough." He picked up the evening paper and shook it open. "Glad I could help."

February: *Jane Eyre* by Charlotte Brontë

Rose

The intermittent fasting book arrived a couple of days later, and Rose sat down to read it straight away. It was one of the more pleasant aspects of being retired – she could plan her days to suit herself. And today, it suited her to read, and to keep on reading, pausing only at long intervals for another infusion of coffee. The more she read, the greater sense it seemed to make. It was the beginning of February now, and Dr Robertson had said her knee operation would probably take place during May. Which gave her three months in which to lose as much weight as she could.

She weighed herself the following morning – 12 stone 6 pounds, far too much for her 5' 5" frame. Then ate breakfast before sitting at her kitchen table to work out a plan of action. Matthew had shifted when he took her shopping to Tuesdays after work, because his Saturdays were so busy with ferrying the children to various activities. So the best days to fast would be Tuesdays and Thursdays, when the fruit would be at its freshest. Like Debbie, she'd decided to eat a ready-made fruit salad for lunch – she couldn't see herself skipping a meal altogether.

Breakfast was the most important meal of the day for her – she was always ravenous when she woke up. What if she served her cereal in one of her small blue and white Chinese porcelain bowls instead of the normal one? That way she'd be able to fool herself into feeling satisfied, having eaten a 'bowlful.' She placed one on her scales, returned them to zero, then filled it with her favourite gluten-free cereal. Fifty grams. That would be enough. But she'd have to skip her normal toast.

One easy way of saving a few calories would be to switch from almond milk to skimmed milk. She found a small jug in her crockery cupboard and filled it with water, before pouring it out into a measuring jug. 300 ml, which should be enough to pour over her cereal in the morning, plus a couple of mugs of coffee. Then she'd switch to herbal tea for the rest of the day. How many calories would that be if it was skimmed milk? She looked it up on her phone – 102.

Oh. The fruit salad for lunch being just over 100 calories, that would only leave 75 calories for dinner – not enough. Blast it! But she was *not* going to skimp on breakfast.

She picked up the book again, turned to the recipe section at the back. Most of the evening meals were at least 250 calories. Perhaps she'd cheat a little, stick to under 700 calories instead of 500. That would have to do. A lot of the breakfast suggestions in the book would work as dinner for her.

Satisfied, she wrote a shopping list for the following day, feeling hopeful for the first time. This diet should be easy to stick to, because she'd only be on it two days a week. But she'd have to be careful on the other days too – she owed it to her knee.

Ginny

Ginny looked out of her bedroom window at the slate-grey sky, listened to the driving rain beating against the window pane. Gah. She'd been stuck in the house for several days now, and had cleaned it from top to bottom in a vain attempt to keep herself occupied. Then she'd started on the cupboards and now all of them, including her walk-in pantry, were spick and span, their contents organised to within an inch of their lives. She was running out of distractions and God alone knew how much this quarter's heating bill was going to be.

"You don't care one way or another, do you, Sofi?" she said to the cat, who was stretched out on the duvet, purring loudly, a picture of feline contentment. "So long as you're warm and fed and fussed over."

Not for the first time, she envied her cat. It must be wonderful to be a pampered, much loved pet. Nothing to worry about, a simple life of food, attention and sleep. She'd read somewhere that many cats sleep for between 12 and 18 hours a day.

"Idle, that's what you are," she said, stroking Sofi's fur.

The cat met her gaze briefly, blinked her sapphire blue eyes, then yawned, showing her little pink tongue. "Meh," she said.

"And 'meh' to you, too."

Ginny shook herself. What to do? *Jane Eyre*. She'd make a start on it and see whether she liked it any better this time round. She walked downstairs, made herself a mug of herbal tea, fetched her Kindle and sat in her favourite chair. Sofi jumped onto her lap, kneading her thighs with her paws, circled a few times, then settled down for a nap.

There was no possibility of taking a walk that day…

Meg

Meg was feeling pleased with herself. The chapter about meeting John and getting married had come together very quickly – she'd been pleasantly surprised by the amount of detail she and John had remembered between them. The next thing to tackle would be the births of Andrew and Jessica – those had been such happy times. She still had a long way to go, but she was beginning to feel hopeful about completing it in time for September. If John was still around. As usual, she dismissed the thought – he was trying so hard to stay sober now. She cast her mind back…

She'd enjoyed being pregnant, suffering few of the more unpleasant symptoms, but the actual births had been something else. She'd ended up with a caesarean section when Andrew had gone into distress after she'd been in labour for more than twelve hours, and she'd had an episiotomy and forceps for Jessica. Not that she'd include *those* details in the memoir – knowing that not only the grandchildren but also the children would find them uneasy reading.

So what to write about? Becoming a mother had changed her life fundamentally. She could remember when Andrew was born, being stunned by the ferocity and completeness of the love she had instantly felt for him. And the same had happened when Jessica came along. Remembering it, she realised that they were the only two people she had ever loved completely and unconditionally. Nothing they did or said had any effect on this total love. And it didn't matter how old they were – if either of them was unhappy, she couldn't be happy. All these years later, she still had to rein in the parental instinct to 'help', in spite of the fact that both of them were quite old enough to sort anything out for themselves.

But she couldn't write about that either – it felt too… vulnerable. And John wouldn't like it. So what to include? She had so many memories of their childhoods – how could she choose among them? She'd ask Rose.

The phone rang and rang. Just as she was about to ring off, her friend answered.

"Hello Rose, it's Meg. Is this a good time to talk?"

"Hang on, Meg, I'll just go through and sit down. My knee's bad today."

"Oh, I'm sorry. D'you want me to ring off?"

"No, that's fine."

There was a pause as Rose (presumably) walked through to her living room. Now that she'd been there, it was easy to visualise it.

"That's better," Rose said. "What can I do for you?"

"I've got to the part in the memoir when Andrew and Jessica were born," Meg said, "and I can't decide which details to include – I've got so many memories of them as children."

"Have you written the memories down on those index cards of yours?"

"Yes."

"Then why don't you lay them all out on a table, see what jumps out at you, then make a chronological list of the memories you want to use?"

Why hadn't she thought of that? "That's a brilliant

idea. Thank you."

"You're welcome. I'm looking forward to hearing it."

Rose

"…and we took Natalie to the hospital last week for a check-up," Debbie said, the joy in her voice ringing down the line, "and they say she's making really solid progress."

"Oh, Debbie!" Rose said. "That's wonderful news. I'm so thrilled for you."

"It's such a relief. They said there was no reason why she shouldn't develop into a normal healthy child eventually." Debbie paused. "Of course, I'll still have to take her for regular check-ups, for the next few years, until they're sure she's okay in every way."

"Why?"

"Because they need to continue to monitor her vision, hearing, speech and motor skills. It's going to take her a while to catch up with normal babies, having been born so early. But they said that there was no reason why she shouldn't have caught up with herself by the time she's two or so."

"Gosh!" Rose said. "It's a long old process, isn't it? I'd no idea it was so complicated."

Debbie sighed. "Yes. We're going to have to take the greatest care of her for at least the first couple of years."

"I'm sure you'll make a wonderful job of it."

"Have you decided to give intermittent fasting a try?" Debbie said, changing the subject.

"Yes," Rose said. "I dropped two and a half pounds in the first week, and a pound and a half this week. Like you,

I decided to have a fresh fruit salad for lunch, rather than only two meals a day, and I'm sticking to between 500 and 700 calories on the fast days. And I'm trying to eat healthily on the other five days. I'm so thrilled – thank you for telling me about it."

"That's great," Debbie said. "Well done. But don't expect to carry on losing at that rate."

"Why not?"

"Well, it might be different for you, but I found that after the first couple of weeks, my weight loss really slowed down – some weeks I only lost half a pound, or stayed the same. I had to keep telling myself that it was heading in the right direction, however slowly."

"Thank you for the warning – I'll bear that in mind. And thank you for letting me know about Natalie – I'm so pleased for you."

And for Daniel – she knew how worried her son had been.

Ginny

Much to her amazement, Ginny was finding *Jane Eyre* far more enjoyable than she remembered. Her first encounter with it had been at school in the late fifties or early sixties, and she'd found its flowery images and romantic sentiments to be way over the top. She'd disliked both Charlotte Brontë's style and her subject matter, being far more interested in the contemporary world.

But this time was different. Some of the long descriptive passages which had so bored her as a schoolgirl now jumped off the page as lyrical evocations of the natural world. Admittedly, she wasn't fond of the God stuff Charlotte Brontë loved to include, but her reverence for nature struck a chord. She began to note down passages she particularly liked, for use in later blog posts. And realised that the reason why they were so successful was because the author stimulated all the reader's senses in her descriptions. Perhaps if she could do the same, she'd get more likes for her own posts. She wouldn't use such flowery language – it wouldn't ring true, but there must be other ways to speak to a reader's senses.

Rose would know – she'd been an English teacher after all. She'd drop her an e-mail.

Hello Rose,

I'm getting a lot more than I expected from *Jane Eyre* – thank you for suggesting it. I particularly like the descriptive passages, and am thinking of trying something similar in my own blog posts (not the same, obviously, but including more description). Do you know of any other ways of speaking to the reader's senses? Or could you recommend some other authors who are good at evoking a setting?

Thank you.

Love,

Ginny xx

The reply came almost straight away.

Dear Ginny,

I'm so glad you're enjoying it – it's one of my favourite 19th century novels. I think the best way of speaking to the reader's senses is to imagine yourself in the place and jot down what would be present to each sense in turn. You could even make notes on your phone at the time you take the photographs. Then (perhaps) use a thesaurus to find alternative words to describe what you've seen, heard etc. The idea is to bring the reader into the landscape you're describing, so that they experience it for themselves.

Or at least, that's what I used to tell my students.

You ask for other authors who are good at evoking a setting: Thomas Hardy is an obvious one – he's famous for his descriptive powers. But if his deep pessimism is not your cup of tea (even I have to be in a fairly upbeat mood to enjoy reading him!) perhaps some of the modern fantasy writers might offer good examples, like Tolkien for Middle-Earth – there are some gorgeous descriptive passages in *The Lord of the Rings.*

See you next week,

Love,
Rose xx

Tolkien. Of course! Why hadn't she thought of that?

Meg

Meg was up early on St Valentine's Day to prepare a special breakfast for John, a tradition she'd followed all their married life. It had begun on their first wedding anniversary, which they'd spent in Paris, staying in the flat of one of John's friends from university in Montparnasse, near the beautiful Luxembourg Gardens. Each morning, they had visited a nearby bakery to pick up some delicious croissants and pain au chocolat, still warm from the oven, and smelling like heaven.

On every anniversary and St Valentine's Day since, they shared the same simple meal. It brought back such happy memories of wandering around the bustling, vibrant streets and fabulous museums of Paris, hand in hand. She laid the kitchen table then put John's card next to his place. The croissants and pain au chocolat were on a baking tray, ready to heat in the oven.

While she waited for him to come downstairs, she fetched the Paris photo album from the spare room and began to jot down her recollections of that lovely week in the journal Rose had given her for Christmas. They'd done so much during that short time, walking miles along the beautiful leafy boulevards, and taking the metro to the more distant sights. Looking at the photos for the first time in decades brought back so many memories – a trip down the Seine on a Bateaux Mouches river boat, which had helped them orientate themselves on the first day; their first sight of the Arc de Triomphe, which she'd seen in so many films; being overawed by the scale of the Eiffel Tower, so much taller in real life than it had looked in pictures, and taking the lift up to the second stage with its gorgeous views over Paris. They had visited Les Invalides, where Napoleon was buried and she still remembered John's annoyance when the guide explained that the great man's tomb was down below, so that anyone looking at it would be bowing to him. The Louvre had been a bit of a disappointment – so full of tourists that it had been difficult to see any of the pictures properly, and she remembered the shock of seeing Da Vinci's *Mona Lisa* – so much smaller than she had expected.

They had spent a day in Montmartre, wandering the streets of the artists' quarter, and had seen the famous Moulin Rouge nightclub (only from the outside) and visited Sacre Coeur, so white and splendid in its magnificent setting. And Notre Dame the following day – Meg had been blown away by the beauty of the soaring Gothic columns and the glorious stained glass. And she had forgotten about visiting La Sainte Chapelle – they'd been there at exactly the right time of day and, when they had stepped off the small spiral staircase leading up to the upper chapel, it had been like walking into a rainbow.

Where was John? She'd left him snoring as usual, but he was normally up by now. Just as she was about to go up and check on him, he stomped into the room, a black scowl on his face. What was wrong with him now? All the lovely memories of Paris fled from her mind.

Rose

Rose was first to arrive at Capuchins. It was her birthday the next day, so she'd decided to let moderation go hang and enjoy a cake or two. And she had no intention of being good on her actual birthday. She'd just have her second fast day on Friday rather than Thursday.

Then Ginny strolled in. As always, Rose admired her friend's seemingly effortless beauty – the floaty clothes she wore, her long silver hair fastened in a loose bun, the grace of her movements. The fruits of decades of yoga teaching and practice. It was difficult not to feel old and dumpy in comparison, although there was only a few months between them in age…. Then she remembered – no comparing. Stop it, Rose.

"Hi, Rose," Ginny said as she sat down at their usual table with her camomile tea. "Any news on the knee operation yet?"

"Not yet. I've got my pre-op appointment on 22nd March, when they'll assess my suitability again, and give me a date. I hope."

"That's good news. How are you feeling about it?"

"More and more terrified, if I'm honest."

"Why on earth?"

"Because it's a major operation and so many things could go wrong."

"Surely they wouldn't have offered it, if the risk was that great."

"Oh, I know," Rose said. "But I'm finding it hard not to catastrophise. What if something goes wrong? I could be worse off than I am now."

Ginny leaned across and hugged her. "If you need to talk," she said, "you know where I am."

Rose hugged her back. "Thank you."

Then Meg walked in, her shoulders hunched, a miserable look on her face. Oh dear. What had happened now?

"Hello, you two," Meg said as she joined them, mug of tea in one hand, and a plate with an almond croissant in the other.

"Hello Meg," Rose said. She had deep shadows under her eyes, as though she hadn't slept for days. "What's up, my dear?"

"John's been doing some research about what might happen to him."

"That's good, isn't it?" But judging by Meg's expression, it obviously wasn't.

Rose took her friend's hand. "What's wrong?"

"What isn't wrong, you mean."

She sounded… angry. What had happened?

"Tell us," Rose said, gently squeezing her hand. "Can we help in any way?"

"It started on Valentine's Day," Meg said, her voice quivering. "I'd prepared a special breakfast for him – it's something we've done for years. But when he came down, he was in a filthy mood. When I asked him what was wrong, he told me, he told me…"

Tears began to trickle down her cheeks. Rose held her

silence, waiting for Meg to continue.

"He told me last month," Meg said, dashing the tears from her eyes, "that he'd been doing some research on the internet and – and, he might have to go to prison. But I didn't dare tell you. Then on Valentine's Day, he found out how much the fine was likely to be – the fat end of a thousand pounds. But I don't care about that – I only care that he doesn't end up in prison."

"Surely not," Ginny said. "Has he got himself a solicitor?"

"Yes, he has, but…"

"Then he'll have someone who knows what they're talking about to defend him," Ginny said. "Why does he think he'll end up in jail?"

Rose winced internally. Ginny was always so… forthright. But Meg didn't seem to notice.

"Because it's not the first time," Meg said, her voice a determined monotone. "He got done for drinking and driving eight years ago, and they're always harsher on repeat offenders."

At the last word, all her attempts at control failed her and she began to sob. "I don't know what to do," she wailed. "If he does go to prison, he might still be there for our golden wedding anniversary."

What to say? Rose put her arm around Meg's shoulders, let her cry her worries out. The storm took a while to subside, but when she felt her friend stiffen under her arm, she let her go.

"I'm sorry," she said, rummaging in her bag for tissues. "What must you think of me?"

"Don't be sorry," Ginny said. "That's what we're here for."

Meg managed a tiny smile. "Thank you both. I feel better for that. I'll keep you both in the loop."

"Any time," Rose said. Time to talk about something else. "What did you think of *Jane Eyre*?"

"I loved it," Meg said. "I've always loved it. It's so romantic, and I love that she married Mr Rochester in the end."

"That's weird," Ginny said. "That's the bit I found infuriating."

"Infuriating?" Meg said, her eyes round with surprise. "Why on earth?"

"It seems like a cop-out," Ginny said. "I love Jane's strength and integrity, especially the part when she sticks to her principles and leaves him, but in the end, she sacrifices her independence and marries him. After all the harm he'd done. It just didn't ring true for me."

Rose couldn't help smiling at her friends' disparate reactions. It reminded her so much of her students. "I think you're both right," she said. "Jane's marriage is true to her Victorian setting, but many of my students felt the same as Ginny."

"What do you think, Rose?" Ginny said.

"It depends on my mood," Rose said. "If I'm feeling romantic, I love the ending, otherwise I also find it annoying. But I suspect that Charlotte Brontë wouldn't have got away with not marrying them off in the end. Not for an 1847 audience."

"Hmph," Ginny said. "I suppose not."

"How are you celebrating your birthday?" Meg said.

"I'm going round to Matthew's for dinner tomorrow," Rose said. "So I'll have to have my second fast day on Friday."

"Fast day?" Meg said. "What's that about?"

"I've been trying intermittent fasting for the past three weeks," Rose said. "Debbie introduced me to it at the end of last month, and it's working really well for me. I've lost five pounds so far."

"How does it work?" Meg said.

"You restrict yourself to between 500 and 600 calories two days a week, then try to eat healthily on the other five."

"That seems awfully low," Ginny said. Rose could see the alarm in her friend's eyes and hastened to reassure her.

"Don't worry," she said. "It's only for two days each week. In theory, I can eat what I like on the other five."

Ginny shook her head. "That wouldn't work for me," she said. "I'd end up sticking to five or six hundred calories every day."

"I guess it wouldn't be everyone's cup of tea," Rose said. "But it's working well for me. I found the first couple of fast days difficult, although I'm allowing myself nearer 700 calories, but I'm getting into the way of it now. The consultant told me to lose as much weight as I could before the operation, and I'm hoping to have dropped a stone by then."

"Have you got a date for it yet?" Meg said.

"Not yet," Rose said, swallowing her irritation. It had been a casual question, after all, not like Matthew's pressure for information. "I've got my pre-op appointment on 22nd March, which means it will probably be at the beginning of May, at the latest. So I've got another two months or so to lose as much weight as I can."

"Well," Ginny said, "so long as you're careful not to take it too far…"

"I won't, I promise."

"You can't say fairer than that," she said, the frown between her eyebrows relaxing.

"What's our book for March, Meg?" Rose said.

"I was so glad when you chose *Jane* Eyre for this month," Meg said. "I'd thought we had to choose modern books all the time. So I've chosen one of my favourite books, *The Daughter of Time* by Josephine Tey."

"Isn't that the one about Richard III?"

"Yes," Meg said. "I started being interested in him a few years ago, when they found his remains in that car park in Leicester."

"It will be fun to read it again," Rose said.

"I've never read it," Ginny said. "Is it a history book?"

"No," Meg said. "It's a detective story, sort of. I hope you'll enjoy it."

Ginny's eyes lit up. "I love detective fiction."

Then she fished in her patchwork backpack, bringing out a small parcel and a card. "Here you are, Rose," she said. "Happy Birthday for tomorrow."

"Thank you," Rose said. She hadn't been expecting this. "Do you want me to save it until then?"

"No, you can open it now."

Rose carefully peeled back the Sellotape and unwrapped it, revealing a small, black cardboard box. Inside was a gorgeous pair of pearl drop earrings, with tiny amethysts linking each pearl to the shepherd's hook.

"Oh, Ginny! They're beautiful. Thank you so much."

Ginny flushed. "I knew you liked pearls, and amethyst is your birthstone."

"They're really pretty – and they'll go with nearly everything."

"I'm so glad," Ginny said.

"And here's my present," Meg said.

It was obviously a book. Rose opened it, to find another cross-stitch title by Brenda Keyes, *Alphabets and Samplers*.

"Oh, that's excellent," she said. "I love her other book, *Traditional Samplers*. Thank you, Meg."

"I asked Karen to find a copy for me," Meg said, "because it's not in print any more. I hope you don't mind it being second-hand?"

She looked so worried. Rose hugged her. "Of course not. The fact that it's from here, where we all meet, makes it even more special. I bought her other one from here too."

Meg's face cleared. "Thank goodness," she said. "That's why I chose it – I knew you liked her designs."

Rose opened it and began to leaf through it. "This is gorgeous," she said. "Thank you again."

Ginny

Ginny and Rose walked out of Capuchins together, Rose to

return to her car, Ginny to her bicycle.

"Forgive me for asking," Ginny said, as they turned into the Shambles, "but I couldn't help noticing you looked angry when Meg asked whether you knew your operation date yet. Is anything wrong?"

"I know," Rose sighed. "I shouldn't have over-reacted to such an innocent question. I hope Meg didn't notice – it wasn't about her."

"Then what was it about?" Ginny said, adding hastily, "but only if you want to tell me."

"It's Matthew. He's been driving me mad, trying to persuade me to pin down the exact date for the operation. I've told him I'll know after the pre-op appointment on the 22nd, but he keeps on nagging me to ring the consultant to find out."

"Why would he do that?"

"He's been the same since he was a little boy," Rose said. "He has such a need to be in control, even of things he has no right to be."

"That sounds quite manipulative."

"You're right. I love him dearly and I really appreciate everything he's done for me since Graham passed, but I'm getting fed up with being pestered – it almost feels like bullying."

"I don't blame you."

"He's so like Graham," Rose said. "I've no idea why some people need to have control over everything."

Ginny winced – that hit home. "I can speak to that," she said. "I'm just the same. You remember when I told you about what happened when Laura died. I felt completely out of control and began to restrict my eating so that I could feel I was in charge of at least something."

"I'm sorry, Ginny, I didn't mean it as a criticism of you."

"And I didn't take it that way," Ginny reassured her. "It's just that I can understand how Matthew feels. Like you said, he's been trying to look after you since Graham passed and I expect he needs to know the date as soon as possible so that he can organise annual leave to be with you after the operation."

Rose flushed. "Oh!" she said. "I hadn't thought of that. You're probably right. But I don't want him to have to use his precious annual leave on me."

"You'll need to have someone on the spot for at least the first while."

"Oh dear, what am I going to do?"

"Well," Ginny said slowly, not sure how Rose would take it. "I'd be happy to come and stay with you for a few days, if that would help?"

Rose's face cleared instantly. "Would you really do that for me?"

"Of course," Ginny said. "I'd be happy to."

"That would be so kind," Rose said. "But what about Sofi?"

"I'm sure my next door neighbour would feed her for me, and she has her cat flap, so she can go in and out as she likes. So I can stay as long as you need me."

"Thank you so much," Rose said. "You've no idea what a weight that is off my mind."

Ginny hugged her. "You're welcome."

"Bless you. I'll let Matthew know."

Rose

Rose rang Matthew just after six.

"Ginny has offered to come and stay with me for a few days, immediately after the operation."

"Has she?" There was no missing the relief in his voice. "That's kind."

"Yes, she's a good friend. And it means you won't have to take any annual leave."

"I'll still take you in on the day of the operation," he said. "But I must admit, it would be fantastic if she could. Sarah and I are planning a special holiday with the kids this summer, to celebrate our silver wedding. Are you sure Ginny doesn't mind?"

"Absolutely sure," Rose said. "I didn't ask her, she offered. Where are you going?"

"We're swithering between Rome and Venice at the moment. It'll be quite expensive for the five of us, but we're planning to go in the first week of the summer holidays. We'll stay in an Airbnb, which will help a bit."

"Won't it be dreadfully hot then?" Rose said.

"Yes, and Sarah's a bit worried for Rosie – you know what fair skin she's got."

"Then why don't you go for the May half term instead? It's nearer your actual anniversary and the weather will be nice and warm, but not as hot as July."

"But you'll only just have had your operation. I can't be out of the country then."

"Before this morning," Rose said, "I'd have said the same. But Ginny drives and she said she'd be happy to stay as long as I need her. So you go ahead and book that holiday for the summer half-term week, and don't worry about me."

"Are you sure, Mum?"

"Positive."

"Okay. Please thank Ginny for me."

"I will."

Rose was so pleased Matthew had fallen in with her plan. She hadn't wanted to have to fight him over this. Then she remembered Meg – what was she going to think? She'd be bound to see it as another example of being an 'unwanted third'. She'd better ring her later, and let her know. How could she reframe it, so Meg wouldn't feel left out? It might be better if she told her face to face. She picked up the phone again.

Meg

"Hello Rose," Meg said, surprised to recognise her friend's voice. She hadn't been expecting a call.

"Can I pop round to see you this evening?"

"Of course – that would be lovely. John will be at his AA group meeting."

"Would 7.30 be okay?"

"Yes, I'll see you then."

And before she could say any more, Rose had rung off. What was this about? Why couldn't Rose have told her whatever it was earlier, at Capuchins?

In the harsh light of the porch, Meg noticed with a pang the shadows under Rose's eyes. What was wrong?

"Come on in and make yourself at home," she said. "I've got the kettle on."

Once they were sitting in the lounge, Rose took a sip of her tea, then said, "I've had some good news, and wanted you to be the first to know."

"I'm all ears."

Her friend seemed to hesitate, then said slowly, "You know I'll need someone to look after me when I've had my knee done?"

"Yes, of course." Her heart sank – this was going to be about Ginny.

"Well, I was talking to Ginny about it on the way back to the car this morning, and she's offered to come and stay with me for a few days, until I'm over the worst."

There was a roaring in Meg's ears and her vision darkened. She knew it! She just knew it!

"Meg? Meg? Are you okay?"

Meg refocussed her eyes, tried to pull herself together.

"I'm fine," she said. Then the words burst out of her, "You know I'd have been happy to help?"

"I would have asked you," Rose said, "but I knew you had John to think about and I didn't want to weigh you down with any more responsibilities. And I live out in the country and you don't drive."

"I would have managed it somehow." It wasn't fair. Ginny was so lucky.

"Don't begrudge Ginny this chance to help," Rose said gently, taking her hand. "She's not as lucky as us – she only has Sofi as family."

Meg's cheeks burned in mortification. For one brief moment, she hated Rose – not for what she'd said, but for the reminder of the idiotic grounds of her own insecurity. When was she going to stop comparing?

Summoning up every ounce of gumption she possessed, she met Rose's eyes and smiled at her. "Of course. I understand."

"Thank you," Rose said. "It means that Matthew will only need to take one day off, to take me into hospital, which is good. He and Sarah are taking the kids to Italy to celebrate their silver wedding, and I've managed to persuade him to do it in the May half term, instead of waiting for the summer holidays."

"Where are they going?"

"Either Rome or Venice. It will depend on where they can book an Airbnb at such short notice."

Meg pasted a determined smile on her face. "How wonderful! I've always wanted to visit Venice."

March: *The Daughter of Time* by Josephine Tey

Rose

By the time 22nd March was on the near horizon, Rose was in what she knew (rationally) was a ridiculous state of fear and apprehension. But reason was fighting a losing battle. Nightmares about all the things which could go wrong were making her sleep uneasy, and during the day, she couldn't stop obsessing about the operation. What if it was a failure? What if she reacted badly to the anaesthetic? What if she caught MRSA while she was at the hospital? What if she ended up worse off than she was now? What if? *What if?*

It was driving her crazy. The week before, unable to bear it alone any longer, she phoned Ginny, not wanting to bother Meg. Meg had enough on her plate already, without having to worry about her. And Matthew wouldn't understand at all.

"Ginny," she said, "are you busy today?"

"No, I was planning a quiet day, but if you need me…"

"Bless you! Would you mind popping round for a coffee? Or I could come to you, if that was easier."

"I'll drive over to you," Ginny said, not asking any questions. "I'll be with you in half an hour."

So kind. It was so wonderful to have a friend she could call on, when her mind was playing such nasty tricks on her. Rose limped through to the kitchen and put the kettle on.

Just over the promised half an hour later, the two of them were comfortably ensconced in armchairs, their drinks on the coffee table between them.

"What's up, Rose?" Ginny said. "You sounded quite frazzled on the phone."

Rose flushed. "I'm getting myself so wound up about the operation," she said. "I keep on catastrophising about all the things which could go wrong, both during and after. It's driving me bananas."

"That's natural enough," Ginny said. "Fear of the unknown can be really hard to deal with."

A surge of gratitude flowed through Rose's heart – it was such a blessing to be understood. She knew that she could share what was on her mind and heart, that Ginny wouldn't judge her. She sat back in her chair and the words began to pour out of her. Ginny listened in silence, sipping her camomile tea, her sapphire blue eyes fixed on Rose's face, giving her the gift of her full attention.

Eventually, she began repeating herself and stopped.

"Sorry about that," she said. "I didn't mean to witter on for so long."

"I don't mind," Ginny said softly.

"It's really helped to be able to tell you about it," Rose said. "I *know* I'm being silly, I keep telling myself I'm being ridiculous, that they wouldn't have offered me the operation unless they thought it would be successful. But I can't seem to stop worrying."

"Not silly at all. I'd be the same myself."

"Thank you, Ginny. You've no idea how much that helps. I've been beating myself up badly about being so irrational."

Ginny leaned across and hugged her. "Beating

yourself up is not allowed," she said. "Like I said, it's quite natural to feel apprehensive before such a big operation."

"Thank you," Rose said again. "I think I'll be able to face it more easily now."

"I wonder," Ginny said, "whether doing some meditation each day would help? I find it wonderfully calming and centring."

"I've never done it before, but I'd be happy to give it a try."

"Would you like me to talk you through it?"

"Yes, please."

"Then find a comfortable position to sit in. Keep both feet planted flat on the floor, have your back as straight as possible, with your shoulders in line with your hips, rest your hands in your lap and close your eyes."

Rose did as she was told and listened to Ginny's voice, so soft and calming.

"We're going to concentrate on following the breath. As you breathe in, feel your lungs expanding, and as you breathe out, expel all your worries, all your fears... Each breath in, a breath of life, each breath out, a breath of calm. When other thoughts intrude, simply acknowledge them, let them go, then return to following your breath..."

Initially, Rose found it so difficult – her mind was all over the place. But as the minutes passed by – she was sharply aware of the ticking of the clock on the mantlepiece, which she usually didn't notice at all – her breathing began to deepen, and her body started to relax. When Ginny brought her back to herself, she was feeling much more serene. She opened her eyes.

"Thank you," she said. "That was really helpful – I've never done anything like it before."

Ginny smiled at her. "I'm glad," she said. "Meditating is an essential part of my life – I do it every morning."

"How long did it last?"

"Only ten minutes. I didn't want to over-face you. But if you commit to doing it each morning, just for ten minutes, I think you'll find it will help. There are various meditation apps you can get on your phone, to talk you through the process, when I'm not there." Her eyes twinkled. "And you could even close your eyes and take a few deep breaths during the day, whenever the worries come."

"I'll give it a go. Thank you so much for being here – you've helped enormously."

"You're welcome."

The pre-operative assessment lasted nearly as long as the initial consultation and involved being shuttled around more than one hospital department. She began at the X-ray Department, where another x-ray of her left knee was taken, and also an MRI scan.

Then she hobbled along what felt like miles of echoing hospital corridors to the Orthopaedic Surgery department, trying to keep out of the way of the staff and patients walking or being pushed the other way, cursing herself for not taking up the X-ray Department's offer of a porter with a wheelchair. At least she'd remembered to bring her stick. By the time she reached Dr Robertson's office, her knee was aching fiercely.

"Hello Rose," Dr Robertson said. "How are you

today?"

Rose limped over to a chair and sat down. "Not so good, I'm afraid."

"I'm sorry to hear that. I just need to examine you again, take some blood and check your blood pressure and weight. Is that okay?"

"Of course."

Rose tried not to wince as the consultant gently manipulated her knee, causing bright red shoots of pain to radiate up and down her leg. It hurt abominably.

Once the other tests were done, Dr Robertson said, "If you could just hop onto the scales, we'll see where you are weight wise."

Rose knew she'd lost half a stone and hoped the scales here would confirm that.

"Well done for losing some weight. Keep on with it, please – you'll be doing your new knee a massive favour."

"Thank you."

"Did you bring your list of current prescriptions with you?"

"Yes, here it is."

Dr Robertson glanced through it. "That's fine, no problems there. Remember to bring enough tablets for a few days in with you, when you come. It will be better if they're in their original boxes."

Rose's head was spinning. "Will I get a list of what I need to bring with me?"

"Yes, don't worry. Everything you need to know will be sent out to you nearer the time."

"Okay."

"Now, have you organised someone to look after you following the operation?"

"Yes. My friend Ginny is coming to stay with me for a few days."

"That's good. In which case, you might like to invite her to come with you to Joint School next week."

"Joint School?" Rose echoed. "What's that?"

"It's a question and answer session we hold for all our knee and hip replacement patients. It's held in the Sheldon lecture theatre here at the hospital and will give you a clearer idea of what's ahead. We recommend that your post-operative carer comes with you."

"What's the exact date please?"

"Next Tuesday, the 26th of March. I'm sorry it's such short notice."

The day before their next book group meeting. "We'll be there."

"Good. It should help to set your mind at rest about what's ahead."

Ginny

Ginny got a phone call from Rose, the day following her friend's pre-op assessment.

"I've got the date for the operation – it's going to be on the 7th of May."

"That's good news," Ginny said. "Let's hope it doesn't get cancelled at the last minute."

"I really hope not. I'm not sure I could bear it. I've got myself psyched up for that date now. And before that, I have to attend a question and answer session at the hospital and bring my carer with me – but it's next Tuesday. She could have given me a bit more notice. Can you make it?"

"Hang on," Ginny said. "I think it's okay, but I'd better check my diary."

She put the phone down on the table and turned to the following week in her Filofax. "Yes, that's fine."

"That's a relief. They call it 'Joint School' and they offer it to all their knee and hip replacement patients."

"It sounds like a good idea," Ginny said. "It'll give you the chance to ask all the questions you like. What time does it start?"

"At nine a.m.," Rose said. "Why?"

"There seems little point in taking both cars. I'll come and pick you up from home, then we'll drive on to the hospital."

"Are you sure? Wouldn't it make more sense for me to drive to your house and park there? I don't want to put you to any trouble."

"It's no trouble at all," Ginny said. "The hospital's on your side of Worcester anyway, and you'd struggle to find a parking space near me at that time on a Monday. So many parents at the local primary school seem to think their little darlings will be tired out by walking to school and they park all over the place."

"That's ridiculous," Rose said. "I used to walk over a mile to school and it never did me any harm."

She sounded tired. "Are you okay?"

A deep sigh echoed down the phone. "More or less. It's just..." and Rose's voice tailed off.

"Just what?"

Another sigh. "I'm still stressing about the operation, even with the daily meditation – what if it goes wrong? I've been doing a bit of googling about knee replacement operations and they're not all successful. I'm in pain at the moment, but I can manage. What if it's worse afterwards, rather than better?"

"Try to keep on with the daily meditation," Ginny said. "Remember, if they thought it wasn't going to work, they wouldn't have offered it to you. And that's what this Joint School is about, isn't it?"

"I know. You're right – I need to pull myself together."

"I'll be there with you. It might be worth writing down any questions you have in advance, so that you don't forget them."

"That's a good idea. I'll do it now. Thank you so much for being there for me."

"You're welcome, my friend."

Meg

John was out at his daily AA meeting when the postman rang the doorbell. When Meg answered, he smiled at her – he was a friendly chap in his fifties who always paused on the doorstep for a snippet of conversation about the day's weather. He was as reliable as a barometer.

"Hello, Bob," she said. "What have you got for me today?"

He held out an official looking buff envelope with

John's name on it. "Lovely sunny morning, isn't it?" he said. "This needs signing for."

He produced the usual small, rectangular device, about the same size and shape as an old-fashioned pocket calculator. "Your initial's M, isn't it?"

"That's right."

He keyed in her details, then turned the machine towards her. She scrawled an illegible signature with the index finger of her right hand – it reminded her of playing with an Etch A Sketch. It never ceased to amaze her that the random squiggles that were the best approximation to her ordinary signature she could produce, were accepted as such.

When John returned an hour or so later, she was sitting at the kitchen table, fathoms deep in her writing, a tepid mug of tea at her elbow. She had found it was her favourite place to write – the table was at just the right height and even in the depths of winter, the room was warm as it faced south. The Aga John had treated her to for their ruby wedding nine years before kept the kitchen toasty during the winter months.

He walked in and dropped a kiss on the top of her head.

She jumped. "You startled me! I didn't hear you come in."

"You were miles away. How's the writing going?"

"Well, thank you. How did AA go?"

"All right, I suppose."

"A letter came for you while you were out," she said, "and I had to sign for it. I think – I think it may be…"

Her voice trailed off as he picked it up and slit it open.

He read it quickly, then tossed it down on the table.

"What is it?" she said.

"The trial date's been set," he said, "for April the 11th."

"That's good, isn't it?"

"I'll have to talk to Simpson," he said, not answering her question, "and see what I'll need to do."

"Whatever happens," Meg said, "I'll be with you."

"Thank you, Meggie."

Ginny

Ginny drove over to Crowle bright and early to collect Rose – it could take a while to park at the hospital and she didn't want them to be late... she knew how slowly her friend was walking at the moment, even with a stick.

Rose was very quiet during the journey and Ginny held her peace. She didn't want to overdo the reassurance, not this early in the day.

"Goodness!" Rose said as they walked into the lecture theatre. "I wasn't expecting so many people."

"Me neither. But I guess it makes sense – it must cost a good bit to put on, so I suspect they only run one once a quarter or so."

There must have been between fifty and a hundred folk, all attending this Joint School. Who knew so many people had this kind of problem? Then Ginny remembered to divide them by two, because of course, half of them would be carers rather than patients. She and Rose found two spare seats and settled down to wait.

A team of people in nurse's uniforms walked in on the dot of 9.00 a.m. One of them strode up to the podium, while the rest found seats behind her.

"Good morning, everyone," the nurse said, "and welcome to Joint School. Today we are going to explain your patient journey, including how to prepare for your knee or hip operation, what to bring with you to hospital, the types of anaesthetic we use, post-operative pain relief, and your recovery both in hospital and at home, including physiotherapy. Don't worry if you haven't brought anything to write with – we'll be giving each of you a detailed booklet to take home with you, which contains all the information you'll need to ensure as positive an outcome as possible. There will be plenty of opportunities to ask any questions you like."

This was going to be interesting. Over the next couple of hours – thankfully broken up by tea and biscuits – the various members of staff took them through all the stages of their forthcoming operations. Models of knee and hip joints were passed around, and a woman about their age who had undergone a successful knee replacement operation gave a short talk about her experience.

Ginny could sense Rose was beginning to relax. Until it came to the part about the actual operation.

"You can choose to remain awake during the operation if you wish," the anaesthetist said. "If you decide on that option, a local anaesthetic will be injected between the bones in your lower back around the nerves of the spinal cord. This will cause temporary numbness and heaviness from the waist down and will allow your surgery to proceed without you feeling any pain. We suggest you bring an MP3 player and headphones with you, so that you have something to listen to during the operation."

"Oh my God!" Rose said, the colour draining from her cheeks. "I don't want to be awake. I can't think of anything worse."

Ginny was about to suggest asking about it, when another patient's hand shot up.

"I don't want to be awake," the woman said. "Can't you put me to sleep?"

"It is now hospital policy," the anaesthetist replied, "not to use a deep general anaesthetic for operations of this kind, to avoid any unpleasant side effects. And it carries far lower risks to the patient. But, if you are feeling anxious about being awake, we can use further sedation, or a light general anaesthetic, which will lower your awareness of what is happening."

"Thank you," she said.

"That's the one for me," Rose said. "I want to have as little awareness as possible, thank you very much."

As they walked back to the car, Ginny said, "That was fascinating, wasn't it?"

"Yes," Rose said. "I'm feeling much better about it, now I understand what's going to happen. And it was so good to be able to talk with other people in the same situation."

She flourished the A4 booklet each the patients had been given. "I'm going to read and re-read every single word in this, so that I can be as well prepared as possible."

"Good idea," Ginny said. "It was pretty thorough,

wasn't it? I was impressed by the woman who'd had the knee operation – she was walking perfectly well."

"I noticed that too. Oh Ginny! I really hope the same will happen for me."

Rose

Rose had thoroughly enjoyed reading *The Daughter of Time* again – it had been years since she'd read it, and she'd forgotten most of the details. Of course, as an English teacher she'd long known that Shakespeare's portrayal of Richard the Third was a caricature written under a Tudor monarch, so it was unrealistic to expect that he could have been objective about the last Plantagenet king. But she hadn't realised (or at least, hadn't remembered) that Shakespeare's primary source of information had been quite so unreliably second-hand. Judging by Tey's account, Archbishop John Morton had been a nasty piece of work.

She was the first to arrive at Capuchins, as usual. Her knee was worse than ever after the visit to Joint School the previous day, so she'd left home early to be able to take her time walking from the car park. She was so grateful that Ginny would be there with her after the operation.

It took every smidgeon of willpower she had not to order one of Karen's delicious cakes, but she knew that every pound she lost would help in the recovery process. She'd been up late the previous evening, reading the Joint School booklet and taking copious notes. No wonder she felt tired.

Next to arrive was Meg. One look at her face told Rose that there had been more bad news about John. How much more could Meg take?

"Hello, Meg," she said, as her friend sat down across from her. "How are you?"

"I'll wait until Ginny arrives, if you don't mind," Meg said. "That way, I'll only have to tell it once."

Oh dear. That didn't sound good.

"Fair enough. I'm sure she'll be here soon. It's five to eleven now."

"Hello, my dears," Ginny said as she joined them, punctual as always. "How are you both?"

Rose smiled at her. "Tired, but okay, thank you," she said. "I was up until gone eleven last night, going through that Joint School booklet with a fine tooth comb, and I've written loads of notes about what I need to have in place beforehand."

"Like what?" Meg said.

"Well," Rose said, "I'll need to make sure that any loose rugs or mats are removed because they're a potential trip hazard. And I'll have to stock up on ready-made meals so that I don't need to do any cooking. The booklet said I'd be on crutches for the first few weeks, so I'm going to ask Matthew to come over nearer the time and help me to move the furniture around a bit, so that I've got more clear space. And they suggest that any pets should be booked into a cattery or kennels, so *they* can't be a trip hazard either. So I ought to arrange that for Bonnie."

"Goodness!" Meg said. "I'd no idea it would be so complicated."

"Nor had I. As I told you, Ginny will be staying with me for a while, so she'll be able to help with meal preparation and shopping, which is a real weight off my mind. But I'll make sure that the house is spick and span before I go in. The booklet also gave a list of what I'll have to take with me to the hospital, so I'll need to have a case packed too."

Rose glanced at Meg to make sure she wasn't upset by the mention of Ginny staying, and was grateful to see that her friend had her emotions well under control. She couldn't deal with an upset Meg just now – she was too tired.

"It'll be a breeze," Ginny said. "I'm sure everything will go well."

Hmph. Rose wasn't sure she agreed with that, but let it go.

"How are things with you, Meg?" she said.

"John's got the date for his trial at the Magistrate's Court," Meg said. "It's going to be on the 11th of April."

"That's soon – only a couple of weeks from now," Ginny commented. "Is he well prepared?"

"Oh yes," Meg said. "He visited Mr Simpson, his solicitor, last week, and knows what he has to do and say."

"Are you going to be there with him?" Rose said.

"Yes," Meg said. "I'm allowed to be there. But John won't be allowed to talk to me, and I've been told I need to remain silent."

"That makes sense," Ginny said. "After all, you're not a witness or anything like that."

"So what are his prospects?" Rose said.

"Mr Simpson *thinks*," Meg said, her lips quivering, "that so long as John pleads guilty, he may get off with a suspended sentence. He's told him that he's going to mention John's illness and that he's attending AA meetings every day, which may mean that the judge will be more lenient with him. After all, he didn't hurt anyone."

"Yes," Ginny said. "If he'd injured anyone, they'd have to be more severe."

Oh dear. Rose noticed the tears welling up in Meg's eyes. Ginny could be a bit more tactful. She rushed into the breach. "We'll just hope for the best."

"It's the waiting that's been so hard," Meg said. "It's been more than three months since – since it happened, and now I can't wait for the trial to be over. It feels like we've been in limbo ever since. I haven't been able to make any plans for this year because I don't know whether John will be around to share them."

Meg bit her lip, but to Rose's surprise, the threatened tears did not fall. This time of trial had strengthened her friend somehow. She took Meg's hand.

"Whatever happens," she said, "we'll be there for you."

Meg squeezed her hand, then withdrew her own. "I know," she said simply, "and that helps more than you know. Rose, you believe in God, don't you?"

"Yes, why?"

"Could you pray for us both on the 11th?"

"Of course I will."

"Thank you," Meg said. "Now, what did you both think of *The Daughter of Time?*"

Rose knew a diversion when she heard it, and obediently followed the proffered lead. "I really enjoyed it," she said. "I hadn't read it for years and years, and had forgotten most of the twists and turns. I find it astonishing that most historians still believe that Richard the Third was such a monster, although there is so much evidence to the contrary."

"But hasn't that changed since he was dug up in that car park in Leicester?" Ginny said. "I thought he'd been rehabilitated since then."

"You would have thought so," Rose said, "but I did some googling about him to check, and the 'wicked uncle who killed his nephews' story is still alive and well. The Wikipedia article was fairly balanced, but the article in the *Encyclopaedia Britannica* still states they were killed in 1483 and that most sources blamed Richard."

"Well," Ginny said, "reading *The Daughter of Time* has certainly changed my mind about him. He seems to have been the best king we never had, if you see what I mean."

"Yes," Meg said. "Even his fiercest critics talk about the good things he did while he was king."

"Thank you, Meg," Ginny said. "I really enjoyed reading it and learned heaps. And it was a cracking yarn too."

Meg smiled. "I'm so glad."

"So," Rose said. "What's our book for April, Ginny?"

"Now that we're allowed to choose older books," Ginny said, grinning at both of them, "I've followed both your examples and chosen *The Heaven Tree* by Edith Pargeter. But it's been out of print for ages, and it's not available on Kindle for some reason. So I scoured the online book stores and managed to find you both a second-hand copy." She fished in her backpack. "Here you are."

She handed a thick, pre-loved paperback to each of them.

"The Heaven Tree trilogy", Rose read aloud from the front cover. "Are you expecting us to read all three, or just the first one?"

"Only the first one," Ginny said. "But finding the individual volumes was even harder, and I'm sure you'll want to read the other two, once you've read the first. It's one of the very few series I come back to, time and again. Edith Pargeter writes beautifully and the story is wonderful."

"Thank you for finding copies for us," Meg said. "How much do I owe you?"

Ginny waved her hand. "Nothing," she said. "Being able to share them with someone else is enough for me. They – Laura loved them."

She sounded so sad. Rose shot her a quick glance, but sensed she didn't want to be questioned. So she changed the subject. "What is a 'heaven tree'?"

Ginny shook her head. "I'm not telling you," she said. "I don't want to spoil the story. I really hope you enjoy it."

"Fair enough," Rose said. "Her name is ringing bells for me, but I can't remember where I've seen it before."

"She wrote the *Brother Cadfael* series," Ginny said. "You know, the ones about the twelfth-century Benedictine monk who was also an amateur detective."

Rose was puzzled. "But surely those are by Ellis Peters," she said. Then the penny dropped. "Wait a minute, they have the same initials. Is Ellis Peters a pseudonym?"

Ginny smiled at her. "Yes. That's where you may have seen her name before."

"Got it," Rose said. "I love the *Brother Cadfael* books. If *The Heaven Tree* is anything like as well-written as them, I'm sure I'm going to enjoy it."

"It's better," Ginny said. "I think they're her best books."

Meg stood up. "I'd better go," she said in a tight, flat voice. "My bus will be leaving in a few minutes. Thank you for the book, Ginny."

"You're welcome," Ginny said. But once Meg had left, she turned to Rose. "Oh dear, I hope I haven't offended her by refusing payment."

"I don't think so," Rose said, trying to reassure her. "She's very uptight at the moment, because of John."

"I hope he doesn't get sent down," Ginny said. "I'm not sure how Meg would cope with that."

"Me neither."

Meg

Meg was more grateful than she had let on for Ginny's generosity. Because what she hadn't told them – what she hadn't dared to tell them – was that John was likely to be fined at least 10% of his annual income, in addition to the sentence. Which would mean there would be little spare cash for extras like new books in the near future. She was so ashamed, fearing they would judge her somehow. Or pity her, which would be even worse.

But she and John would cope – they always did, come hell or high water. But it had to *be* she and John, both of them, together. She wasn't sure she would be able to bear it if he was sent to prison. She could deal with any amount of deprivation, if John was by her side. And they had savings, after all.

Stop it, Meg! The solicitor thought he'd probably get a suspended sentence, so she had to hang on to that. After all, it was only just over two weeks until the trial. Then she'd know. She tried to ignore the now nearly constant roiling in her stomach at the very thought of the trial. She'd been wound up for so long, more than three months now, she could scarcely imagine being able to fully relax again.

As she trudged back to the bus stop, she fought the usual feelings of insecurity and inadequacy. Both Ginny and Rose had read so many more books than she had, had so much more in common with each other, than with her. She tried to remember what Rose had told her, back in December. Something about each of them having different qualities to bring to their friendship, all of which were equally important. She'd written it down as soon as Rose had left, and returned to it often. She'd look it up again.

If only she could believe it. Believe it, Meg. Rose had told her, so it must be true.

April: *The Heaven Tree* by Edith Pargeter

Ginny

I love walking in nature at this time of year – there is so much to see and hear and marvel at. The snowdrops are nearly over, but the annual greening of Spring is well under way as the trees put forth their strength and come out of their long hibernation. In the past few days, I have seen pale yellow primroses, shy sweet violets, sweet-smelling cowslips and wood anemones with their pure white petals.

The delicate pink and white apple blossom on the tree in my back garden has been glorious, and I have one flower-bed full of bright yellow daffodils, which cheer me up every time I look out of my kitchen window. I make sure I keep my bird feeder fully stocked, as many different native birds – robins, blackbirds, goldfinches, blue tits and coal tits, to name but a few – are out and about, courting each other, then building their nests. If you get up early enough, the dawn chorus is wonderful to hear.

Ginny stopped writing and closed down her laptop. She had been longing for the arrival of Spring, after the clocks went forward. She enjoyed the lighter evenings and the slowly lengthening days, could feel her spirits lifting as the days grew gradually warmer. And most of all, she loved being out and about, able to witness the annual greening for herself.

This weather was ridiculous. She glared out of the window, hardly able to see anything for the rain pouring down its panes. The clouds were dark grey, shading to black, covering the entire sky from horizon to horizon. At this rate, her beloved daffodils would be flat as pancakes before the end of the day.

On wild, wet days like this, she wondered why she had chosen nature photography as a hobby. It was so frustrating, knowing that all those wonderful flowers and blossom, trees and birds were out there, but being unable to photograph them all – or indeed, any of them – without getting soaked to the skin. Maybe she needed to treat herself to a proper waterproof coat. But they were so expensive. She'd looked on various 'outdoor clothing' websites and had been horrified by the cost.

Then her cheeks grew warm as she remembered how privileged she really was. Even here in the UK, there were people living out on the streets, for whom *any* waterproof clothing would be a boon and a blessing. Who would love to have a sound roof over their heads, and enough money to pay their bills and food in their cupboards. All of which she took for granted. And here she was, whinging because she couldn't go out because it was raining. Pull yourself together, Ginny.

What to do? The answer came quickly – look for some good poems for her April blog posts. By this time, she had bought herself three poetry collections to help with the blog posts, each of which included a poem for every day of the year, and she had always been able to find something appropriate.

Then she would call it a day and bury herself in *The Heaven Tree.*

Meg

Meg was dreading the trial, now only a few days away. She'd been dreaming – or rather, having nightmares – about it every night for the past week or so. Again this morning, she'd woken up sweating, with tears pouring down her face, as she'd heard the judge pronounce his sentence – nine months in jail. She'd had to flip over onto her stomach and bury her face in the pillow to muffle the cry of pain which would have woken John up.

No more sleep for her. What was the time? She looked blearily at the digital alarm clock on the bedside table, squinting to read its bright red numbers without her glasses. 4.13 am. Oh well, she'd better get up anyway – she didn't dare go back to sleep. If only it was over. The waiting was making her crazy and there was no-one she could tell. Jessica would over-react and she was reluctant to bother Rose, who had her own troubles, with her knee operation coming up fast.

Lying in bed, waiting for her heart rate to slow down, she remembered the conversation (if you could call it a conversation) with John a couple of days before.

"I don't know why you want to be there," he'd said. "It's going to be humiliating enough without my wife witnessing it."

"Because I need to know what happens," she snapped.

"Can't you trust me to tell you the truth?"

Her heart had contracted at the plaintive note in his voice. The honest answer would have been, 'No, I can't. You've hidden so much from me.' But she couldn't quite bear to say that to his face. Not right now. So instead, she said, "Of course I do, but I want to be there just the same. I must know as soon as you do."

"Hmph. I don't suppose I can stop you," he said. "Do what you like."

And he'd stomped off up the stairs to his study.

She dressed quietly, tiptoed downstairs and made herself a coffee. She'd swithered about attending at all, but knew she wouldn't be able to wait patiently at home, for him to tell her whatever partial version of the truth he chose. If he even came home, because if he got a jail sentence, he'd go straight there from the court. *Do not pass Go, do not collect £200.* Please, God, anything but that. She needed to know exactly what happened, expecting the worst, but hoping and praying for the best. Her thoughts went round and round on the same depressing treadmill. It was no good, this was driving her mad. She'd have to talk about it to someone.

Maybe she shouldn't disturb Rose. But she could ring Ginny. As soon as John went out for his AA meeting.

Ginny

Ginny was fathoms deep in *The Heaven Tree* when the phone rang. It took her a few rings to resurface. Then she dashed over to the phone before the answerphone could kick in.

"Hello," she said. Hopefully, she'd be able to get rid of whomever it was in short order and get back to her book.

"Ginny? It's Meg."

Oh. "Hello Meg, how are you?"

"Is this a good time to talk?"

Not really. But Meg wouldn't have rung for nothing. Suppressing a sigh, Ginny said, "Yes, of course. What can I do for you?"

"It's – I've been having nightmares."

"Nightmares? What about?"

"Can't you guess? About John's trial. It's less than a week away now and I'm so frightened he's going to get sent down."

She might have known.

"Do you want me to come over?"

"Oh, Ginny, would you mind? I'd be awfully grateful. John's out at AA for the next hour or so. I would have rung Rose, but she's got so much on her own mind, I didn't like to bother her."

"Where do you live?" Ginny listened as Meg gave her the address, then said, "I'll be with you in fifteen minutes."

Then she rang off, not wanting to hear Meg's effusive thanks, which she didn't deserve. That man was more trouble than he was worth. Let it go, Ginny. Meg doesn't want your judgement, she wants your ears. *The Heaven Tree* would have to wait. She grabbed her coat and backpack and headed for the car.

A quarter of an hour later, she parallel-parked neatly at the kerb in front of Meg's house. There was only room for one car on the drive, and John's car was parked there. Of course, he couldn't drive it any more. It was a good job it was daytime – a lot of folk would be out at work. Otherwise, she would have struggled to find somewhere.

The front door was open already, with Meg framed in it. "Come on in," she said. "Thank you so much for coming."

Ginny followed her friend down the long hallway into the kitchen. It was wonderfully warm in there. She took her coat off, and Meg went to hang it in the hall. Ginny had a good look around – she guessed it had been extended sometime in the past, as most houses of this era had tiny kitchens. But this one was positively spacious, with room for a solid kitchen table and plenty of cupboard and worktop space, all in the same warm wood – oak, for a ducat.

"What a lovely room," she said as Meg walked back in.

"Thank you, it's my favourite place in the house. We had it done nine years ago. Tea or coffee?"

"Do you have any herbal tea?"

"Only peppermint," Meg said. "I hope that's okay?"

"Sure." Ginny waited patiently while Meg bustled around, making the tea and fetching some home-made biscuits from a high cupboard.

"Help yourself," she said.

"Now," Ginny said as Meg finally sat down, "what's he said that's so upset you?"

"He doesn't want me to be at the trial," Meg said in a flat voice. "He thinks it will be humiliating for him. But I can't trust him to tell me the truth if I'm not there."

"That must be so hard," Ginny said. "Not being able

to trust your partner."

Meg bit her lip. "I didn't mean to say that," she said. "It sounds so disloyal."

Ginny wasn't sure what to say – if she agreed with Meg, it would sound like she was criticising her, but if she disagreed, it would invalidate Meg's feelings. She held her silence.

"So I'm going," Meg said. "But every night this week, I've been having nightmares about him being sent down. This morning was a particularly vivid one, and I knew I couldn't go on without at least talking about it with someone I could trust. And you drew the short straw."

Ginny reached across the table, took Meg's hand. "Not at all," she said. "I'm glad you felt you could reach out to me. Is a prison sentence a real danger?"

"I don't know!" Meg burst out, gripping Ginny's hand fiercely. "The solicitor says that he might be able to get him off with a suspended sentence, but I don't know how far I can trust him either."

"Would it help if I came with you?" Ginny said, the words coming out of her mouth before she could censor them.

"To the trial?" Meg looked astonished.

"Yes, if you want me to, and I'm allowed. I can understand why you didn't want to bother Rose, but I'm here for you if you need me."

"Then yes, yes please," Meg said. "I can't ask Jessica, she's too close to it all. Thank you so much."

Ginny hardly recognised herself. First, she had offered to help Rose out after her operation, now she was supporting Meg. It was decades since she'd let another person so far into her life. And now she had two. Two real friends.

Rose

Rose had rather enjoyed reading (and re-reading) Ellis Peters' *Brother Cadfael* books – slim paperbacks set in the mid-twelfth century town of Shrewsbury, their eponymous hero being a monk and mystery solver from the Benedictine Abbey. She'd bought the first one – oh, donkey's years ago – because it had said on the back cover, 'In the bestselling tradition of *The Name of the Rose.*' And she'd been captivated by the Umberto Eco book, back in the mid-eighties.

Only to find that all they had in common were monks as central characters and a Medieval setting. The *Brother Cadfael* books were much less complex, but far more enjoyable, than *The Name of the Rose,* which she'd long since taken to a charity shop. Whereas she still worked her way through the Ellis Peters series periodically, when she needed a dose of gentle escapism.

Like right now. She couldn't believe it had been a whole year since Graham had died. Most days, she managed to put her grief to the back of her mind, but sometimes it hit her like a tidal wave. She ought to be 'over the worst' now, having faced all the horrible firsts without him: first wedding anniversary, first family birthdays, first Christmas. But it still felt as though a limb had been lopped from her deepest self – would she ever feel whole again? Wiping a tear away, she opened *The Heaven Tree.*

Then became glued to her armchair, all else forgotten,

utterly enthralled. Now she understood why Ginny had said it was Edith Pargeter's best book. It was beautifully written, with strong and deep characters, superbly delineated, a complex plot, and gorgeously described settings. This was not just a book, this was literature. It was only when she raised her coffee mug to her lips and found it empty – not, she realised, for the first time – that she came back to herself.

She looked at the brass carriage clock on the mantelpiece – twenty to two. She'd been sitting there for three solid hours. She stretched carefully before levering herself out of the chair and limping through to the kitchen to make herself a belated lunch. And another drink – she was so thirsty.

How could she have reached the age of seventy-seven and never come across these books? She was so glad Ginny had treated her and Meg to the whole trilogy – she was desperate to know how the interactions between Harry, Isambard and Benedetta would play out. And the 'heaven tree' itself – such a beautiful concept. She vaguely remembered having come across a story, ages ago, about a traveller in Medieval times who had come to a town where a cathedral was being built, and asked three people what they were doing and why. The first had said they were being paid to do the work, the second that he was doing it to support his wife and family. But the third, a menial worker, had turned to the traveller with his face alight and said, "I'm building a cathedral to the glory of God."

Harry Talvace's motivation seemed to be the same. The way Pargeter described his love for the stone, his devotion to the task, was wonderful. And it wasn't only the three main characters who were compelling. The secondary ones – Adam, Gilleis, and the Abbot at Shrewsbury, to name but three – were equally well-drawn. It was a long time since she'd enjoyed a reading experience so much.

Wonder what Meg will make of it…

Meg

It had been so kind of Ginny to give her and John a lift to the Magistrate's Court. John could have made an effort to seem grateful. She guessed he was feeling constricted by a shirt and tie and his best suit – it had been years since he'd had to dress so formally, except at funerals. But the solicitor had told him to do it – that it would make a good impression.

They managed to find a space in the Pitchcroft car park, then walked down Castle Street to the Court. Thankfully, it wasn't raining. The Magistrate's Court was an imposing red brick building, with a rounded modern portico of glass and steel. Meg shivered as they walked in – the next couple of hours would seal John's fate.

There was a reception desk in the large foyer. John asked where he might find his solicitor before taking himself off, while Meg and Ginny found out where they needed to wait – in the seats surrounding the walls – and which courtroom the trail was going to take place in. They had an hour to wait.

"I didn't think it was going to be like this," Meg whispered as they took a seat.

"What did you think it would be like?"

"Oh, I don't know. Less modern, I suppose."

A tall man wearing a black gown approached them. He reminded Meg of a vulture. "Good morning, ladies," he said. "Can I help you?"

Meg's mouth was dry with apprehension. She opened her lips to respond, but only a croak came out. Thankfully, Ginny spoke up for her.

"We're here for the trial of John Jeffries, in courtroom 3," she said. "This is his wife, Meg, and I'm here to support her."

The man nodded. "I'm the usher for that courtroom," he said. "I'll call you at the proper time. You are aware that although you are allowed to be present, you mustn't speak to the accused?"

Meg nodded. This was going to be so hard.

"Make yourselves comfortable," the man said. "It shouldn't be too long now."

A few minutes later, he called them into the courtroom, and offered them seats in the public area at the back.

"I thought there would be more people here," Meg said, as she took it in.

"You're thinking of courtrooms you've seen on the telly," Ginny said. "But they're usually based on a Crown Court, where there's a jury too."

"Please be upstanding," the usher said, as the three magistrates – two men and a woman – filed in and took their seats behind a long wooden podium. There was a coat of arms on the tall, well-varnished panel behind them. And below them, a youngish woman in a smart suit. Then there were another two people – both men – facing the magistrates.

She recognised one of them – Mr Simpson – and realised they must be the two solicitors.

She nudged Ginny. "Who do you think the young woman sitting on her own is?" she whispered.

"Probably the Clerk of the Court, or whatever they call them these days."

"What do they do?"

"Advise the magistrates, I think, and make sure that the correct procedures are followed."

"How do you…" Meg began, then fell silent as John was brought in and took the stand.

The prosecuting solicitor rose to his feet. "You are charged with driving or attempting to drive with excess alcohol, under section 5A of the Road Traffic Act 1988, on Thursday 13th December 2018, between 8.40 and 8.50 pm. Please tell the court your name and address, and your date of birth."

John looked so pale, so subdued. Meg could see his knuckles whiten as he gripped the front of the witness stand. He answered the questions in a low voice, not meeting the prosecuting solicitor's eyes.

"How do you plead?" the man said.

John looked at the magistrates. "Guilty, Your Worship."

"Resume your seat, please," the prosecutor said.

Then he turned to face the magistrates. "The case for the prosecution is that on the date and time cited, the defendant lost control of his car near a Zebra crossing on Pheasant Street in Worcester, mounting the pavement and narrowly missing a pedestrian. The car hit a nearby rubbish bin. When police arrived at the scene, the accused was breathalysed twice, in accordance with approved procedures, and the lower reading was 52 micrograms, which is over the legal limit."

The man was speaking in a level tone. But so far as Meg was concerned, he might as well have been shouting, pointing his finger at John. The charge sounded so awful, so final. She knew that John had been right to plead guilty – Mr Simpson had explained it all so clearly – but her heart sank to her boots. Her only hope was that the man would be able to persuade the magistrates that it wouldn't happen again.

The Chairman of the magistrates nodded his thanks. Then their solicitor – John's solicitor – rose to his feet. "My client, Mr John Jeffries, does not deny that the offence took place, and has pleaded guilty to the charge. But there are some mitigating factors which the court needs to take into account."

"Please continue," the magistrate said.

"My client has recently been told that he has ARLD – alcohol-related liver disease – which is a serious medical condition. He has forsworn alcohol since the incident in question, and is attending meetings of Alcoholics Anonymous every day. I urge you to be lenient with my client and not give him a custodial sentence, as his continuing health and wellbeing are contingent on his being able to attend the AA meetings and on the support of his wife and family."

"Why didn't John's solicitor ask someone from the AA to speak up for him?" Ginny whispered, her lips tickling Meg's ear.

"They're not allowed to," Meg replied. "It's part of the 'anonymous' thing."

"Ah, got it."

The prosecuting solicitor stood up.

"Yes?" the Chairman said.

"The court should be aware that this is not the defendant's first drink-driving offence. He was convicted of the same offence eight years ago, and was disqualified from driving for twelve months. The prosecution holds that this repeat offence means he could be a danger to the public, if he is allowed to remain at liberty."

No. This could not be happening. But Mr Simpson was talking again.

"My client," he said, "has convinced me of his very great remorse, and has no intention of ever drinking again. Once again, I urge leniency."

"Do you wish to cross-examine the defendant?"

"No, Your Worship."

"Then we will retire to consider our decision."

"Please be upstanding," the usher's voice boomed out. Meg rose to her feet hastily as the magistrates left the courtroom.

Then everyone sat down again. She sneaked a glance at John. He was sitting with his head bowed, not meeting anyone's eyes. How she wished she could go over to him, offer him the comfort of her presence. But she knew it was not allowed.

"How long d'you think it will take?" she said Ginny.

Ginny shrugged her shoulders. "I've no idea. Not long, I shouldn't think – it's a fairly straightforward case. But like you, I have no experience of this kind of thing."

"Oh, God. He can't be sent down. He mustn't be sent down."

Ginny took her hand and squeezed it. "It's out of our hands now."

Ten minutes passed. Fifteen. How long were they going to take? Meg wanted to scream, to cry, to... anything else than sit here quietly while John's fate was decided. She shouldn't have come.

"Here they are," Ginny said quietly.

Meg struggled to her feet as the magistrates re-entered the room, then sank back into her chair, as everyone else except John sat back down. She scanned the magistrates' faces for some clue – any clue – as to what the verdict might be.

The Chairman spoke. "We have considered the case brought by the prosecution, that the defendant has pleaded guilty to the charge of driving with excess alcohol, and that this is not his first offence. We have further considered the submissions of the defending solicitor, concerning the defendant's future health and wellbeing. Having taken all these factors into account, the defendant's sentence will be as follows."

Oh, God! This was it. There was a roaring in Meg's ears and she fought against it. She couldn't faint, not now. She could tell that Ginny was looking at her, but couldn't turn her head to meet her friend's gaze.

"First," the Chairman continued, the defendant will be disqualified from driving for a period of 36 months, which is the minimum period prescribed for a repeat offence.

Second, he must pay a fine of £704, plus a victim surcharge of £71. He will be expected to pay this sum as soon as possible."

Meg winced – nearly eight hundred pounds. That must have been why John had been asked to complete that means form – Mr. Simpson had explained that he could be fined a percentage of his annual income. This was going to hit them hard. And of course there would be the solicitor to pay as well. They'd have to sell the car, which would help a bit. But she didn't care about all that, so long as John didn't go to prison. She held her breath as the Chairman continued to speak.

"Third, he will be required to undertake a treatment programme for his alcoholism and to serve fifty hours' community service."

Now it was coming. This was the crucial bit.

"Finally, we have decided to send the defendant to prison for six months, the sentence to be suspended for two years. If, during that time, he drives any vehicle whatsoever, he will be deemed in contravention of his sentence and it will be taken extremely seriously. We further expect him to continue to abstain from alcohol and turn up for the treatment programme appointments."

All Meg heard was the first few words. She bowed her head to hide the tears leaking down her cheeks, clapped her hands over her mouth to suppress the wail forcing its way out through her throat. This couldn't be happening. It just couldn't.

Ginny touched her arm. "What's up?"

"Didn't you hear? He's going to prison."

"No," Ginny said, putting her arm around her, "he's not. They've suspended the sentence for two years."

Meg blinked back the tears. She shook her head, scarcely able to take in the enormity of the reprieve. "Really? Are you sure?"

"Absolutely sure. Come on, let's take you home."

She looked over to where John was speaking to his solicitor. She guessed he'd be making arrangements about the fine and the community service. There would be time to talk to him later. He was safe. He was safe. Thank God, thank God.

"Okay, let's go."

Rose

Rose had prayed hard for Meg and John on the morning of the trial, and was struggling to concentrate on anything, as she waited for news. She wanted to pick up the phone so much, but knew it had to be up to Meg to contact her.

Finally, at nearly two in the afternoon, the phone rang. Rose snatched up the receiver.

"Rose Anderson speaking."

"He's not going to jail!" Meg's voice, so full of joy.

Rose allowed her shoulders to sag as the relief flooded through her. "I'm so very glad to hear that," she said. "Tell me all about it."

"Well, he's got a hefty fine to pay, and has to do fifty hours of community service, but they've given him a suspended sentence. I've never been so relieved in all my life."

"I'm so happy for you," Rose said. "I've been thinking about you all day."

"It was all over so quickly. I was so glad that Ginny could come with me – she kept me sane while the magistrates were out making their decision."

"Ginny came with you?"

"Yes, she offered. Oh, Rose, I hope you don't mind. I rang her one day when I was at screaming point, having nightmares every night, and she was so kind."

"Of course I don't mind."

But she did, a little bit. Why hadn't Meg asked her?

Meg was speaking again. "I didn't want to bother you, with the knee operation coming up and all. I know how hard it is for you to walk any distance at the moment."

"I'm glad Ginny could be there for you," Rose said, perhaps a shade too heartily. But Meg didn't seem to notice. "How has John taken it?"

"I think he's relieved, although both of us were dismayed at the size of the fine – nearly £800."

"Ouch, that's a lot of money. But you have some savings, don't you?"

"Yes, and of course we'll have to pay the solicitor too. But we'll manage. We just won't have to buy any extras for the next while. We'll have to sell the car, which should bring in a bit."

"Why on earth?"

"Because he's also been disqualified from driving for three years, as it was a repeat offence."

"Then it's a good job you live on a bus route – I would be really stuck in the same situation."

"That's what I told him, but I think that's the part he's most fed up about. He really loves his car."

Rose had to bite back a sardonic comment, along the lines that John should really rearrange his priorities and think more of his wife and less of his car. Honestly! She privately agreed with Ginny – John was a waste of space.

"I'm glad it's all come out well," she said instead. "See you at Capuchins."

Ginny

Ginny couldn't wait to find out what Rose and Meg had made of *The Heaven Tree*. She cycled down to Capuchins, revelling in the brightness of the Spring sunshine – such a pleasant change after all the recent gloomy weather.

She was, as ever, the last person to arrive. She'd never seen the point of turning up early for appointments or meetings and always aimed to be exactly on time. Sometimes Rose reminded her so much of her own mother, who had always worried about being late – wasting so much nervous energy, exactly like the White Rabbit – and hence arrived everywhere slightly – or even ridiculously – early. Oh well, each to their own.

"Hello, my dears," she said as she sat down. "How are you both?"

Meg beamed at her. "Really good, thank you. I hadn't realised how much strain I'd been under about the trial, until it was over and done. I couldn't settle to anything much, but since then, I've done loads of writing."

"That's excellent news," Ginny said. "Where are you

up to, now?"

"I've covered most of Jessica's and Andrew's childhoods and am about to start a new chapter, when Jessica left for university."

"That's going to be quite difficult to write, I expect," Rose said.

Why? What was the big deal?

Meg touched Rose's hand. "Yes," she said, "I knew you'd understand."

"Understand what?" Ginny said, suppressing her irritation with an effort.

"The pain of letting your children go," Rose said simply. "I can remember Matthew leaving home and feeling as though the bottom had dropped out of my world. And when Daniel left, it was even worse."

"Oh," Ginny said. "I guess I can understand that." Except, not really. Parenthood was a closed book to her. Then had to quash an unexpected pang of regret.

"So," Rose said, "how have you been Ginny?"

"It's been such a joy to have a few days of fine weather this week. I've been getting so frustrated about all the grey days, when it was too wet to get out and take any photographs. My poor daffs were flattened in one particular storm and it took them days to recover."

"It must be very fed-up making," Rose said, "having a hobby which is so dependent on the weather. But surely you have enough photos saved away to keep on writing blog posts?"

"Yes, that's what I've been doing." Enough of the grumbling already. "What did you both think of *The Heaven*

Tree?"

"I absolutely adored it," Rose said, her whole face lighting up. "Thank you so much for introducing us to it. It's been a long time since I've read anything which moved me so much. Her characters are wonderful – so well-written. And not just the main three, but so many of the others too. They lived for me. And I loved the whole concept of the "heaven tree". The settings were wonderfully vivid too – she must have done loads of research to be able to make Paris and the Medieval Marches come alive in readers' minds."

Which was exactly the response Ginny had been hoping for. "Have you started the second one?"

Rose grinned at her. "Not only started, but finished. I'm halfway through *The Scarlet Seed,* and can't wait to find out what happens in the end."

"Have a hankie at the ready," Ginny warned her. "How about you, Meg?"

Meg flushed. "I'm just over halfway through," she said. "I only began to read it after the trial. But I'm really enjoying it so far, except that the print's so small."

"That's good," Ginny said, letting it go. She was glad she now had far more insight into what Meg had been going through. "But have you booked that eye test yet, Meg?"

"No," Meg said. "And I won't be able to for a while now – we won't have enough spare cash to buy new glasses for me. And I can manage well enough for most things."

Ginny was abruptly furious. "That's ridiculous," she snapped. "Your eyesight's really important."

Then bit her tongue as Meg shrank back in her chair.

"I'm sorry," she said. "I didn't mean to shout. I'm just

concerned for you."

"I have to say I'm with Ginny on this one," Rose put in. "Isn't there some way you could pay for them in instalments? I'm sure I've seen that advertised somewhere."

"At the very least," Ginny said, "you should go and get them tested. That doesn't cost anything. And if it's only reading glasses you need, you can pick those up quite cheaply."

Meg shrugged. "Oh, I know you're both right," she said. "I'll see what John says."

See what John says. Bloody John. If it wasn't for him, Meg would be able to afford new glasses easily. But Ginny knew better than to share her thoughts. She changed the subject.

"What have you decided on for our next read, Rose?"

"It's a book Debbie recommended to me," Rose said. "*The Keeper of Lost Things* by Ruth Hogan. It's delightful."

"*The Keeper of Lost Things*," Ginny repeated. "That sounds intriguing. What's it about?"

"Oh no, I'm not giving anything away," Rose said with a laugh. "You'll have to read it and find out."

Oh well. Ginny mentally shrugged her shoulders and gave it up. "I'll get it on my Kindle straight away."

Meg

Rose and Ginny were right. It was ridiculous to risk her eyesight just because they were short of money just now. Meg took off her jacket and hung it in the hall. Squaring her shoulders, she climbed the stairs, then knocked on the door of John's study.

"Come in."

Meg walked into the room and was met by the back of John's head. He was working at his desk. Now or never. Clearing her throat, she said, "I need to ask you something. I've been struggling to read recently – my glasses don't seem to work so well any more. Rose and Ginny think I need to go for an eye test and get some new ones."

"So what's the question?"

Meg felt the first stirrings of annoyance. He could at least stop what he was doing and turn around and face her. But could not prevent the note of apologetic pleading that made its way into her voice. "Well, I know we're a bit strapped for cash at the moment and new specs are so expensive."

John swivelled around in his chair and took both her hands in his, a surprisingly tender expression on his face. He was still so handsome, at least in her eyes.

"I may be a selfish swine at times," he told her, "but how could you believe I'd make an issue of this?"

Meg's eyes filled with tears. "I don't know," she faltered. "I just thought you'd want us to save the money for necessities."

He pulled her towards him, then stood up and folded her in his arms. "We may be a bit broke for now," he said. "But there will always be enough money for me to look after you. Your eyesight *is* a necessity, how could you think otherwise? Of course you should get new glasses. Go and book an eye test straight away."

Meg leaned into his embrace. This was the old John,

the John she had fallen in love with all those years ago. "Thank you, love," she whispered.

For the first time in – oh, a long time, she felt the faintest stirrings of hope and optimism in her heart. Whatever happened, John would be there for her. They would be celebrating their Golden Wedding anniversary together.

May: *The Keeper of Lost Things* by Ruth Hogan

Rose

Rose hadn't the faintest clue where April had gone. She turned over the calendar on her kitchen noticeboard and realised she only had a very few days to go before the operation. Although why this came as a shock, she had no idea – she'd been thinking of little else for weeks.

And she still hadn't completed the silver wedding sampler for Matthew and Sarah. Most of the actual stitching was done, but she still had to finish off the lettering in the centre, then stretch, lace and frame it. Which between them would take at least a few hours. She must have it finished before Saturday, so that she could give it to Matthew when he came over to help her shift the furniture around. So she'd better crack on with it.

She finished framing it late on the Friday evening, just in time. She propped it up on the mantelpiece then stepped back to see it better. Gorgeous – she was delighted with how well it had turned out. She hoped they would love it. No, she was sure they would.

Matthew was due to arrive at ten on this sunny Saturday morning. Rose skimmed through the relevant sections of the booklet once more over breakfast, then made a list of all the things they still needed to do. Much of the preparation had already been done – she'd driven Bonnie to the cattery the previous morning, for a fortnight's stay. And had secured an agreement from the cattery's owner that she could extend it by a week if necessary. The house was as spick and span as she could make it, and the big chest freezer that dominated one corner of her kitchen was full of batch-cooked meals which would just need defrosting, then sticking in the microwave. She'd also rearranged the contents of her kitchen cupboards, which had been a backbreaking job, so that the items she used most often were easily accessible. And to give Ginny a space to store her own food. Such a palaver, but she knew she'd bless herself for doing it, later on.

But she needed Matthew's help with moving the furniture around to make her rooms more easily navigable. The booklet asked, 'Could you organise your home differently or rearrange furniture to make more space and a safer home environment?' and advised her to 'Minimise any hazards or obstacles which may cause you to trip or fall.' So she'd made another list of what needed shifting and hoped it wouldn't take them too long.

There was the doorbell. She limped down the hall and answered the door. "Come on in, love. Would you like a mug of tea?"

"No, thanks," Matthew said. "Let's just get on with it." He sketched a funny little bow. "My muscles are at your service."

The next couple of hours were exhausting, although Matthew did the vast majority of the heavy lifting. By the time they were done, Rose had the satisfaction of knowing that her home was now as safe as she could make it. There were clear pathways around the furniture and her three beloved Persian rugs had been rolled up and stuck in the spare room.

"Thank you, love. I couldn't have done it without you."

He stooped and kissed her cheek. "You're welcome, Mum. See you at seven o'clock on the 7th."

"Wait a moment," she said, suddenly remembering the sampler, "I have something for you and Sarah, for your anniversary."

She fetched it from its hiding place in the drawer of the sideboard and presented it to him.

"Can I open it now?"

"If you like," she said. "But it's not your anniversary for another week and a half."

"Go on, Mum, please?"

"Matthew Anderson, you haven't changed since you were a little boy," she scolded. But didn't really mean it. "Go on then."

He ripped the paper off, then gasped. "Oh, wow! That's beautiful. Did you stitch it yourself?"

"Yes, and framed it too."

He gave her a huge hug which left her breathless. "Thank you, Mum. Sarah's going to love it."

Then he was gone. The house seemed so quiet without him, without even Bonnie. Rose sighed and sank down into her armchair.

She'd packed her case the day before, sticking to the helpful *What to bring into hospital* list in the Information for Patients section. But that could wait. What she wanted now, more than anything, was a belated lunch, followed by a quiet sit down.

Ginny

Ginny too was making her own preparations for her stay at Rose's house. Her neighbour had agreed to feed Sofi twice a day for the first week, after which Ginny reckoned she'd be able to pop home briefly and do it herself. But she needed to have everything in place for that first week.

She wrote one list for clothes and toiletries, then another for what would have to go in her backpack. But she'd leave the actual packing until the day, as she needed daily access to things like her laptop and journal, and there was no point in the clothes getting creased by spending days in a case. She had no idea how long Rose would be in hospital after the operation, so she wasn't sure when she'd first be needed. Doubtless Rose would text her, when the time came. Perhaps she'd better ring her, to check and to wish her luck.

"Hi, Rose, how's it going?"

"Good, thank you. Matthew came over on Saturday and helped me rearrange the furniture, so that it will be easy for me to get around with crutches. Is there any particular food you'd like me to have in for you?"

Ginny hadn't thought of that. She'd better take some food round with her. "No, that's okay. I'll bring round anything I need."

"That seems unfair," Rose said. "I should be paying for it. It's you doing me the favour."

How to say it without upsetting Rose? She'd better just tell the truth, and trust that her friend would understand. "I'm sorry to be a nuisance, but I'm really fussy about everything I eat being organic and sustainable."

There was a brief silence at the other end of the phone. Oh dear, had she offended her?

Then, "Not a nuisance at all. I should have remembered that myself. Bring your own food by all means, but you must let me pay for it."

Such a relief. "Thank you, Rose. I'll take you up on that. Now, when are you going to need me from?"

"I'm not quite sure, yet. It depends on how long they want to keep me in after the operation. From reading the booklet, I have to be able to do certain things like climbing up and down a couple of stairs, before they'll let me come home. But I'll have my mobile with me and will let you know."

"Fair enough. I'll be holding you in my thoughts on the day. I'm sure it's going to go well."

"Thank you. I really hope so."

Rose

Matthew was due to pick Rose up at seven a.m. By which time, she'd been awake for hours and was longing for a cup of coffee. But she'd been instructed to drink only water after midnight, so she'd done what she was told. She'd had a shower and washed her hair – who knew how long it would be before she'd be able to do *that* again.

The mantel clock was just striking seven when the doorbell rang. Thank God he was on time. She'd be warned to be there by seven-thirty on the dot and the traffic into Worcester was always fierce at this time of day.

But they needn't have worried. They reported to

reception a couple of minutes before the half hour and were asked to sit in the waiting room. And then waited, and waited, with (eventually) quite a number of other people who were due to have hip or knee replacements that day, plus their carers. There were the usual questions to answer: Was she feeling well? Yes. Had she been in contact with anyone who had an infectious illness in the last seven days? No. Her blood pressure was taken and she was given an identity band to wear on her wrist.

Then a young man came up to her. "Rose Anderson?"

"Yes, that's me."

"I'm Joseph, and I'll be your anaesthetist today. As your knee replacement is going to be a bit more complicated than a usual one, we're going to use a general anaesthetic. Which knee is it please?"

"The left one," Rose said faintly. A bit more complicated than usual? It was the first she'd heard of that. Her heart sank.

"Could you pull up the leg of your trousers please?"

"Of course." Rose pulled up the wide left leg of her newly-acquired 'loungewear' trousers (not her usual style at all) until her knee was visible. Then watched in bemusement as Joseph marked it with a purple pen. Then he was gone.

"I'm so glad I'm having a general anaesthetic," she said to Matthew. "I really didn't want to be awake while it was happening."

Matthew frowned. "It adds to the risk, Mum."

Rose touched his arm. "I'll be fine, love. Why don't you go to the canteen and have some breakfast? I'll ring you if anything else happens."

"Okay, but be sure you do."

Rose wondered, as she sat and re-read *The Keeper of Lost Things,* why they'd had to come in so early, when it seemed clear that she wasn't going to be operated on for ages. She was about half-way through, and Matthew was long since back from his breakfast, when a nurse came up to her.

"We're ready for you now, Rose," she said.

"You go home now," Rose told her son. "They'll ring you when it's all done."

He stooped and kissed her cheek. "Love you, Mum."

"I love you too."

She was asked to sit in a wheelchair, then taken to a small room called a 'pod', where she changed into a hospital gown, pants and some rather stylish non-slip socks, while the nurse waited on the other side of the curtain. All her clothes and other belongings were put into a sealed crate which she'd see again on the ward, later. Then the nurse covered her with a couple of warm blankets and left.

With no book to entertain her, Rose was bored. Luckily, she only had to wait a few minutes, by which time she was intimately familiar with every detail of the ceiling. At about 12.45, 'only' five hours after she'd arrived, there was another brief flurry of activity when she was moved to the pre-op area upstairs, and transferred to a bed. This was it. They weren't going to cancel it. Her details were checked again, then a canula was put into her hand, which hurt. Hopefully it would be the worst pain she would experience, until afterwards.

"Please would you lean over and hug this pillow?"

was the next, rather unexpected, instruction. Rose did as she was told, but couldn't restrain a gasp when Joseph sprayed her back with some antiseptic spray – it was cold!

A couple of minutes later, he said, "Okay, Rose, I'm going to put some anaesthetic in your spine, which will make you numb from the waist down."

It was a very odd sensation – all she could feel was some tingling, then the heaviness as her lower limbs ceased to be under her control.

"Time to relax, now," Joseph said, and injected her with something via the canula in her hand. She just had time to say a mental, 'Good bye and thanks' to her left knee as everything went black.

Meg

"The varifocal lenses will cost £210," the woman at Vision Express said. "Would you like to choose some frames?"

Meg couldn't believe her ears. Okay, it had been a while since she'd had new glasses, but she hadn't expected this.

"Which are the cheapest ones, please?"

Oh, no you don't," John said from behind her. "None of that, Meggie. You choose some frames you like." Then he bent down and whispered, "Stop worrying – we can afford them."

"You could pay in instalments," the Vision Express woman said, guessing this.

John straightened up, met her eyes. "No, thank you," he said with dignity. "We'd rather pay in one go."

So Meg had obediently chosen the frames she liked. Which had added another hundred pounds or so to the total bill. She was horrified, but John insisted they could afford it.

"After all," he said. "I'm not drinking now, so that's saving a small fortune."

She was so proud of him, so grateful that he was doing this for both of them.

That had been a fortnight ago. Today she was going to collect them, and she couldn't wait.

"Please sit down, Mrs Jeffries," the woman said, "so that I can fit your new glasses properly."

Meg obediently did as she was told, and was thrilled by the difference they made – her fuzzy world suddenly came into sharp and clear focus.

Oh, my goodness," she said. "These are wonderful."

"You'll need to be careful for the first few days," the woman said, "particularly going down the stairs, or stepping off a kerb. It will take your brain a little while to make the adjustment."

And she'd been right. She'd been glad of John's supporting arm as they crossed the road to the bus stop. Her world had seemed to lurch and she couldn't keep her balance.

But she'd soon got accustomed to them. The human brain really was wonderful.

"Thank you so much," she told John a couple of days later. "It's so nice not to have to guess what the dials on the cooker are set to, and to be able to read and use my laptop so easily. I hadn't realised how bad my eyesight had become."

"Good," he said. Then he frowned at her. "But you

should have told me ages ago. I'll make sure you book a regular eye test in future."

"Fair enough. Now, I'm going to settle down with our book for this month."

Rose

Rose awoke in the recovery room and looked blearily at the clock on the wall, squinting to bring it into focus: five past three. She felt exhausted. As soon as she'd been checked over and they were sure she was okay, she was wheeled to the ward on the hospital bed. Her left leg was encased in a foot pump to help her blood circulate and reduce the danger of blood clots. When she peeked under the blankets, her new knee was covered by a long dressing going from just above it down towards her ankle. She felt woozy and supposed it was the painkillers. Must have been, because she felt no pain. So she closed her eyes and dozed for a while. Then felt thirsty, and drank nearly a full jug of water over the rest of the day.

Which led to an embarrassing experience with a bedpan during the night, but she supposed the nurses were used to it. She realised she was on a ward with five other women, all of whom had also had either knee or hip surgery. She found it difficult to sleep – she wasn't used to sharing a room with other people anymore and the normal nightly noises kept disturbing her.

But she must have had some sleep, because she woke up the next morning feeling far more like herself, and ravenous. She ate her gluten-free cereal and toast with relish. Better text Matthew and Ginny… and Meg. She sent the first text to Matthew, then copied and pasted it (with suitable alterations) to the other two.

> Dear Matthew,
> Just to let you know I'm feeling fine and have just eaten breakfast. I'm on a ward with five other women who've had similar surgery and am in no pain.
> Love,
> Mum xx

The next day, the foot pump was gone, but she had to endure a daily blood-thinning injection in her stomach. Dr Robertson came by to let her know the operation had gone well, which was a relief. Then the physiotherapists arrived – a man and a woman. Both of them seemed so young to Rose – but then again, most people did, these days.

"Good morning, Rose," the female physiotherapist said breezily. "I'm Jo and this is Sam and we'll be showing you the exercises you need to do, both here, and once you're back home."

"First of all," Sam said, "let's show you how to get out of bed safely, using your crutches. Then we'll take you through some other exercises."

"It's really important that you do them regularly," Jo put in, "to strengthen your knee and the muscles around it. Here's a sheet to tell you what to do. And you must remember to ice your knee for twenty minutes beforehand."

With an effort, Rose put away a vision of herself with a palette knife and pink icing… "Thank you."

The exercises seemed simple enough, once she got used to them. Although she was a little disheartened by how exhausted she felt afterwards. But relieved to know that she'd be able to go to the loo under her own steam, using the crutches – she had found having to use the bedpan unspeakably humiliating.

Ginny brought Meg to visit in the afternoon.

"How are you feeling?" Meg said, an anxious expression on her face.

"Not too bad at all, thanks. Although I'm still on painkillers. But they're very pleased with how it's gone, so I'm sure it's all going to be fine."

"That's good to hear," Ginny said. "But don't try to run before you can walk. It'll take you a while to get back to normal."

Rose smiled at her ruefully. "I know, and I will be good, I promise."

"I'll see that you are," Ginny said, screwing her face into a ferocious scowl.

Rose burst out laughing. "Thank you. I know I'll be in safe hands."

When her friends had gone, a nurse came and asked her whether she would like a shower. Yes, she would.

Her dressing was wrapped in a waterproof cover to protect it. It was the first time she'd sat down to take a shower and it felt very weird. But she felt so much better afterwards.

Matthew came in the evening, to reassure himself that she was okay, but didn't stay long. He'd never liked being around sick people. She was so glad it would be Ginny looking after her once she was home, rather than her son, dearly though she loved him.

The next couple of days followed a similar pattern. She began to need less pain relief and was encouraged to walk around the ward on her crutches so long as she told one of the nurses. The other women on the ward were doing the same and all of them supported and encouraged each other – so nice.

Each day, she had a session with Jo and Sam, who got her walking up and down the corridor and up and down a step with the crutches. "You'll have to be able to bend your knee 90 degrees before we let you home," Jo told her. Which was a good incentive to practice – kind as everyone had been, she couldn't wait to be back home and to sleep in her own bed, rather than being kept awake by the discordant chorus of snores and sighs.

On the evening of the third day, the head nurse told her she could be discharged the next morning. "But don't worry, we'll give you some strong painkillers, and two weeks' worth of blood-thinning injections. You've been shown how to do them yourself, haven't you?"

"Yes, thank you," Rose said. "And thank you for all your care of me, while I've been here."

The woman smiled at her. "Thank you, I appreciate that."

As soon as she left, Rose rang Ginny. "Please would you pick me up tomorrow morning?"

"What time do you want me?"

"At about nine please."

She was going home – at last.

Ginny

Ginny soon settled in at Rose's house, which surprised her somewhat. Rose had cleared a cupboard for her food and she soon got to know where everything was.

For the first couple of days, Rose hadn't been up to much. Simply getting down the stairs in the morning with Ginny hovering a couple of steps below her, ready to catch her if she fell, had seemed to be as much as she could manage. Once she was installed in her favourite armchair in the living room, with her leg alternately propped up on a pouffe, or bent into a normal sitting position, she had only left it for necessary visits to the loo. Or for the exercises the hospital had told her to do.

"Here's the ice pack," Ginny said. "I've wrapped it in a tea towel."

"Thank you, Ginny," Rose said, smiling up at her, before glancing at the clock. "It's quarter to nine now, so I'll start the exercises at five past."

"Okay, I'll do the washing up, then come in to help you down."

It was quite painful to watch Rose, her dignified friend, sliding from the chair onto the floor, to do her four times daily exercises. Ginny was so glad she was around to help her back up.

"All done for now," she said. "Now, what are you going to do today?"

"I'd like to finish re-reading *The Keeper of Lost Things*," Rose said. "Have you started it yet?"

"No, I haven't. Good idea. I'll pop upstairs and fetch

my Kindle."

They read in companionable silence for a while.

"What do you think of it?" Rose said.

"I'm not sure yet. It seems a bit disconnected. But I am intrigued – I want to find out how it all fits together."

"That's good," Rose said. "I was afraid you'd think it was a bit twee."

"Not at all. Would you like another cup of tea?"

"Yes, please. That would be lovely. Thank you – I don't know how I'd manage without you."

Ginny ducked her head to hide her pleasure. "You're welcome."

Rose

The slow pace of her recovery was beginning to frustrate Rose. The weather had turned warm and fine and she longed to be out in it. But she'd been told to rest, to alternately keep her foot up or sit with her new knee bent, to stay inside the house for the first three weeks, and to do her exercises faithfully, so she was complying. Because she knew it made sense. But it didn't mean she had to like it.

At least she had the French windows in the living room, which meant she could sit near them and feel the warm air on her face. Thanks to Ginny, who had single-handedly lugged another armchair and the pouffe into position for her. And had kept carrying the pouffe to and fro between the two chairs without complaint or comment, as it was easier not to use the chair's reclining function because she needed to alternate sitting with her knee bent and straight. There was more strength in her friend's slim and graceful form than Rose had suspected.

So she had no right to complain, not really. She had books to read and cross-stitch to do. She'd chosen a golden wedding anniversary sampler for Meg and John with Ginny's help, and it had arrived a few days later. It was the most complex pattern she'd ever attempted, and included partial stitches and gold metallic thread, which she suspected was going to be tricky to use. But both she and Ginny had fallen in love with the roses in various shades of gold and deep yellow that formed the border and had decided that Meg would too. Stitching it kept both her hands and her mind occupied.

She was so grateful for her friend's quiet presence. Ginny never tried to jolly her along, was there when Rose needed her, and kept herself occupied when Rose wanted to be alone. She had mown the lawn each week and done some weeding, not to mention hoovering through each day and keeping the kitchen immaculate – all unasked. And had cooked some delicious vegetarian meals, which Rose had thoroughly enjoyed. So very kind. The two of them had settled into a peaceful chummery that she hadn't quite expected. Ginny had fetched Bonnie home from the cattery a fortnight after the operation, and her beloved cat had been good company too, sensing that her mistress needed her presence more than normal.

Her knee was fascinating her. Soon after she had arrived home, the bruising had begun to come out, and by the end of the second day home, her whole leg (or as much of it as she could see for the dressing) was black and blue from thigh to ankle – she'd never seen anything like it. And when the bruises began to fade, there was a rainbow of colours.

Two weeks after being discharged from the hospital, it was time to have the stitches removed and the dressing changed. The thrill of leaving the house was out of all proportion to the event. Ginny drove her to her GP practice, then waited outside the room while the procedure took place.

Which had been a painful process, as there were 32 staples (not stitches, as she'd thought) to be removed, and the practice nurse had not been particularly gentle. Rose had not been able to prevent the tears springing to her eyes. She blinked them away – she wanted to see what her knee looked like.

"It's healing well," the woman said, "so I think we'll replace the dressing with a smaller, waterproof one. Which means you'll be able to have a shower."

On the way home in the car, she told Ginny the good news. "Would you mind standing by while I have a shower? I can't wait to be able to wash my hair and to feel clean!"

Ginny's answering smile was like a clear sunrise. "Of course. That's great news."

Ginny

Ginny found sharing Rose's space easier than she had anticipated. It had been so long since she'd lived with anyone. Of course, she missed Sofi, but had made friends with Rose's Bonnie, a plump ginger tabby who adored having her soft fur stroked and her chin tickled – such a different texture to Sofi's smooth coat. And now that Rose was on the mend, no longer needing her constant presence, she was able to pop home each day to feed and fuss her beloved cat. Ginny guessed it wouldn't be long before Rose could manage without her.

But for now, she was happy – no, more than happy, content – with the present arrangement. Rose was stitching away on Meg's sampler, so Ginny decided to do her daily clean and tidy of the kitchen before starting to prepare the evening meal. They had eaten separately for the first couple of days after Rose got home, but that made no sense to Ginny. So she had persuaded her friend to share her own, fresh-cooked food and Rose had acquiesced with gratitude (but had insisted on paying for the ingredients, which was fair enough). Which meant that when her time at Rose's came to an end, most of the pre-cooked meals her friend had stashed in the freezer before her operation would still be there for her to defrost and microwave warm.

She switched the radio on, and found Radio 2, her favourite station as a background to food preparation. Before long, the vegetarian lasagne, made with gluten-free lasagne sheets, was ready to pop in the oven later on. So she put it away in the fridge and made herself a camomile tea.

She had just sat down at the kitchen table, when she heard the next song begin, *Tell Laura I Love Her* by Ricky Valance. She had avoided listening to it for years – it had been her and Laura's special song. But in a bitter twist of fate, it had been Laura who had died, not her. As Ricky Valance's haunting voice filled the kitchen, Ginny put her head down on her folded arms and wept. It had been so long, and she still missed Laura so very much. Would there ever be a day when her heart did not ache for her lost love?

She was so immersed in her grief that she didn't hear the sound of Rose's single crutch on the tiles of the kitchen floor. She only realised that her friend was there when she felt a gentle hand on her shoulder, heard Rose's soft Highland voice.

"Ginny, my dear, whatever is wrong?"

But her grief had got up a full head of steam and it was some time before she could control her wild sobs enough to answer her. And by that time, her hard-won self-sufficiency was in tatters and she couldn't stop, couldn't even censor the words that came pouring out of her deepest, most private self.

"It's – it was that song," she said, her voice muffled in her folded arms. She couldn't bear to lift her head, meet Rose's gaze. *Tell Laura I Love Her.* I haven't heard it for years. It was our special song and it reminded me how very much I loved her. How much I still miss her, even after all this time."

"Oh, love, I know," Rose said softly, holding her hand. "I do understand – there are days when I miss Graham so much I hardly know what to do with myself."

Ginny raised her head and saw that Rose's eyes were sparkling with unshed tears. Her loss was so much more recent – how could she, Ginny, be so self-indulgent?

"It's been nearly twenty-five years," she said, "since she – since she died. You would have thought that by this time, I'd have got over it. I feel so stupid, breaking down like this." Especially in front of you.

"You mustn't say that. Grief is never stupid and it has no time limit. Would you," and Rose paused before continuing, "would you like to talk about her?""

Ginny took a deep breath, scanned her friend's face, and saw nothing but the deepest empathy there. "Yes," she said, "I think I would. Thank you."

Meg

The doorbell rang and Meg rushed down the hall to answer it, knowing it would be Ginny. Exactly on time, as always. They had decided to hold this month's book group meeting at Rose's house and Ginny had offered to collect her. So kind.

"Ginny!" she said. "It's lovely to see you. How's Rose?"

"Much better," Ginny said. "She can manage with only one crutch now, so I won't be staying there much longer."

"Where are you going?" Meg asked, as they took the road into the city centre. "This isn't the way to Rose's house, is it?"

"I thought we could drop in at Capuchin's on the way, to buy some cakes and let Karen know why we're not there today. I told Rose we might be a bit late back."

"That's a good idea – we wouldn't want Karen to think we've deserted her."

"Exactly what I thought."

Meg had to practically trot to keep up with Ginny's long legs as they headed down the Shambles towards Friar Street. It was a beautiful sunny morning and by the time they arrived at Capuchin's, she was feeling more than warm, and wishing she hadn't worn a jacket.

"Here we are," Ginny said, over her shoulder. Then she frowned. "Are you all right, Meg?"

"I'm not used to walking that fast," Meg said, a little breathlessly.

Ginny's face softened. "I'm sorry – I tend to forget that not everyone rushes along like I do."

"It's okay. It's just that my legs are a lot shorter than yours."

"Let's go in and choose some cakes."

"Hello, you two," Karen said. "No Rose today?"

"No," Meg said, "she had a knee replacement operation at the beginning of the month, so we're holding this month's book group at her house. But we'd like to buy some cakes to take with us, please."

"So that will be gluten-free carrot cake for Rose, and a piece of my coffee and walnut cake for you," Karen said, a twinkle in her eye. "How about you, Ginny?"

"I'll pass, thanks," Ginny said. Then her expression changed, became lighter, more open. "Actually, I think I will have a cake this time – we need to celebrate Rose's recovery."

Meg watched her choose a pear and ginger slice. This was new – Ginny never had cake. Maybe she was easing up on herself. Best not to say anything, perhaps.

They reached Rose's house at about ten past eleven. It was good to see her almost back to her old self, with some colour in her cheeks again. She had looked very pale and wan in the hospital.

"You're looking really well," Meg said, moving forward to hug her friend. "It's so good to see you."

Rose returned her embrace. "And it's lovely to see

you too," she said. "Come away in."

Ginny disappeared into the kitchen to make the drinks, and Rose led Meg into the living room.

"How have you been?"

"I'm fine, thanks," Meg said. "I'm making real headway with the memoir now – I think I'm going to finish it on time. And Ginny has offered to scan some photos in for me."

"That's kind of her," Rose said. "Adding photos will make all the difference. Have you brought along a chapter to read to us?"

Meg blushed. "I have, actually. But enough of me – how are you?"

"Good, thank you. Ginny has been so kind – I've been waited on hand and foot. But now I'm really on the mend, so she'll be going home next week."

"I'll be going home once you've had your first physio appointment," Ginny said as she walked in with a tray of mugs and plates, the cake box balanced on top of the plates, "and not before. Meg, would you take the cakes, please?"

"What's this?" Rose said. "Cakes? It'll be as good as being at Capuchin's."

"We stopped off there on the way," Ginny said, as she put the tray down on the coffee table and began to dole out the drinks, "to let Karen know why we wouldn't be there. She sends you her best wishes."

"Ah, that's kind," Rose said. "I'm planning to be back next month."

Meg opened the cake box. "Here we are," she said, "cakes for everyone."

Rose's eyebrows shot up as Meg opened the box to reveal three cakes, but she didn't say anything. Ginny took her slice, flushing slightly. "I thought it was time to lighten up a bit," she said.

Rose reached across and touched Ginny's arm. "Good for you."

What was going on here? Meg shrugged – Ginny would let her know in her own good time. Or not. Let's change the subject. "When is your first physio appointment?" she asked Rose.

"On Friday. Ginny's taking me to the outpatients' physiotherapy department at Worcestershire Royal for an initial assessment. Then I expect I'll be going to their regular knee clinic sessions."

"When will you be able to drive again?" Meg said.

"I'm hoping by the middle of June," Rose said, "or at least, by the first week of July, which will be eight weeks after the operation. Luckily, my car's an automatic, so there isn't much for my left leg to do. It'll depend on my progress."

"Fair enough," Meg said. "But don't overdo it – better to go slow and steady, and heal properly, rather than rushing ahead and overstraining your knee."

Rose gave her a rueful smile. "I know, I'll be sensible. Now, what did you both think of *The Keeper of Lost Things*?"

"I loved it," Meg said, "and it was such a joy to be able to read it easily, without having to squint and strain my eyes."

"Yes," Rose said, "I noticed your new glasses – they really suit you."

"Thank you," Meg said. "John was furious with me

when he realised how much I'd been struggling. I was going to go for the cheapest frames, but he insisted I choose some I liked."

"Good for him," Ginny said. "You can't take risks with your eyesight."

"I did find the book very confusing at first," Meg said, not wanting to hear Ginny being judgemental about John, "the way she kept hopping around between the Eunice story and the Laura story."

"Me too," Ginny said, "but it was wonderful how she wove all the different plot strands together at the end."

"I'm so glad," Rose said. "I think it's astonishing for a debut novel. I fell in love with it the first time I read it, and will definitely be keeping an eye out for her next book."

"What's the book for June, Meg?" Ginny said.

"I've chosen another Liz Gilbert book. I hope that's not against the rules?"

"No, of course, not," Rose said. "Which one have you chosen?"

"Her bestseller, *Eat, Pray, Love,*" Meg said. "I've only seen the film, so I thought it would be fun to read the book. We owe her so much."

"I've not read it either," Rose said. "How about you, Ginny?"

"I read it when it came out," Ginny said, a faint frown between her eyebrows, "but I suspect it would be good for me to read it again."

"Then we're agreed," Rose said. "Thank you, Meg. Now, let's hear that chapter of yours."

June: *Eat, Pray, Love* by Elizabeth Gilbert

Ginny

It appeared that God (whoever She was) had a sense of humour. Why that book? And why now? Ginny slammed her car door, then locked it with the key fob, before stalking into the house. It made her think of Humphrey Bogart in *Casablanca*: of all the books in all the world, why did Meg have to choose that one?

Like millions of other women, Ginny had read *Eat, Pray, Love* when it first came out in the mid-noughties, and had envied Liz Gilbert's ability to uproot herself from her daily life and take off on a voyage of self-discovery. Her own journey felt more like a free-fall into darkness.

At that time, Ginny would have loved to be able to walk away from the mess that was her post-Laura life. She'd been in her early sixties then, convinced that her only chance of happiness had died with her beloved. Who would have thought that, a decade later, she would have two new friends, whose friendships she was coming to value more and more? Maybe there was some hope for her, in spite of everything.

She'd start to read it later. For now, she had some housework to do and a new blog post to write before heading back over to Rose's.

Meg

Meg worried all the way home about Ginny's reaction to hearing her book choice for the next month. She tried to start a conversation once or twice during the journey back into Worcester, but got nowhere, so she relapsed uneasily into silence. 'I suspect it would be good for me to read it again.' What did that mean?

And she couldn't even ring Rose to ask her, because Ginny was staying there, and would hear the conversation (or at least, Rose's side of it). An e-mail would have to do.

> Dear Rose,
> I'm a bit worried at how Ginny reacted when I told you both my book choice for this month. She didn't seem at all happy about it, and when I tried to talk in the car on the way home, it was obvious she wasn't in the mood... What have I done wrong? I thought it was a happy book.
> Love,
> Meg x

She decided to type up the latest chapter of her memoir while she waited for a reply. Although her typing was of the hunt and peck variety, she was getting quite fast at it now. Maybe she'd teach herself to touch type one day. She was deep into the work when the laptop chimed to notify her of an incoming e-mail – yes, it was from Rose. She clicked on the link.

> Dear Meg,
> Yes, I noticed that too, but no doubt Ginny will let us know in her own good

time. You haven't done anything wrong – it is a perfectly valid choice. Don't worry so much!

How's the great work going? I really enjoyed that last chapter you shared with us – you have a definite gift for making your reader 'see' what you're describing.

I've got my assessment appointment with the physiotherapist the day after tomorrow. I expect I'll have to go for weekly sessions for a while, but I can feel that my knee is getting better all the time.

Love,

Rose xx

Feeling reassured, Meg switched back to Word. Rose was right – she was far too sensitive to unspoken words. She glanced up at the kitchen clock and gasped – it was gone half past three already. She'd better get a wiggle on if she wanted to finish this typing before she began to prepare dinner.

Rose

Rose had truly appreciated Ginny's presence during the first wobbly weeks of her recovery, yet it also felt good to feel independent again. Ginny had taken her for her first physio appointment on 1st June, then packed up her things and returned home. She would still be seeing her once a week, as her friend had kindly offered to give her a regular lift to the Knee Clinic sessions, as well as hoovering through and cleaning the bathroom and downstairs loo on their return, but otherwise, she was on her own.

The sessions at the Knee Clinic were almost like circuit training, which she had done many years ago at the local gym. She had to climb up and down a short flight of stairs, walk forwards and backwards, attempt balancing on one foot or on a balance board (which she found particularly taxing, as she wobbled all over the place) and even had to cycle on a static bike. The only relief was a one-on-one chat with the physiotherapist, Diane, who seemed to be pleased with her progress. And she was still doing the exercises at home, which were becoming increasingly easy.

Each day, blessing the kindly weather, she made herself walk from one end of the quiet close she lived in (only a couple of hundred yards) to the other, then back again. The first time she tried it, she had to use two crutches. It was a lovely way to reconnect with her neighbours and she looked forward to the daily conversations about their gardens and her own progress, as she graduated to one crutch, then only a stick. Her nearest neighbour, Joyce, had volunteered to trundle her wheelie bins out on a Wednesday evening, then back round to the back garden after the bin men had paid their weekly visit. People were so kind.

"How long will it be before you're allowed to drive again?" Joyce asked her one Tuesday morning. She had got into the habit of dropping in to see Rose, to check whether she needed anything from the supermarket.

"By the beginning of July, with any luck. I've got an appointment to see the consultant on the 4th, and I hope it's going to be my very own Independence Day."

Joyce smiled at her. "That's great news. Do you need anything from Tesco's today?"

Rose shook her head. "No, thank you. Matthew is doing my weekly shop at the moment, so I'm fine."

"Well, you know where to find me if you need anything."

"Thank you. I'm most grateful."

"That's what neighbours are for."

Ginny

"Rose," Ginny said, as they drove back to Crowle after Rose's latest knee clinic session, "would it be okay if I stayed for lunch?"

She could hear the curiosity in her friend's voice as she answered, "Yes, of course. Any particular reason?"

It had taken a lot of guts to decide to reach out to Rose. Ginny was more used to looking after herself, to not allowing anyone close. But since that memorable day last month, when she'd spilled out the story of her life with Laura, she knew she could trust Rose with anything. Which was a whole new feeling.

"I'd rather talk about it over lunch, if you don't mind."

Rose gave her a quick, sideways look, then nodded. "Fair enough. How does cheese on toast sound?"

"Perfect. I got quite used to your gluten-free toast when I was staying with you."

Rose laughed. "Yes, it's not too bad toasted. But it's like soggy cotton wool otherwise."

Ginny shuddered. "I'll take your word for it."

Back at the house, they prepared the simple meal in perfect amity – Ginny grated the cheese and prepared a small side salad for them both, while Rose laid the table before putting the toast under the grill, and the kettle on to boil – coffee for her and a herbal tea for Ginny.

"You seem to be moving a lot more easily now," Ginny said, watching her move around the kitchen. "It looks like the physio's doing you good."

"Yes, I always feel better after a session at the clinic. And I'll sleep like a log tonight."

They ate in silence for a little while, then Ginny pushed her plate aside. It was now or never.

"Have you read *Eat, Pray, Love* yet?"

"Yes, I really enjoyed it. Why?"

"Because it's really got to me," Ginny blurted out, "just like I knew it would. I couldn't believe it when Meg chose it for our group this month."

Rose didn't say anything, sipping her coffee. She was good at that – it made Ginny want to confide in her, throwing her words into Rose's silence, knowing that she would be held, that her friend wouldn't judge, wouldn't try to fix her.

"I'm so like her in some ways," she began, "and so different in others. We both do yoga, are both attracted to Eastern mysticism, and her instinct to leave her messy life behind in an effort to find who she really was, resonates with me. A lot."

Rose nodded. "I can see the parallels," she said. "So how are you different?"

"Well, for a start, I would *never* over-eat to comfort myself, like Liz does in the Italy section. Yet I envy her the ability to let go of controlling as much as she can — I find it nearly impossible. Some of the things she wrote about her monkey mind in meditation really made me laugh — I recognised it so intimately. But she conquered it in the end, and found her moment of transcendence. And I — I never have. By the end of the book, she seems to have found a balance between her heart and her head that I'd do anything to have for myself. Hang on, let me find the place."

Rose waited patiently while she flipped through the pages "Here it is," she said. "'The best we can do, then, in response to our incomprehensible and dangerous world, is to practice holding equilibrium internally — no matter what insanity is transpiring out there.'"

"Hmm," Rose said. "Are you saying you've never found that equilibrium?"

Ginny shook her head. "Not since Laura died. It was as though my heart, my still centre, had been ripped out of me."

Rose took her hand, then squeezed it. "So what are you planning to do about it?"

Okay, that was unexpected. "I hadn't thought of it like that. What do you think I should do?"

"Uh-uh," Rose shook her head, "it's not my life. If you really want to grow and change, it's going to have to come from you, not because I've made a suggestion."

Ginny pillowed her chin in her hands, and gazed off into space. An idea presented itself. She dismissed it. It was insistent. She sat up straight and met her friend's eyes.

"You're not going to believe this," she said. "I'm not sure I believe it myself. No, it would be impossible..."

"Why? Most things are possible if we plan them well enough."

"It's – well, I thought... I thought, 'I want to go to India for a month, to travel around, soak up the atmosphere, visit some temples.' And I could take Graham's camera with me – I bet I could get some fantastic photos from a trip like that."

"So what's stopping you?"

Ginny gaped at her. "You mean, you're not going to try to talk me out of it?"

"Why on earth would I do that?" Rose said. "It sounds like it could be a fabulous, once-in-a-lifetime experience, like your year in California."

Ginny could feel a fire warming her belly as Rose's words sank in. "You're right," she said. "It could be. Of course, I'll have to do a lot of research, plan a route, find out when would be the best time of year to go, stuff like that. But wow! It sounds so exciting!"

"Then go for it, my dear," Rose said. "It's never too late for a new adventure. It sounds like Liz Gilbert has even more to answer for."

"Wait till I tell Meg!"

Rose

Rose was feeling much more like herself by mid-June, and invited Daniel and Debbie and the children to come over for

Sunday lunch. Ginny had generously offered to come and help her do the preparation – she didn't feel up to standing for so long while her knee was still healing – and now the joint of pork was roasting in the oven, and the veg were in pans of water on top of the stove, all ready to cook. She'd decided that a ready-made frozen dessert would do this once, and had transferred it to the fridge the previous day to defrost.

It seemed an age since she'd seen Daniel and the rest of them – not since Easter, at the beginning of April, although they had connected regularly on FaceTime. Little Natalie was nearly eight months old now – she'd be sitting up by herself, might even be trying to crawl. And it would be good to see Jake and Davy – they changed so quickly at their ages.

The doorbell rang. Rose walked as quickly as she could to answer it – she was only using a stick in the house now – and was enveloped in Daniel's strong arms as he hugged all the breath out of her.

"Oh, it's so good to see you all," she said, as she was hugged by Debbie and the boys in their turn. "Come away in."

Daniel strode up the hall towards the kitchen. "I'll get us all something to drink," he said. "What would you like, Mum?"

"Tea, please."

Rose shepherded the rest of them into the living room, then settled into her reclining chair.

"How have you been?" Debbie said. "Is your knee really getting better?"

"Much better, thank you. I'm doing my exercises faithfully and walk around the close each day. I'm hoping to be driving again by the beginning of next month." Then she turned to Jake and Davy, "And how are you two?"

"Good, thanks, Granny," Jake said.

Rose waited, but apparently there was no more. Oh, dear. She could see the start of pre-teen non-communication – both Matthew and Daniel had been the same.

"That's good," she said. "How about you, Davy?"

"We've been learning about the Ancient Egyptians at school," Davy said. "All about pyramids and mummies."

"That sounds fascinating. Are you enjoying it?"

He shrugged, his young face serious. "I s'pose. Can we go and play now, please?"

Rose had long kept a stash of toys – board games, jigsaws, an old Playmobil pirate ship that had belonged to Daniel, and a bucket of Lego – in a particular cupboard in the dining room, as she knew from long experience that both boys would soon be bored with adult talk. And she had invested in a second-hand doll's house for Rosie, although as Matthew's family lived so close, she usually visited them. But it would come in useful for Natalie, a few years down the line.

"Of course you can. Off you go."

"Thanks, Granny," Davy said. Then the two of them raced off into the dining room.

While Rose was talking with the boys, Debbie had propped Natalie in one corner of the sofa, then took a big blanket out of her baby bag and put it down on the floor, together with a selection of brightly-coloured toys. She plonked her daughter down in the middle of them and

Natalie gave them both a happy smile before starting to play.

"She's cut her first teeth!" Rose said.

"Yes," Debbie said proudly, beaming at her daughter, "she's doing really well."

"And her hair's growing so much now," Rose said, eyeing the fine golden brown curls on her grand-daughter's head, "bless her!"

"Yes, she's going to be beautiful," Debbie said.

"I think you're right," Rose said softly. "I'm so very glad."

Just then, Daniel arrived with a tray of hot drinks. "Sorry it took so long," he said. "You've moved things round in the kitchen, so I had to hunt for the tea and coffee."

"Sorry, Daniel – I've needed to be able to get at the stuff I use most often easily while my knee's getting better."

He planted a kiss on her head. "Not to worry – I found it all in the end. How are you doing?"

"As I was telling Debbie, I'm hoping to be driving again by the beginning of next month."

"That's great news. Well done."

"I'm aiming to have lunch at one," Rose said. "Would you mind giving me a hand, Daniel? It's the first time I've cooked a roast dinner from scratch since the operation, and even today, Ginny came over this morning to help me with the prep, so it's all ready to go."

"Of course I will," he said. "Ginny – she's one of your book group friends, isn't it?"

"Yes, she's lovely. She stayed with me for the first few weeks, so that Matthew could go to Rome with Sarah and the kids at half-term."

"That was good of her."

"Yes," Rose said. "She and Meg and I have grown very close these past few months."

"I'm so pleased," Daniel said, "that you've made some new friends since Dad..." his voice tailed off.

A pang of grief. It was amazing how it could still creep up on her unawares. But she didn't want Daniel to know, so she met his eyes, forced herself to smile. "Yes, I'm very lucky."

Meg

It was interesting, Meg thought as she gazed off into the middle distance, her biro beating a staccato tattoo on the kitchen table, how her writing had evolved over the past few months. When she first began, it had been a self-conscious, almost painful process, as she questioned each word.

Yet as her self-confidence as a writer grew, her style had morphed into something more like her speaking voice and sometimes, now, the words came easily, pouring from the end of her pen as fast as she could write them.

She knew this was only the first draft, but it was an achievement to have written it at all. A couple of years ago, before she had met Rose and Ginny, it would never have occurred to her to write anything more than the odd poem. And now she was loving it: the chance it gave her to express herself, to be herself.

She was about to start the final chapter, which was going to be about becoming a grandmother – perhaps the favourite era of her life so far. She'd divided the book into ten chapters of roughly seven years each – although this last one was going to reach further back to Katie's birth, more than nine years ago.

She picked up her pen and began to write. *Becoming a Nana was (and is) one of the high points of my life. When I saw the first photo of my daughter cradling her daughter in her arms, my heart overflowed with joy...*

The phone rang. Drat it. Sighing, Meg walked over to the kitchen counter to answer it.

"Hello."

"Mum." It was Jessica's voice and that one word was enough for Meg to realise that she was on the edge of wild tears. Her heart began to beat faster.

"What's wrong, darling?"

"It's – it's Katie," Jessica said. "She's been so sick, and she's in tears from the pain, and I think, I'm afraid..."

Then she burst into tears. Oh God, what was wrong?

"*What* do you think?"

"I – I think she's got meningitis. She's got those dark spots they talk about. The doctor's on her way to the house."

Meg felt the tears rising behind her own eyes and blinked them back fiercely. She had to be the strong one now.

"Would you like me to come over? I could be there in half an hour."

If the buses were running to time. Not for the first time, Meg mentally cursed John for losing his driving licence. Not that he was here, anyway – he was out at his AA group.

"Oh, Mum, would you?" There was no missing the relief in Jessica's voice. "If she has to go to hospital, I'll need you to pick Becky up from school, then look after her. Mark's not due back from work for hours."

"I'll be with you as soon as I possibly can."

Ginny

Ginny was about to sit down in front of her laptop to write her latest blog post when her mobile rang.

"Ginny? It's Meg."

"Hi, Meg, what's up?"

"Could you," Ginny could hear the hesitation in her friend's voice, "do me a massive favour?"

"It depends what it is." Ginny couldn't resist teasing Meg sometimes. And was shocked to hear a sob at the other end of the phone.

"I'm sorry," she said. "Of course I will. What d'you want me to do?"

"Would you possibly be able to drive me over to Jessica's? Katie's really poorly – Jessica thinks it may be meningitis, and she needs me to look after Becky, in case…"

Meg's voice tailed off. Meningitis. That sounded serious.

"Of course. I'm on my way."

Ginny grabbed her bag, fished around for her keys, then bolted out of the door. It shouldn't take her more than ten minutes to get to Meg's, traffic permitting. Where did Jessica live? She seemed to remember Meg saying it was over the river somewhere.

Meg was waiting outside the house for her.

"What's the postcode?" Ginny said.

Meg told her and Ginny set her sat nav. "We should be there in about twenty minutes, if the traffic over the river isn't too busy."

"Oh, Ginny! Thank you so much for coming. I wouldn't have asked, but with John not driving at the moment, and the buses are so unreliable…"

"Not a problem," Ginny said. "I'm glad to be able to help."

When they reached the house, there was already a car parked outside and Ginny dropped Meg off, then cruised along the street, trying to find a place to park. Then she walked back and rang Jessica's doorbell.

"Come on in," Meg said. "The doctor's already here."

The two of them walked into the front room, where the doctor was talking to a young woman, who must be Jessica.

"She needs to go to hospital, Mrs. Dunstan. I don't think it's meningitis, but we have to be sure. I'll ring ahead to make sure she is admitted straight away."

Jessica's face was so white Ginny was afraid she was going to pass out.

"I'll pick Becky up from school," Meg told her daughter. "You take Katie to the General."

Ginny admired her friend's calm manner, as Jessica visibly took heart from it. She knew that Meg was in bits, but she wasn't showing it.

Once the doctor, Jessica and Katie had left, Ginny put her arm around Meg. "Is there anything else I can do?"

Meg shook her head. "No, thank you. You've been a complete star, bringing me here, but I can manage now. I'll ring John to let him know where I am – he should be back from his AA group by this time, then I'll go and collect Becky. Luckily, the school is quite close."

"Fair enough," Ginny said. "But please let me know what happens."

"Of course I will. And, thank you so much for bringing me – it would have taken me far longer to get here by bus."

Meg

Meg was in the middle of making Becky's tea when her mobile rang.

"Yes?" she said. "Who is it?"

"It's me." Jessica's voice. She sounded a bit more cheerful.

"What have they said?"

"It's not meningitis."

Oh, thank God for that. "Then what is it?"

"Some weird illness I've never heard of before. It's called Henoch Schönlein Purpura."

"That's a new one on me too," Meg said, relief flooding through her. "What did they say about it?"

"It's still quite serious, but she should recover completely. The main symptoms are just what she's had – the tummy pain, sickness and those red spots. And her joints are so painful too – they said it's like she's got acute arthritis."

"Poor little Katie!" Meg said. "That sounds horrible. But you have to hang on to the fact that she should recover completely. Don't worry about Becky – I'm just about to give her tea and I've told her that Katie is poorly, and that you've gone to the hospital to be with her. She was a bit upset at first, but I've let her watch *Beauty and the Beast* and given her some ice cream. I'll stay until Mark gets home."

"I rang him from the hospital," Jessica said, "so he should be back soon. Thank you so much for looking after Becky for me."

"That's what Nanas are for."

Ginny

Ginny couldn't settle to anything. Why hadn't Meg rung her? She was probably still at Jessica's, but she could at least have sent a text.

Just then, her phone pinged – an incoming message. Yes, it was from Meg. Fingers trembling, Ginny opened it.

Dear Ginny,

Sorry to keep you in suspense for so long, but I was waiting to hear from Jessica. It's *not* meningitis – thank God! She has 'heenock shernline', something or other (probably not how you spell it, but that was how it sounded when Jessica told me) – I'd never heard of it before, but apparently it happens most often to children aged between two and eleven. Poor little Katie is quite poorly, and they're keeping her in overnight, but she should be completely better in a couple of weeks, they think.

Thank you again for coming to the rescue.

Love, Meg xx

Not meningitis – such a relief. She would google 'heenock shernline' and see what came up… Henoch-Schönlein Purpura – that must be it. Ginny's eyes widened as she read the symptoms – poor little Katie – no wonder she had felt so rotten. She hoped the kidneys wouldn't be affected. Meg hadn't mentioned anything, but the test results might not have come back yet. Such an awful thing to happen, right out of the blue.

Doubtless she'd hear more next week, at book group. She sent Meg a non-committal reply, just saying how glad she was that it wasn't meningitis.

Rose

It felt so good to be back in circulation. She still needed a stick to walk with, and Sarah had kindly picked her up, then dropped her at Capuchins, because she wasn't allowed to drive for another week yet. But the pain was far less, unless she overdid it.

"Hello, Rose," Karen said, "how is the knee?"

"Much better, thank you." How kind of her to ask. "Please may I have my usual?"

"One latte and one piece of carrot cake coming right up."

Rose smiled at her, then walked over to their usual table and settled down to wait for the others.

Meg was the next to arrive, as usual. She bustled in, beaming when she saw Rose waiting for her.

"Hello, Rose. I'll be with you in a minute."

As soon as Meg sat down, Rose said, "How's Katie?"

"I'd rather wait for Ginny to arrive," Meg said, "instead of telling it twice."

"Fair enough. How are you then?"

"I've nearly finished the first draft of the memoir," Meg said, "and I have a favour to ask you."

"A favour?"

"Yes. Once I've revised it, would you mind reading through it and seeing what you think? I'd really value your opinion, both as a friend and an English teacher."

"Of course, I'd be happy to."

The Capuchins' doorbell glingled and Ginny strolled in. Rose was looking forward to seeing Meg's face when she heard the results of her book choice.

"Hello, my dears," Ginny said breezily as she sat down. "How's Katie, Meg?"

"Better than she was, but still not right. Poor little mite! For the first few days, Jessica had to carry her everywhere."

"Why on earth?"

"Because of the pain in her joints. But that seems to have died down now and the rash is beginning to fade. The good news is, her kidneys weren't involved. She's on the high road to recovery now and is starting to enjoy being off school."

"That's good to hear," Rose said. "It sounds like a horrible disease."

Meg shuddered. "It is," she said, "but it could have been a lot worse. If her kidneys had been affected, it could have had a permanent effect on her. Anyway, enough of that. How did you both enjoy *Eat, Pray, Love?*"

Rose held her silence, expecting Ginny to jump in first. Which she did.

"Well," she said, "Liz Gilbert has done it again."

Meg frowned. "What do you mean?"

"Re-reading it has given me an idea," Ginny said. "I've decided to go to India for a month, on a spiritual journey of my own."

Meg gaped at her. "Truly? What brought that on?"

"You know I've always been interested in Eastern mysticism because of my yoga? Well, reading about Liz's adventures in India has made me long to do the same – to travel around, soak up the atmosphere and visit some of the famous cities, like Amritsar and Varanasi. I might even get as far as Dharamsala. And of course, I want to see the Taj Mahal."

"Wow!" Meg said. "Good for you. When are you planning to go?"

"I've been doing some research, and the best time for Westerners to visit seems to be late Autumn, but I'm in the early planning stage at the moment as most of the tours seem to offer either Varanasi, or Amritsar and Dharamshala and I want to visit all three. So I may have to find a tour operator who does bespoke private tours."

"Isn't that going to be dreadfully expensive?" Rose

said.

"Yes, but like you said, it's going to be a once-in-a-lifetime experience, so I don't care. I've got some savings stashed away, which should cover the cost."

"Are you going on your own?" Meg said.

"Yes," Ginny said, "but I don't mind. I've been alone for twenty-five years now, so I'm used to my own company."

Rose touched her hand. "You're not alone now. You've got us."

Ginny flushed, obviously touched. "I know, and I'm so grateful for your friendship. For both of your friendships. It's made more difference than you know, being able to share my life with the two of you." She paused, then continued, "In fact, it's exactly twenty-five years today since Laura passed – I never thought I'd be able to allow anyone into my life again. I was so afraid that if I did, I would lose them. You two have taught me that the risk is worthwhile – that even if I–I lose one of you, it will have been worth it for the happiness you've brought me."

Ginny ducked her head, seemingly unable to meet their eyes. Rose squeezed her hand.

"I feel the same," she said. "Without you and Meg, I'm not sure how I'd have got through the first year without Graham. It's made a massive difference, knowing that I could share my grief with people who would understand."

"Me too," Meg put in. "I was thinking only the other day that I'd never have had the courage to write my memoir if you two hadn't shown me there was more to life that just being a wife and mother. I feel like a different person altogether. Stronger, somehow."

Ginny met Meg's gaze. "I saw that the other day," she said, "when you were able to put your own fears aside to be strong for Jessica."

It was Meg's turn to flush. "Thank you. I really appreciate that."

Ginny withdrew her hand from Rose's clasp. Rose sensed she was feeling overwhelmed by all this talk about the value of friendship, so she changed the subject.

"What's our book for July?"

Ginny flashed her a grateful look before answering. "It's one of my favourite books of all time," she said. "*Neverwhere* by Neil Gaiman."

"*Neverwhere* – what a weird title," Meg said. "What's it about?"

"It's a fantasy," Ginny said, "set in an alternative London."

That rang a bell somewhere. "Wasn't there a television adaptation of it, ages ago?" Rose said.

"Yes, there was, in the nineties, I think, and it was an excellent one. But the book's even better."

"I've hardly read any fantasy," Meg said. "I must be one of the few people of our generation who never managed to get through *Lord of the Rings,* though I quite enjoyed the films. There were just too many characters with such weird names and I kept getting muddled up."

Ginny grinned at her. "Horses for courses," she said. "I adore reading fantasy, escaping into an entirely different world. But I hope you'll enjoy *Neverwhere,* Meg. It's set a bit closer to home and there certainly aren't as many characters as there are in *The Lord of the Rings.*"

"I'll give it a go," Meg said. "That's what this group's been all about, isn't it? Introducing us to new ways of seeing the world."

"You're right," Rose said. "I'm looking forward to it."

Meg

It took Meg more than a week to read through her memoir, tweaking this, altering that, fiercely doubting herself the whole time. But eventually, she felt it was as good as she could make it (apart from the photos, which Ginny had promised to help her with). It was time to send it to Rose.

> Dear Rose,
> Here it is. I've now read it through so many times, I can't be objective about it anymore. I'd be so grateful if you would read it through and bear these questions in mind:
> 1 Does the story flow – does it make sense?
> 2 Have I got the balance between my memories and what was happening in the UK at the time right? Have I left anything important out?
> 3 Are there any sections you particularly enjoyed? Why?
> 4 Are there any sections you didn't enjoy? Why?
> I know it's only for the family, but I want to be proud of what I've written and at the moment I'm not at all sure about it.

Love,
Meg xx

Even writing the e-mail took forever. This was so scary – what if Rose thought it was rubbish? What would she do then? It was far too late to start again from scratch – their Golden Wedding Anniversary was only two and a half months away, and this had taken far longer than that to write. She held her breath, and pressed SEND.

That was it. It was gone. It was too late to wish it back. She had complete faith in her friend's ability to put her right, if necessary – after all, Rose had been an English teacher. But she prayed there wouldn't be too much to rewrite. She wasn't sure she could bear to hear it was not good enough to share. That would be so devastating, after all her hard work. She hoped that Rose would be gentle with her.

July: *Neverwhere* by Neil Gaiman

Rose

Rose settled down in her favourite armchair near the French doors at the back of the house, which she'd opened wide to catch the breeze (if any). It was both hot and muggy, as July days in England so often are. But they were saying on the news that this heatwave was as bad as 1976, which would take some doing. Hosepipe bans were in force everywhere and she blessed the hunch which had nudged her to buy a new electric fan a few weeks before, when the hot weather had begun. It was at least moving the air around. She had a tall glass of blackcurrant squash jostling with ice cubes at her elbow, her pen in hand and a notepad by her side, and was settling down to read Meg's memoir. She hadn't got very far – only the first couple of pages – before she realised that she needed to have a conversation with her friend about what she was actually after. She picked up the phone to ring her, then realised it would make more sense to do it by e-mail, so she'd have a permanent record of Meg's answers.

> Dear Meg,
> I've just sat down to start going through your memoir, and realised that I need to clarify what you want me to do:
> 1 Do you want me to correct any typos / grammatical errors, or just point them out?
> 2 Shall I produce a list of suggested changes, or would you rather I used the

Comments feature, which allows me to make suggestions or ask questions in the margin of the MS? Because if you want me to use the Comments feature, I'll read it on my laptop.

3 Or do you simply want me to answer the questions you sent me in your e-mail, which are about the content rather than the writing?

Please let me know – I want to do the best job for you that I can.

Love,

Rose x

She sent Meg a text to let her know she'd sent her an e-mail, knowing all too well that her friend didn't check her e-mails regularly. Then opened *Neverwhere* on her Kindle while she waited for a reply.

It didn't take long to come…

Dear Rose,

Oh dear, I hadn't thought about any of that. Thank you so much for checking. I didn't even know Word had a Comments feature! But the answer to your questions are:

1 Yes, please – I think I assumed you'd be doing this, what with you being an English teacher. I think I'd prefer you to point them out, because that way, I'll learn more.

2 I dithered about this – my first

inclination was to have a list to work from, because I'm still quite scared of Word. But I guess it would be better to have the comments directly in the MS. So that, please.

3 Those, and the other things you've suggested, please.

I really appreciate you going to so much trouble for me – I hope it doesn't take you too long.

Love,

Meg xx

Rose sighed quietly to herself. She'd more or less suspected that would be the way Meg's mind was working. Good job she'd checked. She'd better fetch her laptop and the lap-tray.

Ginny

Ginny was feeling hot and bothered. She enjoyed the warmer summer months usually, but this muggy heat was ridiculous. She was sitting at her dining room table in front of her laptop, wearing her floatiest dress, made of Indian cotton, and as little else as was decent. She ground her teeth in frustration. Why was it so difficult to find a tour operator who would visit all the parts of India she wanted to see? There were half a dozen places she definitely wanted to visit: Varanasi, Rishikesh, Amritsar, Dharamshala, Shimla and the Taj Mahal in Agra. And she quite fancied seeing Mumbai. But no matter how hard she looked, most of the tours seemed to include a maximum combination of four of them. And it looked as though she'd have to decide which festivals (if any) she wanted to experience, as the three she was interested in, the Hindu festival of Holi, the Sikh festival of Vaisakhi and the Buddhist festival of Vesak, were in successive months in the spring, and she definitely couldn't afford to stay for two months. Or, if she went in November, which was supposed to be one of the best months, weather-wise, she could be there for Diwali. She definitely didn't want to be there during the monsoon season, which ran from June to September. Then again, maybe it would be better to avoid places like Amritsar during Vaisakhi, as it was bound to be booked up months and months in advance. This was more complicated than she'd thought.

Maybe if she searched 'bespoke tours of India'.

Bingo! Straightaway she found a company that offered tailor-made tours, and the more she looked around their website, the better she felt. It sounded like her dream might be possible, after all. She clicked on the link to be sent a brochure, then filled out her details. This was more like it.

She stood up and stretched. She'd been stuck in front of her laptop for hours, and the weather was cooling down a little. Time to go for an evening walk. Grabbing her back pack and Graham's camera, she headed out.

Meg

It was so good of Rose to take so much care over the reading of her memoir. But then, Rose was always kind. Meg counted herself blessed to have her as a friend.

She remembered Ginny's offer to help her with the photos, but wasn't sure where to start. She'd used the family photo albums to give her ideas for the writing, but hadn't kept track of which ones had inspired her, and was now kicking herself for not having photographed them on her phone when she'd originally found them. Which now meant she'd have to search for them all over again.

Now, how to work out which ones she needed to find? The best way would be to read through the memoir one more time, taking notes for possible photos (or of photos she knew she had, somewhere) as she went along. Then she could type it up in a long list, which would include where she thought each particular photo might be. Blimey, this could take a while...

Which it did. It took her three long evenings to work her way through the whole MS, and the best part of a morning to type her scribbled notes up into a table with four columns: Status, Page Number, Subject of Photo, and Possible Source. She was so proud of herself for working out how to create a table on her own, although she'd had to ask John about adding extra rows. By the time she was done, she had listed nearly a hundred photos she was sure she had... somewhere. She knew exactly where to find some of them – on the wall in the lounge, for example. But the possible source for others was worryingly vague: "J/A photo albums" meant somewhere in the many albums she had compiled over the years for each child, Jessica or Andrew. And others she was sure she did not have, like photos of her primary and secondary schools. How on earth was she going to find those?

She certainly wasn't going to be able to travel up to Yorkshire to take them, even if the schools still existed…

It was no good – she'd have to ask John. Meg walked up the stairs and knocked on the door of John's study.

"Come."

"I've got a problem," Meg said.

"What sort of problem?" John said, looking up from the accounts he was auditing for the golf club, held down with paperweights to stop the breeze from the electric fan blowing them everywhere.

Meg flourished the list at him. "I've come up with a list of the photos I need to include in the memoir and Ginny's promised to help me edit them and put them in the right places. But I don't know where to find some of them."

"Aren't they all in our photo albums?"

"Most of them are, but some aren't. For instance, I'd like to include photos of my primary and secondary schools, and I've no idea how to get hold of them. I don't even know if they're still open. And even if they are, they're bound to have added new buildings since I was at school."

"My darling Meggie," John said, smiling in that superior way he had, "how often do I need to tell you? You can find *anything* on the internet."

Meg ground her teeth. Why did he have to be so bloody patronising?

She bowed her head – there was no point in picking a row with him, not today. "Thanks, John. Where do you think I should look?"

"Go onto Google Images and put in the name of the school. Then, when you find the image you want, right click on it, then choose 'save image as' to save it on your laptop."

Why hadn't she thought of that for herself? "Of course. I'll do that. Thank you."

"Any time."

Rose

Rose was finding Meg's memoir fascinating. Having lived through the same time period herself, it was interesting to see how different Meg's experiences were to her own. Of course, she was a few years older than her friend, but their lives could not have been more dissimilar, particularly during their growing-up years. Part of it was because Meg had been born three years after the Second World War ended, and her memories were of being a child in the fifties, and a teenager in the sixties, whereas Rose could remember the austere second half of the forties. The other main difference came from where each of them had grown up – she in the rural Highlands of Scotland, Meg in a bustling town in Yorkshire.

Meg wrote vividly, even if her spelling and grammar were often wild, and sometimes included a lot of descriptive detail, which was good, if occasionally confusing to a reader who hadn't shared the context. But at other times, she suffered from what Rose thought of as 'white room syndrome'. Often, when she was writing about a past event, or retailing a conversation, it might have been happening anywhere because no physical details of the background or the people concerned were included. How was she going to explain that, without hurting Meg's feelings? This was going to take some careful consideration, because the last thing she wanted to do was to knock Meg's confidence. It was quite something to have written an entire book – Rose wanted to applaud that, while helping her to make it as readable and interesting as possible. She'd have to be lavish in her praise of the good bits, while ensuring that she also pointed out what needed amending, such as grammar and spelling. Although she had decided to quietly amend some – or even all – of the latter without comment. It was going to be a delicate balancing act, particularly in the light of how fragile Meg's self-esteem could be.

And time was running out – it was nearly halfway through July now and Meg and John's Golden Wedding anniversary was in mid-September. Rose knew that Meg was planning to ask Ginny to help inserting some photos, so it was up to her to help her produce a final version of the words as soon as possible. She'd better crack on with it, doing some every day until she reached the end. She'd both comment in the margins, but also produce some notes for Meg to read alongside, for wider principles.

Onward.

Ginny

Ginny was just about to start cleaning the bathroom when her phone rang.

"Hello?"

"Ginny? It's Meg."

"Hello, Meg. What can I do for you?"

"Well," and Meg's voice sounded hesitant, uncertain. "You remember you offered to help me with the photos for my memoir?"

"Yes, of course. Are you there yet?"

"I think so, nearly," Meg said. "Rose is working her way through the manuscript and she's promised to get it back to me by the beginning of August. But I'm struggling a bit with the photos."

"What kind of help? I can't do much until we've got the finished script to work with."

"It's taken me ages to find all the photos I want to include, but I think I've managed it. I've taken photos of the photos, if you see what I mean, so they're all on my phone. But I've got no idea how to get them onto my laptop."

Was that all? Ginny had to stop herself asking the question out loud. She couldn't understand why Meg didn't know this stuff – it was so simple. Shut up, Ginny – Meg's your friend.

"What kind of phone do you have?" she said. "An Apple or an android?"

"An iPhone. Why?"

"Because I have an iPhone too, so I can tell you how to do it over the phone."

"Thank you. I'd ask John, but this hot weather's having a bad effect on him. He's either grumbling about not being able to enjoy a long, cold G and T, or so patronising he sets my teeth on edge. So I find it hard to ask him favours…." Meg's voice tailed off.

Ginny scowled. Meg did not deserve to be treated like that. But all she said was, "Yes, I see what you mean. Of course I don't mind helping you. Do you have your phone on you?"

"Yes, I'm ringing you on it."

Oh. That was going to complicate things. She couldn't see Meg managing to keep switching between screens to follow the instructions.

"I tell you what, why don't I come over and help you? It'll be easier to show you in person."

"Oh, would you? I'd really appreciate it."

"I'll finish cleaning the bathroom, then drive over to yours."

"Thank you so much. You're a true friend."

Rose

Rose sometimes wondered how on earth she had ever had time to work. She had expected to have far too many empty hours to fill when she retired, but it hadn't worked out that way. She was almost as busy as she ever had been. And she knew that at least part of that was to keep herself occupied so as to fill the empty evenings, which she had been expecting to spend with Graham… But at least she could choose what she did these days, and when.

As the heatwave ground relentlessly on, she had begun to organise her time differently, waking up early doors to get some editing done, when her mind was most alert, having a long Mediterranean-style siesta during the hottest hours of the day, then working on Meg and John's sampler in the evenings.

She had nearly reached the end of Meg's sixth chapter when the phone rang.

"Rose Anderson speaking."

"Hello Rose, it's Debbie."

"How lovely to hear from you. How is everyone?"

"Hot," Debbie said, and Rose could hear the weariness in her voice. "None of us are sleeping well, and poor little Natalie is struggling to cope."

"Oh, no! Is she okay?"

"She is now, but she gave us a proper scare. She wouldn't drink her milk, hardly ate, came out in a prickly heat rash, and was so miserable. Poor little mite. I ended up taking her to A&E."

"What did they tell you to do?"

"Oh, the usual things. Dress her in as little as possible, have an electric fan going at all times, and keep the curtains closed to keep the heat out."

"How has that worked?"

"A combination of all of them, plus a cool sponge bath when necessary, has done the trick. Also, I'm taking her to the library as often as I can."

"The library? Why on earth?"

"Air conditioning. It's delightfully cool in there. Even the boys don't mind a quiet hour or so there, most days. It's too hot for their usual summer occupations. They're both doing the Summer Reading Challenge again this year."

"Hasn't Jake aged out of it?" Rose said. "I thought it was only for primary school children."

"It is, mainly, but the library staff are brilliant at finding new books for him to read."

"I bet it's given Davy's reading a good shove-on."

"Yes, it has. It always does. And we've been visiting the swimming baths at least once a week. Natalie loves it, bless her."

"Let's hope the weather breaks soon," Rose said. "It's been almost tropical."

"Yes, roll on winter," Debbie said.

"Did you ring for any particular reason?"

"No, I just wanted to check that you were okay, bearing up."

"Bless you, that was kind. But I'm fine. I've got a big standing fan that I keep going all day – and most of the night too. And I only have me to look after."

"You ought to come over to visit us, now that you're driving again. The boys would love to see you."

"I might just do that," Rose said. "But not for the next couple of weeks. I'm editing a friend's book at the moment and I've got to get it done by the end of the month."

"What's it about?"

"It's the story of her life. It's her Golden Wedding in September and she decided to write it for the grandchildren."

"What a lovely idea! You should do the same – I know the boys would love it, and Matthew's three as well."

"Perhaps I'll give it a go," Rose said. "It would give me something to do in the long winter evenings."

"Please think about it," Debbie said. "I'd love to read about your life too." Then her voice changed. "That's Natalie – she's just woken up. I'd better go. 'Bye Rose."

Rose put down the receiver and gazed off into space. It was a thought, a definite thought.

Meg

Meg was about to do the breakfast dishes when her mobile phone beeped. Who would be sending her a text at this time of the morning? Rose.

> Dear Meg,
> Just to let you know I've finished going through your MS now and have really enjoyed reading it. Would you like me to just send it to you, or would you prefer to have a talk about it? Or perhaps that would be better once you've had a chance to read through my comments? Let me know.
> Love, Rose xx

> Dear Rose,
> Just send it please. Like you say, I think it would be better for me to read through the comments first, then have a talk with you. But I'm glad you enjoyed it. Thank you so much for doing all this for me.
> Love, Meg x

Meg's stomach clenched. Was Rose simply being kind, when she said she'd enjoyed reading it? There was obviously quite a lot wrong with it, or she wouldn't have suggested they needed to talk. It took every ounce of Protestant work ethic Meg possessed not to drop everything and log into her laptop. But she knew that if she got today's morning jobs done first –

washing up, putting a load of washing on, cleaning the kitchen floor – she'd be able to concentrate on what Rose had said. Otherwise, the undone tasks would keep distracting her. It shouldn't take too long...

An hour later, John put his head round the kitchen door. "I'm off to AA," he said.

"Okay, love, see you later."

Good. He'd be out of the way and she could read in peace. Ten minutes later, all her tasks were done. She made herself a large mug of tea, grabbed the biscuit tin from the cupboard and walked through to the lounge, a whole flight of butterflies swooping around in her stomach. She opened her laptop.

Here it was. With two attachments. Meg scanned Rose's e-mail quickly. Ah, she'd made comments in the MS as they had agreed, but also written some notes. What to open first? The notes.

A neat heading. *Notes on 'The Wonder and Marvel of an Ordinary Life'.* Meg scrolled down through it – it looked as though Rose had made notes on each chapter. Then at the end, another section: *General Observations.* Meg closed her eyes and sent up a little prayer, that Rose had liked it. Then opened them again, and began to read.

General Observations

First, and most important, I really enjoyed reading your memoir. You write vividly and have a gift for carrying the reader along with you. But there are a few things I've noticed (and marked up in the comments) which might help to make it easier for a modern reader (particularly the grandchildren) to understand:

- <u>Grammar and spelling</u>: I've corrected these as I went through, as you asked, without commenting on them, but I've been careful not to alter the meaning of your words.

- <u>Description</u>: there are some vivid descriptive passages, but sometimes, you refer to something which very much belongs to the time you're talking about, which I think the family might struggle to understand without a bit of explanation. For example, in Chapter 2 you mention fuzzy felts and hula hoops – I remember them clearly, but they probably only know of hula hoops as an alternative snack! So perhaps you could add a line of explanation in those places.

- <u>White room syndrome</u>: sometimes, when you're writing about an event or a conversation, they seem to be taking place in isolation – you haven't added any context to explain where this is happening or what people were doing. Again, a

line or two added in would help to
bring them to life for your readers.

- <u>Head-hopping</u>: You've quite rightly
decided to use your own viewpoint
for this memoir. But sometimes,
you tell us what other people are
thinking, which you couldn't
possibly know. Again, I've made a
comment where this has happened.

But all in all, it's great. I hope that, taken
together with the comments in the MS
itself, it should be fairly simple for you to
amend it as you see fit. WELL DONE!

Meg let out a breath she hadn't realised she'd been
holding. Rose had enjoyed it – thank goodness! She was so
grateful for Rose's comments, although she wasn't quite sure
what she meant by 'head-hopping'. Doubtless it would
become clear when she worked her way through the MS. And
she still had more than a month to get it done, and get the
photos inserted where they belonged. Then she'd have to find
someone to print it.

She refused to worry about that for now. The first
hurdle was over – Rose, whose views she respected so much,
had enjoyed it.

Ginny

Contrary to her usual practice, Ginny decided to drive into
the centre of Worcester rather than cycling. She didn't want

to arrive at Capuchins beet-red and flustered. As a result, she was there way too early. However, the ceiling fans were doing sterling work in keeping the shop cool, which was a relief.

"Hello Karen," she said, striding up to the counter. "Do you do iced tea?"

Karen grinned at her. "I'm selling practically nothing else at the moment," she said. "My freezer is working overtime to produce all the ice cubes."

"Excellent. I'll have one of those then."

She dropped her backpack into her usual seat, then sloped across the room to browse the bookshelves until the others arrived. What to choose for next time's book group? She hoped Rose and Meg had enjoyed *Neverwhere*. She didn't find a fiction title which tickled her fancy, but did come across a book about editing photos, which would come in useful when she was helping Meg, later on. So she bought it, then sat at the table, sipping her iced tea, while she waited for the others to arrive.

Rose was first. Although she still walked with a stick, she was scarcely limping at all. Which was so good to see.

"Hello, Ginny, what are you doing here this early?"

"I decided to drive rather than cycling because of the heat, then had a minor brainstorm and left home at my usual time."

Rose laughed. "I don't blame you. I can't wait for this weather to break."

"I've had an idea for Meg's birthday." Ginny said.

"Ooh, what?"

"You know they're a bit strapped for cash at the moment?"

"Yes."

"Well, I thought, why don't we offer to pay to have Meg's memoir printed?"

To her relief, Rose's face lit up. "That's a brilliant idea," she said. "Let's tell her at the end of our meeting. I can easily save what I've bought her for Christmas."

"I'm so glad you agree with me. It may be pricey, but I'd love to help her out, and this seems a painless way of doing it."

"Hush, here she is," Rose said. "Hello, Meg."

Meg walked up to the table and gave Rose a huge hug.

"What's that for?" Rose said, returning it.

"I just wanted to thank you for going through the memoir," Meg said. "Your comments have been so helpful."

"That's good," Rose said. "Go and get your coffee, then we'll hear all about it."

She grinned at Ginny, as Meg bustled up to the counter. "She's going to be equally grateful to you, once the photos are edited and added."

"I hope so. I went over last week to help her transfer them all from her phone to her laptop. So they're ready to be edited, then inserted."

"That was kind of you. She still gets so flustered with computers."

"So, Meg," Ginny said, as her friend sat down, "it sounds like you're ready to make a start on the photos."

Meg beamed at her. "Yes, I am. Thank you so much for your help."

"When would you like me to come over?"

"Could you make it next Tuesday?" Meg said. "John

will be out playing golf with his mates, so we'll have the house to ourselves."

Ginny fished her Filofax out of her backpack. "Yes, Tuesday's free. What time would you like me to come?"

"About 11, if that's okay with you."

"That's fine," Ginny said, scribbling it down.

"How's the revision going?" Rose said.

"Really well, thank you," Meg said. "I've printed out your comments and I'm working my way through the MS page by page, making all the changes. I hadn't realised it was going to be such a major production, but I'm really glad I'm doing it – it's going to be much better once I've finished. I hadn't thought of half the things you've commented on."

"It's been a pleasure," Rose said. "A second pair of eyes always helps."

"So," Ginny said. "What did you both think of *Neverwhere?*"

"I absolutely adored it," Rose said. "I'll never be able to use the London Underground again without thinking about it."

"It took me a while to get into it," Meg said. "Fantasy isn't usually my thing, but the way he combined the fantasy bits with our London was brilliant. I ended up really enjoying it."

"I'm so glad," Ginny said. "I've loved it for years. I watched the television series again a couple of weeks ago – I've got it on DVD – and that brings it alive."

"I'd love to see that," Rose said.

"Would you like to borrow it?"

"Yes, please."

"Then follow me back home after the meeting and I'll lend it to you."

There was a pause as they all finished their drinks and ordered another round of iced tea or coffee.

"I've got heaps to tell you about my India trip," Ginny said. "It took me ages to find a tour operator who did tailor-made private tours, but I've managed it. I'm going for three weeks in November, to coincide with Diwali, and I'm so excited."

"Which places will you be visiting?" Rose said.

"I'm going to Varanasi to pay homage to the Ganges, Rishikesh because of the Beatles and my yoga, then up to Shimla and Dharamshala – I couldn't go to India without visiting the home of Tibetan Buddhism – then back down to the Taj Mahal in Agra, and Jaipur, then to Amritsar to see the Golden Temple of the Sikhs, before finishing off in Mumbai."

"Wow! That sounds fantastic," Rose said. "I quite envy you. But I know I'll never be able to do a holiday like that now – I know my limits."

"You'll have to take loads of photos," Meg said, "then make them into a photo book when you get back, so you can tell us all about it."

"There's going to be a lot of travelling," Ginny told them, "and I'll need to make sure I've had all the requisite jabs. But I love Indian food and I've always had what my mother used to call a 'cast iron stomach', so I hope I'll be able to enjoy it."

"I'm sure you will," Rose said with a smile.

"It's costing me a small fortune," Ginny said. "But I

don't care. It's going to be the trip of a lifetime."

"Good for you," Rose said.

"What's our book for August, Rose?" Meg said.

"I've decided on *The Handmaid's Tale* by Margaret Attwood," Rose said. "It's quite a disturbing read, but one of the best dystopian novels I've ever read. In fact, reading *Neverwhere* gave me the idea of choosing it."

"Why on earth?" Meg said.

"Because in one sense, London Below is another kind of dystopia."

"I suppose so," Ginny said. "*The Handmaid's Tale* is one of those books I've never quite got round to – thanks for suggesting it."

"You're welcome. Although, I think it will make you angry."

"Why's that?" Ginny said.

"I don't want to spoil the story for you," Rose said. "It's one of those books that changes how you think. That's all I'm going to say."

"Sounds intriguing," Ginny said.

She caught Rose's eye and raised her eyebrows. Rose gave her a tiny nod. She rummaged in her backpack and brought out a card.

"Happy Birthday, Meg."

Rose took her own card out of her bag and handed it over too.

Meg's face fell. "We haven't bought you normal presents this year," Ginny said hastily, not able to bear the sadness in her face, "because we've decided to give you something between us."

Immediately, Meg's face brightened. "I thought you'd forgotten."

"Of course not," Rose said, putting her hand over Meg's. "It was Ginny's idea, but I think it's a brilliant one. Ginny, over to you."

Ginny turned to face Meg, unable to eke out the suspense any longer. "We've decided to pay to have the memoir printed as our joint birthday present."

Meg's hands flew to her cheeks as her eyes filled with tears. "Thank you both so much! I've been worrying about how I was going to be able to afford it."

"Worry no more," Ginny said. "We're picking up the tab. Just let us know how many copies you want doing and we'll get them done in good time for your Golden Wedding."

"That's brilliant," Meg said, getting up and giving them each a hug. "It's so generous of you both. Are you sure you can afford it?"

"Absolutely sure," Rose said.

Rose

Rose was still mulling over the suggestion from Debbie the following Sunday, while she was driving over to Matthew and Sarah's for lunch. It had been a while, because of her knee – Matthew and Sarah, Jamie and Rosie had visited her a few times while she couldn't drive, but she hadn't seen Ben for ages.

Why hadn't she said anything about Debbie's idea to Ginny and Meg? After all, it had been her editing of Meg's memoir that had inspired Debbie to suggest that she wrote her own.

She slowed down to navigate the narrow, hump-backed bridge and was so grateful that she had; seconds later, she was nearly mown down by an idiot on a motorbike, who came roaring over the hump and missed her car by inches. He could have killed her – or, more likely, the smash could have killed him.

Which didn't make her feel any better. She unclenched her white-knuckled fingers from the steering wheel and carried on, nosing her car slowly over the bridge. Her heart was going twenty to the dozen and she was shaking from reaction, and drove more slowly than normal for the rest of the way. She decided not to tell Matthew and Sarah – she didn't want to rouse Matthew's over-protective instincts.

But when Sarah answered the door, she took one look at her face and said, "Rose! Whatever's wrong? Come in and sit down."

So much for that resolution. Rose forced a smile, but was grateful it was Sarah.

"I had a narrow miss with a motorbike," she said, hearing the thinness in her own voice, "at the humpbacked bridge near the Tibberton turn-off. It shook me up a little."

"What a horrible thing to happen!" Sarah said. "I'm so sorry. You sit there and I'll get you a nice, hot cup of tea."

Rose grabbed Sarah's hand as she was leaving. "Please don't tell Matthew," she said. "He'll only worry himself needlessly, and I'm all right."

"Don't you think he ought to know?"

"No. Like I said, he'd only worry, and I can't have him fussing around me."

Sarah's eyebrows shot up, but she only said, "Okay, if that's the way you want it."

"Thank you."

Just then, Jamie and Rosie came running in, and hugged her as though they hadn't seen her since Christmas.

"Granny! It's lovely to see you," Rosie said.

"And it's lovely to see you too, and you, Jamie. Are you enjoying the holidays?"

She let them prattle on about their latest exploits, which were a lovely antidote to her recent scare. By the time Sarah came in with the tea, she was feeling calm again.

"And we're going to Drayton Manor Park next week," Jamie said, "for a whole day."

"That sounds wonderful," Rose said, smiling at her grandson's excitement. "Is Mummy taking you?"

"Yes," Sarah said. "We're going with Jamie's friend, Sam, and his sister, Sophie, who's a year younger than Rosie. I've been friends with their Mum, Jill, since I was pregnant with Jamie."

"I hope you all have a lovely time," Rose said. "Is Ben coming too?"

"He hasn't decided yet," Sarah said, a sad expression coming over her face. "He used to love it when he was a little boy."

"Well, I hope the weather cools down a bit before then. It's fierce out there today."

"Don't worry, Rose. I'll be taking plenty of suncream, sunhats and big water bottles for all of us."

Just then, Matthew stuck his head round the door. "Hello, Mum," he said. Then to everyone, "lunch is on the table."

Rose got quite a shock when Ben slouched into the kitchen-diner, the ever-present baseball cap on his head. He must have grown three or four inches since she'd last seen him a few months ago.

"Hello, Ben," she said. "How are you?"

And got another shock when a man's deep voice came out of his mouth. "Okay thanks, Granny." His boy's treble was gone forever.

By the time lunch was finished, Rose was worn out. She was no longer used to the volume of noise Matthew's young family could make, when they were all together. Everyone talked over the top of everyone else, and she found it hard to follow the conversation. Time to go home.

On the way back, she suddenly remembered the memoir idea. Why hadn't she mentioned it to Matthew and Sarah? Perhaps it was a silly idea, after all. And she didn't want Meg to think she was copying her.

Which was an even sillier notion. Of course Meg wouldn't think that. Yes, she'd do it. But not until she'd finished Meg and John's sampler. That must come first. In the meantime, it wouldn't do any harm to mull it over in her mind, decide how she'd like to arrange it... When she got home, she took out a notebook and began to scribble down some ideas.

August: *The Handmaid's Tale* by Margaret Atwood

Meg

Ginny had persuaded Meg it would be best to do the photo editing and insertion round at her house, rather than Meg's. For two reasons. First, Ginny had a special photo editing programme on her own laptop and it would be easy to transfer individual photos round there, and second, Meg didn't want John wandering in and making caustic comments.

So a few days after her birthday, Meg packed her laptop, mouse, marked up manuscript and list of photos into her shopping bag and took the bus round to Ginny's.

"Come on in," Ginny said. "I'm looking forward to this."

Meg hugged her. "I am too – I'm so excited."

Ginny led her into the kitchen and they set their laptops up on the kitchen table. "You'll need to log into my wi-fi," Ginny said, "so that we can e-mail back and forth if we need to."

"How do I do that?"

"I'll fetch the password."

Cool drinks to hand, the two of them set to work. Each photo was scrutinised, then edited as necessary, before being inserted at the exact spot in the text. Meg was fascinated by Ginny's expertise – she had tried to insert a photo into the MS herself and had ended up with huge, unbudgeable gaps, when the photos were too big to fit in the place she wanted them to. She had thought that they'd have to put in a few pages of photos after each chapter. But this wasn't how Ginny had decided to do it. She'd asked her to put an asterisk next to the text each photo would be illustrating and Meg hadn't understood why, but had done what she was told.

Watching her friend work was an education. Mainly working at Meg's laptop, she inserted each photo, then wrapped the text around it, so that it was right next door to the story it was illustrating, before adding a caption. It took a good while, especially when Ginny decided that the photo needed more editing than the inbuilt software could cope with. When that happened, she asked Meg to e-mail the photo across to her own laptop, then opened it and used Photoshop to enhance it. But the results were amazing – faded photos Meg had despaired of, thinking they would spoil the look of the book, were brought back to vibrant life.

They stopped part way through for a scratch lunch of cheese and salad baguettes, with another cold drink.

"This is delicious," Meg said, biting into her baguette. "Thank you."

"You're welcome," Ginny said. "I think we've broken the back of it now. The rest should only take us another couple of hours."

"Honestly, I'm so grateful. You're making a brilliant job of them."

"I'm happy to help. I can't wait to see your family's faces when they receive them."

"They're going to be thrilled, I know it."

Back to work. By the time they were done, Meg's back was aching from sitting in one position for so long. But her heart was exulting – the illustrated memoir looked fabulous.

"Do you want to use particular photos for the back and front covers?" Ginny said.

"Oh! I hadn't thought of that. Yes, that would be great."

"Which ones then?"

"The back cover's easy," Meg said. "I'd like to use the photo of all of us together, that Richard took on my 70th birthday. He set up a tripod and did it on a timer, so that he could be in it too."

"What about the front cover?"

"I don't know… what do you think?"

"It has to be something that summarises what the memoir's about – the wonder and marvel of an ordinary life."

As soon as Ginny said that, the idea came. "Would it be possible," Meg said, a little hesitantly, "to have a circle of photos, each in a round frame, with the title in the middle? Then I could use seven different ones, one for each decade of my life."

Ginny blew her cheeks out. "Blimey," she said. "That could be complicated."

Meg hastened to apologise. "I'm sorry," she said. "You've done enough already. Forget about it. I'll try to think of something else."

"Uh-uh," Ginny said, wagging a finger at her. "I *like* complicated. I'm sure there will be a way to do it."

And there was. It took another hour to get it done to Ginny's satisfaction, but by the time she was finished, Meg was beyond thrilled.

"Oh, Ginny," she said. "It looks fantastic. Thank you

so much."

Ginny grinned at her. "It does, rather, doesn't it?"

"What do I have to do next?"

"We'll turn it all into a PDF, then you can send it to Dropbox and I'll collect it."

"Dropbox? What's that?"

"It's a file hosting service. We should be able to set up a free account for you. Move over."

And in less time than it took to tell, Ginny had set up a Dropbox account on Meg's laptop and sent the precious manuscript to it.

"Now it's up to me," she said. "Rose and I have agreed that I'll organise the printing and we'll split the cost two ways."

"I can't tell you how grateful I am to you both," Meg said.

"We're happy to do it for you. Now, how many copies do you want?"

"Let me think. One for me and John, one for Jessica and Mark, one for Andrew and Richard, and one each for Katie and Becky. Oh, and one each for you and Rose." She counted up on her fingers. "That's seven."

"Seven it is," Ginny said. "Leave it with me."

Ginny

"Come on," Ginny said as Meg packed up her stuff, ready to leave. "I'll give you a lift home. You can't wait for the bus in this."

'This' being a sudden, fierce downpour, which had

turned the August sky almost black.

"Thank you," Meg panted, as they ran for the car. "I'd have been soaked to the skin in this little lot."

"No trouble," Ginny said gruffly. She hated being thanked for small kindnesses.

Once they were in the car, she had to turn her headlights on – to be seen, rather than to see – which was ridiculous at this time of year. "It won't take many minutes."

There was silence in the car as they drove through the rain-slicked streets, darkly reflective in the headlights' beams, the windscreen wipers going twenty to the dozen. She needed all her concentration to see where they were going, and to avoid the idiots driving far too close in this kind of weather.

It had been a good day, but an exhausting one. As she dropped off an effusively grateful Meg outside her house, the tiredness suddenly hit her. It had been a long time since she'd shared her private space with someone else for so many hours – Meg had arrived just after half-past nine and it was now nearly six.

But she couldn't have done the editing work round at Meg's. Her one experience of her friend's house had been when she'd picked her up before John's trial, and she had found it overwhelming. Meg was a great collector of ornaments and knick-knacks – every available flat surface was crowded with figurines and framed photographs. As a result of which, Ginny had been entirely unable to relax while she was there. The house had made her feel cramped and claustrophobic, even though it was almost certainly larger than her own neat home.

Her own taste was far more pared back – minimal,

that was the word. Each room had one or two pictures – although she had been tempted lately to print out a couple of her best flower photos on A4 art paper and display them in plain wooden frames. But generally, she preferred her wall art to be carefully chosen and even more carefully placed, to show them off to their best effect. And of course, she loved her house plants.

And she wasn't a collector, which Meg obviously was. Her own few ornaments had each been selected for the memories they held – like the gorgeous brass singing bowl, which reminded her of Laura. They'd bought it at an antiques fair years ago and Ginny loved the way it sang. And the wooden mantel clock – one of the few items she'd kept from her parents' home.

It was fascinating, how the interiors of Meg's, Rose's, and her own homes expressed their differing personalities, with Meg's kaleidoscopic displays at one end of the spectrum and her own spare minimalism at the other. Rose was somewhere in between – she had some ornaments and photos, and more wall art than Ginny, but all presented with impeccable taste. She'd enjoyed spending those weeks living with Rose far more than she had expected. She'd come to feel at home there.

Oh well. Each to their own. No doubt her own house felt heartlessly spartan to Meg.

Rose

"So it's going to cost nearly £275 between the two of us," Ginny said.

Rose transferred the phone to her other ear and groped for a chair. "Ouch," she said, "I didn't think it was going to cost that much."

"Are you still up for splitting the cost?"

"Of course. I just wasn't expecting it to be so expensive."

"I think it's on account of all the photos – colour printing costs so much more – and also that Meg wants hard covers, rather than paperbacks."

"I don't blame her – they're going to be family heirlooms, after all. And I suppose when you think about it that way, £275 isn't much… When do you want me to transfer the cash to your account? I'll need your banking details."

"Thank you," Ginny said. "Any time now would be good. I've already sent it to the printer. Have you got pen and paper handy?"

"Hang on a tick… yes, I have now."

Ginny told her the account details, then asked, "How's the sampler coming along?"

"Really well, thank you. But it's taking longer than I thought it would – it's the most intricate design I've attempted."

"In what way?"

"Do you remember the sampler I chose, with three big golden yellow roses in each corner?"

Ginny murmured her assent. "Well, each rose has more than two hundred stitches in five different shades of yellow, gold and cream, and I've decided to include part-stitches rather than following the pattern, which leaves empty triangles inside the backstitch borders, which I think looks tacky and amateurish. And the leaf border is similarly complicated. I've done three of the four three-rose corners now and most of the rest of the border. So I ought to have it finished in good time."

"It sounds gorgeous."

"What are you giving them?"

"I've been quite sneaky," Ginny said, her voice clanging with satisfaction. "When I was helping Meg to add all the photos to her book, I saved a selection away and am going to create a photographic collage of their lives, then frame it in a gold-coloured frame."

"She'll love that, I'm sure," Rose said. "You'll have to come round to mine to give me a sneak preview when it's done and I'll do the same for you."

"It's a date," Ginny said. "How are you otherwise?"

"So relieved that the heatwave has finally ended. I was beginning to think I'd never be cool again."

Ginny laughed. "Me too. It's been too hot even for me."

"How are you going to manage in India then?"

"It won't apply. The weather will be in the mid-20s for most of it in November. I'm getting so excited about it now."

"I don't blame you – it sounds fabulous."

"Well, I'd better crack on if I want to get this sampler done," Rose said. "See you in a couple of weeks."

"Looking forward to it."

Meg

Now that John couldn't drive, Meg was having to do a food shop more frequently, as there was a limit to what her faithful shopping trolley could hold. But this particular trip was for pleasure, rather than business – she'd decided to bake a rather special multi-tiered cake for their anniversary celebration, and needed to do a trial run before the big day. She trudged back to the bus-stop nearest the supermarket, lugging her wheeled shopping trolley behind her, her mind full of cake, and the trolley full of ingredients.

It was getting late and she knew that John would be home from AA by now, and would be counting on his supper being on the table at its usual time. It had taken longer than she had expected to locate one or two of the more unusual ingredients on the supermarket shelves, like the black treacle.

She had nearly reached the bus-stop when one of the trolley's little wheels caught in some uneven paving and stuck. Annoyed, she tugged at it and it abruptly came free, cannoning into the back of her legs and sending her flying. Instinctively, she threw out her free hand to save herself, but that was a mistake. She landed on it heavily and wrong, folding it underneath her.

The pain was immediate and agonising and she couldn't help crying out, hot tears springing to her eyes. She rolled off it and tried to sit up, which wasn't easy with only one good hand. Then she realised that her handbag had flown off her shoulder and burst open on the pavement, scattering its contents far and wide – her purse, her bus pass, her phone – everything. She tried to reach her mobile, so that she could ring John, but it was out of reach.

At least her expensive new varifocals hadn't broken. They were still on the bridge of her nose, a little askew, but intact.

Then she heard heavily booted feet nearby. She looked up and saw a hulking young man, wearing distressed jeans and a hoodie, striding towards her. Both his nose and his left eyebrow were pierced and she could see tattoos on his neck. Oh God! Was he going to mug her?

"You all right, love? You came one hell of a purler."

She looked again, and saw the concern in his eyes. "No, I'm not. I think – I think my wrist is broken."

She held it out to him and they both looked at it. Already it was red and swollen, and didn't look like a normal wrist at all.

"Hang on, love. Don't try to move. Kev!" This last over his shoulder to an equally tough looking young man. "This lady's broke her wrist. Pick up the stuff from her handbag and put it all back in."

"Thank you," Meg said faintly. She was shivering in spite of the warmth of the afternoon, and her head was beginning to swim. She couldn't faint, not now.

"I'm Jordan," her rescuer said. "You'd better take those rings off, before your hand swells up too much."

Meg did as she was told, glad that he'd thought of it – she wouldn't have done.

"I'm going to ring for an ambulance," he said. "Hang on in there."

A couple of minutes later, he knelt down beside her. "All done," he said. "How are you feeling?"

Meg shook her head. It was all she could do not to scream with the pain.

He patted her shoulder awkwardly. "I'll stay with you until the ambulance arrives."

"Thank you," Meg managed to say. "You're so kind."

"No worries," he said. "I'd want someone to help my Gran if she was in trouble. Is there anyone else I can ring?"

"My husband, John. John Jeffries. His number's in my mobile."

Jordan handed her bag to her, which had been roughly packed by his friend, who was now hovering in the background. Meg rootled around for her phone with her good hand, trying to ignore the agony in her other wrist.

"Oh no!" she said. "The screen's smashed."

"No worries," he said again. "Tell me his number and I'll ring him on mine."

And he did. He couldn't have been kinder if he'd been her own Andrew. Forty minutes later, there was still no sign of an ambulance, but John arrived.

Rose

"…and I was so frightened when he came up to me," Meg continued. "But I needn't have been – he was so kind. He waited with me until John arrived and couldn't have been kinder if I'd been his own grandmother."

"I'm so glad he was there," Rose said. "Most people are decent when it comes to the crunch. Such a horrible experience, though."

She could only too easily imagine herself in Meg's

situation – even with her new knee, she was still afraid of falling, of injuring herself. The fruits of getting older. "So what happened next?"

"It took ages for the ambulance to arrive, but it came in the end. My wrist was so painful – the worst pain I've ever experienced, outside of labour."

"What did they say at the hospital?"

"I've somehow managed to break two bones at once, and it's going to have to be in plaster for weeks."

"Oh, no! And with your anniversary coming up too."

"Exactly. The only reason I was out shopping in the first place was to buy ingredients for a trial run for the anniversary cake. It's going to be almost impossible to do all the baking with only one hand. I was looking forward to it so much, and now…"

Meg's voice choked on a sob. "Hey, hey," Rose said. "Don't cry. How long did the hospital say it would take to get better?"

"Six to eight weeks, which is long after our anniversary."

"Don't worry, I'm sure Ginny and I can pitch in to help, and Jessica too."

"Would you really? Oh, that would be wonderful. Thank you so much."

"Of course we will," Rose said briskly. "I know you'd help me if I was in the same boat and I'm sure Ginny will want to do whatever she can, too."

"You've no idea what a weight off my mind that is," Meg said.

"What about this month's book club meeting?" Rose

said, changing the subject. "Do you want us to come round to you? Or I could pick you up from home and bring you to Capuchins."

"I think I'd rather have it at Capuchin's," Meg said.

"Then I'll pick you up at 10.30. Do you want me to let Ginny know?"

"Yes, please."

Rose sighed as she replaced the receiver. As much as Meg might rant about John's many shortcomings as a husband, at least she still had him around... No, that wasn't fair. It wasn't Meg's fault that Graham had died. What kind of friend was she, anyway? Rose pulled herself together.

This called for hot chocolate – hang the diet for once. What's more, it called for hot chocolate made with milk, boiled on the hob. Nothing less than its sweet, indulgent creaminess was needed to dissolve the wave of bitter grief that threatened to overwhelm her.

Enough already. Of course she still missed him, even eighteen months on. It wouldn't be natural not to. But she was lucky, really. Rose knew that if she'd had a fall, she would have been able to call Matthew or Sarah. Or Ginny, if they were both at work. So many elderly women had no-one to call on.

She walked across to the kitchen sink to splash cold water on her face, then whirled as she heard the hiss of boiling milk. She snatched the milk pan off the hob just in time to prevent it going everywhere. Then poured it into the largest mug she could find, added several teaspoons of hot chocolate, before taking it through to the lounge to savour, slowly.

She'd better finish re-reading *The Handmaid's Tale* – it was book group next Wednesday.

Meg

"Oh my goodness! What happened to you?" Ginny said as she joined Meg and Rose at their usual table in Capuchins.

"My shopping trolley tripped me up a week or so ago," Meg said, "and I've broken two bones in my wrist."

"Your shopping trolley tripped you up? How on earth?"

"Not a supermarket trolley," Meg said, grinning as she realised what Ginny was thinking. "It's one of those shopping bags on wheels, and one of them got stuck in the pavement. I tugged on it and it came free and flew into the back of my legs, knocking me over."

"Ah, I see. Poor you. What a horrible thing to happen."

"Yes," Rose put in, "and it means she won't be able to do much if any of the preparation for the anniversary party, which is less than a month away."

"We'll help," Ginny said.

"I hoped you'd say that," Rose said. "We're all yours, Meg. Just let us know what you need us to do, and we'll be there."

"Bless you both," Meg said, a warm glow in her heart. "Jessica's coming over at the weekend to help me plan everything, so I'll let you know what I need after that."

"Fair enough," Rose said. "What did you both think

of *The Handmaid's Tale?*"

"I found it horrifying," Ginny said. "That women should have all their rights taken away from them, and be owned by a man they have to have sex with. Reading it made me feel... I don't know, dirty. And it made me more passionate than ever for feminism."

Rose nodded. "I agree. Although it's only a story, it made me remember how lucky we are here, to have more or less equal rights with men."

Ginny snorted. "More in theory than in practice. There's still a long way to go before women can go out at night without fear. There are still far too many women being taken advantage of by unscrupulous men."

"You sound so fierce," Meg said.

"I feel fierce," Ginny said, "every time I read about a woman being raped or abducted or abused by a man. It still happens far too often."

"I think I can understand," Meg said. "After all, I was frightened of Jordan when he first came up to me."

"Jordan? Who's that?"

"He's the young man who helped me after my fall. When I saw him coming towards me, I was afraid he was going to mug me. But he was so kind – he looked after me until John came, and rang the ambulance and everything."

"Yes," Rose said. "It's good to remember that most people are kind and decent. And that the bad people are the outliers rather than the norm."

Ginny shrugged, seemingly unconvinced. "I guess so. It still makes my blood boil, though. Why are some men so predatory?"

"I don't know," Rose said. "But I do sometimes wonder how different our world would be if it was run by women instead of by men."

Huh? Meg couldn't imagine it. But Ginny was gazing off into space, her eyes far away.

"Penny for them?" Meg said.

Ginny grinned at her. "I was just thinking how very different things would be. Women are so much less aggressive than men, much keener to preserve relationships than to destroy them. And not so territorial."

"Hmm," Rose said. "I'm not so sure about that. I'm pretty certain that if the family or close friends of any woman were threatened, most women I know would leap to their defence, and fight to the death to protect them."

"Ye-es," Ginny said. "I guess so. Perhaps acquisitive would be a better word than territorial. But the point I'm making is, she wouldn't be the aggressor. Most wars today seem to be caused by governments greedy for land and power. And most governments are overwhelmingly male."

Rose sighed. "I can't disagree with that. And it's the women who are left to pick up the pieces afterwards, and build new lives for themselves and their families."

"Exactly," Ginny said. "Women are so much more practical than most men."

Meg didn't like the contempt in Ginny's voice – surely all men weren't like that? Her own Andrew certainly wasn't. She was about to open her lips and say so, but too late. Ginny swept on regardless.

"Talking about powerful women, I was scrolling through the environment posts in my Instagram feed the other day, and came across one by a Swedish teenager, Greta Thunberg, who's decided to skip school to draw attention to the climate change crisis."

"How does that work?" Meg said. "I can't see the link between them."

"She sitting outside the Swedish Parliament building," Ginny said, "with a placard reading, 'Skolstrejk för Klimatet'. And I loved what she'd written in the caption – hang on, let me bring it up on my phone."

There was a short silence while Ginny retrieved the post. Then she passed it first to Rose, who then passed it to Meg. Meg saw a picture of a very ordinary looking mid-teen child with long blonde plaits, wearing leopard print trousers and a blue hoodie, a placard in front of her. Then she read the caption: 'We children don't usually do what you grown-ups tell us to do. We do as you do. And since you don't give a shit about my future, I don't give a shit either.' Charming.

"It's only been a week since she started," Ginny said, her voice warm with enthusiasm, "and already her post's gone viral. She's planning to sit out there every day, handing out home-made leaflets, until the Swedish government agrees to implement the Paris Agreement."

"What's the Paris Agreement?" Meg said, puzzled. Then winced internally as Ginny scowled at her.

"Haven't you heard of it?"

Meg hated the scorn in her friend's voice.

"Hang on, Ginny," Rose said, "that's not entirely fair. It's not Meg's fault she doesn't know about it."

Ginny's cheeks flushed, and she nodded to both of them. "Sorry, Meg. It's hard for me to remember that not everyone is as passionate about saving the world as I am. Okay. The Paris Agreement," she continued in a calmer voice, "was signed at the end of 2015 by nearly 200 countries, and is a legally binding international treaty on climate change, which should have come into force in November 2016. But so many countries have been dragging their feet, because adopting it will mean making major changes to the way we all live."

"What sort of changes?"

"For a start, we need to stop relying on fossil fuels for our energy and switch to renewable sources. We need to shift to electric cars, rather than gas guzzlers, and learn to shop only from sustainable, fair-traded suppliers. And stop eating meat. And start repairing our stuff rather than throwing it out. And find ways to right the imbalances between the decadent West and the developing world. Oh, there are so many changes people could make. But most folk seem unable to see beyond their own short-term comfort. What they don't seem to understand is that if we carry on as we are, there won't *be* a habitable planet for our grandchildren."

Rose was nodding her agreement. Meg felt so stupid. She'd never even thought about any of this. Was it really true?

"But if it's as bad as you say," she said timidly, "what can we do to make a difference?"

"Everyone can do their bit," Ginny said passionately. "Did you know that doing something as simple as switching to a vegetarian diet would have a massive impact on the amounts of methane in the atmosphere?"

"Give up meat?" Meg said, dismayed. "I'm not sure that John would be able to do that. And I love cooking my Sunday roast."

Ginny snapped her fingers impatiently. "Even cutting down would help," she said. "Perhaps you could try being vegetarian during the week, and only eat meat at the weekends."

"Hmm, I guess so."

"What about flying?" Rose said. "Isn't that one of the worst things we can do?"

Ginny sat back in her chair. "I know," she said. "It's making me feel really guilty about my India plans. Perhaps I should cancel them. Because it won't only be the flights out and back – the distances are so vast over there, I'll be flying between places too."

"Couldn't you ask to go by train?" Meg said.

Ginny's face brightened immediately. "That's a brilliant idea. Thank you!"

Rose changed the subject. Meg envied her ability to do this tactfully, without seeming pushy. "What's next month's book, Ginny?"

"I haven't quite decided yet," Ginny said. "I've just finished reading *The Overstory* by Richard Powers. I haven't read a book that has excited me so much for ages. But I'm not sure it will be your cup of tea – either of you."

"Why?" Meg said. "What's it about?"

"It's quite complicated," Ginny said. "It's about nine very different people, who for one reason or another decide that they need to do something to save trees from being exploited by human beings. Because, you know, forests are the lungs of the Earth, and we're losing them at a frightening rate."

Meg groaned silently. It sounded both heavy and

boring. "So why haven't you decided yet?"

"Well, it's only available in hardback at the moment," Ginny said. "But I'd be happy to lend you my copy."

"Let's give it a try," Rose said. "I enjoy a challenge."

Ginny

Rose and Meg left Capuchins first. Ginny bought herself another herbal tea, and sat at their table, deep in thought. She hadn't handled that at all well. Poor Meg! She hadn't deserved being ranted at like that. How to make amends?

Perhaps she was wrong to want them to read *The Overstory*. Even she had found it hard going at times, with all the switching between viewpoints. So she knew that Meg at least would find it a tough read. What could she choose instead, to make it up to her, without seeming obvious? She put her cup back down and strode up to the counter.

"Karen, do you have any good reads about the environment?"

"That's a pretty big subject. What do you mean?"

"Oh, something that gives an overview of the issues without being too heavy. I want to make it my read for next month's book club meeting. I'd thought of making them read Richard Powers' *The Overstory*, but I think they'd both find it too heavy."

"Yeah, I struggled with that one – I gave up two-thirds of the way through." She raised the flap of the counter and came out into the shop. "Let's have a look."

She walked over to the science and nature shelf and ran her fingers along the spines of the books. "Gotcha," she said, hooking out a slim paperback, and handing it to Ginny with a broad grin. "This came in last week, and I had a quick look through it. I think it may be exactly what you're looking for."

Enough: Breaking Free from the World of Excess by John Naish. Ginny turned to the introduction and started to read. Oh my, this was perfect. His writing was wryly amusing and got his message across without preaching.

"Bless you," she said. "This looks perfect. Let's see… when was it published?" She flipped to the back of the title page. "Hmm, 2008. I hope it's still in print."

She pulled out her phone and looked it up on Amazon. It was. Excellent. "I'll have this copy please," she told Karen. "And I'll let the other two know I've changed my mind. I know that Meg at least will be relieved."

"Always happy to help," Karen said. "I've enjoyed having your reading group in here."

Ginny smiled at her. "We wouldn't consider going anywhere else." She stowed the book away in her backpack and continued, "See you next month."

Rose

Rose's phone pinged as she drew up on her drive after dropping Meg home. Ginny. What could she want to say so soon after their meeting?

> Hello Rose and Meg,
> DON'T order *The Overstory!* I'm texting you
> both straight away in the hope that you

haven't already done so. Karen has helped me find a perfectly brilliant alternative, which is much more readable. It's called *Enough: Breaking Free from the World of Excess,* and is by a guy called John Naish. I read the introduction in Capuchins' and think you'll both really enjoy it.

Love,

Ginny x

PS Please text me back to let me know you've read this in time.

Well, that was a relief. She hadn't been looking forward to a heavy read, even if Ginny had recommended it. She'd order it straight away, after texting Ginny back.

She had been quite worried about the future of their little group earlier after Ginny's rant and Meg's obvious discomfort. They were so very different from each other – Ginny tall, elegant, independent, self-confident, yet introverted, and Meg so much the opposite: short and cuddly, family-orientated and with dismally low self-esteem. She seemed to be the glue who held the three of them together. Meg had been quite upset in the car on the way home and Rose had had to soothe her, while simultaneously thinking that Ginny had been out of line.

But it seemed that Ginny had realised this, and that the alternative book was her way of trying to make amends. Which was good. She valued their friendship enormously and wasn't sure how she would have got through the last eighteen months without the pair of them.

She'd better have some lunch. Lesley had changed her piano lesson to this afternoon, as one of her students needed a lift to her piano exam at Rose's usual time. It was a nuisance having it on the same day as book group, but it was the only time Lesley had available. Oh well, it was only for once.

"Thank you for being flexible, Rose," Lesley said as she walked in. "Neither of Kyle's parents could get time off work to take him to his exam tomorrow, so I said I'd pick him up from school and take him, then deliver him back home. His mum will be back by then."

"Not a problem," Rose said. "I remember only too well the difficulties of juggling work with child responsibilities."

She sat down at the piano and looked at her teacher, now almost another friend. "What are we doing today?"

"I think," Lesley said, "that you're ready to start working towards your Grade I exam. Your playing has come on by leaps and bounds since you started with me a year ago."

This was a bombshell. She hadn't even considered the possibility of doing exams. When she told Lesley that, her teacher's response was typically breezy.

"Nonsense. So many of my adult learners say that. But I honestly believe that it will help to motivate you to keep practising every day. What do you say?"

Rose thought for a moment, then shrugged mentally. In for a penny, in for a pound. "Well, if you really think it would be good for me… What does it involve exactly?"

"Excellent. I've got you a copy of the current Grade I

syllabus and I thought we could choose your three pieces and make a start on the first one today. I've got a CD with all of them on which we can listen to, and you can choose which ones appeal to you."

Rose took the book from her and began to look through it. "It looks like a lot more than three pieces. I don't know anything about arpeggios or broken chords. And what's an 'aural test'?"

"I don't think you'll find the arpeggios and broken chords difficult," Lesley said. "You've always been good at your scales and they're quite similar. And an aural test is simply checking how well you hear and understand music; the examiner will ask you to guess the time signature to a piece of music and clap the beat; to sing back a tune like an echo; and to recognise articulation, speed and dynamics when you hear them."

Rose's heart sank – this sounded complicated. "Do you really think I'm ready?"

"I wouldn't have suggested it, otherwise," Lesley said. "If we start working towards it now, you should be ready to sit the exam next March."

"Okay, you've sold me."

"Excellent," Lesley said again. "Let's listen to those pieces."

There were three pieces to choose – one from each of three categories. After listening to them all, they agreed on *The Agincourt Song*, a 15th century English carol which had such a rousing, strong, rhythmic tune; a soulful legato piece with gentle dynamics called *The Lonely Road* by Felix Swinstead; and *Happy Day* by Ian King, which had a swing rhythm and a jaunty tune which lifted Rose's spirits. Plus which, it was in G Major, so only one sharp to worry about.

Rose left feeling quite excited – this was going to be a great challenge, but fun too.

September: *Enough: Breaking Free from a World of Excess* by John Naish

Meg

In spite of having to operate one-handed, Meg's preparations for the Big Day were coming along nicely. Which was a good job – it was September tomorrow and their 'do' was planned for Saturday the 8th, three days before their actual anniversary. Luckily it wasn't the wrist on her writing hand that was in plaster, so she was still able to make copious lists. She currently had three different ones on the go: To Do, Food Shopping, and Other Preparation. The second one was currently blank, a situation she planned to remedy today, when Jessica came round.

John was being surprisingly solicitous about her injury – there was hope for him yet. He'd promised to do all the shopping and Jessica, Rose and Ginny had all offered to help with getting the house spruced up ready for the party. It would be a bit cramped, but Meg didn't care. It would be so wonderful to have all the family and her two best friends there on her special day. She caught herself – on her and John's special day.

The doorbell rang. John was out at his AA meeting, so Meg rushed down the hall to answer the doorbell. "Jessica! Come in, darling."

Jessica hugged her carefully. "Hi, Mum. Here I am, ready and willing to do whatever you need me to."

"Bless you, love. Come into the kitchen and I'll make us a cup of tea."

"No," and Jessica frowned at her, "*you* sit down and *I'll* make the tea."

Meg smiled to herself. Her daughter reminded her so much of John sometimes – dictatorial, that was the word.

"It's only shop-bought biscuits, I'm afraid," Meg said. "They're in the usual tin."

"Triple chocolate chip cookies – nom, nom!" Jessica said, and took two before handing the tin to Meg.

"I've been doing a lot of planning," Meg told her, absent-mindedly helping herself to a biscuit before putting the lid back on the tin. "and I've decided who to invite, and have some thoughts about the food I want to provide – although I'd like some ideas for Katie and Becky."

"That's easy," Jessica said with a grin, "in lieu of Nana's biscuits, anything with chocolate would go down fine."

"But they can't just eat chocolate," Meg protested. "What about savouries?"

"Let me think… if we cook a pizza, they'd enjoy slices of that, and both of them love cheese. Hang on," and her face brightened, "I've had a brilliant idea! You could go with a sixties theme and do things like cheddar and pineapple on sticks – oh, and cocktail sausages on sticks too. I think it would be great fun to have the sort of food that was around at parties when you and Dad were courting. Apart from that, crisps and nice biscuits and grapes should be plenty. The girls will be too excited to eat much, I expect."

"I really like your idea of doing sixties food," Meg said thoughtfully. "Let me see… I remember little sausage rolls being popular, and mini pork pies, and Scotch eggs, and

I think plain quiches were just coming in. We could buy all those at the supermarket. And we could get a grapefruit, cut it in half and stick the cheddar and pineapple on sticks and sausages on sticks in the halves. That used to be really trendy. And a couple of baguettes – we used to call them French sticks – sliced thin and spread with butter. Oh, and some green olives."

"We'd better provide a few more healthy choices," Jessica said, "for the folk who don't want to die of cholesterol poisoning."

"I see your point. And of course there's Ginny to think about too – she's vegetarian, and Rose is coeliac. I'll have to make sure we have something nice for them too. Sainsburys probably does a gluten-free vegetarian quiche, and we could provide carrots and peppers and things and a couple of dips, and a rice salad. And it would be wonderful if you could make some cheese straws – home-made ones are so much tastier than shop-bought ones."

"Ginny and Rose are coming too?" Jessica said, surprised. "I thought it was going to be just family."

"Rose and Ginny are the best friends I've had in years. They've stood by me through thick and thin this last year or so. It wouldn't seem right not to invite them."

"Fair enough." Jessica shrugged. "Two more won't make much difference."

As they'd been talking, she'd been writing down what Meg had said. She passed the list across the table. "Anything else you can think of?"

"Well, there's the cake," Meg said. "I'm really fed up that I won't be able to bake it myself, but I'm grateful to you for stepping in. I've already written a list of ingredients and copied the recipe out for you. Here it is." And she gave the list to her daughter. "And of course, being a fruit cake, you can make it a few days in advance."

Jessica's eyes widened as she read. "Wow! This looks complicated. But I'm sure I'll manage, with a few days' grace."

"I'd already bought some of the ingredients," Meg said, "when I had that fall. I've marked them on the list with a star. Let me know what the total bill comes to and I'll ask your Dad to transfer the money to your account."

Jessica nodded. "Fair enough. What about drinks?"

Meg met her gaze. "I've decided to stick with alcohol-free Prosecco – I think it's called Nosecco. They do it in both white and rosé varieties. I don't want to have any booze in the house, on your Dad's account. He's been so good these past few months, it wouldn't be fair to tempt him."

"Sounds fine to me," Jessica said. "Mark and Andrew and your friends will all be driving anyway, so it will save them from being tempted too. But we'd better provide coke or lemonade for the girls."

"I feel so much better now that's all sorted out," Meg said.

"What else do you need me to do?"

"If you could possibly come round the day before and help me with the final clean, that would be great. I can do things like dusting one-handed, but we'll have to lug every chair we own down the stairs to seat everyone. But your Dad will help too."

"Hopefully, this nice weather will continue till then,

and we'll be able to use the garden as well," Jessica said.

"That's a good idea."

"I'll take the day off work on the Friday, and come round as soon as the girls are at school... Talking of which, I'd better fly. It's time to pick them up from the holiday club – last session of the holidays."

She dropped a kiss on Meg's head and was off down the hall at a gallop.

Rose

Rose was feeling rather excited. Ginny had just rung to ask whether she could drop by to give her a sneak preview of Meg's memoir in book form. Good job she'd finished the sampler in time to reciprocate the favour.

Come away in," she said, when her friend rang the doorbell. "What would you like to drink?"

"Something long and cold, if you have it, please," Ginny said. "The worst of the heat may be over, but it's still warm out, behind glass."

"Come into the kitchen, we can sit there."

One long cold drink later, Ginny sat back with a sigh. "That hit the spot," she said. "Thank you."

"You're welcome. I hope you're not going to keep me on tenterhooks any longer. I can't wait to see it. It's been ages since I've read it."

"Oh, of course, I'd forgotten you'd edited it for her. Here it is."

Ginny produced a thick A4 book in a handsome binding out of her backpack and passed it across.

Rose opened it eagerly and began to leaf through it. "It looks wonderful with all the photographs in," she said, smiling at Ginny. "Meg is going to be thrilled, and I think her family will be too."

She handed it back reluctantly and Ginny stowed it away in her pack. "I'm going round early on the day to drop all the copies off, but I wanted you to see it first."

"That was kind. I've got something to show you too," Rose said, trying but failing to keep the triumph out of her voice. "I've finished the sampler!"

"What? Framed as well?"

"Yes, stretched, laced, and framed. Hang on, I'll go and fetch it." Rose took up her stick, which had been leaning in the corner of the kitchen. She wasn't sure she'd ever feel entirely secure without it. "Back in a tick."

"Here we are," she said, giving it to Ginny. "What do you think?"

"Oh, it's gorgeous! I hope they'll appreciate how much work has gone into it. It's a work of art."

"Thank you, my friend, that means a lot," Rose said, feeling her cheeks grow warm. "It was great fun to do."

"Has she asked you to do anything for the day?" Ginny said. "She's asked me to bring along my favourite vegetarian sweet and she'll pay me for it."

"Same here, but coeliac," Rose replied. "I asked whether there was any housework she needed doing, and she told me Jessica had it all in hand."

"That's good," Ginny said. "Have you started to read the John Naish book yet?"

"Started, and finished. I absolutely loved it, even if it

is a bit out of date. If he ever does a second edition, it'd have to include all sorts of new things that weren't around in the noughties, like smart phones and social media. But I loved the underlying message and it's really made me think."

"Good. That was what I hoped." Ginny stood up. "I'd better go now – Sofi will be wanting her tea."

Rose laughed. "Cats are such tyrants."

Meg

Meg peeped around the bedroom curtains and sighed with relief. A beautiful blue sky day, with high, white, wispy clouds. This day had to be perfect. What time was it? Quarter to eight. She'd better get on – everyone was due to arrive at 11.30 and she wanted to be ready for them.

Dressing in what she called her 'housework clothes' – a faded pair of elasticated-waist trousers and a blouse that had seen better days – she crept downstairs and breakfasted as quickly as possible. Fortunately, the kitchen was at the opposite corner of the house to their bedroom, so she wouldn't disturb John with her preparations.

By 9.30, the kitchen was as immaculate as she could make it with one hand, and all the food was ready – either sitting in the fridge or waiting to be cooked. She sat down at the kitchen table with a well-earned cup of tea and nibbled on a couple of chocolate digestives.

John walked in, yawning. "Blimey," he said, looking around. "What time did you get up?"

"I couldn't sleep, so I came down and started work. Sit down and I'll get you your breakfast."

He kissed her cheek. "Bless you, Meggie. You don't need to worry – it's all going to go well."

"I really hope so," she said. "It's not every day we celebrate our Golden Wedding."

She left him eating, and began the final tidy round and hoover through. Then went back to check that John had cleared up after himself – he had, which was a surprise. Which left a scant half hour to get herself ready. Things being as they were, she hadn't been able to afford a new dress for the occasion, but she'd found a pretty one at the back of the wardrobe, and washed and ironed it. Now, make-up or no make-up? She never wore any usually, but this was a special occasion…. No, she'd only forget and rub her eyes or something and smudge it all. In the end, she stuck to her usual lipstick. Then walked back downstairs, her tummy all a flutter, to wait in the lounge for the first arrival.

As she'd hoped, it was Ginny, holding a gorgeous bouquet of bright sunflowers, yellow gerberas, paler yellow alstroemerias and golden yellow roses. "Thank you," she said, hugging her. "They're beautiful."

"The books are in the car," Ginny said. "D'you want me to bring them in now, so that you can hide them somewhere?"

"That's a great idea, thank you. I can't wait to see them. It was so good of you and Rose to pay for them."

"I thought you might like to write in each one," Ginny said. "Where can we do that?"

"In the dining room, I think. But I must put these into water first. This way."

She was halfway through writing the inscriptions,

fighting against an almost irresistible urge to browse through the books, when the doorbell rang again. John could answer it. She rushed through the rest of the inscriptions, then she and Ginny hid the books in the sideboard, before joining the party.

And was nearly bowled over by Katie and Becky dashing up to hug her. "Hello, darlings," she said. "I'm so glad to see you."

"Steady on, you two," Mark said from behind them. "Don't knock Nana down."

Just then, the doorbell went again and Andrew and Richard arrived, followed shortly afterwards by Rose, who was carrying a large, flat, rectangular parcel.

"Hello Meg," she said, and Meg smelled her signature perfume as Rose leaned in for a kiss. "Happy Anniversary!"

"Come on in," Meg said. "Everyone's here now."

"Sorry if I'm a bit late – it was hard to find somewhere to park."

"You're not at all late – Andrew and Richard have only just arrived."

Meg led the way into the lounge, where everyone was assembled, every available seat occupied, and the two little ones sharing the footstool. As she looked around the room, her heart was full. This was going to be such a special day.

"Present time, I think," Jessica said. "Sit down, Mum. It's our time to treat you and Dad."

Meg sat next to John on the sofa, her heart beating fast, not at all sure what to expect.

"Here's our contribution," Jessica said, handing over a soft, squishy parcel. Meg tore open the paper, to reveal a cushion made of cream silk. "Thank you, darling," she said, a little confused.

"Silly Nana," Katie said. "You have to turn it over."

Meg did what she was told and gasped. On the other side of the cushion was a stylised family tree all done in gold embroidery, with her and John's names at the top, and the rest of the family's lower down, and the date at the bottom. "Oh! That's lovely," she said. "Look, John."

"It *is* lovely," he said, giving Jessica a hug, "thank you, love."

"Our turn now," Andrew said. "This is from Richard and me."

'This' was a large, square parcel. Once again, Meg ripped off the paper, to find a navy blue box.

"Look inside, look inside," Becky said, dancing up and down on the balls of her feet.

Meg took the lid off the box. "Careful, Mum," Andrew said. "It's fragile."

Her fingers trembling, she reached in, and drew out a glass dome, under which an exquisite golden rose bloomed. "Ah, that's beautiful," she said.

"It's a real rose, which they've somehow preserved in gold," Andrew said. "I thought you'd like it."

"Like it? I love it!" Meg placed it carefully on a side table, so that everyone could admire it.

"My turn now," Rose said. "Happy Anniversary, Meg and John."

Meg had been wondering what was inside Rose's mysterious parcel. Now she'd find out.

"Oh, Rose," she said, as the sampler was revealed,

"did you stitch this yourself? It's wonderful!"

Rose smiled at her. "I did indeed," she said. "I'm glad you like it."

"It's fabulous," Meg said. "We'll put it over the mantelpiece, to remind us of this day."

Just then, Ginny came back into the room – Meg hadn't noticed her leaving. "Here's my contribution," she said. Another large, flat parcel.

Meg opened it, to reveal a wonderful photo collage of her and John's lives over the last fifty years, all set in a large Perspex frame. "Where did you find all these?"

Ginny's grin was triumphant. "I saved them away when you weren't looking."

Everyone else apart from Rose was looking confused. "Come on," Meg said to Ginny, "I think it's time."

The two of them fetched the memoirs from the dining room and Meg began to hand them out – one for John, and one each for Mark and Jessica, Katie, Becky, Andrew and Richard, Rose, and Ginny.

"Wow!" Andrew said. "You've finished it. I like the title, *The Wonder and Marvel of an Ordinary Life*." He opened his copy and began to leaf through it. "This is marvellous, Mum."

"Rose helped me to revise it and Ginny was my photo wizard. Which is where she found all those photos. Thank you, Ginny. The collage is such a lovely surprise."

The room was almost silent as everyone began to look through their books, Meg looking over John's shoulder at their copy.

"What do you think, love?" she said.

"I think," he said, giving her a big hug, "that I have a very talented wife. And here's my present to you, Meggie darling."

He reached into his pocket and produced a small, square parcel. "With all my love," he said.

Inside was a gold chain with a twisted rope design, on which six rings were strung. When Meg looked closely, she realised that each ring had a name engraved on it – John, Meg, Andrew, Jessica, Katie, Becky.

"This is perfect," she said, kissing him warmly. "I'm going to put it on right now."

It was time. She looked around for Jessica and gave her a tiny nod. Her daughter slipped out with her son-in-law, returning a few minutes later with two bottles of Nosecco, which had been chilling in the fridge, eight champagne glasses, and two tall tumblers filled with Diet Coke.

Mark gave the girls their drinks and began to fill the adults' glasses, and Jessica tapped one of the glasses so it rang. "If I could have your attention, please?"

The hubbub of conversation quietened.

"We're here today," Jessica said, "to celebrate the Golden Wedding anniversary of two very special people. Mum, Dad, Nana, Papa, Meg, John, I hope you both know how very much you mean to us – we're so lucky to have you as our parents, in-laws, grandparents, and friends. Ladies and gentlemen, please be upstanding and raise your glasses in a toast: we wish you both many more happy, healthy years together. I give you, Meg and John."

"Meg and John," everyone echoed, then drained their glasses before sitting back down. Meg squeezed John's hand.

She vowed to fix this moment in her memory, so she could revisit it any time she felt sad. It had been a perfect day.

Ginny

Ginny had decided to move her birthday celebration this year to Capuchins, at their normal book group meeting – nothing should detract from Meg's anniversary bash. She dropped in to see Karen the week before, to ask whether she could produce a special carrot cake for the occasion.

Now – most unusually – she was here first, before Meg and even before Rose. She paid in advance for their first drinks.

"When d'you want me to bring the cake out?" Karen said.

"When they're both here, please."

Rose and Meg arrived together – Rose must have given Meg a lift again. Why hadn't she thought to offer? Oh well.

"Hello, you two," Ginny said. "Come and sit down – the drinks are on me today."

Then she winked at Karen, who brought out the cake.

"What's all this?" Meg said.

"My birthday cake," Ginny said. "I thought we could celebrate it here today."

"What a lovely idea!" Rose said. "Thank you."

"Karen made it specially for us, so it's guaranteed gluten-free and vegetarian." Ginny cut three generous slices. "Here you are."

"Oh," Meg said, after taking a large bite, "this is

delicious. Would you let me have the recipe, please, Karen?"

"Of course," Karen said, a pleased smile on her face.

"This month has been all celebrations," Rose said. "First, Meg and John's anniversary, and now your birthday." She delved into her bag, and brought out a large, book-shaped parcel. "Happy Birthday, Ginny."

Ginny opened it, then gasped. It was a copy of *India* by Olivier Follmi. "Oh, this is perfect! I've read about him – he's the Dalai Lama's official photographer." She began to leaf through it, savouring the beautiful images.

"I hope you don't mind it being second-hand," Rose said. "It's not in print anymore."

"Not at all – I wouldn't have known if you hadn't told me. This is going to give me so much inspiration."

Rose smiled. "That's what I hoped."

"My turn now," Meg said, handing over a smaller parcel. "I asked Rose, so I hope it's the right one."

Ginny opened it to find a polarising filter for Graham's camera. "Excellent," she said. "That's going to come in so useful in November. Thank you. I'm getting so excited about it now. I've asked the travel company and they've managed to organise some of the internal trips to be by rail, so I don't feel quite so guilty."

"That's good," Rose said. "I quite envy you – I'll be working hard by then."

"Why on earth?"

"Lesley's decided I'm ready to do my Grade I piano exam. I've started on my first piece and she's planning to enter me in March. Which means I'm going to have to be a bit more committed to daily practice."

"That's exciting," Meg said.

"Hmm," Rose said. "That's one way of putting it. I'm more petrified than excited at the moment."

"You'll be fine," Ginny said. "I've long known that you can achieve anything you put your mind to. Look at Meg's beautiful anniversary sampler."

"Yes," Meg said. "So many people have admired it. John's put it up over the fireplace, so I can feast my eyes on it every day."

Rose flushed. "Thank you," she said. "It was a joy to stitch."

"So," Ginny said, "what did you both think of *Enough?*"

"I found it fascinating," Rose said, "even though it's a bit out of date now. It's made me think about what I consume and why I consume it in a new way. I've made a resolution not to buy any new clothes, and to weed out the ones that no longer fit me before giving them to charity. And to be more careful about the food I buy."

"That's a great start," Ginny said. "How about you, Meg?"

"Well," and Meg smiled a little sadly, "John and I need to be careful what we spend at the moment, so reading it's helped me to reframe having to economise into something positive. And like Rose, I'm looking more carefully at where our food comes from."

"I'm trying to find contact details for him," Ginny said, "so that I can drop him an e-mail suggesting an updated edition. Because the world's changed so much since 2008 – social media, the climate crisis getting so much more acute, and so on."

"I'd buy that," Rose said.

She drained her cup and stood up. "Another drink, everyone?"

"Yes, please," Meg and Ginny chorused, then laughed.

They sat and chatted for a while longer, and Ginny was filled with a powerful surge of affection for these two women, who had become real friends for her. They each had another slice of cake, and Ginny offered one to Karen.

"What's our book for next month, Meg?"

Meg took a small hardback book out of her bag. "I thought this," she said, showing it to them. "It seems to follow on from *Enough*."

"*The Little Book of Hygge*" Ginny read. "I love the cover."

"I've seen it in Waterstone's," Rose said. "What's it about?"

"I don't want to give too much away," Meg said. "But it's about appreciating the simple things in life, more or less."

"That sounds perfect," Rose said.

Rose

It had taken Rose a while to get round to re-reading Meg's memoir. Ginny's meticulous placing of the photographs made such a difference – they brought the text to life.

When she reached the end, she found a short list of acknowledgements, which hadn't been there when she'd edited and proofread it.

"This memoir would never have seen the light of day without the encouragement and help of my two dear friends: Rose Anderson, who turned my rough draft into something readable, and Ginny Lambert, who edited and inserted the photos so beautifully. Both have been hugely supportive all the way through the writing process.

I'd also like to thank Elizabeth Gilbert, author of *Big Magic: Creative Living without Fear,* who (although she'll never know it) inspired me to write it in the first place; and William Martin, author of *The Parent's Tao Te Ching: Ancient Advice for Modern Parents,* for generously allowing me to adapt his words for my title.

And of course, this memoir wouldn't exist at all without you, the members of my beloved family: John Jeffries, my husband of fifty years; my daughter, Jessica, her husband, Mark, and Katie and Becky, my gorgeous grandchildren; my son, Andrew and his husband, Richard. I love you all so much.

August 2018"

Tears pricked Rose's eyes as she read – her own experience of writing an autobiography (if she ever did) would be so different, because she had no Graham to share it with. Was she brave enough to start writing it? Reading Meg's memoir made her realise that she'd be spending much of the time writing about her life with Graham – was she ready to do that? Or would it be more painful than cathartic? In a way, it would be a tribute to their lives together, without which the rest of her family would not exist.

She shook herself: she had a duty to Graham's memory too – she wanted him to live on, not only in her heart and mind, but also in the grandchildren's. Ben and Jake, maybe even Jamie, would have true recollections of him, but she wanted Rosie and Natalie to know him too.

She'd start tomorrow.

ABOUT THE AUTHOR

Sue Woolley lives in Northamptonshire with her husband and cat. Her first novel, *One Foot in Front of the Other,* was published by Hachette Headline in 2020, and she has also written a fantasy trilogy, *The Stones of Veylindré,* published by Scimitar Edge in 2023 and 2024.